The Karenina Chronicles

A Waterspell Novel

Deborah J. Lightfoot

Seven Rivers
Publishing

Seven Rivers Publishing
P.O. Box 682
Crowley, Texas 76036
www.waterspell.net

Cover design by Tatiana Vila, Vila Design
www.viladesign.net

The Karenina Chronicles: A Waterspell Novel (Book 5) / Deborah J. Lightfoot
First paperback edition: November 2023
First electronic edition: December 2023

Summary: In the grip of a grief-fueled wanderlust after the death of her Earthly husband, Lady Karenina of Ruain—Nina to family and friends—escapes into unfamiliar lands, a harsh and distant country peopled with enigmatic characters: the Leviathan, the Nomad, the Outcast, and the Wolf. In their company she finds adventure, danger, champions, and rogues—some of the latter worth killing, but at least one worth loving.

ISBN 978-1-7377173-3-1 (Paperback)
ISBN 978-1-7377173-4-8 (Ebook)
ISBN 978-1-7377173-5-5 (Audiobook)

This book was written by a human, not AI.

The Karenina Chronicles

A Waterspell Novel

BOOKS of WATERSPELL

Original Series
Book 1: The Warlock
Book 2: The Wysard
Book 3: The Wisewoman
Book 4: The Witch

Nina Series
The Karenina Chronicles
The Fires of Farsinchia

For all who have lost their way and found it again.

With special thanks to Martin, Sharon, and Kathy for protecting me from the self-doubt demon.

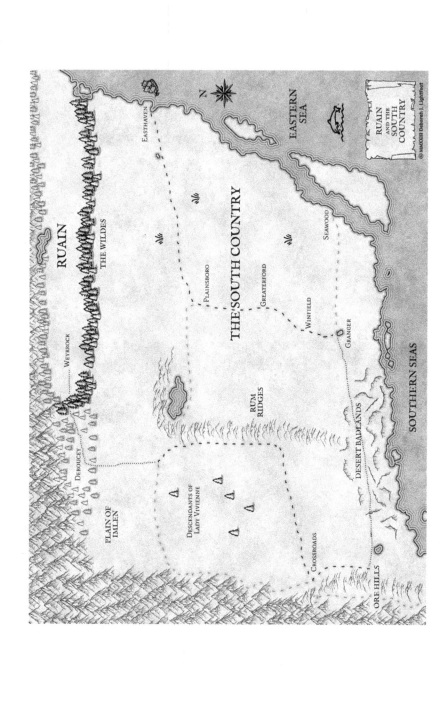

RUAIN

THE WILDES

EASTERN SEA

EASTHAVEN

N

PLAINSSBORO

THE SOUTH COUNTRY

GREATERFORD

SEAWOOD

WINFIELD

WEYRROCK

GRANGER

DEBOUCET

RUM
RIDGES

DESERT BADLANDS

SOUTHERN SEAS

PLAIN OF
IMLEN

DESCENDANTS OF
LADY VIVIENNE

CROSSROADS

ORE HILLS

RUAIN
AND THE
SOUTH
COUNTRY

© MMXXIII Deborah J. Lightfoot

Contents

The Karenina Chronicles

THIS BOOK is more properly titled *The Second Chronicles of Karenina*. The original volume resides in the great library at Weyrrock, hidden in the secret province of Ruain. Known as *The Book of the Two Kareninas*, that work is a collection of personal letters that were exchanged between Lady Karenina and her parents during the decades of Nina's otherworldly sojourn across the void. The collection is privately held and has not been made public.

This present volume tells of Lady Nina's further travels, how she left the island world and journeyed far from her ancestral home, encountering new perils and adventures at every turn. Her restless flight from the grief of widowhood draws her down a long road through unfamiliar lands where she finds mystery, danger, family, friends, and rogues —some of the latter worth killing, but at least one worth loving.

Part I
The Leviathan

Chapter One

Karenina fought down the urge to conjure a monster wave, a wall of water high and violent enough to seriously challenge her little brother. Dalton the weather-mage had handled everything she'd summoned against him from the otherwise placid waters of the Eastern Sea. His eyes had widened at the unexpected ocean disturbances, the sudden surges and gaping maelstroms that popped into being without warning just ahead of his ship. Each time, Dalton magicked away the threat, uncoiling the whirlpools with a flick of his wrist, or smoothing the swells like he smoothed his white-blond hair.

Not once had the mage turned from his place in the ship's prow to shoot Nina a suspicious look or even a questioning one.

Does it not occur to this innocent boy, she wondered, *that he never had these problems until he took a water-sylph on board?*

Nina stepped up beside her fair-haired brother, smiling at him. As she gripped the rail, the wind whipped her long raven tresses around her face and stung her eyes.

Dalton grinned back, his smile expressing only an excited and fond delight at having his big sister with him on this voyage. His smile remained in place as he returned his watchful gaze to the now-calm ocean that lay between them and their next port of call.

I might have been a 'sea goddess' on that world called Earth, Nina mused, studying her weather-working brother, *but it's Dalton who is in his ele-*

ment here on these deep waters of Ladrehdin. I doubt I could best him even with a tidal wave.

She planted a sisterly kiss on the *wysard*'s wind-burned cheek, briefly blinding Dalton as her hair whipped across his eyes. Then Nina stepped down from the foredeck and left the ship's master to continue his lookout for those odd ocean turbulences that seemed to come from nowhere.

Stop teasing him, she ordered herself. *You're acting like a child. Even by the reckoning of Earthly time, you're too old for childishness.*

And if Dalton figured out that the rogue waves and sudden whirlpools were Nina's doing, he might not appreciate the joke. She barely knew this second of her brothers, but it hadn't taken her long to conclude that Dalton was the straightest of straight arrows. At home in Ruain, he was their father's chief steward, overseer of the annual harvests, master of the ports, administrator of the province's outbound shipments of grain and goods. When he chose to sail with his trade ships, Dalton was not only master of the fleet but also the weather-working *wysard* at their head who ensured they had favorable winds at all points along the coast. If he caught on to Nina's little game of "quell the wave and quash the whirlpool," Dalton might be the opposite of amused.

He might throw you overboard for putting his ship in peril, Nina thought. She chuckled. Straight-arrow Dalton would never do that. But even if he did, Nina the water-sylph was a remarkably strong swimmer. Drop her anywhere along this coastline of Ladrehdin, and she'd make it to shore before her little brother dropped anchor in the nearest harbor.

Belowdecks in her cabin, Nina worked the tangles from her wind-blown hair. Combed out, her glossy black mane fell below her shoulders. She pulled it up into a sleek ponytail, the quickest and easiest "formal" hairstyle she could manage on her own. Though why Dalton insisted on dressing for dinner aboard ship was beyond her. Nina supposed he had picked up the custom from the wealthy merchants he dealt with on his southern sailings.

He certainly didn't get it from our parents, she thought, and smiled at the memory of rushed, often chaotic but always happy mealtimes at the old stone manor called Weyrrock. During her girlhood there, meals had seldom been formal occasions. Any time the northern weather permitted, the family ate outdoors in the garden or under the trees. When winter's biting winds forced them inside, they would gather, the five of them, around a rough-hewn trestle table in a kitchen ruled by Myra the housekeeper.

Even after many years away from that table, Nina could picture it, could see her younger self sitting at the right hand of Master Welwyn, her beloved tutor and governor. To Welwyn's left squirmed the red-headed child of fire, the boy Galen—the brother with whom Nina had grown up, and the only one of her three brethren that she really knew.

Facing them across the table, sitting side by side on the bench opposite Master Welwyn and his pupils, were the lord and lady of Ruain. As Nina pictured the pair in her mind's eye, she saw the attention of them both fixed on their two young children, and both parents bursting with questions. Over bowls of stew and baskets of hot bread, Lord Verek and Lady Carin would ask the novice *wysards* about their day's lessons. What had they learned? What had they seen, read, done, and mastered since dawn?

A boundless curiosity underlay those questions, such a depth of genuine interest that the inquiries never felt like interrogations. The questions, rather, formed an invitation which Nina and Galen noisily accepted. Speaking as often as not with their mouths full, tripping over their words in their eagerness, the children would babble about the new spells they'd learned, the ancient tales they had read, the wild animals they'd tracked through the oakwoods, or the powerful herbs they had gathered in shadowy forest glades.

Their parents soaked up their chatter as bread absorbs broth. If there was to be any lecturing about table manners or any instilling of the social graces, it was Master Welwyn who saw to such niceties. Never once, to Nina's recollection, had Lord Verek or Lady Carin demanded silence or "proper decorum" from their children.

No, thought Nina, *wherever Dalton picked up this silly habit of dressing for dinner, he didn't get it from our parents.* Unless, she mused, they had amended their way of parenting after seeing how their first two off-spring turned out.

Nina donned the only dress that she'd packed for this journey, then made her way to the main cabin to join Dalton and his ship's officers for dinner. Except for a quick breakfast at dawn tomorrow, this would be her final meal aboard. By daybreak, so Dalton had informed her, they would reach the ship's southernmost destination: a coastal town called Easthaven. There, well beyond the borders of her ancestral lands, with the province of Ruain lying hidden and secret behind her, Nina would disembark and head out on her grand scheme of visiting all of her far-flung Ladrehdinian kindred.

But on the morrow, as it happened, her further travels had to wait a few hours. Dalton insisted on coming ashore with her in the early dawn, determined to show Nina the two most remarkable pieces of art that he had discovered on his previous voyages to the port of East-haven.

"What, my Honored Sister, does *that* bring to your mind?" he demanded, pointing up at a sinuous sculpture which towered over the mouth of the town's protected, natural harbor.

The monument rose at the bluff end of a long arm of land that curved around the bay like a mother's arm around a child. One end of the sculpture extended out over the water in a tangle of bronze filaments that showed green with age. On the statue's shoreward side, more bronze strands like the twisting, coiling tendrils of innumerable vines anchored the huge sculpture amid the rocks. Massed between the two ends of the structure, jumbles of filaments reached for the sky, a maze of metal tendrils so skillfully forged and interwoven that the rigid bronze seemed to writhe and sway in the sea breezes.

As she studied the lofty framework, with the morning sun rising above a distant bank of clouds and shining full upon the sculpture, Nina picked out bright embellishments, fashioned from quartz perhaps, or moonstones. As they caught the new day's light, the gems flickered and sparked like fireflies.

Even brighter were the red tongues that flared against the massed green tendrils. Gleaming bloodstones, garnets, and crimson granite had been carved into great flames evoking fire. These spouted from the stone-chiseled figure of a sailing vessel, creating the effect of a fireship colliding with the sculpture, ramming its base. Where the red flames erupting from the vessel seemed to burn the writhing tendrils, the green patina on the bronze gave way to charcoal black.

"What am I looking at?" Nina asked as she and her brother stood gazing up at the maze of metal, granite, and gemstones. "Those twisted pieces look like they're growing up out of the rock—like stems of ivy or honeysuckle. But from here, the ship that's setting fire to all those twisted stems looks huge. Which would make that tangle of metal vines even bigger. What's it supposed to be?"

"It's strangleweed," Dalton replied. "It's a memorial to when East-haven fought off a massive invasion of devil's guts."

"Devil's guts! Bunched up *that* high?" Nina turned to stare at her brother. "Local folklore, is it? Even for a fairy tale, I'd say the sculptor exaggerated a mite."

Dalton shook his head. "They believe it here. The people talk about an invasion of strangleweed that almost buried the town." He gestured up at the monument. "I hiked up there once and read the plaque on the side of the ship. It says that a particularly nasty variety of devil's guts came down from the north and made a great green tangle, a wall of weed so thick and tough that it blocked the harbor mouth. No ship of Easthaven could go to sea. But then the harbormaster had the idea of filling an old boat with wood, setting it on fire, and ramming it into the weed. That's how they cleared their harbor." Dalton grinned. "The story goes that the old man's name was Sutton—and to this day every third boy born in Easthaven is named Sutton. Both of the merchants I'll deal with today are called that. I've had to rename them to keep my account books straight. The mill owner is Silky Sutton, and the fellow who tries to overcharge me for limes and tamarinds is Sourpuss Sutton."

Dalton's smile faded, and he looked a little worried. "You won't tell them, will you? I wouldn't want to give offense."

Nina laughed. "I'll not breathe a word, little brother. I doubt I'll have the pleasure of meeting your Suttons. This is a fine morning for riding, and I'm keen to be on the road." She patted the purse at her belt. "I'll be off as soon as I get a horse."

"As it happens, I know the best horse-trader in town," Dalton said as they faced away from the strangleweed sculpture and walked inland along the waterfront. "But first, there's something else I must show you. It's up this hill." He gestured at a gentle knoll that rose behind the docks. Atop the knoll stood a three-story, whitewashed building.

It proved to be an inn called, rather unimaginatively, the Harbor Hill. Its wagon yard was noisy with travelers repacking their belongings, hitching up their teams, and bidding farewell to their night's neighbors before resuming their separate journeys. Dalton led Nina through the graveled yard and up the inn's front steps, past more travelers who were rushing to be on their way in the cool freshness of the spring morning.

Off the busy lobby, a door opened to an almost silent dining room where only a few guests still lingered over breakfast. One of the serving maids bobbed a shy curtsy as Dalton walked past. Across the room, a tall, redheaded wench stood in a kitchen doorway staring bold as brass at the captain. The redhead's eyes narrowed and her expression hardened as she glanced at Nina.

"I can see you're a regular customer here." Nina stepped up beside Dalton to whisper in his ear, then nod toward the kitchen wench. "I think you'd best be telling your 'friend,' quick as you can, that I'm your long-lost sister, not your new lover. Else she might knife me in a fit of jealousy. What a face that woman is making!"

Dalton turned beet red. Bronzed though he was from his years under the sun, riding the breadth of Ruain when he wasn't sailing the Eastern Sea, he flushed scarlet to the roots of his pale hair. "I, uh ... she's, uh ...," he stammered, then stopped, wringing his hands.

Nina giggled at his embarrassment. "Maybe you're not such a straight-arrow after all, little brother." She punched him in the shoulder. "I'm beginning to think the chief steward of Ruain lets his hair down in Easthaven."

"I, uh," Dalton stammered again, but got no further.

She grinned at him. "Show me whatever you wanted me to see here—assuming, of course, that I haven't already spotted the object of your interest—and then go explain things to your redhead before she comes over here with a meat cleaver."

"I, uh," Dalton said for a third time. "It's here," he finally managed in a faint murmur and turned toward the dining room's back wall. He pointed at a framed sketch that hung amid dozens of similar drawings. Some were skillfully rendered; others, the work of amateurs. Several of the sketches were ancient, to judge by the style of the art, the garments and hairdos of their subjects, and the portraits' yellowed backgrounds. Others in the collection appeared new, freshly sketched on crisp white sailcloth.

The drawing that Dalton pointed out was neither new nor archaic, but it had hung on the wall long enough to be faded. Dust had gathered on its frame. Evidently this wall of portraits did not get the daily scrubbing that was now happening in the dining room at Nina's back. A bevy of white-capped maids cleared now-vacated tables, throwing uneaten breakfast scraps into pails that were destined for pig troughs behind the inn's kitchens. An older, gray-haired man pushed a broom across the flagstone floor, shouting "Step aside, missy!" and "Look lively, girl!" to the young creatures who were doing their best to stay out of the curmudgeon's way.

Dalton beelined through the general confusion to have a word with the redhead. He pulled the wench into a quiet corner and spoke urgently to her, gesturing toward Nina and the wall of portraits.

Nina chuckled, then turned back to the wall to give her full attention to the sketch that Dalton had pointed out. It was by no means a masterful work of art, but she would have to be blind to not recognize the face that looked out from that faded sketch. It was her own face. Or rather, it was the visage she would wear if she were male, and a little older, and long accustomed to barking orders at underlings. The eyes in the sketch were her dark, glinting eyes. The crow-black hair was her hair. The shape of the face, the nose, even the proud tilt of the head: all hers.

"Nerissa," called Dalton, interrupting Nina's study of the portrait as he approached through the bustle of table-wiping and floor-brooming. With him he brought the redhead, who was, Nina silently conceded, rather pretty now that a delighted smile had replaced the woman's scowl. "May I present to you my friend Tilda? Tilda love, this is my sister Nerissa," Dalton said, repeating the false name that Nina had adopted to guard her privacy on her southern travels.

"Charmed, I'm sure," Nina murmured, fighting to keep her smug amusement from showing. "Any 'friend' of Damon's has my regard."

As soon as she said it, Nina wondered if she had blundered. *Damon* was the name her brother used beyond the borders of Ruain. It was the name known by the foreign merchants with whom he traded. But perhaps among the trollops with whom he cavorted, her fair-haired brother called himself differently.

Tilda, however, only grinned more broadly. She knew the name.

"Pleasure's mine, mistress," the redhead simpered with a pronounced local accent. "Damon says 'tis your first visit to Easthaven. Will you stay here at the inn?"

Nina shook her head. "The road beckons and I must hurry on. But before I go," she added, turning back to the expanse of framed portraits, "pray tell me: Who are these people? Why are they pictured like this?"

The redhead shrugged. "Them's just some fancy folk who've taken a meal here. Nobles and such. Rich folk and posh 'uns." Tilda ran an indifferent eye over the portraits. Her gaze lingered on none of them, not even on the sketch that so closely resembled the dark-eyed, raven-haired woman in front of her. Posh folks did not interest Tilda. "I never seen any of 'em, myself. 'Course, they's all dead now, most likely. Them pictures been hanging on that wall forever."

They are not all dead, Nina thought, recalling the vitally alive patriarch who had pressed gold into her hands to finance her arguably reckless journey across the southlands.

"Tilda! Get back to work, woman."

The redhead jumped as the broom-wielding curmudgeon yelled at her from across the room. She turned to yell back. "I'm takin' these people's orders for tea, you old crab!"

Swinging around to face Nina again, Tilda muttered, "Grumpy coot's been here 'bout as long as them pictures. He'll drop dead one of these days, still pushing that fragging broom."

Nina smiled, glad for this chance to be rid of the woman. "Please do not let me keep you from your duties. I shan't have tea, thank you. But I would like to study these portraits for another minute, if that will not inconvenience you or your maids."

Tilda puffed up with self-importance, visibly pleased by Nina's suggestion that she had authority over the bevy of serving girls and was not just another among their number. The redhead bobbed a haughty little curtsy, then headed back to the sweltering kitchen, escorted partway by Dalton. Nina saw the two of them whispering together before they separated and he returned to stand with her at the portrait wall.

"She has no idea, does she," Nina muttered. "No idea who you are or where you come from."

Dalton grinned, red-faced. "I'm only Captain Damon to her. Just another seafarer who passes through Easthaven from time to time." He looked down at his feet. "I hope you don't think the less of me."

Nina laughed. "On the contrary! I am delighted to discover that you are flesh and blood. The way everyone talks about you at home, I had begun to think you were a paragon—our father's perfect steward, Ruain's infallible weather-mage, the unsinkable master of the Eastern Sea." She chuckled. "How many mistresses do you keep in these coastal towns? One in every port?"

Dalton shuffled his feet and began a weak protest, but Nina waved him to silence. "I'm teasing, brother. Your love life is your business and none of mine. Nor shall our parents hear of it, not from me anyway."

She tapped her teeth with her thumbnail, then added, "I would only caution you to take care what seeds you plant. Any child you father could possess the Gift to a great or minor degree. If that child receives no proper instruction in spellcraft, disaster and destruction may follow as your by-blow comes of age."

Dalton's flush deepened beneath his outdoorsman's tan. "I take pre-cautions," he muttered. "Our father has given me herbs."

"O ho!" Nina exclaimed. "So at least one of our parents knows of your southern liaisons." She laughed again. "Let us speak of it no more. You have set my mind at ease, little brother. I should have guessed that our faultless steward of the north would not fail to responsibly manage his foreign affairs." She clapped Dalton on the shoulder, dismissing the subject of "affairs," and turned back to the wall of portraits.

"This certainly is our honored father, sovereign lord of Ruain." Nina pointed at the faded sketch from which a black-haired man stared out with a piercingly direct gaze. "But scrawled below the drawing is the appellation 'Lord Forester.' Is that the artist who made this sketch? Or did our father take that name during his time here?" Nina scanned the portraits to the left and the right, seeking some clue by which to date the drawing. "Which begs a further question: *when* was he here?"

"Many years ago, I believe," Dalton replied, quick to embrace this new subject. "I have asked, but he's never told me much. Just that he and our mother passed through here once, on their way back to Ruain from the lowlands village, Granger, where our mother grew up."

"And to which I am bound," Nina said, turning to leave. "The morn-ing is wasting: I'm fain to be away. Pray take me to your horse-trader and then be about your business, captain. You mustn't keep the Suttons waiting."

Or your mistress either, Nina added silently, catching sight of the brassy Tilda stepping through the back door of the kitchen, a slops bucket in each hand. *Drisha's teeth!* Nina thought. *Could you not have set your sights higher, Dalton? Seduced the rich widow of an Easthaven merchant, perhaps?*

But the heart wants what the heart wants. Nina recalled her long marriage to a man of the distant world where she had lived for the bet-ter part of a century, as reckoned by the passage of time in that faraway place. She had watched her husband, a captive of his mortal years, grow old and die, while she herself—a creature of magic—had hardly aged. *Wysards* live long.

Which explains, she thought, *the fading of that portrait in the Harbor Hill dining room.* The maker of that drawing was undoubtedly long dead, as was every other individual to whom Lord Verek and Lady Carin had spoken during their long-ago visit to this coastal town.

What a strange thing time is, Nina thought as she and Dalton walked up the high street of Easthaven and stopped at a large paddock where a dozen horses grazed the new spring grass. On the ocean planet called Earth, she was a great-grandmother many times over. But here in this strange town of her own homeworld, this place that retained a forgotten trace of her parents' long-past visit, Nina felt like a girl again. Like the stubborn twelve-year-old who had ridden alone from Weyrrock all the way across her father's lands to swim in the Eastern Sea.

On her present journey, however, she would be riding a strange horse, not the levelheaded warmblood of her girlhood, the gray called Ghost. She would be riding alone in a southern land she knew almost nothing about. And this time, Nina would be riding *away* from the ocean, not toward it.

With the thought came a twinge of anxiety. It flitted past, ignored for the moment, but notable as the first inkling of hesitation she had felt since declaring her intention of visiting every limb in her family tree.

Nina gave Dalton a last hug, then swung into the saddle of the alert, bright-eyed roan she had picked out from the dozen animals in the horse-trader's paddock. As she reined the gelding around to head out of town, she felt for the sling she wore concealed under her linen tunic. She checked that her throwing-knife and her rapier were securely sheathed at her belt. Her bow—an elegant recurved weapon handcrafted by her father—rested in a saddle scabbard with her quiver slung near at hand, close by her waterskin.

I haven't been armed like this, Nina realized, *since I bested the Ronnat boys that time in the woods—that time of testing when I showed Papa that I could take care of myself.*

"Now's your chance to prove it again," Nina muttered. Only this time, Lord Verek would not be there to magick her attackers to stone, should the need arise.

Stop doubting yourself, Nina snapped inwardly, surprised by the twitch of uncertainty that again made itself felt. *You handled every threat on Earth, and in the beginning there were many. Pirates, even! Drisha's teeth. Before the pirates, there was a* demon, *for pity's sake. You will handle whatever comes your way, out on these bleak grasslands. The power of water is great, and it is yours to command.*

From Easthaven she rode west and a little south, following the highroad out of town. In the cool morning with the sun at her back, Nina gazed ahead at a seemingly endless plain of low grass and stunted trees. Already feeling out of her element, she twisted in the saddle to seek the ocean behind her. But no glimpse of blue water did she spy. Though she could still smell it, that wonderfully familiar salt tang, the scent of the ocean was rapidly giving way to the acrid smell of sage and creosote-bush.

Nina reined in. For a long moment she sat in the silence of the thornscrub, taking deep breaths of the dusty air that hung over the hard-packed road. If she turned back now, she would be in plenty of time to rejoin Dalton in Easthaven, to reboard his ship and sail with him back to Ruain.

"Certainly not," she muttered to the empty landscape, impatient with the misgivings that had crept upon her. Nina swung down from the saddle. Grasshoppers scattered before her as she stooped to pick up quantities of the small round stones that littered the roadway's edge. "I've got family in this country," she went on speaking softly into the stillness. "I have every right and reason to be here. To my kindred I *will* take myself. Woe be to any southlander who might try to hinder me."

Nina pulled her sling from beneath her shirt, armed it with a stone from the roadside, whirled and let fly. The stone sailed hard and fast, and smashed a dry limb from a prickly tree.

The crack of the impact split the sunlit silence. Nina's new horse snorted—

—and bolted, straight back through the scrub toward the magical ocean she had just left.

Chapter Two

She might have chased the animal all the way to the coast, had the reins not snagged in the twisted limbs of a low-growing tree. As it was, Nina caught the horse before she was much winded. She stroked the animal's neck, soothing it, and stood with it beside the stunted tree, speaking to the roan for really the first time. When she'd purchased it, she had said no word to the gelding except to call its name, which the horse-dealer had told her, fittingly enough, was "Traveller."

"Well, Trav," Nina murmured. "We have not made a great start, you and I. Let's try again."

From her saddlebags she took an apple, one of a bagful that she'd brought from the ship's stores to provision the first part of her journey. As the gelding crunched the sweet fruit, Nina showed the animal her sling. She rubbed the leather strap along the horse's cheek and jaw, then looped the weapon's braided cords over the roan's neck. When Trav finished his apple, Nina held the sling for him to nuzzle and snuff.

"Nothing scary about it, see? Unless you're on the receiving end of one of these." Nina stooped for another of the small white rocks that lay everywhere. The stones practically covered every inch of ground that wasn't occupied by a gnarled shrub or a clump of tough grass.

Slowly she whirled the loaded sling, near Traveller's head but at sufficient distance to avoid alarming him. When he seemed to accept its twirling presence, she increased the speed until the sling whirred through the air with the sound of angry hornets.

Thus, Nina was perfectly positioned to meet the attack that came from the nearby roadway in the form of a man riding toward her, brandishing a sword.

"I'll have that horse, wench," he shouted as he spurred his mount. "While I'm about it, gypsy slut, I'll have you too."

"I think not," Nina muttered.

She took a step toward him to better align on her target, and loosed the stone. It flew straight and hard, and struck the man's shoulder with a crunching *thump* that spoke of broken bones.

He screamed as he tumbled from his saddle, his sword flying free. The man's horse raced away, heading straight up the road to Easthaven. No scrubby trees grew in the middle of the road: with nothing to catch its reins, that horse would likely run until it reached the town. Or the seashore.

Nina bent for another stone. Rearmed, she walked to pick up the man's sword from the dusty verge. Examining the weapon with a practiced eye—her father had been her weapons master, and from him Nina had learned much—she curled her lip in a sneer.

"This blade would not serve for pig-sticking," she said. "But I expect it'll do for cutting the balls off a would-be rapist. Shall we see?"

From where he lay on the road's hard surface, squeezing his broken shoulder with one hand while grabbing at his crotch with the other, the man flung curses at her. Nina knew them all, and more. She had been collecting colorful swearwords since her childhood, and to the common profanities of Ladrehdin she'd added a choice selection of coarse language from the ocean world of her married years.

She laughed at the man. "I won't waste the effort on a coward like you. But know this: If I ever lay eyes on you again, I *will* geld you." Nina whirled her sling again and popped the stone straight between the man's legs. His shriek of agony said the missile had done about as much damage as a castration knife would have. She smiled.

As a final act of dismissal, Nina snapped the man's cheap sword across her knee and flung the two halves to either side of the road. Returning to Traveller—who had watched the brief confrontation with interest, alert but not frightened—Nina remounted and resumed her southwestward course.

She did not glance back. If someone happened along this road in time to save the man from thirst and his injuries, so be it. He would undoubtedly account for his situation by claiming that his horse had thrown and then trampled him. A would-be rapist and thief would shy from admitting that his intended victim had bested him and left him where he fell.

But if no one found the fellow before he perished in the sun?

Nina shrugged. "Let Drisha's will be done," she muttered as she leaned to pat Trav's neck.

* * *

When the cool morning gave way to a warm spring noontime, Nina stopped to rest the horse and eat her lunch. She took a moment to tie up her long, braided hair and tuck it under a cap so her raven tresses would not announce so loudly that she was a woman traveling alone. She filled a pouch with the smooth round stones that were so plentiful beside the road, and so perfect for her sling. Nina kept the weapon handy, draped around her neck outside—not under—her shirt.

"Thank you, Honored Mother," she breathed in a rush of gratitude, "for teaching me the best weapon I could wield in this scrub." Lady Carin was expert with the sling, and she had taught her five children to make and use one. Never suspecting, Nina thought, that her firstborn would need to knock a scoundrel out of his saddle before she was a day's ride along the same road that Carin had once traveled.

Thinking of her mother brought thoughts, also, of that lady's struggles with the faculty of memory. Carin's trips through the formless void had profoundly altered her perception of time, leaving her unsure of when and where events in her life had occurred. She had described it to Nina as being unstuck in time, as though she had drifted both forward and backward during her transits of the void. Memories had drifted as well. In more than a few instances, Carin's memories had come apart, breaking up, leaving pieces of themselves scattered along a time "line" that was decidedly not linear, but coiled and twisting back on itself.

Now as Nina rode through the afternoon, truly alone with her thoughts for the first time in weeks, she felt a growing suspicion that something of the sort might be happening to her own memories. She had lived for decades on that ocean world called Earth. She'd married a man of that world, and together they had raised almost more children than Nina could count. Her eldest offspring had produced children of their own while Nina still nursed her littlest ones. The generations had blended until hardly anyone in her huge Earthly family could be bothered to keep track of who had sprung from which branch of the matriarchal tree.

That had been her life. On Earth, Nina had been the queen of her family, the protector of her island home, confidante of dolphins, healer of oceans: a master *wysard* who commanded the forces of the deep. On Earth—by the Powers—she had been like a goddess.

But now? Who was she now? Only a woman who had forsaken her home? A wanderer who traveled a lonely road on a sentimental journey, hoping to reclaim a bit of her childhood?

There was more to this journey, however, than nostalgia for her youth. As much as she wanted to see Galen again, to reminisce with him—and to meet for the first time their youngest brother, the south-country stonemason named Legary—Nina's strongly felt family ties were not the only invisible strands pulling her down this road. Ever since the death of her Earthly husband, Makani, Nina had been gripped by a wanderlust that first propelled her the length and breadth of the archipelago where she had spent her married life. After a time, too restless to remain in those islands without her beloved man, Nina had jumped the void to return to her homeworld.

Even in Ruain, however, she'd been unable to settle. She had insisted on traveling from one end of that province to the other, retracing the journey she'd made in girlhood. But upon reaching Ruain's easternmost shores, she had impulsively hopped on a ship and headed south, declaring her intention of visiting every one of her scattered Ladreh-dinian kindred.

Impulsive? *Call it foolhardy,* Nina admitted, staring around at the near-desolation of the scrubland through which she now rode. *Breath and blood,* she swore silently. *It's horribly dry out here.*

A sudden longing for water—the element of her wizardry—had Nina flinging up her arm in the beckoning motion that she'd used since childhood to call forth waves of billowing magic. With every wizardly fiber of her being, she commanded the waters to rise from the dusty soil alongside the road.

They refused. No drop answered her summons.

Nina reined up, gasping in surprise and sharp confusion. Never before had the magic failed her. Only weeks ago on Earth, she'd conjured waves capable of sinking ships. Just yesterday in her home waters of Ladrehdin, she'd spun whirlpools to pit her magic against the wizardry of a powerful weather-mage, Dalton the sea captain. Why, now, were her powers forsaking her?

"Turn back," Nina muttered. "Return to the ocean before you choke on this dust. Make haste to reclaim who you are ... or who you were."

She made no move, however, to rein Traveller around. When the horse tired of standing in the road, he began to amble along, drawn to the clumps of wiry grass that grew in the verge. Nina hardly noticed. She sat frozen in the saddle while Trav grazed his way slowly southward. Neither her gaze nor her mind seemed able to focus. Her thoughts, darting everywhere, would not form decisions; her impulses, now wildly contradictory, would not produce actions.

Only her instincts functioned as they should. They warned Nina that two riders were approaching. The men rode single file, although the road was wide enough to accommodate a pair abreast. Their brisk advance jolted Nina from her daze. She unlooped her sling and reached for a stone from her munitions.

These wayfarers, however, appeared to pose no threat. The rider in the lead carried no visible weapon. His clothing—tailored jacket and trousers, and round-brimmed hat perched staidly atop his head—suggested an individual of sober consequence. Perhaps he was a lawyer,

Nina thought as she eyed him and his bulging saddlebags. Those and a water costrel were his only luggage. Everything else that a traveler might need, including pots for cooking and blankets for sleeping, trailed along behind him, carried by the overloaded horse which bore the second man of the party. That fellow, shabbily dressed and far thinner than the portly figure in the lead, barely had room amongst the packs for his scarecrow frame.

As the first rider neared Nina, he kept to his expeditious pace and stayed on his side of the road. The man barely glanced at her but touched the brim of his hat in a brief, wordless salute. She acknowledged him with an equally silent nod. The second man, however, gazed openly at Nina, the look on his face blending surprise with admiration. She stared back, feeling her eyes narrow as the man's gaze lingered long. Then the scarecrow seemed to catch himself, to realize that he had overstepped the bounds of propriety.

"Beg pardon, my lady," the scarecrow mumbled as he dropped his gaze and reined his horse to a saunter, and then to a halt as he continued speaking. "I mean no disrespect, but this road is no place for a lady alone, 'specially with night to fall afore you may hope to reach shelter, the way you're headed. Ride now with my master and me, on up to Easthaven." He gestured toward the lead rider who had rapidly drawn away, disappearing into the dust stirred up by his passage. "I'd be honored to offer you my protection—such as it is."

The man peered at the packs which hemmed him on all sides. If he had a sword or even a knife, it must be as deeply buried as he was.

Nina inclined her head. "I thank you, sir," she said, her tone courteous. "But my way lies opposite: inland, not to Easthaven. From that port I have come this very day."

Until she said it, she hadn't known her decision. She hadn't realized that her darting thoughts and conflicting impulses had sorted themselves and made their choice. She would continue this journey away from the sea, away from the magic of water—even if her compulsive wanderlust cost her her powers.

Her would-be protector slumped in his saddle, as far as his jammed-together packs would allow. He looked so crestfallen that Nina was moved to slip her rapier partway out of its scabbard to show him the blade.

"I assure you, I am not defenseless," she said with a smile as she replaced the blade and hefted her sling. "I have unhorsed more than one man with only a well-aimed stone. My mother taught me." Nina jerked her thumb over her shoulder, to where the lawyer had disappeared. "I must delay you no longer. Your master will miss you."

"That he will. He'll be quick with a curse and a sharpish cut to my wages if I make him wait for his comforts." The man tried to pat one of the bulging packs but he couldn't follow through because another overstuffed sack blocked the bend of his elbow. He sighed.

"Defenseless or no," the fellow added as he prodded his horse into motion, "most every traveler wants company of an evening. My master and me, we overtook a wagonload of folk this day. They was in no great rush, back along this road. Ride on quick-like now," he advised, "and mayhap you'll meet with them afore it's full dark. There was a woman or two with 'em, and they looked to be decent folk. Better company for ye, anyways, than *some* that might be wanting to join you tonight."

The scarecrow's face reddened as he tipped his shabby hat to Nina and urged his horse to a trot, to lumber after his master. Briefly she watched the man go, touched by his concern for her safety and amused by the liberty he had taken in referring to the dubious "company" Nina might attract tonight. Oblique though his comment was, he'd blushed to dare such familiarity with a strange woman met in passing on a public road.

But if I'm smart, I will take his advice and find decent company before nightfall, Nina conceded with a glance at the westering sun. Among the many lessons she had learned from the sea creatures of Earth's great Pacific Ocean: There was safety in numbers.

Miles later in a deepening dusk, Nina called a greeting as she emerged from the shadows of scattered trees into the light of the campfire that had drawn her a short way off the road. "Good evening to you all."

She ran an appraising glance over those at the fireside. Two men and two women scrambled to their feet. Nina reined up at a prudent distance. "I do not ask for food," she hastened to assure them. "I have my own provisions ... even some apples that I will gladly give the children if I may be permitted to camp near you tonight."

An excited murmur rose from the young ones at the fire, a mob of eight urchins, the youngest barely out of diapers, the eldest a boy about fourteen. Some were fair-haired; others dark and so dissimilar in their looks, Nina doubted they shared kinship. More likely, these were two unrelated families who had met on the road and thrown in together.

Opting for all the honesty advisable when dealing with a crowd of strangers, she added: "A woman traveling alone wants the company of respectable folk. I will count myself fortunate if I may share your fire this evening."

The men exchanged glances, their suspicions as obvious as their hesitation. Nina didn't blame them. They might reasonably wonder whether she was, in fact, a woman alone. Thieves could hide in the trees behind her, using her as bait, waiting for the wayfaring families to drop their guard.

Before either man could challenge her, however, a matronly woman stepped forward and motioned for Nina to dismount.

"Welcome, child!" the woman called, startling Nina. She had not thought anyone in the cosmos, with the exception of Lady Carin her mother, would ever again address her as "child." She was too old for that.

But, she reconsidered, *wysards do not age as mortals age.* And in the void between the worlds, that strange nothingness she'd recently traversed, time lost all comprehendible meaning. It hung suspended or curved back on itself, sometimes catching in its wake those few voyagers who dared to cross the void, but other times leaving no mark upon them. She had returned to her ancestral home in the province of Ruain looking hardly older than when she'd left it. If the woman who now beckoned her toward the crackling campfire thought her young enough to be called "child," Nina would make no protest. This, she suspected, would not be the last time on her journey that she would benefit from the sympathy of strangers.

With her thanks and a smile, Nina handed down the sack of apples. While the young ones devoured the treats, she tended her horse, taking care with Traveller's hooves to be certain no stone from the road's rocky verge had lodged in his feet. This new horse of hers had a long journey ahead: south to Granger to meet Legary, the baby brother she'd never laid eyes on. Then west across the desert to reunite with Galen, the firedrake with whom she shared memories of childhood. What mischief the pair of them had made, flames and floods within the walls of Weyrrock.

Nina grinned, remembering.

The sound of running water drew her to a small spring. It fed a pond and watered a grassy strip where the campers had staked their horses. While Trav slaked his thirst, Nina refilled her waterskin. She tethered the gelding to graze apart from the other animals. Shouldering her gear then, she went to join her new companions at their evening fire.

"Sit with me," the matronly woman said, waving her into the circle of flickering light. "We've a stew simmering, and you are welcome to a bowlful."

Nina settled beside her. From her bags, she pulled a round of cheese. "Will you take a wedge of this in return?" she asked the woman. "It's my favorite, flavored with mustard seed and ale."

No one declined as Nina cut and passed around hunks of a delicacy that must be unknown to these plains dwellers. The hard cheese that she'd lifted from the ship's galley before disembarking that morning was wildly expensive. Few outside the House of Verek had ever tasted it. A connoisseur would have paid a fortune for the wedges that disappeared down the gullets of Nina's supper companions.

The gift had the intended effect. Any remaining suspicions were dispelled, and tongues were loosened. Nina learned that her initial impression was correct: the two families were not related, only traveled together for safety. Both were making for Easthaven, seeking better opportunities in that lively seaport. The younger children in the mob of eight belonged to the friendly matron, and hers appeared to be the better-off of the two families. The older boy and his siblings had the gaunt, half-feral look of the chronically underfed. When the stew was served, those children wolfed down their portions like a pack of starvelings.

Nina pretended not to notice. But afterward, when the children were at the pond washing themselves and their supper bowls, she leaned to whisper to the matron. "Those younglings seem undernourished. Is their father so shiftless, that he cannot put food in the mouths of his babes?"

The matron sighed. "That man is a wastrel," she whispered back. "His hungering children would eat us into the poorhouse if we allowed it. I could wish that we had not met them on the road. But we've only our three young ones to feed, and they have six hungry mouths. So my husband and I have shared with them all that we can spare." Again she sighed. "Tomorrow, Drisha willing, we reach Easthaven and part company. There's plenty of work to be had in that town, or so we've been told, for anyone willing to put their shoulder to the wheel."

Nina nodded. "Only this morning, I saw for myself how busy it is. Ships coming and going. Travelers passing through. Any kind of work that anyone might want could be found there." She paused, frowning. "Your friends ... they have six children, you say? You've the three, but I counted only five at their wagon."

"There is a sixth," the matron whispered, looking around to be sure she was not overheard. "It's a girl. Never leaves their wagon. I have never seen her sit up. Her mother takes her a little food—not enough to keep a bird alive." The woman dropped her voice still lower. "Every day since I found out about her, I have hoped she would not die while we're on the road together. She is sure to pass soon. But I would rather my young ones not witness a child near their own age, a sack of bones dead and buried in a roadside grave. Drisha forgive me, but that's how I feel about it."

"No blame to you, mistress," Nina murmured. "Any mother would want to shield her children from life's cruelties." She paused, then added, "I have skill with herbs and healing. Perhaps I can help. Will you walk me to the wagon where the girl lies?"

The matron hesitated, as if reluctant to further involve herself in the woes of people who would again be strangers once they reached their destination tomorrow. But after a moment she nodded. With Nina she rose from the fire, and led the way to the two parked wagons.

"Isobel," the matron called softly to the bone-thin woman who was spreading threadbare blankets on the ground. Her children piled into the frayed woolens, curling up together like a litter of puppies. Their mother, an inelegant woman with a lovely name, had stooped to smooth the hair from a child's forehead. But she straightened like a startled squirrel when Nina and the matron approached her.

"Isobel, dear," the matron repeated, her tone soothing as if coaxing a skittish animal. "We've had more luck than we knew this evening. Not only does this lady share her wonderful food with us, she knows about herbs. Like a wisewoman. She offers to extend what healing she may to your poor sick daughter."

For a moment, skittishness seemed poised to become flight: Isobel looked frightened, as if she nursed a terrible secret that was now exposed. The woman threw an anxious glance over her shoulder— seeking her husband, Nina thought. That man was not in view. But a rumble of coarse laughter drifted from the shadows beyond the camp-fire, suggesting that the two men of the party were out there together, in near darkness under the trees.

Drinking, I'll wager, Nina supposed. *And gambling,* she added silently as the sound of rattled dice reached her.

Nina glanced at the matron and saw a grimace cross that woman's face. *The sooner she separates her man from the influence of that wastrel, and her children from the shiftless one's starvelings, the happier she will be,* Nina thought, not without sympathy.

Returning her attention to Isobel, she flashed the nervous creature a reassuring smile. "From the time I was old enough to pick flowers and dig roots, I was taught the arts of healing and the uses of herbs," Nina said. "I can make no promises, you understand. But if you will allow me to examine your daughter, perhaps I may prescribe some remedy." Nina held up the satchel she had grabbed from her gear on the way to this meeting by the wagons. The satchel held a considerable variety of dried plants and bottled tonics. "I can but try, with all that I have, to ease your girl's suffering."

Isobel hesitated anew. She cast another wary glance in the direction of the men's increasingly raucous laughter. But then she nodded. Stepping to the rear of her family's wagon, she pulled back a heavy blanket that lay draped over a frame of peeled sticks. The frame enclosed a snug space that made a small, private compartment.

Curled into that space was a tiny girl. Or more the skeleton of a tiny girl, Nina thought as she climbed into the wagon and kneeled beside the child. No flesh clung to those bones. The skin was stretched tight across the child's skull, betraying a deformity in the underlying structure. Arms like twigs protruded from the sleeves of a loose shift. A gap in the garment's front revealed ribs as sharply defined as the ridges of a washboard.

Nina looked no further. She did not lift the blanket to examine the child's shrunken belly or matchstick legs. She could picture them without looking, and could foresee the child's future: starvation this severe must end in death, and soon. The wonder was that the girl still breathed. Nina pressed her ear to the bony ribcage and caught the faintest sound of a barely beating heart, an organ that labored against impossible odds, struggling valiantly but deserving the rest it would soon attain.

She swung down from the wagon and helped Isobel stretch the blanket back over the frame, to re-enclose the dying girl in her private, womblike space. The matron had stepped away by this time, retreating to the far side of her own wagon to see to her own younglings' bedtimes—and to distance herself, Nina thought, from the tragedy next door.

Leaving the matron to her evening's occupations, Nina walked with Isobel to the pond. Neither of them spoke, but they seemed to agree without words that they needed privacy together. When they stood among the tethered horses, assured of being neither seen nor heard, Nina wrapped her arms around the thin, careworn woman and hugged her.

Isobel stood stiffly in her embrace, as if unaccustomed to compassion. But then the woman melted into Nina's arms, clinging to her and sobbing noiselessly. Isobel cried while the stars wheeled overhead and her five barely surviving children slept, and her feckless husband laughed over his game of dice. She cried until she had no more tears to shed. When Nina released her, the woman stepped back far enough to bring up her apron to dry her eyes, but not so far that she would miss Nina's whisper.

"When you reach Easthaven," Nina said, "seek out an inn called the Harbor Hill. Ask for Tilda. Tell her that you are sent by the sister of Captain Damon, esteemed seafarer. Say that the captain wishes her to give you wholesome employment—nothing improper or indecent, for you are a respectable woman. Say that she is to find suitable accommodation for you and your children." Nina glanced into the shadowy distance, past the parked wagons, as another peal of rough laughter split the night. "Your husband will receive neither aid nor recommendation from me, for I cannot countenance a man who lets his children starve while he gambles away what little he has. How you deal with him is your concern. If you'll accept a word of advice, however, you will leave him at your first opportunity."

Isobel made no reply to this: the woman had yet to utter a sound. But standing so close to her, Nina felt the intensity with which Isobel absorbed everything she said.

"If you choose to stay with a man who cannot feed his family, you plainly have no business bringing another child into that family," Nina continued. "At first light tomorrow, as soon as the sky brightens enough that you can distinguish one green thing from another, come to me. I will show you the herb that women have used for millennia to spare themselves the ordeal of childbirth. It is found all over. I saw patches of it growing by the roadside today. I smell it even now, and know that we will find it under our feet in the morning. Come to me then and I will show you how to harvest and prepare it, so that you do not birth another child that cannot be fed."

Still Isobel did not speak. But in the fragrant darkness beside the pond, Nina felt the woman take her hand, gripping with slender, bony fingers.

In the gesture, Nina read gratitude. She had not misjudged the situation: Isobel was stretched to the breaking point, mothering the children she already had. She wanted no more, could stand no more heartbreak, could barely endure the cries of hunger from the unfed mouths of her scrawny brood. Most assuredly, the woman could not bear another child and watch it starve to death. That worthless husband of hers might force her to lie with him, careless of the sorrow to be sown with his seed. But Nina could show the woman how to rid herself of the unwanted results.

She pulled Isobel close and whispered into her ear. "Your little girl will draw her last breath before the sun sets tomorrow. Be glad of it. Send her wrapped in your love to rejoin the circle of life. Do not tarry to grieve, but take your living children east, and there make a new beginning. Come to me at first light for the means to free yourself."

Chapter Three

In the gray dawn, Nina sat on the pond bank catching a pale glimmer of light off the water. With paper and pencil from her bags, she scribbled a note of introduction for Isobel to take to Dalton's mistress in Easthaven. Having heard no word pass the woman's lips yesterday, Nina thought it likely that Isobel was mute. If that were so, then only a written note would accomplish her purpose in sending the woman to Tilda for aid.

She was putting the final line to the message when a soft disturbance rose on the pond's far side. Sleepy twitterings and the faint rustling of wings betrayed the presence of waterfowl.

Nina rose stealthily, pocketed the note, and took the sling from around her neck. As she crept toward the awakening flock, a stand of prairie willows provided cover. One final step took her into the clear. She whirled her sling and slammed a stone into the breast of a bird that had launched itself from the water, its wings flapping frantically. The bird tumbled from the sky, smacking the damp sand only feet from Nina. It had barely come to rest before she was sailing another stone into the flock.

Birds erupted from the water then, squawking, colliding with each other. Before the last of the flock could take wing and fly beyond the reach of the dozen or more stones she flung into their midst, Nina had downed enough of the big-bodied, meaty waterbirds to feed every camper who had been startled awake by the noise of the slaughter.

One of those campers was the boy of fourteen, Isobel's flaxen-haired eldest. He stood across the pond from Nina, his gaping stare visible in the growing light of this new day.

She beckoned to him and the boy came at a run, his thin legs carrying him around the pond with the speed of an antelope. He was too thin, too underfed to have stamina. His sprint left him gasping for breath. But Nina saw the spark in his eye, the light of curiosity, his desire to learn. He wanted to know the means by which he might bring down the meat that would keep him and his family alive. This boy was ready—past ready—to step into the role unfilled by his father.

"It's a sling," Nina said, showing him the weapon's braided hemp cords and its stone-holding pocket of leather. "Easy to make. Not so easy to use. Help me carry these birds to your mother, dress them—do you know how?—and I'll give you a lesson in slinging."

The boy did know how to dress waterfowl. His siblings, some of them still half asleep, pitched in to help. They plucked the feathers, chopped off the heads and feet, pulled the entrails out. The children saved anything remotely edible. Nina averted her gaze as one of the girls took special care with each small avian skull, cracking them open one by one and slurping down the brains, raw.

Soon the children had three of the birds roasting over a new-built fire. Leaving them to tend their breakfast feast, Nina drew the eldest boy aside and put her sling into his hands.

He proved to be a quick learner. Before the morning sun had cleared the mist from the pond's surface, he was whirling the weapon in smooth arcs, though mostly botching the timing of his releases. But clearly he understood the basics of this simple stone-throwing device. With practice—many hours of practice—this boy might be knocking birds from the sky, even bringing down antelope.

The slinging lesson ended with the boy once again out of breath. To build muscle and stamina, he desperately needed daily nourishment, as did all his kin. Nina sent him to eat fire-roasted waterfowl while she kept her appointment with the boy's mother. The meeting she had planned for first light had been delayed by the morning's bird hunt and weapons training.

Nina found Isobel with the matron, handing that woman one of the dressed birds, offering it in partial payment for the quantities of her neighbor's food that her brood had consumed.

"You needn't," the matron was saying as Nina joined them. "Keep it for your children."

Isobel, silent as ever, shook her head and held out the plucked carcass, insistent.

"Very well," the matron said. "I thank you. Now we're off. My husband is eager to reach Easthaven in good time today. Pleasant travels to you."

With those few words of parting—or dismissal—the woman turned away from both Isobel and Nina. She wedged the dressed meat into a corner of her fully loaded wagon, then hoisted herself into the driver's seat. Her husband slumped beside her, looking anything but eager. His hat was pulled low over his eyes, and as his wife snapped the reins to start the wagon rolling, his hands came up to hold his head as though he feared it might shake loose.

Hung over, I'll wager, Nina thought, remembering the rough laughter that had drifted through their night's encampment, the two drunken gamblers braying like donkeys.

Which reminds me, she thought then. *Where, this fine spring morning, is Isobel's worthless husband? Still sleeping it off?* Herself awake since the predawn, she had not yet laid eyes on that man.

Shrugging, she returned the matron's brief wave of farewell, not much surprised that all of that woman's friendliness from last night seemed to have evaporated at sunrise. Pity had moved the matron to do what she could for the unfortunate Isobel, for as long as the vagaries of travel had thrown them together. But now her journey's end was in sight, and the matron—quite sensibly—wanted her family on the road, her husband parted from a bad influence, and her children spared the tears of a funeral. This day would end the suffering of the tiny skeleton that lay in the only wagon remaining at this waterhole.

If fate refuses to take that child, I will release her myself, Nina silently vowed. She'd seen water hemlock growing under the willows at the pond's edge. It would do.

But first, she owed Isobel that other herb, the one she had spoken of last night, the one by which a woman could decide for herself when and with whom to have children.

"I haven't forgotten," she said, turning to the thin, haggard woman who stood watching the matron disappear down the dusty road. "That plant I was telling you about—a patch of it grows by the water. We'll pick it for a tea to wash down your breakfast." The woman seemed only half aware as Nina took her arm and guided her to the pond. "Hurry," Nina urged her, "before your children finish off every scrap and leave you no bite. You must eat too, you know."

Isobel made no acknowledgment, but she went where Nina led. She seemed to regain some of her focus, to be more wholly present in the moment, when Nina drew her down to the pond bank. With much repetition to be certain the lessons stuck, Nina showed the woman the herb, how to identify it, and how to strip its leaves so that some of the stem's peel remained attached.

"You'll need both," she explained. "They work together, leaves and stem, so be sure to catch a little of the stalk in every cup you brew. Drink a cup each day if you can," she added. "That is safest ... especially if your man is the insistent type."

At this, Isobel looked up and locked gazes with her. But Nina could not be certain what she read in the woman's eyes. Anguish? Resignation? Or was that a touch of defiance, perhaps a glint of satisfaction?

Isobel filled her apron skirt with the herb's leaves and stems, then creaked upright, her movements stiff like those of a woman thrice her age. Nina followed her back to the campfire and watched her prepare the tea. As it brewed, the woman picked slivers of flesh from the bones that her brood had gnawed and discarded.

"That won't do!" Nina protested. "You must eat, Isobel. Would you starve yourself and leave your children motherless?"

The woman's reply was to sip tea from a battered tin mug. But when her son twisted a drumstick from a roasted bird and handed it to her, Isobel put down her mug and bit deeply. Hot juices trickled down her chin.

Which reminded Nina that she had not yet breakfasted today, herself.

She left her companions to enjoy their feast—every morsel of it supplied by Nina—and drew aside to make her own meal on dry bread and cheese from her saddlebags. Also from her bags she took her spare sling. Though the weapon was simple and relatively quick to construct, she liked having a spare immediately at hand. But she would part with her second sling this morning, gifting it to Isobel's son if he wanted it.

Her meager breakfast done, Nina dusted bread crumbs from her hands and got to her feet. She looked across to Isobel's wagon, expecting to see the family packing up, harnessing their horses and stowing the children. But most of the young ones were on their knees now, digging in the rocky ground.

Her puzzlement at this lasted only an instant. Nina spotted Isobel and the eldest boy standing behind the wagon. From its bed, the boy lifted a tiny, blanket-wrapped bundle. He carried the bundle to the freshly dug grave, and without ceremony his siblings heaped stones over their dead sister. Isobel stayed at the wagon, dry-eyed, never glancing at Nina.

Nina kept her distance, watching with her hand over her heart, respecting the right of these people to bury their dead undisturbed by outsiders. But with his part in the "funeral" now concluded, the boy came straight to her.

"I found this," he announced. His voice was bright, no grief in it as he stood before her and pulled something from his pocket. "Is it good? Make a sling, will it?"

The boy opened his fist to reveal a piece of leather the size and shape of the tongue from a boot. It was old leather, dark, stained from long use. But as the boy showed it to her, Nina saw how supple it was. The piece was perfectly appropriate for shaping into a sling pocket.

"It's very good," she said. "Trim it here"—she pointed—"and shave this side to make an oval." From under her jacket, she brought out the spare sling she had meant to give to this boy. Now the gift seemed unnecessary. Nina used it only to guide him in finishing his handiwork. "Be sure to make the cords long enough—like so." She laid the weapon full upon the ground and stretched out its cords, demonstrating as she spoke.

The boy crouched to place his piece of leather over the pocket of Nina's spare sling. Then he sat flat in the dirt, his legs together and extended alongside the cords, using his outstretched limbs like a yardstick to gauge the lengths required. Satisfied with his measurements, he bounded up, grabbed his scrap of leather and turned away, seemingly ready to end his acquaintance with Nina without further ado.

"Wait!" she called. "I have something for your mother."

From her trousers pocket, Nina pulled out the note she'd scribbled in the early dawn. "I wish for your mother to take this to Easthaven and give it to a woman she will meet there. A woman I have told her of." Nina glanced at the sun, which by now had climbed well up the sky. "You are getting a late start this morning, but I believe you may still reach Harbor Hill today if you delay no longer."

She looked over the boy's shoulder to see his siblings still piling rocks on their sister's grave. In these few minutes, they had done a respectable job of burying it under layers of stone. The efficiency with which the children conducted the burial suggested this was not the first sibling they had laid in the ground. Nina observed that Isobel had left the wagon. The woman moved more slowly than her children in piling rocks upon the mound, but she had joined the effort.

Which was more than could be said for the woman's husband. Nina scanned the area from the wagon to the now-cold campfire. She took in the still-tethered horses of the wagon team, grazing undisturbed along the pond's edge. She cast her gaze across to the water's far bank, and yet saw no trace of Isobel's husband.

"Where is your father?" Nina abruptly demanded. She grabbed for the boy's arm as he made to turn away from her again. "Will he not help to bury his own dead child?"

The boy shrugged. "Pappy ne'er liked 'er," he muttered. "Said she were a wrong 'un." He tapped his head—exactly where Nina had noted a deformity on the little girl's skull.

The boy pulled away and trotted back to his siblings. The burial was done, and they were breaking camp. Into the now-roomier bed of their wagon, the children tossed dented cookpots, ragged clothing, frayed blankets. The boy brought up the family's horses. No one paid the least attention to Nina any longer. She stood alone in the fast-disappearing camp, apparently forgotten and entirely unthanked for either the breakfast feast or the note of introduction.

It was not the family's ingratitude, however, that made her frown as she went to saddle her horse and load her gear. A suspicion was growing, one Nina felt compelled to investigate.

Mounting, she reined Traveller away from the campsite and away from the nearby road. Slowly, Nina made her way around the pond—all the way around, past the willows and the shallow end where the waterbirds had fallen to her marksmanship.

Beyond that point, with something like three-quarters of her circuit complete, Nina saw it: a body in the water. It lay head down, nothing showing but the feet and those barely visible, tangled in mats of pond-side greenery. The feet, judging by their size and blocky shape, were a man's. They were bare, uncovered by boots or even stockings.

"So here you are, worthless husband of Isobel," Nina muttered to the corpse. She kept her voice low, though she was now entirely alone at the pond. While she circled it, seeking this confirmation of what she suspected, the dead man's family had hitched up and cleared out. As she glanced up past the grassy patch their horses had grazed, Nina saw nothing now at the deserted campsite, not even a wisp of smoke from the cold, dead fire.

"What happened to you last night?" she asked, returning her attention to the corpse. "Did you trip on those weeds and pitch facedown into the water? Were you too drunk to haul yourself out?"

And from where had the liquor come? How had this wastrel got his hands on enough of it to get that drunk?

Recalling the matron's husband and how that man had hidden under his hat as they fled this place, Nina could guess: That man had supplied the strong spirits, and with his drinking companion he had laughed and joked and played at dice until the small hours. But then what? Had the matron's husband staggered back to the wagons but left Isobel's man to weave his drunken way toward a drowning death?

"Or did you quarrel over dice?" Nina wondered aloud, still addressing the corpse. "Did your chum strike you? Did he put you in the water?"

At what point had the wastrel's son found his father lying dead and relieved the corpse of its boots? Nina could not doubt that the piece of leather the boy had shown her, the leather meant for a sling pocket, had been cut from the tongue of one of those missing boots.

She drew a sharp breath as her conjecturing expanded to include the boy and his mother. Perhaps Nina was unfairly accusing the matron's husband. Hadn't Isobel had good reason to hate the man who would not feed his children? Perhaps that quietly desperate woman had lashed out last night, pushed past the breaking point by the wastrel's drunken laughter as their starved daughter lay breathing her last.

Or had Isobel's son knocked his father into the water and held him down with cold singleness of purpose? Remembering the boy's excitement over the tongue of leather, Nina could believe that he'd had more use for his father's boots than for the man himself. She winced as she recalled her own enthusiasm for the boy's "find," how she'd declared the leather "perfect" for shaping a sling pocket.

"Drisha's knuckles," she muttered as she stared at the barefoot corpse. "I meant only to give the boy some means of putting meat on the family table. Did I unwittingly encourage an act of murder?"

Shaking her head at the sea of speculation she had conjured, Nina turned away from the corpse, unable to choose a most-probable cause of death from among the possibilities. She rode the rest of the way around the pond, examining its edge, looking for additional evidence but finding nothing conclusive. She ended the circuit back at the cold campfire.

Gnawed bird-bones lay scattered in its ashes. Nina dismounted to rake them up and throw them in the pond. The corpse that lay mostly underwater at the pond's weedy edge, a short walk from this ash heap, would draw scavengers. The man's family had made a passable effort to properly bury his daughter, but they had left the wastrel to rot where he'd fallen.

"So be it," Nina muttered as she wiped her hands. If his family owed him nothing, then neither did she. But she wanted no scraps, not even burnt bones, left where they might bring scavengers to sniff around the tiny body under the piled rocks.

She stood at the grave, her head bowed, and whispered lines that she had memorized long ago from the *Book of Archamon*. "Life is a circle," Nina recited. "A flaming arc that we know, rounding to a dark sweep of time that we cannot know. We neither join the circle nor leave it. We are forever the circle, and it forever us."

The ancient benediction seemed to hang in the air, and then filter down through the mounded stones.

Nina raised her head and stepped away. She swung into the saddle, ready to resume her interrupted journey. Her road lay beyond the scatter of thorn trees that screened off the pond. She headed back through those trees, retracing her path from last evening when she'd been drawn to a troubled family by the flickering of their campfire.

But as she reached the road Nina reined up again, her gaze caught by a folded piece of paper that a light breeze had carried into the brushy verge.

With a frown, she swung down to retrieve the paper, knowing without unfolding it that she held the note of introduction she had scribbled for Isobel. Had it been lost from the boy's pocket? Or did Isobel cast it away?

Nina sighed. No point wasting a good sheet of writing paper. She tucked the note into her saddlebag, remounted, and reined Traveller southwestward. In that direction lay the hamlet of Granger—the unassuming place where her mother had long ago been a servant, and where Nina's youngest brother now lived.

"Trav, my friend," Nina said as the roan settled into a comfortable, ground-covering walk. "We're getting a shamefully late start today, and it's because I stuck my nose where it had no business to be. Kick me, will you, the next time I decide to meddle in the affairs of strangers."

Traveller blew softly through his nostrils and gave a slight bob of his head. Nina smiled. She and this horse were going to get on fine together.

Chapter Four

Her resolve to keep to herself lasted all of that afternoon. Nina said no word to any rider she met on the road. Most of them were equally silent, though two or three offered a quick salutation—"Good day" or "Go with Drisha"—as they touched their riding crops to their hat brims. Several horsemen overtook Nina, going the same way she was but at greater speed. These spurred past without a word. With her braided hair tucked into a slouchy cap, and her rapier hanging from her belt, Nina would look like a young man to any wayfarer approaching at her back. That was as she wished.

She herself overtook no one until the day was nearly done. Pushing Trav too hard this early in their journey would be madness. A worn-out horse could collapse under her at the very moment she needed his best speed. So Nina let the roan set his own pace, which proved nimble enough to suit her leisurely plans for this expedition, and also speedy enough to eventually catch up with the colorful wagon that she had trailed for miles.

As she approached the wagon, Nina studied the objects dangling from every side. There were the usual pots and pans of the itinerant tinker or tinsmith. Among those, however, hung objects of better quality and greater interest, including horse bridles trimmed with brass medallions finely cast. Beside them swayed children's toys crafted of wood, intricately carved and gaily painted: balls and bats, toy swords, lifelike dolls richly dressed. The westering sun also picked out bright enamels and jewel tones: ladies' ornaments were strung on velvet cords, interspersed with delicate bells that jingled with every roll of the wagon's wheels. Nina marveled that any merchant would carry such a variety, and would display his wares so openly, practically inviting thieves to fall upon him.

She glanced ahead at the driver and his companion, and caught her breath as the massiveness of the second man was revealed. Trailing behind the pair mile after mile, studying them from a distance that had only slowly diminished, Nina had supposed the driver to be unusually small. And his companion, she had thought, must be wearing a cloak that billowed around him, its folds creating an illusion of hugeness.

But no: the second man was in fact a giant. No cloak covered the sleeveless shirt that displayed his bulging muscles. His powerful shoulders rippled like a bull's. From his enormous bald head, two colossal ears stuck out like the shells of giant marine clams. He sat motionless beside the driver, dwarfing that man, although Nina could now see that the driver was himself a fellow of ample size. No wonder the merchant was unconcerned about displaying his wares so boldly. The hulking giant sent a clear message to any would-be thief: pilfer at your peril.

Reflexively, Nina loosened the throwing knife at her belt, but her only thought was to move away from the wagon. Continuing to ride close behind it was out of the question. The pair might think she was attempting to grab the dangling treasures. Her only choices were to fall back or hasten ahead. She rejected the yield-the-way option: retreat would be spineless, and in any case the driver and his bodyguard might misinterpret such a move as fresh preparation for a rearward assault. So Nina did the only thing remaining. She nudged Traveller to a quicker pace, and rounded the wagon at a brisk, confident walk until she was abreast of its driver.

As she moved alongside the man, meaning to give him the slightest nod with the quickest glance that civility demanded, Nina found herself staring instead. The driver was so ugly, he was charming. His wrinkled face and sagging jowls were more doglike than human. The expression in his clear brown eyes—friendly, but a tad imploring—added to the doggish impression, as did the man's flowing locks. Streaming over his shoulders, his tawny hair resembled the silky coat of a hound bred for cold climates. Nina was reaching to pet the man before she knew what she was doing.

With a gasp, she jerked away and laid her hand upon the hilt of her knife.

The man laughed, plainly aware of the effect produced by his appearance.

"Good afternoon, my lady," he boomed, his voice a hound's deep baying. "I seen you back yonder, following us all this while like you've no place to be and no reason to get there. But evening's coming on, and this way's no place for a lady after dark." He nodded at the empty road that stretched ahead. "You're welcome to camp with Grog and me tonight."

Nina needed a moment to realize that "Grog" was the giant's name, not an invitation to get drunk with this doggish fellow. She needed a further moment to weigh her options. The sun would set within the hour, and she did not relish the thought of continuing in the dark. But what trouble would she be inviting, to share a fire tonight with a hound and a giant?

The man grinned.

"Be at your ease, my lady," he boomed. "In all the southland you'll not find a more honest fellow than Grog here." The man reached to pat the giant's bare, bulging shoulder. "Too, if you were to speak the name Nimrod—that's me—anywhere between here and the coast, or down as far as Granger, you'd hear hardly a complaining word." He chuckled as he added, "A few might say I drive a hard bargain, but that's no sin in a traveling shopkeeper. A man's gotta eat. And Grog here"—again he gave the giant an affectionate pat—"Grog eats for five."

"I, um, don't doubt it," Nina half stammered, finding her voice for the first time since rounding the wagon and facing the hound-dog driver. "As it happens," she said, "I have a brother in Granger, and it's to his house that I am bound."

Nina considered hiding Legary's identity behind a false name, for surely this roving trader would know the master mason of Granger. If the stories about Legary were even partly true—all the stories Nina had heard over the years, of the prodigious feats performed by the stone-crafter *wysard*—then her brother was a legendary figure known to all in the south. To claim that she was close kin to such a famous individual might make this "Nimrod" think she was a scheming imposter.

On the other hand, her claim of illustrious kinship might ensure the good behavior of the hound and the giant if she shared a camp with them tonight.

"Perhaps you know my brother, or know of him," Nina said, deciding to risk the name. "Legary the stonemason has an outsized reputation in these parts, if I may judge by the tales I heard these past years when I was living ... away from here."

"Legary!" the hound exclaimed. "You are Master Legary's little sister?"

Big sister, Nina started to correct him. But why say more than she must to this stranger? If she had emerged from the otherworldly void looking younger than her baby brother, thanks to the void's warping of time, then why argue?

"I have that honor," she replied, smiling at the hound-dog's surprise. "But though Master Legary and I have had much news of each other, and have followed each other's lives as best we can, we have never met face-to-face. We are not close in age. Decades lie between the day of my brother's birth and the hour of my coming into this world."

"You're the sister who went to teach in the mountains! That right?"

Nina could not hide her shock or subdue the reflex it produced. She jerked the reins, and Trav swerved away from the wagon. Within two steps, she and the horse had recovered. As they resumed their post by the driver's side, Nimrod appeared to read nothing in her stumble. Perhaps it had seemed to be only a horse's misstep on an uneven roadway.

But Nina's thoughts were still stumbling, tumbling over each other.

Did Legary place such trust in this south-country merchant, that he would speak openly to him of a master *wysard* of Ruain? Would Legary engage in gossip about his true baby sister, Vivienne the extraordinarily gifted daughter of House Verek? That lady had indeed journeyed to the western mountains to teach wizardly apprentices the *art magick*. More importantly, to Nina's way of thinking, Vivienne was destined to take her father's place as the head of their ancient house. What business did Legary have, telling any outsider where the members of that great family went or what they did with their lives?

But consider, Nina thought then. *You have revealed to this puggish outsider your own family ties. You readily told him where you are going. Does this man have the power of loosening tongues? Does he charm the unwary into telling too much?*

Nina shot Nimrod a cautious glance. But she elected to answer his question with the truth, seeking to draw him out and learn what else he might know.

"I'm not the sister who went to the mountains," she said. "I'm the one who went to sea."

Nimrod threw back his head and howled. "The sea goddess!" he boomed, laughing. "By the marrow of me! I never thought I would fall in with a sea goddess out here on these dry plains. You are quite the fish out of water, aren't you, my lady!"

Nina's astonishment was complete. Legary, evidently, had told this fellow everything.

So much for the spell of omission, she thought. Her stonecrafter brother had apparently been incapable of omitting any detail about the hidden—or formerly hidden—province of Ruain. Nina could not help gaping at Nimrod, so staggered was she to discover that this mortal male knew so much about her and her wizardly family.

What was more, even the silent Grog had responded to his companion's bellow of "sea goddess." The hulking colossus had sat unmoving this whole time, never glancing Nina's way. But now he turned his huge head on his almost absent neck, and peered at Nina with limpid blue eyes.

Meeting his gaze was like falling into tidewater pools. Nina felt transported back to the Eastern Sea from which she had lately come. Or perhaps if she swam in those blue pools long enough, she'd be flung all the way across the void, to land with a *plop* in the great Pacific Ocean that had ringed her other life.

But then Grog blinked, sweeping his thick eyelids over those magical orbs, breaking contact with Nina's gaze before she was lost in the depths. The big man swiveled his head to the fore, to resume his study of the featureless roadway up ahead, a road that was getting hard to see. Dusk was falling.

"We'll pull in there," Nimrod said. He pointed to thin shadows that loomed against the sunset. "If memory serves, there's a fine little spring down off the road yonder. A patch of grass too, enough for these animals."

Into the shadows Nina followed him, halting with him in a grove of spiky trees. The trees formed a loose wall around a bubbling spring. Enclosed by that wall, a water-fed meadow offered grazing for Traveller and for the merchant's wagon team.

The care of her horse and the business of setting up camp gave Nina a chance to calm her thoughts and form her questions. She had many. Until she knew more of this fellow Nimrod, she was not prepared to trust him to the extent that Legary evidently had. Nina frowned as she stripped her gear off Trav. How unsettling, to think that a brother she had never met would talk about her outside the confines of family. Just how much might Nimrod know about her life beyond the void?

When she'd finished grooming, watering and pasturing her horse, Nina claimed a place by the spring and watched the hound and the giant. Nimrod kept up a constant banter while they unhitched and unharnessed their team. Then the man turned to rummaging in his wagon. From under his assorted wares, he pulled out pounds of fresh vegetables and a side of beef.

In contrast to his talkative companion, the giant uttered no word. Grog clomped to the spring bearing cookpots and bedrolls, and got a fire blazing across from Nina in an old ring of soot-blackened stones.

Nina eyed the big man. He could break her in two as easily as he snapped lengths of wood for the fire. But in the giant's blue eyes she had seen a vast gentleness—a mildness of temper allied with prodigious strength.

Like a whale, she thought, studying the colossus in the firelight. *Like those humpback whales I swam alongside on my ocean world.* Those leviathans could have killed her with one flip of a tremendous fin or a slap of their tail. But they took care to never harm the diminutive swimmer at their side.

"Feeding this fellow is no easy task," Nimrod boomed. The hound startled Nina from her thoughts as he approached with armloads of beetroots. He dumped the roots beside the spring and reached for a cookpot. "I couldn't help noticing that gleaming knife at your belt," he said, grinning. "Put it to good use, won't you, and help me peel these for our supper."

Nina obliged. At the hound-dog's side she worked, and cautiously began to voice her questions.

"Pray tell me, Master Merchant. What did you mean a while ago, when you called me 'the sea goddess'?" Nina strove to keep her tone light and conversational. "I have been to sea, that much is true. I've come ashore only lately. But that hardly makes me a goddess of the deep." She glanced at him. "I am surprised to hear myself spoken of in such a way."

Nimrod chuckled. "A grand title, is it not? I got it from your brother. It's what he calls his sister the seafarer." The hound grinned as he returned Nina's glance. "I suppose Legary thought 'sea goddess' sounded better than 'common sailor.' When he told me he had a sister who went to sea, I pictured a battle-axe—a woman built along the lines of our friend Grog here." With the stick upon which he had skewered vegetables, Nimrod pointed at the giant. "I thought a woman who chose a maritime life must be a tough old leatherback. Legary's tongue was firmly in his cheek, or so I had presumed, when he called you the sea goddess.

"But now that I've met you," Nimrod added, giving Nina a long look, "I see that your brother spoke the plainest truth. By Drisha's old bones! Many a goddess of legend would wither in your glow."

From most men, those words—accompanied by such a direct gaze as Nimrod's—would be deemed either flattery or impudence, depending on the mood and the character of she who received the compliment. But coming from the doggish merchant, the remark was like a hound's happy smile. It communicated friendly respect.

Nina gave a brief nod of acknowledgment, and relaxed a little. Nimrod's explanation of the "sea goddess" label suggested that Legary might not have been an irresponsible blabbermouth after all. Perhaps there had been no harm in him mentioning a sister who took a teaching job in the mountains, and another sister who had seawater in her veins.

But destruction be upon him, Nina silently swore, *if he has babbled about his sisters' wizardly gifts:* one of them a worker of water-magic so potent, she healed a world with it; and the other an adept with powers to rival the great *wysards* of Archamon's day. No mere mortal needed to know those details about the two daughters of House Verek.

While the supper cooked—the meat in a pan so large, Grog alone could lift it—Nina posed the merchant another question. She needed to know more about this odd man who claimed friendship with her baby brother.

"I confess," she said, "you are the first person named 'Nimrod' that I have met in all my travels. I *have* heard the word used before ... but never favorably. It is often applied to those who are considered fools or half-wits. You will forgive me for mentioning it. I only wish you to know, that if I am slow to address you by the name your mother gave you, it is because I am certain you are *not* half-witted."

"But I *am* very foolish," Nimrod boomed. He laughed as though he didn't care if every cutthroat from here to the coast heard him and came slinking into their camp. "You may believe me, lady of the water, when I tell you that I come by the name honestly. But it is not the name my mother gave me." He winked. "Mayhap I'll tell you, someday, what I am truly called. For now, though, I beg you will use the common name by which I am known throughout these parts."

Nina frowned at the man's evasiveness, but also at his casual use of a term so insulting, it tended to choke in her throat. "Would it offend you," she proposed after a brief silence, "if I addressed you as 'Roddy'? It is a name I heard in my sea-voyaging." She gestured in the general direction of the deep water she had left only yesterday.

"Roddy!" the man exclaimed. "By Drisha, I rather like that." He repeated the word as if tasting it. Then he nodded. "My lady, I am honored by this new name you give me." His grin widened. "Mayhap it will catch on. By year's end I might be a new man in every market town from the Eastern Sea to the southern briny."

But still you will hide your true identity behind a false name, Nina thought, eyeing him, *for names have power.*

Did "Roddy" know what she herself was called? He had not asked, but had Legary told him? As Nina turned the roasting vegetables, she considered giving Roddy her assumed name. How would he react if she introduced herself as "Nerissa," the name she meant to use among strangers?

Volunteer nothing, she decided. *Let him ask, if he wants your name. Reveal no more than you must.*

"How fortunate I am, Master Roddy," she said, smiling at him over the campfire, "to have fallen in with such an experienced long-distance traveler as yourself. Tell me if you please: How did you meet my brother Legary? Is he a customer of yours?"

"More a supplier of goods than a customer," Roddy replied. "Your brother crafts, from the most beautiful red-rose granite, the finest mortars and pestles that I have ever seen or sold. From the best rock also, Legary shapes sling-bullets to fly fast and true." Roddy gestured at the weapon that hung around Nina's neck. "Remind me in the morning and I'll dig some out for you. I have bags of them in the wagon. They don't sell as well as his mortars do. Few in this plains country have skill with the sling, more's the pity." Roddy clicked his tongue. "Since meeting your brother—and witnessing his expertise with the weapon—I have endeavored to interest folks in it, up and down my trade route. There's many a down-and-out family that would eat better if they had a slinger putting wild game on their supper table."

Nina nodded. "I had occasion, very recently, to tutor a boy in sling-craft. He and his family were half starved. They'll have an easier time now, I hope, if the young man does not abandon his practice before he figures out what he's doing."

And if he uses the weapon only on small game, Nina added silently. Her thoughts flashed to the drowned father and his missing boots. Briefly she considered telling Roddy her suspicions about that death. Nina had no evidence except the dead man's missing footwear and the piece of leather the boy had brandished. For her own peace of mind, she would prefer to banish the boy and the boot from her thoughts. But the question she'd asked herself this morning continued to press her: Had she encouraged—and armed—a fourteen-year-old killer?

None of that affair, however, concerned either Roddy or her brother Legary. Nina's attention snapped back to the merchant as he asked about the tradition of slinging in her family.

"From childhood," Nina answered him, "I was trained in the use of the sling." She touched the cords that dangled down her front. "I imagine that Legary received the same instruction in his own youth, although I was not there to witness it."

"If you're as skilled with that weapon as your brother," Roddy responded, "then our friend Grog can have a holiday." He chuckled. "The fellow eats as often as he can, but he seems never to sleep. Maybe he'll catch forty winks tonight, though, with you here to sting the hide of any thief bold or daft enough to creep upon us in the dark." Roddy turned to Grog. "How's that sound, big fellow? Shall you leave the night watch to the lady?"

A grunt came from the hulk who sat tending the fire. It was the first sound Nina had heard Grog make. In the flickering light, the giant's features were those of an ogre.

Nina glanced at him, then away. From Roddy she accepted a plate of skewered vegetables and salty beef. She set to with a will and ate heartily of the only hot meal she'd had today. Her appetite, however, was nothing compared to Grog's. The big man did eat for five, even tipping up the huge cookpot to pour the renderings down his throat once the beef was gone.

As she watched Grog from the corner of her eye, Nina couldn't help feeling sympathy for Roddy, for what it must cost the merchant to feed his bodyguard. Whatever price Roddy got for his goods from one market town to the next, it must take every penny to buy rations for a giant.

* * *

The sun was hours above the horizon before they got on the road the next day. Preparing breakfast for such a voracious eater as Grog took time. While Roddy fixed a meal even larger than last night's beef-and-beetroot supper, Nina saddled Traveller and went hunting.

In the scrub beyond the thorny grove, no great distance from camp, she spotted a herd of the fleet-footed antelope that dotted these plains. Her quick bowshots downed two. Traveller stood braced as Nina heaved the carcasses onto his back. The horse's nostrils flared at the scent of hot blood, but he did not shy from the load.

"Next time I'm in Easthaven," Nina murmured as she walked at Trav's head, leading him back to camp, "I will pay my compliments to that horse trader. He sold me a sensible companion for my foolish journey." But in truth, Nina doubted she would ever see Easthaven again. A return to that seaport seemed unlikely, if she stuck to her plan to travel westward from Granger, across to the desert hills where Galen lived.

And from there, Nina meant to wend her way northeastward, stopping to visit far-flung branches of the Verek family tree before eventually reentering the magical land of Ruain. She was only now beginning to realize that her grand tour might take quite a long time to complete. What was "time," however, to a *wysard?* Its passage held fewer terrors for the adept than for the merely mortal.

But was she still a *wysard?*

Nina paused behind a thicket of trees, screened from the merchant's camp in the grove. With one hand on her horse's reins and the other held high, she attempted to invoke the water magic that had never failed her until she came south.

But again it refused. No drop answered her summons.

It's the shock of separation, nothing more, Nina told herself, chewing her lip. *Think where you are, how strange this land is.*

For the first time in her life, she was away from water. From the age of thirteen, Nina had lived on an island surrounded by a vast ocean.

Only days ago she'd been shipboard, sailing the Eastern Sea of her native world and conjuring great waves. Even when she'd been home in Weyrrock, far inland at the manor house, water had been a constant and magical presence. The old stone mansion was built on a flowing spring of natural potency.

I need time to adjust to this waterless scrubland, that's all, she thought as she rounded the trees and continued toward camp. But the thought carried no real conviction. These plains were not waterless. They were pockmarked with ponds and spring-fed pools—plenty of water for Nina to conjure with.

Except that she lacked the power to do so.

I'll manage without magic, Nina vowed in silence, her lips clamped together. *My mother crossed this southland on foot, carrying only flint, steel, and her sling. I will not shame myself by admitting failure, a scant three days in.*

Grog's eyes lit up at the sight of the two slain antelope that Nina brought into camp. A toothy grin split the giant's face. He clomped over to grab the animals, one in each huge hand, holding them by the scruff as though they weighed no more than kittens. Traveller jigged a step, startled by the giant's approach and the eager way the fellow snatched the carcasses from his back. But the horse soon settled, relieved to be unburdened.

To judge by the flurry of activity that greeted Nina's return to the now-cold fire ring, Grog had eaten his lavish breakfast, and with his companion he was breaking camp. Roddy crouched at the spring, scrubbing pans. The giant had been untethering the wagon team. At sight of the fresh game, however, Grog abandoned the horses, leaving them where they stood. He hurried to disappear beyond the trees, as though wanting privacy for what came next.

Nina stared after him, astonished by the speed with which the muscle-bound giant had moved ... and appalled by thoughts of what Grog might be doing with those two bloody carcasses.

"Roddy," she said, and turned to the merchant who was stacking the clean breakfast gear in the wagon. "Will he ... um ... will he eat them raw?"

The merchant smiled. "Partly. If our big friend could talk—and I'm not saying, mind you, that he cannot, although I have never heard more than a grunt from him. But if Grog were to speechify on the great culinary moments of his life, I believe he would name fresh antelope liver as the most delectable morsel ever to pass his lips." Roddy chuckled. "He'll be looking to you now, to keep him well supplied. And from me you will have unending thanks if you can down enough of those animals to relieve the strain on my purse." The merchant patted his money belt. "It's a great service you'll do me, lady, to fill his belly with wild game."

It seemed that two raw livers, on top of the huge breakfast he had already consumed, were enough to satisfy the giant that morning. Grog emerged from the sheltering trees carrying both carcasses, the animals now gutted, headless, and skinned, all but the livers saved for a future meal. While Nina packed her personal gear and made ready to resume the journey, Roddy and Grog washed and wrapped the dressed carcasses. They loaded the meat into the wagon, then finally hitched up their horses.

The sun was creeping toward noon before they got back on the road, but no one seemed to mind. Roddy kept the wagon rolling at the same leisurely pace as yesterday, and Nina rode alongside wherever the roadway's width permitted it.

Occasionally she veered off into the scrublands that stretched to the horizon on either side. Antelope had scattered from view, but Nina flushed a covey of prairie chickens out of the brush. With a thunderous whir of wings, the birds exploded from hiding and fluttered low over the grass, easy targets. Nina's sling-work brought down half the flock.

She cut across the open country to rejoin the road not far behind the slow-moving wagon. Trav brought her up alongside Roddy's bodyguard. Grog seemed unimpressed by the fifteen dead chickens that Nina tossed into the wagon behind him. Roddy, however, let out a whoop.

"My profits increase!" he boomed. "That's one more meal I shan't have to buy."

Nina rode around behind the wagon to come up on its other side, the better to speak with the merchant. Grog was not a conversationalist. Though it seemed discourteous to talk about the big man while he sat silent but hearing every word, Nina had a question for Roddy concerning the giant's seeming inability to rustle up his own grub.

"If you think he'd like it," she said, turning to the merchant, "I could take Grog hunting with me. Give him pointers on tracking game. I expect he wouldn't have to get really close to bring down a buck antelope. With his muscles, he could throw a rock from any distance and crack open a skull."

Mentally picturing such a hunt, Nina added, "If he even needed the rock, that is. Sit him down beside a waterhole where the antelope come to drink of an evening, let him get still as a stone, the way he is now"— Nina nodded at the motionless hulk on the seat beside Roddy—"and then when the herd comes close: *Bam.* One good blow from that man's fist would snap an antelope's neck."

Grog responded to this suggestion with a moan of what sounded like horror.

Roddy patted the giant's leather-clad knee. "It's all right," he murmured. "You'll not be doing any of that. The lady meant no offense, I'm sure. It's just that she does not know your ways."

Nina clapped a hand over her mouth, aghast at the reaction to her words. "Forgive me!" she exclaimed, lowering her fingers enough to splutter out an apology. "I was only trying to help him get enough to eat."

"All's well," Roddy said, turning back to her. "Speak of it no more." He reinforced the warning with a shake of his head and a small motion of one hand, like a gesture of erasing or rubbing out.

Nina heeded his admonition. After a moment of awkward silence, during which she cast around for a safe topic, she launched into a discourse on the sea life that she had known and befriended during her oceanic sojourn. Nina spoke of swimming with whales and manta rays ... of playing catch with dolphins ... of sitting on the beach with her feet in the water while small fish nibbled her bare toes. She told of fish massing, huge schools of them flashing this way and that as though controlled by a single mind. Nina talked of coral reefs and their brilliant inhabitants, pushing the common tongue of Ladrehdin to its limits in her attempts to describe the colors of those creatures. They had been every shade of pink, green, purple, blue, red, gold, lilac ... their patterns spotted, banded, and striped.

By the time she finished her travelogue, Roddy was smiling again. Beside him on the wagon seat, Grog seemed to have melted into a contented lump, so relaxed was the big fellow. He'd hung on her every word.

Studying him, Nina again wondered: What was it about Grog that reminded her of the whales she had once swum with? Why did he seem a gentle leviathan who was as far removed from his proper element as Nina felt estranged from her own?

And how had he ended up as the silent partner of a traveling merchant? she wondered silently.

That evening, Nina left the men making camp while she rode alone into the twilight, her bow in her hand. A full moon aided her hunt. She rode with the rising orb at her back and traveled a distance onto the plain before she spotted her prey, and heard it: the grunting of hogs. The moon picked out a small herd rooting for tubers.

With a single arrow, Nina downed a yearling boar. Its sudden death sent the herd into swinish hysterics, and threatened to send them after her. She answered with her sling, flinging stones not with lethal force, but hard enough to smart. The hogs soon tired of the pelting and trotted off into the scrub, grunting with anger but leaving her to claim her kill.

Nina found, however, that she could not lift the carcass onto her horse. The boar was too heavy. Unthwarted, she fished in her saddlebags for a coil of stout rope, something else she had pinched from Dalton's ship.

Traveller seemed dubious when Nina got the rope around the boar's back legs and, remounted, asked the horse to drag the lifeless, stinking lump. Patiently she coaxed as he pulled the bulky carcass through brambles.

But if the horse had doubts, they were nothing to Grog's misgivings. The giant flatly rejected the hog that Nina hauled into camp.

"Ugh," the big man grunted, and turned away radiating disgust.

Nina felt the force of his rebuff as if it had been the slap of a whale's fin. Scowling, she watched him hunker at the fire. All fifteen of her prairie chickens were roasting there, along with a sizable hunk of the antelope that she'd previously brought him. With or without the hog, they would eat well tonight. But Nina—and Trav—had expended a not inconsiderable effort to deliver that carcass to the table. Rejected though it was, she was loath to drag it back through the moonlit brambles and dump it for the vultures to feast upon at daybreak.

"So," she addressed Roddy as the merchant came to inspect the trussed-up carcass. "Am I to butcher this creature myself?"

He scratched behind his ear. "Only if you intend to consume the entire thing on your own. I should have warned you," he said, "but it never entered my thoughts that you would hunt such large game. The wild pigs in this brush can be dangerous. I would recommend keeping clear of them—especially since pork is the one meat that our friend will not eat. Out of respect for him, neither do I consume it. Not in his presence, anyway."

Nina would have thrown up her hands, had she not been holding the tow-rope as well as her horse's reins.

"That's twice today that I have offended the fellow," she muttered, too softly for Grog to hear over the crackling of fire and the hiss of roasting meat. "First I want him to hunt for himself—a prospect that appears to horrify him. Now I've gone out on his behalf, only to bring him meat that he despises." She jerked her chin at the lump on the ground. "There's no help for it, I suppose, but to haul this thing back where it came from. Though I count it a shame to have killed for no purpose."

"The meat need not be wasted," Roddy replied, smiling up at Nina. "Perhaps you have not noticed, but we do not camp alone tonight." He gestured at the tall brush that screened them from the road. "Just down there, a family pulled in shortly after you had left us this evening. I daresay they'll esteem the gift of more meat than they have likely seen in a month. If your horse can be persuaded to drag the beast a little farther, then take it to our neighbors and be done with your toils tonight."

With a brief flattening of his ears, Trav communicated his resentment of this new task. But he went at it with stoic determination. Horse and rider were welcomed into the adjacent camp, where a family of six could hardly believe their good fortune. The father of the brood would not accept the meat as a gift but insisted on paying for it to the extent he was able.

Thus, a few coins jingled in Nina's pocket when she led Traveller back to her party's side of twin, spring-fed waterholes. As the first to arrive, Roddy had claimed the upstream pool, a rock-rimmed basin into which fresh water bubbled from a stony fracture. The neighbors had camped lower down, where the upper pool dripped into a depressed, slightly boggy area. Nina tethered Trav at the natural dividing line between the two camps. As she unsaddled and groomed the horse, she apologized for riding him all day and then asking him to drag stinking meat for an hour past sundown.

Her grumpy mood was not improved when she returned to the fire to find only three birds remaining of the fifteen she'd bagged early in the day. Granted, the prairie chickens were small and less meaty than domesticated fowl. But Grog seemed to regard a dozen of them as no more than an appetizer. He'd taken that many for his portion, and was now devouring an antelope's hindquarter.

Roddy chuckled as he served Nina half of what meat was left. He split the remaining chickens with her and added a small loaf of bread, cut and filled with shreds of antelope.

"Eat, my lady," he said in his usual booming voice. "You must be starved after your labors."

To be sure, Nina was ravenous. She had eaten nothing since breakfast, so intent had she been on stalking the scrublands for game.

No pork for you, huh? she thought, eyeing the colossus who was licking his fingers after gnawing clean the antelope's bones. *No hunting for you, either? From tomorrow, big fellow, you will eat what I bring in, or you'll watch me hunt for no one except myself. Find your own raw liver.*

Grog appeared to be unaware of Nina's scrutiny. But perhaps he read something in her silence, or he felt the irritation that must emanate from her like heat from the campfire—heat that had him sweating. Grog had been at that fire all evening, tending roasted chicken and spitted antelope. Sweat ran down his face. But rather than back away, he held his hands near the fire and inspected them by its light. His fingers glistened with saliva and with fat from the meat that he'd clawed off the bone and stuffed into his mouth.

"Ugh," the giant grunted, repeating the sound of disgust he'd directed at the hog.

The fellow hoisted himself up and towered over the fire, his sweat dripping. Grog shot a glance at Nina, the look in his round eyes shy, almost entreating. Then he clomped away, heading as far from the bubbling spring as he could get without crowding their neighbors' encampment. In the shadows beyond the firelight, he stripped down and splashed into the horses' watering hole. Moonlight glinted from the drops the big man flung in all directions.

Nina dropped her gaze, giving the giant his privacy. She shifted around toward Roddy.

"What was all of that about today," she asked, low-voiced, "when I offered to take Grog hunting? The way that fellow loves meat, I thought he would jump at the chance. Instead, he seemed insulted." Nina raised an eyebrow. "What's his story? He will eat meat but he won't lift a finger to hunt it? Where I'm from, some would call that unsporting."

Roddy sighed. The man glanced in Grog's direction, as if to be certain his friend could not overhear.

No chance of that, Nina thought as she followed Roddy's gaze and saw the giant scrape at the folds in his huge, clamshell ears. Grog was dipping first one ear and then the other into the water, filling and emptying each by turns, as if each protuberance was in fact the half-shell of a giant clam.

"He can't hear us," Nina whispered. "Tell me about him so maybe I can keep from upsetting him again." She rubbed her lower lip. "I'm not keen on the idea of an upset giant."

Roddy turned back to her. The look he gave Nina was the most serious expression she had seen on the merchant's puggish face.

"My lady, Grog's relationship with meat is ... complicated," the man said, his voice hushed—proving that he could speak in tones lower than a bellow. "As you have seen, our friend does crave meat at every meal. But Grog is shamed by the bloody work of butchering it, which is why he will not disembowel game out in the open, but hides the act from view as he did this morning."

Roddy paused, locking gazes with Nina as if to be sure she fully absorbed his words. "Far worse than butchering it, however, is killing it," he murmured. "Under no circumstance would the fellow kill his own meat. I do believe our friend would starve before he would take the life of any animal. The thought appalls him. My dear huntress, you shocked him to his core with your suggestion that he might break an animal's neck bare-handed."

Nina stared at the merchant, her mind filling with the implications. A natural next question rose in her thoughts, but she hesitated to ask it.

"Then he's not ...," she muttered, and trailed off, wanting to soften her words but finding that she must speak frankly. "Then he's not doing an honest job as your bodyguard, Master Merchant. He seems an imposter. How is he earning his keep? If Grog cannot kill an animal, how can he protect you from thieves and cutthroats? As I know from my life over the sea"—Nina waved in a vaguely easterly direction—"it is sometimes necessary to kill an attacker to preserve one's own life, or the lives of others."

Roddy stroked his beard, which was tawny like his ruff but shot through with gray. "As I say, with Grog it's complicated," he muttered. "The truth is, he's quite capable of killing men. I have seen him do it— but only when the fools gave him no choice." The merchant paused, a weary nod of his head suggesting that he called up dark memories of past violence. "Grog has not been driven to kill a man for a long time now. These days, folks up and down this road know better than to provoke him—and newcomers soon learn."

Roddy crooked a grin as he added, "With that great hulking fellow watching over us, my lady, you can be sure: neither you nor I have aught to fear from cutthroats. Just don't be expecting Grog to join you in the hunt, is all. He can't do it."

Nina paused to take this in. Grog was proving to be ever more surprising. With a nod of thanks, she accepted the cup of after-dinner tea that Roddy handed her. She took a sip, then asked, "How did you two meet? Are there others like him out here in this scrub?"

Roddy shook his head. "He does not come from here. In truth, I cannot say where he *does* hail from. I found him in Easthaven." The merchant studied Nina. "When your ship docked there, did you notice that long spit of land? How it curves out from the shore like an arm embracing the harbor?"

Nina nodded. "My ship's captain made sure I saw it. He pointed out a monument that was raised long ago at the tip-end of that arm. There's a fanciful tale goes with that shrine, so I understand."

Roddy rubbed his jaw with his thumb. "I was half thinking that *you* were the captain of your ship," he said, squinting at her. "Now that I've met you, I find it hard to picture you as a common sailor. It's clear to me why Legary preferred the term 'sea goddess'."

Nina brushed the comment aside. She wanted to be the one asking the questions, not answering them.

"On that particular voyage, I was neither sailor nor captain. Only a passenger eager to disembark and be on my way." She glanced at the waterhole where Grog still sat, unmoving now, his bald head and massive shoulders gleaming in the moonlight like water-washed boulders.

Returning her gaze to Roddy, she said, "But you were telling me how you met your big friend. Did you find Grog in that harbor?"

The merchant nodded. "I spotted him far out on that spit of land. He was sitting in the shade of that old monument. The fellow looked as forlorn as a beached whale."

Nina nearly choked on her tea in her hurry to swallow so she could speak.

"You see it too!" she spluttered, leaning toward Roddy. "I've swum with whales, I know what they are. In appearance, Grog looks nothing like a whale. He's more of a bull. Even so, he has stirred a strong impression in my mind, like a leviathan of the deep."

Roddy eyed Nina thoughtfully. "Yes," he muttered. "One creature of the ocean perceives another."

"What? Do you mean he's a seafarer?" Nina paused, then added, "Or are you saying that Grog came *out* of the ocean."

The merchant shrugged. "I cannot say anything with certainty. Grog speaks no word to me. From him, I have learned nothing of his antecedents. Nor have I met anyone who can shed light on his origins. I know only what I've learned of him through our long acquaintance, since that day I approached him, there at the ocean's edge, and offered him my hand." Roddy peered at Nina in the firelight. "You are the only person—besides myself—that I have seen Grog take a shine to. His friendship is a rare and precious thing. I hope you will value it and trust in it, as I have."

Under Roddy's puppy-dog gaze, Nina felt ashamed of the irritation she had displayed earlier this evening, over that rejected hog. She nodded, contrite. "I thank you, Master Merchant. You have aided my understanding of our big friend." Nina glanced past Roddy, her gaze caught by lumbering movements at the waterhole. "I believe Grog has finished his bath. My turn now. I stink after handling that boar."

Nina stood and went to the packs she had stripped from her tired horse. She pulled out a clean shirt and stockings, and straightened to see Grog climbing the gentle slope from the downstream pool. He was fully dressed in his same nondescript apparel—the only clothes he owned, most likely, for garments big enough to fit him would not be easy to find.

When Grog came up to Nina he hesitated, as though hoping she might speak. Instead, Nina stuck out her hand, a silent offer of apology for every time she had offended or distressed him that day.

With painstaking care, the giant accepted. He extended only two fingers and his thumb, but those wrapped Nina's entire hand. His mitts were enormous and stony hard. Yet his touch was light, conveying immense power perfectly controlled ... like a whale gliding alongside her, careful not to break her.

Grog uttered a soft grunt of what seemed contentment. He released Nina's hand and gave her a nod. The fellow barely had a neck, so a nod of his huge head involved the whole of his upper body.

Curiously honored by the gesture, Nina nodded back. Her gaze followed the big man as he climbed on up to their campsite. A moment later she headed the other way, down to the moonlit waterhole to bathe away the pig stink.

Chapter Five

A time or two in the days that followed, Nina thought of leaving her strange new companions and continuing alone. But a deepening fascination with Grog kept her near, as did her need to sound out Roddy about what else he might know of herself and her siblings. Legary had taken the merchant surprisingly far into his confidence, but Nina was still making up her mind about the doggish fellow. What was Roddy's interest in the children of House Verek, and what reason did the man have for concealing his true name?

Thus the days passed, and she continued in company with the hound and the giant. Nina fell naturally into the rhythm of their travel. Almost every morning while Roddy prepared an enormous breakfast, she went hunting. If she bagged an antelope, Grog would snatch it away into the brush, disappearing from sight as he eviscerated the carcass and gorged on the still-hot liver. The rest of the meat, Roddy stowed for that night's supper.

The routine meant they never got under way until the sun was well up. Despite their late starts, however, the party made decent time on the road. They passed through a landscape that gradually softened. Brambly scrub and dry brush gave way to greener grasslands and scattered farms. The road curved past haystacks, skirted thinly spaced cottages and stone-walled fields, and eventually rambled through the outlying precincts to deliver Roddy's party into the middle of a bustling township.

"Welcome to Plainsboro," the merchant boomed. The sweep of his arm encompassed a market square that was noisy with hagglers and bright with the colorful wares of sundry traders. "I trust you will find this outpost of civilization to your liking. We'll be here a day or two. I can recommend a stable for your horse and suitable quarters for yourself, if such appeal to you."

Those things did indeed appeal. Nina was soon ensconced in a private guesthouse among lush gardens on the well-to-do side of town. Traveller was housed in stables of palatial grandeur, attended by grooms who rubbed him down and massaged his legs until the roan almost purred with pleasure.

For her own pampering, Nina had a proper bath in a proper tub with hot water, soap, and a sweet-smelling lotion to smooth the tangles from her long, freshly washed hair. She also engaged a laundress to scrub the dirt and sweat from her clothes.

Late in the afternoon of their arrival, Nina twisted a scarf around her still-damp mane, donned clean garments, and went shopping. The southern sun dictated her first purchase: a broad-brimmed straw hat. Mindful of the strain on her purse—what she was paying for her lodgings and for Trav's care—Nina meant to spend nothing more on herself. But she could not resist a silky blouse in an icy shade of blue. The fabric promised cool comfort. Spring was on the cusp of summer, with the weather warming and the power of the sun intensifying every day that her party pushed on to the south and west.

With her personal buying complete, Nina ambled up and down the streets of Plainsboro. She poked into odd shops and market stalls, knowing what she sought but doubting she would find it. At last, however, a satisfactory article turned up in a tent shop—an establishment, Nina realized in hindsight, that should have been the first place she looked.

Back in her lodgings, she dropped off her new hat and blouse and took the time to fold her third purchase into a bulky bundle. Nina unwrapped her hair and combed her raven tresses into waves. As dusk approached, she went looking for her companions.

She found them closing up shop for the evening. The merchant grinned from ear to ear, and even Grog looked pleased.

"You've done a brisk trade today, I take it," Nina greeted the pair. "Turned a profit, I'm thinking. No cat that stole the cream ever looked more satisfied with himself."

Roddy laughed. "The gods of commerce have smiled upon me in this fair town." He nodded at the bundle Nina carried. "It appears you have transacted business of your own ... crossed a fortunate palm with silver somewhere in this burg. May I stow your purchase in the wagon, then escort you to supper?" Roddy gestured at an eatery across from the wagons and the awnings that sheltered his wares and those of other merchants. "Your property will be safe. We'll dine just there at the corner, where I am known to the proprietor. A steady diet of fresh antelope," he added, "leaves a man wanting a change, don't you know."

"As does your cooking!" Nina retorted. "Lead on, Master Nimrod. Introduce me to the culinary delights of this place. But," she said as the merchant took the bundle from her hands, "I do not wish that item left in your wagon. Bring it with us. When we have dined, I will present it to Grog."

The merchant's eyebrows shot up, giving him the look of a curious dog. From Grog came a grunt of surprise. But Nina only smiled and said no more as Roddy offered his arm and escorted her to supper.

Their meal was heavy on meat: goat, beef, pork, chicken, and even antelope were on the bill of fare. More appealing to Nina were the leafy greens and root vegetables, many prepared in novel ways. She filled her plate with spiced beets and sweetened potatoes, sprouts baked with goat cheese, green salads tossed with groundnuts. To wash it all down, she had her choice of local wines, but Nina declined alcohol and drank only tea. In this foreign town among strangers, she must keep her wits about her. Especially since a trio of hard-eyed toughs were spending the evening leering at Roddy's party.

The merchant had chosen a table under the stars, well away from the eatery's kitchens and the long bar where the noisiest patrons were ordering endless rounds of beer and laughing loudly at bad jokes. As Nina ran her gaze over the crowd of diners and drinkers—a crowd that swelled as the evening progressed—she could perceive a dividing line, an invisible but definite partition that separated the rowdy crowd at the bar from the more sedate diners in her tree-shaded section of the grounds. The trio of toughs occupied a table that straddled the boundary line. Their backs were to the bar, their faces turned to the genteel side. From their table, they could study every diner in the more respectable half of the crowd.

Choosing their targets, Nina thought with a sidelong glance at the three. *They're looking for wealth and perhaps for weakness ... deciding who they'll waylay tonight.*

Roddy's party assuredly did not appear weak—not with Grog hulking over their table, plunked on a bench that could barely support his weight. The giant kept to the shadows as best he could. Roddy had chosen their table, the eatery's most remote, with an eye to keeping the big man as far from neighboring diners as possible. Even so, Grog was an unmissable presence. Everyone there, except perhaps the drunkest patrons at the bar, had noticed the colossus who put away prodigious amounts of meat. He ate every kind on offer—except, Nina noticed, the pork.

Either those ruffians don't know about Grog, she thought, slanting another glance at the leering trio, *or they're willing to take him on for a chance at Roddy's money.*

Even a casual observer would have seen how freely the merchant spent his profits. Besides the endless servings of meat that slid down Grog's gullet, Roddy ordered the eatery's best wine—a bottle he drank by himself, since neither Grog nor Nina partook. The merchant also bought wine for neighboring tables. He seemed to know most of the diners there. Many of them stopped by his table to exchange greetings, drink Roddy's health, or share news. Most of the well-wishers cast oblique glances at Grog, but none said anything to him.

Everyone who came by, however, demanded that Roddy introduce his newest companion. Nina was the focus of much curiosity and blatantly open stares. She was not the only woman dining that evening. Couples and foursomes occupied tables on the respectable side. Across the dividing line, several women leaned against the bar, and more than a few of those rowdy-side doxies wore daggers on their belts.

Among all the female patrons, however, only Nina had a rapier sheathed at her side. She'd left her bow and quiver at the guesthouse but she was fully armed otherwise, with her sling around her neck and her throwing knife in her belt.

"My friends," Roddy boomed in answer to inquiries about Nina's identity, his typical bellow intensified by the wine he had guzzled. "I have the pleasure and the honor to introduce to you Lady Archer, who is traveling from the coast to join family in the south. This lady has paid me a great compliment, condescending to ride with my wagon and endure the witless company of a poor itinerant merchant."

Hardly witless, Nina thought as she exchanged civilities with Roddy's acquaintances. She had not asked the man to guard her privacy, to keep secret her name or that of her brother Legary. Roddy, however, was a man of discretion. He had assigned her a false identity and blurred the starting place and endpoint of her journey, folding Easthaven and Granger into "the coast" and "the south"—all the detail these strangers needed.

The man's no more witless than he is poor, Nina mused, keeping her thoughts to herself but hearing them confirmed, with laughter and mockery, by all who heard Roddy's protestations of poverty and stupidity.

"A poor merchant indeed!" exclaimed a well-dressed fellow with a neatly curled mustache and gold rings on his fingers. The man pointed at the table that groaned under the weight of all the dishes and drinks Roddy had ordered. "So lacking in funds is Nimrod the simpleton, he must content himself and his friends with dry crusts for supper."

The gold-bedecked man roared as though he had delivered the punch line of a clever joke. Roddy joined in, bellowing laughter.

Nina only smiled. She watched Roddy's well-wishers drift away, back to their own tables or out into the night. Most took their leave with respectful salutes, leaving her in no doubt that "Nimrod" was a figure of consequence in this town: widely known, well liked, highly regarded.

As the dinner crowd thinned but Grog went on eating, Roddy lingered over his wine and Nina took another cup of tea. The eatery's respectable side emptied out, while the rowdy crowd at the bar grew noisier and more quarrelsome. Nina glanced over at the tough trio. Those thugs still loitered, nursing their drinks ... biding their time. Without doubt they had heard the jokes about Roddy's "poverty." The merchant and his well-wishers had been loud enough that every patron in the place must have heard them.

Roddy did not follow Nina's glance. He did not twist in his chair to peer toward the bar, where a drunken argument had erupted. But the man seemed to know exactly what—and who—Nina was looking at.

"Persistent, aren't they," Roddy muttered, his voice a ghost of his usual boom. "Been staring over here all evening."

"They want your money," Nina whispered as she pretended to sip her tea.

Roddy snorted. "More than that, my lady. More, and worse. They want *you*. Do those men not make the hackles rise on the back of your neck? They should. They're predators. Rapists. I have never laid eyes on those particular devils before, but I know their type."

Slowly, Nina nodded. Now that every table stood empty between herself and the thugs, she could feel it: the savagery, the brutishness that pulsed below the men's greed. Greed was commonplace, a vice of many. But these vipers were after more than money. Now in the relative silence of the dining side, she could not only feel their intentions toward her, she could hear what they said, their lewd remarks, their graphically obscene mutters about her body and what they meant to do to it.

They require a lesson in respect, Nina thought. As she fingered the sling around her neck, she recalled the attacker on the road from Easthaven, the man she had left lying in the dust with broken bones, no horse, and a stone-bruised ballsack.

Roddy nodded as if he had followed every thought in Nina's head.

"Show those scoundrels your skill with that weapon," the merchant whispered. He indicated Nina's sling with the slightest tip of his head. "Let them see that their quarry has teeth. We will be spared much unpleasantness, I believe, by a timely display of your mastery." Roddy tilted his head again, this time more emphatically to indicate the colossus who sat across from him.

Grog was still eating. The giant had consumed every scrap of meat, and now he was sampling the cold, leftover vegetables. He did not much like them, Nina thought, judging by his guttural grunts of disfavor.

The big man had seemed not to notice the three waiting villains. Grog gave no sign that he had heard what Roddy said. Nina could not fail, however, to read the warning in the merchant's words and gestures:

If she did not deal with the villains, Grog would. When the trio made their move, the instant they came for either herself or Roddy, those scoundrels would die. Quite possibly they would be torn apart, their limbs scattered across the tables of Roddy's favorite eatery.

We can't have that, Nina thought. *The mess might displease the proprietor.* And might get Roddy and Grog banned, forbidden to dine there ever again on their regular trips through Plainsboro.

Nina smiled. Lazily she stood up and stretched, making a show of calling it a night, bidding her companions farewell. She was still smiling when she spun away from the table, a sudden whirlwind of motion.

No one watching could have followed the speed with which she drew her knife and threw it. Nina buried the blade deep in a leg of the table where the scoundrels sat. The blade pinned one man's boot to the supporting trestle. It caught the fellow's flesh as well, to judge by the shriek that burst from the man's throat.

Before his two companions could do more than recoil in surprise, Nina had her sling whirling. She slammed a stone into an overhanging tree. A branch broke with a sharp crack and the sound of splintering. It plummeted down and crashed upon the table with bruising force. One man was knocked to the ground. The third found himself still seated, but pinned between the branch and the table.

Nina looped her sling around her neck, tucking it out of sight as she stalked to confront the men. She yanked her knife from the table leg and put the blade to the throat of the man from whom she had already drawn blood. Nina looked him in the eyes. He shrank from her: predator had become prey. From her years on Earth, Nina knew the power of the look she had inherited from her wizardly father, Verek. That darkly brilliant, piercing gaze, focused as she was now focusing it, would strike terror in any mortal man.

"You offend me," Nina said, her voice carrying to every corner of the eatery. "All evening you have sat here leering at me, offering me insult. From no man do I tolerate such impudence." Slowly, deliberately, Nina cleaned her blade on the man's shirt collar, wiping his blood off as she stared him down. He winced and looked away, his breath coming in shallow gasps.

Nina glanced around the table, pinning each man with the anger of her gaze. "Baseborn creatures!" she snarled. "But even such as you, the lowest of the low—even you can learn proper manners if the lesson is driven home." By the light of the few candles that still burned on nearby tables, Nina saw the blood drain from each man's face as she shifted her knife to her free hand and drew her sword. "Know this, each of you," she said, making short, mock thrusts at the men's faces. "Cast a wanton eye in my direction ever again, and I shall put it out."

The drinkers at the bar had been watching all of this. All in that crowd had fallen silent at the first shriek and the bit-off curses from the direction of the scoundrels' table. Now they erupted in cheers for Nina and jeers for the men.

"That's telling 'em, lady!" cried one wobbly drunk. In the act of raising his tankard to salute Nina, the man toppled over.

"Tuck your tails 'tween your legs, boys!" shouted another bar rat. "Hide your balls afore she cuts 'em off."

"I'll help her cut!" retorted a female voice. "I'll geld the bastards this instant. No woman's safe from those devils." Nina couldn't pick out the speaker at the crowded bar, but she thought it was one of the women who carried a dagger. A woman, Nina thought, who had some familiarity with rapacious men.

"Boy!" bellowed Roddy, from so near that he startled Nina. The merchant had come to stand with her at the scoundrels' table. He summoned a youth who had been stacking dirty dishes on the respectable side. "Run fetch the sheriff, lad," he said. "These men are thieves and pickpockets. They tried to lift my purse, but I was too quick for them." Roddy jangled a bag of coins in one fist as he shook his other at the trio.

"They've stolen my liquor, too!" cried a portly fellow who came out from behind the bar. The fellow pointed an accusatory finger at the men. "They been guzzlin' liquor they ain't paid for. Glass after glass of it."

This was a bald-faced lie as far as Nina could see. She had observed the men nursing single mugs of beer all evening. Moreover, they had never left their table, never gotten close enough to Roddy to pick his pocket.

But the merchant's allegation had the intended effect. As soon as the portly fellow—evidently the eatery's proprietor—leveled his own charge of theft, new cries arose from the drunks at the bar. They called the men everything from card cheats to horse thieves. By the time the errand boy had returned with the sheriff and two deputies, the crowd stood massed around the scoundrels, raining abuse upon the three and preventing their escape.

Roddy chuckled. "Well done, my lady," he murmured. "A hot spark you struck to light that fire. Those curs have plenty of enemies in this town but no friends. I'll wager the sheriff has been itching to lock them up. Now he has a surfeit of reasons."

The merchant and Nina returned to their table on the genteel side of the premises, to find Grog hunched over the bundle that Nina had bought for him. As she walked up, the big man shot her a questioning look. His aspect was so wistful, so eloquently expressive compared to his usual stoicism, Nina's heart nearly burst.

"Forgive me!" she exclaimed. "In the uproar, I forgot. Go on, Grog—open it. It's yours. I hope you like it."

The giant's face brightened like a child's. Nina expected the hulking fellow to rip open the bundle, and she hoped the fabric could stand the mauling. But Grog undid the gift as though it were made of spun sugar. He loosened each fold and smoothed the material against his broad chest until he had freed enough of the cloth that he was obliged to stand and let the fabric unroll itself to its full length.

Revealed was a tentlike expanse woven not of canvas, but of a smooth, lustrous fabric that any nobleman would have been proud to wear, had it been cut for a tunic or a summer cloak. What Grog held was yards of cloth, wide enough to slip over his protruding ears and wrap comfortably around his huge frame.

"I thought you might like a change," Nina said as she showed the big fellow how his head would fit through an opening in the tent's center. "Put it on like a pullover, then bring the ends around and tie them. See?" With quick turns of the silky fabric, and judicious tucks here and there to tidy away the excess as she stood on tiptoe to extend her reach, Nina soon had the giant arrayed in his new finery.

"I wondered about the color," she commented. Nina stepped back and eyed her handiwork, first critically, then with satisfaction at the effect she had achieved. "In the tent shop, that cloth looked very dark, almost black. But here under the stars, it's a pewter gray. Much better for summer, I would think, when the sun beats down." Nina shrugged. "We'll need daylight to know what color it really is. But for now: How does it feel? Comfortable? Do you like it?"

The giant nodded vigorously—as vigorously as he could, given his lack of a neck. With grave formality, Grog extended two fingers and a thumb to shake Nina's hand—a gesture of such sincerity, one might think he was binding himself with a blood-oath.

"You put me to shame, my lady," Roddy murmured, watching with a smile as Grog released Nina's hand and resumed smoothing his sleek new garment. "Never once had it entered my mind that the fellow might want a change of clothes. He's never given me a sign, not so much as glanced in the door of a tailor's shop." The merchant shook his head. "But you are quite right, of course, and I have been blind. Though it's said that clothes don't make the man, garments are without doubt essential to any man's dignity."

Grog did look surprisingly dignified in his wrap-around apparel. The fabric caught the stars and draped him in their light. Thus enfolded, he seemed to cut an even larger figure, as though his already impressive dimensions were billowing out like a cloak in a breeze. In Grog's silhouette tonight there was something heroic rather than hulking. Nina studied her big friend, and wondered: *What is he? Where does he belong?*

"Deputy!" bellowed Roddy. His summons boomed out from beside her, interrupting Nina's thoughts.

The merchant beckoned to one of the sheriff's men who was taking statements from "witnesses" at the bar—although Nina doubted that any of them were sober enough to give a true account of tonight's events. They had heard her rebuke the leering trio and had cheered her for it, but no observer—drunk or sober—could have followed the speed of her knife-work or her slinging. The ensuing flurry of accusations against the toughs had been all the excuse the sheriff needed, however, to take the trio into custody. The men, now shackled, were being marched away. But at Roddy's call, one of the deputies abandoned the supposed witnesses. He rushed over from the bar, doffed his cap, and bowed.

The deputy's regard confirmed the belief that had grown in Nina's mind through the evening: "Nimrod" held great sway in the town of Plainsboro. He was far more than a traveling merchant. He had money, status, and influence.

"Evening, sir," the man said as he snapped to attention.

Roddy clapped him on the shoulder. "Fine work tonight, deputy." The merchant grinned. "All the town will sleep more soundly, knowing those rogues are behind bars. But now, my good man, do your further duty and see this lady safely to the Widow Griffin's." Roddy indicated Nina in the manner of a merchant displaying valuables. "I charge you to allow no harm or insult near this gentlewoman. Do not leave her side until she is securely locked behind the widow's doors."

The deputy bowed again, to Nina this time. "Your servant, my lady. I shall be honored to escort you." The man puffed up with self-importance as he threw back his shoulders and jammed his cap on his head.

As if I needed an escort, Nina thought with a wry smile. She rested a hand on the hilt of her rapier. *But let the men feel useful and important.*

She bade her companions good-night. "I will see you in the morning." Nina gestured at Roddy's wagon where it waited with others across the market square, and where the merchant and his bodyguard would spend the night, protecting Roddy's wares. "If either of you can get out of your bedrolls, that is," she added, "after all the food and drink the pair of you put away this evening."

Roddy chuckled. "We'll be up before the sun, preparing for another day's brisk trade. I must hasten ere tomorrow's dawn to make a pleasing display of my most beautiful jewels and ladies' adornments, to be ready for the crowds that will come. For word will spread among the ladies of this town, and they will wish to glimpse the raven-haired swordswoman who schooled three ruffians." The merchant winked. "Your presence at my humble stall will be most welcome at whatever hour you choose to join us, my lady."

* * *

Roddy's prediction, that every woman in town would come to gawk at her, almost persuaded Nina to hide in her lodgings all day. But the morning, cool and fresh, drew her out against her will. Her feet carried her back to the market square, with detours along the way to check on her stabled horse and consult a farrier about reshoeing Traveller for the road ahead. After satisfying herself that the horse was in good hands, Nina found the rest of the morning hanging heavy. No other occupation presented itself except to meander down to the bustling square.

As she threaded her way through the crowds and approached Roddy's wagon, she heard the merchant haggling with a customer over the price of some trinket. Nina slipped quietly around the wagon's tailboard and found Grog sitting like a statue in the shade of an awning. He wore his new finery, though wrapped and knotted less neatly than Nina had arranged the garment last night. He'd obviously had it off, and had removed his coarse undershirt to don the fine fabric next to his bare skin. When he spotted Nina rounding the wagon's back corner, Grog came out of his stone-still pose and raised one hand to smooth the satiny material against his muscle-bound chest.

"By the Powers," Nina said, using the magian oath reflexively without considering that "By Drisha" might be more suitable here among the ungifted denizens of the southland. "I have never seen cloth of such changeable color. Depending on the light, it can be blue-black or pewter gray or hunter green. In the brightness of this morning, I see hints of purple and violet. Quite regal you look in it—a veritable titan."

Grog bared his teeth in what Nina interpreted as the giant's attempt at a smile. But a passing youngster glimpsed those huge gnashers, and ran shrieking.

"Don't be alarming the customers," Roddy muttered as he came to join them, having concluded the sale of the trinket. He patted a blocky shoulder of the sitting colossus, then winked at Nina. "You brighten our morning and bring me luck. I profited handsomely on that little bauble, parting with it for considerably more than I paid. And now I am reminded: Did I not promise to equip you with the exquisite sling-bullets that I buy from your brother? I am sure you know how great is Legary's skill with stone. But perhaps even you will be astounded by the examples of his handiwork that I can show you."

So speaking, Roddy dug into his jampacked wagon, tossing aside teapots, shoehorns, and painted toys as he burrowed. At last he pulled out a plain burlap bag and thrust it into Nina's hands.

"Perhaps you would care to test your brother's work." Roddy gestured at the grassy commons that stretched along one side of the market square. "The youngsters are playing at swords and steeds over yonder. How honored they would be if you joined their games."

Though suspecting that the merchant wished to manipulate her into displaying her skill with a sling more publicly than she had done last night, Nina was nonetheless intrigued by the contents of Roddy's burlap bag. She plumped the heavy sack on the ground and squatted in the shade beside Grog to examine its contents.

It held only stones, but not the stones of nature's shaping. Each cobble had been knapped and worked by an expert hand. Some were perfect spheres; others almond-shaped. Most had images etched into their otherwise smooth surfaces. Nina picked out forked lightning, flaming arrows, soaring eagles. Some of the sling-bullets also bore words in the common script of Ladrehdin. "Catch," read one. "Take that!" and "Got you!" taunted others. All were shaped from rocks and minerals that appeared to have been chosen for their colors as well as their hardness. From the pile at Nina's feet peeked red travertine, striped flint, jet-black ironstone, and purple quartz.

"Do you see," Roddy asked from over Nina's shoulder, "that your brother has drilled holes in the smaller ones? I beg you will sling a few of those at the targets on the greensward, so as to give me your thoughts on the reason for the holes." The merchant gestured at the mounded sling-stones Nina was examining. "I've had knaves say to me that the drilled stones are damaged or defective. But knowing the pride that Master Legary takes in his work, I cannot accept the naysayers' verdict. Such claims are made, I suspect, by those who wish to cheapen the goods and thus lower the price they'll pay."

Nina nodded, only half listening to the merchant's patter. She opened her belt pouch and dumped out the round, white stones that she had collected at the roadside. Missiles that she'd earlier deemed perfect now seemed crude, ungainly when viewed against Legary's exquisite craftsmanship. Nina refilled her pouch with the beautifully worked and colorful sling-bullets, choosing from among them the smaller, drilled stones. She had no illusions about Roddy's motives in showing them to her: he was nudging her in a direction that would ultimately benefit his finances. But Nina could not resist trying out Legary's handiwork.

As Roddy turned away to greet a new customer, Nina left the merchant's wagon and threaded her way through the crowded market, past throngs of shoppers. Beyond the stalls of Roddy's competitors, she emerged at the edge of the grassy commons. There, hay bales had been stacked as practice targets to occupy restless youngsters. She watched a pack of urchins charge from one stack to the next, stabbing the targets with their wooden swords. The clumsy young warriors stormed the line, screeching with the excitement of their game, stumbling over each other in their haste.

Nina waited until the pack had reached the endmost haystack, a distance that put the whole of the commons between herself and the children. Though she had absolute confidence in her slinging skills, she would not risk an errant throw with untested ammunition. When the way stood open between her and the targets, Nina let fly at the nearest, her whirl and release lightning quick.

The effect startled even her. A piercingly sharp whistle split the air—not at all the usual *whoosh* of a sling-stone in flight. The shriek cut off abruptly as the missile reached its target and penetrated the tightly stacked hay. The whistling had been loud enough, however, and unfamiliar enough to turn heads throughout the commons and the square.

"What was *that?*" cried the urchins. As one, they abandoned their games and came bounding across the field to Nina. The pack surrounded her, every child shouting questions and entreaties. "Did you do that, lady? Do it again! What's that in your hand? Show us!"

As she surveyed the eager faces of her encircling audience, a corner of Nina's memory urged caution. *Remember the boy*, it whispered ... *that boy who so coveted a sling, he used his dead father's boots to make one.*

But her mob of admirers would not be denied. The children clamored until Nina lined them up where they could safely watch her demonstrate slinging. She whirled dozens of the whistling stones, slamming them into targets all down the line of hay bales. Her audience squealed with glee at the ear-piercing shriek of each stone in flight. By the time Nina called a halt, the commotion had attracted a great crowd of onlookers. With a promise to stage another exhibition later on, she waved the gawkers along to Roddy's wagon to buy his sling-bullets. Well before the close of business that day, her admirers had depleted the merchant's stock of suddenly popular stone munitions.

"You sly dog!" Nina growled at the man, with grudging respect for both his skill as a manipulator and his money-making talents. "You'd heard that whistle before, hadn't you. You knew it would be the sound of silver hitting your coffers if I slung those things in public."

Roddy chuckled. "Your brother demonstrated his handiwork when he consigned his wares to me. Quite remarkable, eh, the noise those bullets make. One slinger letting loose with those would feign an army." The merchant grinned at her. "I spoke the plain truth, however, when I told you of the skeptics who scorn Legary's work, who mistake the cleverness of his design, who see only holes in stones. But after what the doubters saw—and heard—today, they have become believers." Roddy's grin widened. "As profitable as this day has been, tomorrow must surpass it. For no man's arm is strong enough, nor his throw fast enough, to make those stones scream as you did with your expert slinging. The crowds will be back."

They were. Next day, Nina was out in the morning sun giving another exhibition. She started with the drilled whistlers to announce that lessons had begun, but soon switched to the "undamaged" stones: those without holes flew silently, and thus were better suited for hunting. Determined to shun spectacle in favor of practicality, Nina demonstrated how wild game could be brought down with a simple homemade sling. Not for the first time, she marveled that such a basic, easily constructed weapon had remained little more than a novelty in this south country, never passing into widespread use. A good slinger, or so she hinted to her audience, could always put meat on the family table—not bought dearly at the butcher's, but taken from the land: rabbit, wildfowl, wild goat, antelope.

"Why should any child go hungry," Nina said, projecting her voice to carry through the crowd, "when great herds of wild game graze your fair lands? Those who master this simple tool need never starve, nor watch their children waste away. Join me under the trees yonder"—she pointed to the shaded edge of the commons—"and see how easily you may equip yourself with a device so valuable, it has been used in this world since time immemorial."

The crowds not only accepted her invitation, they brought their own materials with which to make their slings. Roddy, not one to forgo an opportunity, had been busily trading with his fellow merchants, snapping up their stocks of flax and hemp cordage, and paying street urchins to scrounge for scraps of leather that could be cut for sling pockets. He turned a tidy profit, selling these strings and scraps to the enthusiastic neophytes who crowded around "Lady Nerissa Archer's" outdoor school.

A table and chair were procured for Nina, brought over from the corner eatery, and there she sat all day patiently demonstrating the techniques of sling construction. Under her tutelage, scores of pupils shaped their leather scraps, braided their cords, and knotted the pieces together into serviceable weaponry. By mid-afternoon, the commons swarmed with beginners all trying to hit the same haystack targets that Nina had unerringly bull's-eyed. So many of the enthusiasts' throws went astray, however, landing variously in merchants' stalls and bartenders' bottle shelves, that the crowds were eventually chased away by frowning sellers and shopkeepers.

"No more," declared an exhausted Nina that evening. "I'm worn out with this town and these people. With or without you, Master Roddy, I'm off in the morning."

Chapter Six

Sunrise of the new day found Nina astride Traveller heading south, and riding once more beside the merchant's wagon. Roddy had concluded his business in Plainsboro—in a manner most satisfactory, he said.

Thanks to me, Nina thought as she studied the merchant's doggish profile and his smug grin. *He's leaving town a richer man, and I'm the cause.*

Nina had intended to demand her fair share of the profits from Roddy's sales of sling-bullets and scrap leather. But upon vacating her lodgings that morning, she had found the bill already settled. The merchant had paid for her room and board at the Widow Griffin's, and he'd paid Traveller's expenses, too. Roddy had discharged the farrier's bill for the horse's new shoes, and he'd covered the costs of the animal's feed and stabling. All told, those bills came to substantially more than Nina would have demanded as her fee for boosting the merchant's business.

Nevertheless, she refused to tell the man "Thank you." Nina's indignation smoldered, that Roddy had manipulated her so brazenly.

But for a worthy cause, she consoled herself. *Perhaps some of those people will make slingers of themselves and feed the hungry children of the poor.*

Roddy's sudden laughter interrupted Nina's brooding. With a flicker of suspicion that she deemed fully justified, she twisted in her saddle to see what had amused the fellow.

"As much as I will miss your company, my lady," Roddy said, winking at her, "it is well that we must part ways in Granger when I deliver you safely."

Before Nina could protest that she wasn't being "delivered" anywhere, and she didn't need Roddy to be safe on the road, the merchant emitted another burst of laughter but with such a conspiratorial glance her way, Nina couldn't help smiling, like she was in on the joke—though she did not know what the joke *was*.

Roddy cleared up the mystery.

"The butchers, my lady!" he chortled. "How their faces darkened and their frowns deepened at every word of that fine speech you gave in the market, when you exhorted the populace to kill their own meat and not buy it 'dearly'!" He guffawed. "You were too intent on your pupils and your mission to notice the angry looks of those whose profits you undercut. My dear lady, you wore out your welcome there." Roddy chuckled. "The farmers who supply the butchers may also take offense, when the orders stop coming for meat on the hoof. We three made our escape in good time, before the pitchforks and the cleavers came out. You'll not be wanting to show your face in Plainsboro, Lady Archer, for quite some time to come."

"I've no intention of ever returning there," Nina retorted. "As I have told you: from Granger my way lies west. The butchers of these plains will *not* see me again."

Hoping that would be the case, Nina stuck close to Roddy's wagon all that morning. From time to time she glanced over her shoulder, half expecting mobs of pitchfork-wielding farmers and armed butchers.

I have much to learn about the ways of commerce, she silently conceded. *Barely has my journey begun, and I'm interfering with people's livelihoods while enriching a wily merchant and spending money that I don't have.* The truth was, Nina could not have settled her bills at the lodging house and the stables with only the money she had brought from home, the coins her father had given her. She'd spent most of that in Easthaven buying her horse.

I've worked for a living but never for wages, she realized, recalling her years on the ocean world. There beyond the void, Nina had been fed, clothed, and housed by a community that relied on her knowledge of herbs and healing. She'd earned her keep by tending all manner of illnesses and injuries, restoring to health nearly every patient in her care. Only rarely had Nina's abilities as a healer failed her on Earth. Wherever an ember of life smoldered, she had fought for its preservation with all the skill and the magic at her command, and she'd almost always emerged victorious.

The people of her islands had rewarded her by supplying Nina with all she needed. Then when she married a boy of those islands, and together they restored the old family home of Nina's Earthly grandparents, the gardens and orchards of that secluded house had sustained Nina and her husband through the many years of their marriage. Blessed by tropical sunshine and plentiful rains, those gardens had produced bountiful surpluses, which Nina and Makani had traded for whatever else they required.

A barter system, Nina thought. *That's what I'm used to. It's all I really know. Money is a mystery to me.* She'd had no need of it on Earth. Even here in her homeworld of Ladrehdin, she'd had very little experience with coinage. Even Nina's father had not fully appreciated how much silver and gold his wayfaring daughter would need, once Nina left his lands in the magical north and entered the mundane, mercantile south. She smiled, remembering how casually Lord Verek had dug into his coin purse and produced a little gold to help Nina on her way.

"Here," he'd said, pressing it into her hands. "Take some money, for you'll need a horse and something to eat."

Had you any idea, Honored Father, thought Nina with affection for the master of Ruain, and with a little pang of homesickness too, for that distant, secret province, *that I would spend almost all you gave me on one good horse, obliging me thenceforward to work for my supper?*

And work she had, almost nonstop since her first night on the road. Bow in hand, Nina had ranged the prairielands for wild game to feed herself and her companions. She'd sold an unwanted hog for a few coins. She'd put herself on display in Plainsboro, staging a performance like an itinerant juggler. In the market square she'd put on a show, and people had paid for the entertainment.

"Oh!" Nina blurted as a new thought occurred. She had not intended to share her musings with Roddy, or with the silent, motionless bodyguard who sat on the wagon seat beside him. But a sudden realization, or suspicion, jolted the exclamation from her.

"Penny for your thoughts," Roddy said, startling Nina with yet another reference to money, as though the merchant had been following her train of thought these past several miles. And now he was offering to pay her for it.

But a man like him would *assign a monetary value to nearly everything,* she told herself, to keep from crediting Roddy with the power of mind-reading.

She turned to him. "Plainsboro taught me a lesson," Nina admitted. "In your company, Master Merchant, I have learned that things which are freely given may be perceived as less valuable than those which command a great price." Nina related the story of Isobel and the discarded note of introduction. "At the time," she said, "I thought the woman and her son had scorned my words because they could not read. But perhaps they thought my recommendation worthless because I had not demanded payment for it."

Roddy chuckled. "I'm pleased that I have aided your understanding of avarice. It's a vice you will encounter in your peregrinations." His grin became wistful as he added, "But Drisha knows this world needs the do-gooders who will extend a helping hand. Pray tell me of the woman in Easthaven to whom you would have sent the beleaguered Isobel. My route takes me regularly to the coast, and I am eager to know of such a generous soul in that pitiless place."

Nina did not get far into her description of Tilda—brassy, red-haired, the jealous type—before Roddy was roaring with laughter.

"The Captain's mistress!" he exclaimed. "Oh my dear, how you have misjudged *that* one! No stranger—worthy of aid or otherwise—could hope to impose upon the 'kindness' of that woman. I have never known Tilda to give a crust of bread to a starving beggar. She would not throw a drowning man a rope." Roddy chuckled. "But clearly she possesses merits in certain other respects—merits esteemed by her mysterious lover, the sea captain who hails from parts unknown and waits upon her when he's in port." The merchant grinned at Nina. "How did you make the acquaintance of Tilda? And why in the name of all that's holy would you have thought her likely to embrace a needy mother with a pack of whelps?"

Nina scowled at Roddy's amusement over her "do-gooder" naivety. But she was secretly pleased the merchant seemed unaware that the mysterious sea captain from unknown places was her brother, and was therefore the brother of the master stonecrafter of Granger. If Legary had not revealed to Roddy his connection to Dalton, then Nina must keep the brothers' secret.

With a gesture of annoyance, she brushed aside Roddy's question. "I spent scarcely two hours in Easthaven and spoke to hardly anyone— only a dealer in horses, and the woman at the inn who offered me tea. Plainly, I had no reason to expect anything from that woman, nor from any resident of her city. How foolish of me to suggest that a wretched mother of five starvelings might find a friend in that place, when I myself had none there."

In the face of Nina's brittle sarcasm, Roddy looked uncomfortable, as though he feared he had genuinely offended her. Nina gave him no chance, however, to comment or apologize, for her thoughts had glanced from the desperate mother to the cold-blooded son who had stripped the boots from a dead man's feet. Tersely, she told Roddy about the boy's fascination with her slinging and how she had encouraged his desire to master the weapon. Nina described her discovery of the father's drowned remains. She shared her conviction that the boy, in making a sling of his own, had used leather from the man's boots.

"I acknowledge that I have no hard evidence of murder," Nina added, shifting in her saddle to address the merchant eye to eye. "I have only my suspicions, and those derive from what I saw, heard, and felt in the presence of that youth and his unspeaking mother. The boy seemed altogether untroubled by the death of his sire ... I detected little emotion of any kind in that child. Toward me, he showed no gratitude for the lessons in slinging, nor for the waterfowl that fed his family."

Nina paused, her mind on that roadside encounter. Reliving it now from the wider perspective that time and distance afforded, she found the boy's behavior even more disturbing. Only briefly had she seen a flicker of any feeling in that boy's face. And that had been a flash of pride, or satisfaction, when he revealed to her a piece of leather that he had sliced from his dead father's boot.

Roddy cleared his throat with a soft, puppyish growl.

"I confess, my lady," he said, smiling at her again but speaking in tones lower than his usual thunder, "I see little which is worrisome in what you have told me. Young people are notorious ingrates—unappreciative by their natures. It's no surprise that the boy failed to thank you for what you gave him." The merchant clucked his tongue. "As for the drowned wastrel: accidents happen, especially to drunks. If he served only himself and not his family, then I can well imagine that his widow and his son would shed no tears. Neither would they leave a serviceable pair of boots to rot in the mud."

"You weren't there," Nina snapped. "You didn't meet those people or see what I saw."

"By the marrow of my bones," the merchant boomed, louder now and sounding exasperated. "Lady Archer, I make you a promise. When next I am in Easthaven I will alert the constabulary to watch for a penniless widow who arrived with five starvelings in tow, one of those a novice slinger of about fourteen summers who did not grieve for the father who let his family go hungry. Will that satisfy you?"

"You're laughing at me," Nina muttered. She wished she had never raised the subject, never shared her misgivings about the piteous, gaunt family that she had met for only a passing moment but could not forget.

A shout from up ahead brought her head around. Nina was reaching for her bow but stopped at an answering bellow from Roddy.

"Here now!" the merchant thundered as he guided his horses off the road into a patch of prairie myrtles. "Make room." Roddy pulled up in the shade close beside the wagon of the man who had called out to him.

"About time, you old mongrel!" exclaimed that man, a sparely built individual with wild hair and arms too long for his body. "I was near to giving up and selling your consignment out from under you."

"Do that, and Grog goes hungry," Roddy retorted.

"Any later, and he would've," the man grumbled. "If I'd found this grub edible, I might have eaten it myself. How Grog stomachs it, I'll never know." The man glanced at Roddy's bodyguard. Grog was neatly attired this morning in the new apparel Nina had purchased for him.

"Top of the day to you, big fella," the man called across to the giant. "You're looking spruce. Dressed up for the lady, are ya?"

The man shifted his gaze from Grog to stare with frank interest at Nina as she rode up on the giant's side of Roddy's wagon. She was starting to bristle at the overly direct way in which the stranger ogled her, but then Grog made answer for them both. The giant swung his massive head toward the man, fixed the depths of his enormous round eyes upon the fellow, and grunted out a *"Numph"* that carried a clear note of warning.

The man heard and comprehended. He ducked his head with a nervous twitch as he tipped his hat in respectful salute. Then the fellow rushed his attention back to Roddy and to completing the business at hand.

That business involved a great quantity of brined beef, whole sides of it to be shifted from the man's wagon into Roddy's. *So this is how the hound feeds the leviathan,* Nina thought as she watched the transfer, *when there is no huntress in his party to bring meat to his camp.* From what passed between Roddy and his supplier, she gathered that this was their regular arrangement. The merchant's route along this road south from Plainsboro was so fixed and predictable, the man with the meat knew exactly when and where to await Roddy to offload it.

Grog, his muscles rippling, made quick work of the task. As he shouldered the beef, he gave the supplier no notice beyond the one cautionary grunt he'd directed toward the man.

Nina followed the giant's example. While the men busied around the parked wagons, she dismounted and led Traveller deep into the shady verge, drawn to a trickle of water. A spring seeped into a depression barely large enough to give the horse a drink. Nina and Trav refreshed themselves there, and the horse grazed on moist vegetation until the business with the meat was concluded.

"I'm going hunting," Nina called when Roddy and Grog were again seated in their wagon and back on the road. "If I bag nothing but a chipmunk, it will taste better than what you just bought, Master Merchant. What a poor use of all that money I made you in Plainsboro."

Roddy only chuckled and waved her on her way. But Grog looked longingly after Nina as she swung into the saddle and headed for open country. She knew what the big fellow wanted, and she did not disappoint him. Hours later near the close of day, Nina brought two antelope into the camp her companions had made, miles down the road. Grog did his secret work of butchering the animals—and eating liver—while screened from view by tall rushes on the banks of a good-sized watering hole.

All in all, Nina thought from her seat on the ground, her back against her saddle as she watched the men prepare a huge supper at their evening fire, *I haven't done badly, falling in with these fellows. I hunt; they cook. Much better that, than the other way around.*

On the downside, however, it was a slow way to travel. Nina would have been farther south by now if she hadn't been ambling along at the pace of this unhurried merchant and his voracious bodyguard. At the rate she was going, summer would blaze at its fiercest by the time she reached Granger. Pushing on westward from there, across the desert to the Ore Hills where her brother Galen lived, might be impossible in sunbaked heat—especially for a water-sylph who could not summon water.

Maybe I ought to stay in Granger, Nina thought, *and wait to go west in the fall. Rather than impose on a brother I don't know, I could find work and get my own place. If grandmother Merriam and grandaunt Megella could earn their bread as wisewomen in these southern plains, so could I.*

Nina fell asleep that night remembering the book of herbal remedies that had come down to her from her foremother Merriam. Merri had deserted her northern husband and fled south to make a life for herself in these grasslands. As the wisewoman of a town called Winfield, she had gained a reputation throughout the region as a skilled healer. Everything Merri knew of herbs and remedies, she had immortalized in a book of recipes that now resided in the great library of House

Verek. Nina had committed that book to memory. Into this south country—so unfamiliar to her but known to her forebears—Nina carried the lore of generations of healers and herbalists. If the need arose, she could make her living as Merri and Meg had made theirs long before Nina came to retrace their steps—drawn down their old path by hardly more than a whim.

Honestly, she asked herself just before sleep took her. *What* are *you doing here?*

The answer came as a single word, a word that glided up from her subconscious and slipped into her drowsing mind: *Family.*

Their faces drifted into her dreams ... dreams that took her back to the huge family she had left behind on her ocean world, and on back farther to the small, tightknit family Nina had known as a child when it had been only her parents, herself, and Galen. To her fondness for those, she'd recently added an attachment to her only sister, Vivienne, and a teasing sort of affection for their middle brother, the serious but surprisingly roguish Captain Dalton.

But Legary the Younger—namesake of the man Merriam had deserted—remained a stranger to Nina, a stranger and a mystery. All she knew of him came from tales relayed in letters—stories recounted thirdhand. Why she felt so compelled to meet him face-to-face, to talk with him and come to know him, Nina would have struggled to say even if she'd been awake. But blood called to blood so strongly, she had committed herself to this journey of family reconnection, for however long it might last, and however deep into the unknown it might take her.

Even if it stripped from her the Gift of magic.

Chapter Seven

N ina was not again called upon to parade her skill with the sling. Roddy had sold his entire stock of stone bullets, and thus he could not press her into demonstrating the novelty of whistling munitions. She was at leisure to explore each new hamlet they entered. As her funds allowed, she replenished her supplies of the cheese and dried fruits she liked to nibble while out hunting. The tidbits made a change from the monotonous meat-and-tuber meals that Roddy prepared morning and night when they were on the road.

In each town, happily, the merchant treated his companions to good suppers at his favorite inns. Roddy was known in every market square. As in Plainsboro, local notables went out of their way to visit his wagon or his supper table.

At every stop, Nina made the rounds of the village commons, seeking a resident healer or wisewoman. She would need to know the competition if future circumstances obliged her to take up the trade. From apothecary shops she acquired samples of locally grown herbs and inquired of the sellers how to use them. Although some of the advice struck her as wrongheaded, even dangerous, Nina encountered no herb with which she was wholly unfamiliar. Her years-long study of Merriam's recipes had acquainted her with the medicinal properties of every common plant of these grasslands.

As Roddy concluded his business in each town and the three of them continued southward, Nina's confidence grew that she could fund her further travels to any extent necessary, when the time came to part from the merchant. For Roddy had made it clear that his route ended at Granger. There, he would meet with Legary and others, and restock his wagon with whatever goods the merchant thought he could sell—especially those new and novel wares, like carved sling-bullets, that were produced by the town's artisans. But soon enough, the itinerant dealer would turn around and be on his way north again, back along the road as it curved gradually eastward and returned him to the coast.

"I'm sure I speak for Grog as well as myself, Lady Archer, when I say that you will be missed," Roddy commented on their last night of road-side camping. They were due to reach Winfield on the morrow, and Nina had told him she would leave him there while she rode alone to Granger. That near to the end of her journey—this first leg of it, any-way—Nina could not stand to twiddle her thumbs in the market while waiting for the merchant to transact his business and move along.

"This is not good-bye," she promised. "I will see you and Grog when you get to Granger. The suspense is killing me, though, and I must press on to find that brother of mine who is a stranger to me."

Roddy regarded her with puppy-dog eyes. "Your company has been most welcome, these many days and miles." The merchant stroked his tawny, graying beard. Then he chuckled and winked. "Grog will pine, don't you know, for antelope livers. He's eaten better on this trip than ever he did since falling in with me. You've been a good friend to that poor, lost fellow."

"Lost?" Nina echoed. "Hasn't he found a home with you?"

The merchant did not immediately reply. He scratched behind his ear and looked thoughtful.

"Would you tell me again," he asked, "what you see when you look at that fellow? That is, what he brings to your mind?"

"A whale," Nina said. "Not because he's enormous, but because his strength is tempered with gentleness. When I went over the sea"—she waved in a vaguely easterly direction, as always when she mentioned her previous home—"I would swim with the leviathans of the deep. As tiny as I was alongside their tremendous bulk, they acknowledged my presence, saw in me a fellow being, and took care to avoid harming me." Nina paused, remembering. "The first time I met Grog's gaze, I saw in his eyes that same gentleness and that same recognition." She shook her head. "I cannot explain it. He's clearly not a whale, but there is that about him which puts me in mind of one."

Roddy nodded, and smiled. "Then it may surprise you, lady of far oceans, to learn that I do *not* see a graceful creature of the depths when I look at our friend. I see a rock troll."

"A troll!" Nina exclaimed. "That's harsh."

The merchant laughed. "Would you not say the fellow is big, strong, and slow enough to pass for one of those mythical beings? In particular, I recall old tales about the mountain-folk: giants who lived in caves high in the snowy peaks of western Ladrehdin. It was said they drew nourishment from the living rock, grinding boulders into flour with their massive stony teeth."

"We're far from the mountains," Nina pointed out. "I've not noticed any snowy peaks or troll-sized caves in these parts. And aren't trolls supposed to turn to stone when sunlight touches them? For many days I have ridden under sunny skies with you and Grog, and I have not observed the fellow beginning to petrify."

Roddy chuckled. "Nor have I. Nonetheless, it is a curious fact about Grog: ask any person what they see when they look upon him, and you will get a different answer. Some say he's a tree, a towering figure with bent limbs and feet like gnarled roots. Others see him as a great bull, thick with muscles, his voice a wordless bellow. You view him as a whale. To my eyes he is a creature of rock, all hard edges as though hewn from stone."

"If that's how you see him," Nina slowly replied, digesting the merchant's words, "then I wonder that you had the courage to go near him when you found him alone in the Easthaven harbor. Most people would run from a rock troll."

"Be assured that I approached with caution," Roddy said, winking. "If he'd been standing, showing me his full height, I might have raced away with all the speed my horses could give. But he was sitting, a lonely figure with his back to me, looking forlorn and very lost. When I came up behind him, as near as I dared to that great hulking form, and I spoke a kind word, Grog did not seem startled by my presence. He did not bolt to his feet, but merely shuffled around—more slowly than time itself—to eventually give me a look so wistful, my heart went out to him. Seeing the bewilderment in his deep blue eyes, I could not fear him. I could only ask if he would like to come with me." Roddy tilted his head like a curious pup. "To this day, I do not know if he understood my words or only felt the sincerity of my concern for him."

"But surely," Nina put in, "Grog comprehends very well the common tongue of this world. Though he speaks nothing, I am certain he understands all that I say to him."

The merchant nodded. "Now, yes, he understands our speech full well. But when I first discovered him, the fellow was like a lost infant, knowing nothing, communicating nothing—except a great need to eat." Roddy chuckled. "I'd not been long in Grog's company before I realized what an insatiable appetite the fellow has."

"Like he can't get enough," Nina murmured, catching at a thought not fully formed but seeded in her mind by Roddy's words. "Like he needs something he's not getting, but he doesn't know what it is or where to find it."

"Exactly right, my lady!" Roddy exclaimed, leaning toward her. "That, in brief, is the mystery that I have been trying to solve since I met our friend. What does he need? Where is he going, or where *should* he be going? How can I help him return to wherever he belongs?" The merchant shook his head. "This is no life for the fellow, traveling my same road up and down—up to the coast, back through the plains, then do it all again." Roddy scratched behind his ear like a hound relieving an itch. "It's a fine life for me. I've got the thrill of the chase, nosing out bargains, cocking an ear for lucrative gossip, digging for profits." He grinned. "It's a great game to me, and I've made a good living by it."

Like a dog chasing a stick, Nina thought. *He doesn't tire of playing his favorite game.*

"But you think Grog needs more than you can give him," she said, prodding the merchant. "You think he belongs ... somewhere else."

"I'm certain of it." Roddy's grin faded. He looked troubled. "For years I've searched for clues, for signs that would tell me who or what the fellow really is. I've tried jogging his memory—assuming that Grog retains any remembrance of his past existence. In every market in every town, I've bought the most exotic goods on offer, hoping that some object or material would take his fancy. That he would recognize some item or article that would point to his proper home."

"But he never has?"

Roddy shook his head. "Nothing that's passed through my hands has interested him. He seems to not see the garish baubles, the painted toys, the gleaming copper pots. The brightest and best of my wares are lost on him." The merchant clucked his tongue. "It's only *your* gift that's caught his eye."

"*My Gift?*" Nina gasped. She stared at the merchant, confounded by this seeming reference to her magian heritage.

"That cloth," Roddy said. He cocked an eyebrow at her. "That tent, or whatever it was you gave him."

"Oh!" Nina exclaimed. "His overshirt." She nodded, relieved. "He does seem to like it."

She glanced around, seeking the giant who had absented himself for longer than usual this evening. Grog still remained out of sight, hidden in a willow grove on a far edge of tonight's campsite. Movement among the slender branches assured Nina that the shy leviathan was still at his task, carving up the three antelope she had brought in just before sundown. The animals were her parting gift to Grog before she galloped on ahead of Roddy and his bodyguard tomorrow.

"If there's a clue in that fabric," Nina said, returning her gaze to the merchant, "if it offers some hint about Grog's origins, I can't see it. The cloth, as far as I know, is nothing exotic, but was made where I bought it." She shrugged. "It's a clever weave, though, changing colors with every change of light. Like a chameleon."

"A what?"

Nina mentally cursed her slip. The merchant had seemed to accept her story about living abroad, "over the sea" in some vaguely distant island region of Ladrehdin. Roddy had not questioned her closely, and

Nina had striven to avoid any reference to her Earthly home that might arouse his curiosity. *Chameleon*, however, was one such reference. Ladrehdin had no creature by that name or possessing its abilities.

"*Kuh-mee-lee-uhn*," she repeated, sounding it out for Roddy. "They're interesting reptiles. They can change color to blend into the background, or stand out if they mean to scare a rival or attract a mate. I saw a few on an island I once visited. Far from here." She gave an indifferent wave, hoping to discourage further questions. "That fabric I picked up for Grog reminded me of them, is all."

"Hmm," Roddy murmured. "I almost envy you, Lady of the Water. What wonderful things you have seen." He winked. "But I'm a man who likes the feel of solid ground under my feet and under my wheels. I'll stick to the hard dry road and leave the seafaring to adventurous types like yourself."

Roddy stroked his beard as he added, "I'm thinking there's something of your '*kuh-mee-lee-uhn*' in our friend Grog. Does he not change his 'skin' in similar fashion? To all who see him, he appears in different guise: a leviathan to you, a troll to me." The merchant nodded as if warming to this idea. "Perhaps on your travels you visited the very island from whence our friend hails."

Nina started to protest, to say that she was quite certain no giants were living "over the sea" in her home beyond the void. But Grog chose that moment to return to their campfire. He carried armloads of dressed antelope. His fine new shirt, Nina saw as he came into the firelight, was stained with the animals' blood. She sighed.

No further opportunities presented themselves that evening for Roddy to advance his theories about Grog's origins. And as the next day dawned, Nina took care to be unavailable for further questioning or additional private conversation with the merchant. She'd already said more than she should about a land so distant and alien that no one in this rustic southland could begin to understand it.

It's good that I'm to part from Roddy soon, Nina thought as she saddled her horse and made ready for the day's travel. The merchant had said they would reach Winfield by noon, and there he and Grog would break their journey for an indeterminate time. They'd set up their wagon and stay for as long as the customers came. But Nina would continue on to Granger.

That, at least, was her plan. No part of the day, however, went to plan, except that they did reach the outskirts of Winfield as the sun neared its zenith.

The orb shone upon a scene of chaos and terror. People stood or kneeled in a tight ring. Some shouted across at others in the circle, some yelled commands over their shoulders, and others screamed downward into the ground. Their frantic cries were swallowed up by what seemed a great rift, a hole in the bedrock under the crowd's feet.

"Where is he?" a woman shrieked. "I can't see him!"

"Get a rope!" shouted a man as he pushed one onlooker out of the circle and away from the hole. He gestured for the fellow to go. "*Now, you fool!*" the man barked when the errand-runner stood frozen in his tracks, seemingly too dazed to move.

As the merchant's party drew nearer, all of them—Nina, Roddy, and Grog—stared at the knot of people, trying to make sense of what was happening. The knot broke up in sudden panicked haste when a cloud of white vapor belched from the rift. The vapor sent people reeling, stumbling over each other in their rush to escape it. Screams of pain replaced the cries of alarm: that white cloud was steam, searingly hot. As Nina reined her horse in retreat, she felt the blistering heat of the steam cloud and caught the stink of sulphur. Bedrock had split open in this place, sundering a path to the bowels of the world.

"Grog! Stop!"

The thunder of Roddy's outcry brought Nina's head around. She twisted in her saddle to see the usually ponderous, slow-moving giant leap from the wagon and race to the chasm's edge, his thick legs pounding the ground. Without an instant's hesitation, Grog jumped into the rift.

"No!" Nina shrieked in a cry so piercing that several onlookers whirled to seek the source. Their openmouthed stares followed her as she dropped from her horse's back and chased the now-disappeared giant.

"Don't do it, my lady!" Roddy boomed after her. Nina ignored him.

At the chasm's edge in a miasma of hot, sulfurous fumes, she skidded to a stop and stood choking. For a moment she could see nothing in the fissure's depths, although the noontime sun shone straight down into it. But then the wisps of vapor drifted clear on a rising breeze. The fumes swirled upward, above the crack and above Nina's head, as cool, breathable air swept aside the haze and opened a view into the cleft's interior.

Grog was there, deep in the fissure, scrabbling at a pile of stones and flinging them aside as if they weighed nothing. He uncovered a hollowed-out space, an opening like a shallow cave in one wall of the cleft. From it, Grog withdrew a human figure: limp, certainly unconscious and possibly dead. But tenderly the giant cradled the victim and commenced climbing out.

"Thank the Powers!" Nina exclaimed as she watched her muscle-bound friend clamber upward with more speed than she had thought he could manage. "Hurry, Grog! Any moment, this crack could belch another cloud of blistering reek."

"An excellent reason for you to *back away!*" boomed Roddy from several steps behind her. "Get out of danger. Let Grog see to himself."

But Nina stayed where she was, crouched on the chasm's rim and reaching for the giant—though certainly she hadn't the strength to help him climb out.

Grog proved to need no help. He gained the upper edge and all but vaulted from the fissure. Nina shot up from her crouch and rushed to embrace him.

The giant not only returned her embrace, he wrapped his free arm around her and picked her up bodily. With the unconscious man tucked against his other side, Grog rushed them both to the knot of onlookers.

Some of those individuals fell back at his foot-pounding approach, their alarm plastered across their faces. But others stepped forward to meet him. They reached to take the limp form of the man Grog had pulled from the abyss.

"Thank you, friend!" cried a woman who clasped the man to her bosom. She rocked the unconscious figure in her arms as she sat on the ground surrounded by gawkers and well-wishers.

Grog made no acknowledgment of the woman's gratitude. As he turned away from her and the others, he gently released Nina and set her on her feet. He took a step back to stand towering over her, meeting her upturned gaze. Once more Nina felt drawn into the depths of Grog's wide blue eyes.

"Owm," the giant grunted. He raised a heavy arm to point at the fissure behind him. Steam was again rising from that cleft, and Nina detected a rumbling in the rock under her feet.

"I don't understand 'owm'," she murmured, "but that was a brave thing you did, Grog, going down to get that man. Let's leave now," she added, "before it explodes again. We're too close."

She reached for the giant's hand and tried pulling him away. It was like tugging on a mountain. Grog did not move.

"Owm," he repeated. Holding Nina's hand in his gentle, two-fingered grip, Grog bowed to her, bending his body over their hand-clasp. As he straightened, he again caught her eye. In his gaze Nina saw a brightness, a gleam of some emotion she had never before detected in him. Was it excitement? Eagerness? Happiness?

The giant dropped Nina's hand and wheeled away from her. Before she knew what he was about, Grog had launched himself into a run, straight at the chasm's steaming edge.

"No!" she shouted. "Stop!"

But the leviathan was gone. He'd dropped feet-first into the fissure. As the chasm swallowed him, it erupted with scalding, suffocating vapors.

Under Nina, a violent tremor shook the rocks. It knocked her to the ground. Precious moments passed as she struggled to regain her footing. But even when she'd pushed herself upright, she could not move toward the rift that roared and hissed with the sound of escaping steam and sulphur. Something held her, pinned her in place, unyielding despite her frantic efforts to free herself.

"Stop!" Roddy shouted into her ear. "Grog is gone. You cannot bring him back."

Only gradually did Nina realize that it was the merchant who held her. The man had both arms wrapped around her, clamping her against him with husky strength. She tried kicking, tried stamping his feet, tried head-butting him. Roddy's grasp never slackened. He held her back from certain death, yelling at her to "Show some sense!" By turns he shouted and cajoled. "There's nothing you can do," he repeated in Nina's ear until finally she stopped fighting him.

"Why?" she wailed as she turned in Roddy's arms and buried her face in his ruff of hair. "Why did Grog do that?"

For a time the merchant made no reply. He stroked Nina's raven braid and held her as she sobbed, her face pressed to his shoulder. But presently, when Nina's weeping had abated somewhat, Roddy held her away from him and stared into her eyes.

"Did you see?" he murmured. "Just as Grog leapt into the chasm: did you see him take the form of a rock troll?" Roddy tilted his head, looking like an inquisitive hound as he studied Nina's face. "I myself have never seen it more clearly. Everything the fellow had ever shown me of a form seemingly cut from granite—every detail came to sharp focus at the moment he made that jump." Roddy smiled. "I do believe our big friend has gone home."

"Home!" Nina exclaimed, aghast and wanting to protest that none but demon-spawn might call the bowels of the world their "home." But then she paused, and slowly nodded.

"That's what Grog said to me," she muttered. "I think he was trying to tell me. He made a sound I didn't understand, but maybe 'owm' was as close as he could get to the word he wanted."

Roddy continued to gaze at her, now tilting his head doglike on the other side. "To have shaped even a semblance of our speech must be counted a momentous thing, I believe, in one who cannot call this upper realm his proper abode, or the people of this surface world his preferred society. But my lady, I must know," the merchant persisted. "Did you see? At the final moment, did he remain for you a leviathan of the deep? Or did you glimpse the creature shaped from rock?"

Nina inclined her own head now, brow furrowed with concentration, calling to her mind every detail of Grog's leave-taking. She had been so startled by him picking her up and carrying her like a rag doll, those seconds of near helplessness came to her now as indistinct impressions: She'd felt the giant's sinews wrap her like ropes of flint. But then Grog had set Nina on her feet, locked her gaze with his, and tried to make her understand: "Owm." That singular moment of communion ended with the giant turning away from her, briefly showing Nina his profile before he sprang away, a majestic figure racing to reclaim what he had lost.

She closed her eyes to picture the giant as he had appeared in that fraction of a moment. Nina saw the chiseled outline of Grog's face ... the blocky shape of his shoulders. When he'd turned fully away and she viewed him from the back, there was the giant's bald head sitting atop his neck like a boulder. His ears, which Nina had previously likened to the shells of giant clams, seemed in that instant to be buttresses carved of stone.

"Not a whale," she muttered. Nina opened her eyes and stared at Roddy. "Definitely not a whale when he jumped. I caught only a glimpse, but yes: I saw the man of rock."

Roddy scratched behind one ear. "I don't know why I needed to hear it, why it seems so important. But I am pleased that you beheld our friend in what I believe to be his true form. Or as true to the fellow's essential nature as any of us may discern, when we look upon a being so foreign to the world we know."

And to other worlds besides, Nina thought. She imagined the stir that would have rippled through her Earthly home, had any of those islands coughed up a creature like Grog. *They might have done, if giants actually lurked beneath those isles,* Nina mused as she recalled the volcanoes that regularly belched the contents of that world's bowels.

"But now, my lady," Roddy said, interrupting Nina's thoughts. "Let's get on into Winfield and find you a bath. You'll pardon me for saying it, but you stink, my dear. You reek of sulphur and brimstone."

* * *

Hours later, Nina emerged from her lodging house, having scrubbed until her skin was tender but still catching whiffs of sulphur as though she had it up her nose. Her hair, Nina discovered when she undid the braid to wash the stink from her mane, was singed. She also had patches of peeling skin: not from contact with scalding steam, she didn't think, but from the bitter vapors swirling around the chasm's rim. She might even have been touched with sulfurous acid when Grog picked her up. The giant could not have avoided getting it on him when he was down in the smoking chasm, rescuing that very fortunate young man.

For such were the tidings Nina gleaned from the guesthouse laundress when she handed that woman the clothes she'd been wearing. All around town, the woman reported, tongues were wagging on one topic only: the youth who was swallowed up, and the brave giant who saved his life. Consciousness had returned to the limp form Grog raised from the abyss. The young man would recover fully, predicted Nina's informant.

"Drisha be praised," the woman exclaimed. "Providence saved that boy from boiling like a chicken in a pot. By rights he should be dead, but Drisha decided otherwise."

Maybe Drisha had a hand in it, Nina silently conceded. *But I'll split the credit between Grog and the Powers: the Powers for sheltering that young man in a little cave behind heaped stones so he wouldn't burn in that first blast of steam. And then Grog, the only living being who could have dropped into that deadly abyss and resurfaced with that boy in his hand.*

Nina shared none of this with the laundress, only asked the woman's opinion: Could her clothes be salvaged?

The woman sniffed as she held Nina's reeking apparel at arm's length. "I think not, mistress," she said. "There's naught to be done with these but throw 'em on a bonfire."

Nina had to agree. With a sigh, she gave up the icy blue blouse that she'd bought in Plainsboro. Dressed in older clothes, she went to check on her horse.

She had abandoned Traveller the moment Grog left the wagon to race toward what had seemed his undoubtable death. The horse, being a sensible creature, had bolted in the opposite direction. But Trav possessed an inquisitive streak, too, and perhaps he did harbor some affection for his rider. For the horse had not run clean out of Roddy's sight, but had paused at a prudent distance to assess the situation. The merchant, having kept his wits about him in the midst of general mayhem, collared a farmboy who was coming in from nearby fields, drawn by the commotion.

"You there!" Roddy boomed, his bellow carrying above the eruptions from the chasm. "Catch that horse," he ordered the lad. "Take him to the best stable in town and there's a gold piece in it for you."

"Yes, sir!" the boy exclaimed, losing all interest in the abyss as this opportunity fell into his hands, straight from the heavens as it seemed. Here was a chance to earn more in half an hour than the boy could make all summer, working the fields. He did not scorn this godsend. With the soothing voice and easy manner of one who knows horses, the boy soon had Traveller safely collected and stabled.

That's where Nina found her horse, well groomed and housed in a roomy stall with hay and fresh water. Traveller greeted her with drowsy contentment, giving no sign that events had rattled his nerves.

"Thank you for not leaving me," Nina muttered. "I've lost a good friend today, Trav, and I couldn't bear to lose another." She buried her face in the horse's mane and let one last tear trickle down.

From the stable, Nina wandered along to the market square, where Roddy was holding court. It seemed everyone in Winfield had heard the story of Grog's heroism, and they'd come to Roddy to rehash the event. Nina hung at the back of the crowd, close enough to hear but keeping to herself. She would not discuss Grog for the entertainment of strangers.

When daylight began to fade, the crowd thinned around Roddy's wagon, everyone having chin-wagged until they'd worn out the topic. As the locals drifted away to their evening meals, Nina slipped under the awning that sheltered the merchant's wagon.

Roddy greeted her with a wistful smile. "The story's already grown with the telling," he said. "Four span have been added to Grog's height, and he's been proclaimed a god of the underworld. Which he might be, for all I know."

"I'm glad they're praising him," Nina said. "Some of them were formerly inclined to dislike or distrust him, I suspect. Having grown so accustomed to Grog hulking over me, I had become blind to how uncanny he was. Or is," Nina amended, though finding it difficult to accept that the giant could still be alive in the smoldering abyss.

She said as much. "All the old stories that I've ever heard depict the underworld as the realm of demons and devils, a place of torture for the lost souls of the dead. Do you honestly think, Master Merchant, that your bodyguard could hail from such a place? Is he down there now, battling demons—maybe eating their livers?"

Roddy scratched behind one ear. "I can't speak about the demons, my dear. But I know what I saw. When Grog leapt into the chasm, he was stone like the bedrock of this world." The merchant went on scratching, his head atilt. He studied Nina. "You may feel that you've lost a friend. But I've a suspicion you will see him again ere your travels are done."

Nina stared at the merchant. "Why would you think that?" she demanded. "I can't go where he's gone. It's death to such a one as I. If you're right about him—that Grog has no proper place in this upper realm—then he's back in his own world, and I must stay here in mine."

"Ah," Roddy said, stroking his beard now and smiling at her. "But do you not think that your world and Grog's may safely meet at certain times in special places? Before you turn your back on Winfield and go to your brother, I suggest that you revisit the scene of our friend's heroics. There, you will see a sight that may build your hopes for an eventual reunion."

Chapter Eight

The sun had barely cleared the horizon next morning when Nina was out viewing the chasm that had swallowed her friend. What she found in place of a steaming fissure rocked her back on her heels. Overnight, the crack in the ground had filled with water to within several feet of its brim: clear blue, fresh water. Instead of a stinking pit belching clouds of scalding steam and suffocating fumes, now on its outskirts the town had a lake.

Early though the hour was, many locals strolled along the lake's rim and paused to peer into the water. The onlookers marveled, but none dipped their toes. The lake was so new and the manner of its formation so bizarre, no one had worked up the courage yet, to go for a swim.

They'd have to be a strong swimmer, Nina thought as she crouched at the water's edge, *and they better have somebody ready with a rope to pull them out.* For there was no lakeshore or gradual incline, no easy slope leading into the water. The walls of the rift went straight down, a sheer drop, dizzily vertical. Even Nina, naiad that she was, would hesitate to dive in, for scrambling out again would be almost impossible without a ladder.

In any case, far too many people milled around for her to strip to her underthings and try it. So Nina contented herself with a walk around the rim, leading her horse and stopping occasionally to pick up chunks of the pure sulphur that yesterday's explosions had ejected from the fissure. In Nina's stock of medicines and remedies were several that needed best-quality sulphur as an ingredient.

She had nearly completed her circuit of the new lake when she saw it: a scrap of cloth, charred along one edge, half buried under a good-sized stone that, until yesterday, had been deep underground. She gasped. Going down on her knees, Nina worked the cloth free and held it to the rising sun. Despite the damage it had sustained, the fabric was distinctly recognizable. She held in her hand a half-burnt scrap of the overshirt her friend had been wearing when he leapt into the abyss—the gift Nina had given him, the gift Grog had accepted with quiet gratitude and clear pleasure.

Through a burst of fresh tears, Nina fumbled open her saddlebags and stowed away the fabric and the precious sulphur—two last mementos of her lost friend. Then she swung into the saddle. Hardly able to see for weeping, she headed for the main road south, the road to Granger. Traveller took her through Winfield at a gallop, scattering chickens and pedestrians. Annoyed locals flung curses after her.

Nina didn't care, and she did not slow until Trav decided he'd prefer a saner pace. Well south of Winfield, the horse dropped to a steady walk that ate up the miles, carrying her along until hunger pangs penetrated far enough into Nina's sorrow to remind her that both she and Trav needed food and rest.

She reined up and sat with her eyes closed. Her tears had dried, and her emotions were spent. On her own again for the first time in weeks, Nina was conscious of one chapter closing and another opening. Grog was gone, and late last evening she had bidden Roddy farewell, after taking a final meal with the merchant ...

... And taking from him, also, the silver and gold Roddy had insisted on giving her.

"Lady, I pay my debts," he'd barked when Nina made to refuse the money. "I give you only what is owed for the wild game you delivered to my wagon. How could I stay in business if I refused to pay my suppliers fairly and honestly? Do not mistake me for a charitable man," Roddy had said, shaking a bag of coins at her. "I drive a hard bargain. This is payment for the fresh meat at only the same rate that I give for salted. Here also is your commission on the sale of your brother's sling-bullets."

"But you already paid me for that," Nina protested. "Or we traded. You covered my room and board in Plainsboro, remember? Traveller's feed bill, too."

The merchant laughed. "You poor innocent sea goddess who has so little grasp of landward things and what they're worth!" he exclaimed. "As those who know me better would assure you: I have deducted to the penny everything that I have laid out for your expenses, at every moment of our association. This"—Roddy shook the bag at her again—"this is the modest sum I find myself owing you, when both sides of the ledger are totted up."

Though skeptical of the merchant's accounting, and feeling that she was in fact the recipient of his charity, Nina had accepted the money, giving him both her thanks and a hug. They had parted with a promise to call upon one another when Roddy made his way to Granger.

"That might not be anytime soon," the merchant had hedged. "Winfield has always been a lucrative stop on my itinerary, and this month promises to be extraordinarily profitable." With a grin, he'd added, "Our friend Grog is now a legend in these parts, and as a known associate of said legend, I can ride the fellow's coattails."

Nina frowned, wishing that Roddy would show more respect and less avarice in the matter of their departed friend. Evidently, however, no possible circumstance could arise, no calamity could befall, that would discourage the merchant from pursuing profit.

The sound of an approaching haycart prodded Nina from her musings. She nudged Traveller to a walk and left the roadway, heading for a stand of prairie myrtles some distance off.

Partway there, she came upon a gully slicing through the flatlands. Nina guided Trav down into it, drawn by the promise of water. Though she might lack command of her magian powers these days, she still had a nose for water—a trait inherited from her mother. Lady Carin had recounted to Nina how she'd followed her instincts to locate the water she'd needed, on her long-ago walk across these same grasslands.

In a mile or so, the gully opened out to a water-filled depression hardly deserving the title of pond, but offering welcome respite from the noontime heat. Nina dismounted and pulled her packs from the horse's back. She made a meal on bread and cheese while Trav drank from the pond and grazed the wiry grass that greened its banks. Down in the gully all was peaceful. Birds sang and butterflies flitted past. Nina lingered long. She'd had little solitude thus far in her journey, and she hadn't realized until now that she was craving it.

Before sundown tomorrow she would be in Granger, meeting the brother she knew only from stories and sketches. Upon the common ground of their shared ancestry, they might spend the summer together then, trading tales, filling in the blanks, catching up on family doings.

The prospect delighted Nina. Wasn't family reconnection the whole point of this journey? But some part of her also shied away. Legary of Granger was reputed to be a great *wysard*, an adept possessing powers to rival the legendary magician for whom he had been named. Nina's youngest brother had literally moved mountains, or so she'd been told. He'd transmuted boulders into soldiers and sent them like an army against a despot. What would he make of his big sister, the former "sea goddess" who had lost her water-working magic? Would he sneer at her? Look down his nose at her?

Nina sat up from her slouch against a grassy hummock. She put away her uneaten bread and cleaned her hands on a patch of moss. Getting to her feet, she approached the shallow pond as if it were a *wysard*'s well, a fountainhead of purest, potent magic. At its edge Nina knelt in respectful humility. The Powers, after all, were to be found in all of Nature, whether the setting be modest or sublime.

"I ask your mercy," she murmured, fixing her gaze on the water's surface but feeling below it, dipping into it with what magian sensibilities she still possessed. "I pray you will look with favor upon a servant of the Power who has strayed far from her elemental source. Here in these grasslands, I cannot touch the ocean. The sea's mighty waves do not break upon this ground. But still this land knows the blessings of water. Wellsprings rise amid brambles, streams flow, ponds fill with the life-giving element."

Nina closed her eyes and bowed low over the little pond, so low that her brow touched its surface.

"Hear my plea," she whispered. "In every drop is the strength of the whole. I pray to find that strength once more. May the Elemental Ones extend to me your favor, as the ancient Powers have nurtured me since I was but a mote in my mother's womb."

Bent over the pond's edge, Nina held the pose until something brushed against her forehead where it dipped into the water. It felt like a kiss, at first. But then the touch became a sensation less pleasant. It pinched, or bit. She straightened, and raised a hand to feel for whatever had attached itself to her brow.

Her fingers met soft sliminess.

Gingerly, Nina peeled away the slimy thing, wincing as it dug in and resisted removal. When finally she'd worked it loose, she held in her hand a creature midway between a leech and an eel. It groped along her fingers, seeking to reaffix itself.

"Ugh," Nina grunted. But she resisted the urge to fling away the slimy lumpkin. Though she could not guess whether it was meant as a blessing or—as appeared more likely—a curse, it had seemingly come to her from the Powers in answer to her appeal. So Nina only held her hand over the water and spread her fingers. She breathed a sigh of relief when the clingy little creature let go and dropped back into the pond.

She gathered her gear and went to collect Traveller. After strapping her bags in place behind her saddle, Nina checked the horse's muzzle to be sure no leech-thing had attached itself while the animal slaked its thirst. Satisfied that neither of them were burdened with parasites, she mounted and rode up out of the gully. It no longer seemed a pleasant, tranquil place for solitary reflection.

* * *

In late afternoon of the following day, Nina reached Granger. The town struck her as unremarkable, only a modest collection of structures rising from the surrounding grasslands and laid out along a narrow market square. The only building with any height above double storeys was the mill that loomed on the town's far edge. Nina glimpsed a great waterwheel turning steadily, sunlight flashing from it in an unvarying rhythm as it slowly spun 'round.

She did not need to ask the way to the master stonemason's workshop. Legary's place of business fronted the square, standing out among its neighbors as one of the more prosperous-looking enterprises. Displayed out front were a great many stonecrafts: decorative doorposts and fireplaces, elaborate hitchracks, utilitarian water troughs, intricately carved grave markers.

Nina paused at the edge of the grassy commons to study the works of her brother the mason. Somehow she'd expected more. Such was Legary's reputation in Ruain, she'd pictured him living in a castle surrounded by magnificent statuary, on a huge estate enclosed by a soaring wall of rock that he'd conjured into place with his formidable wizardly powers.

There could be no doubt, however, that this relatively modest shop was her brother's. A superbly sculpted rock slate hung without visible means of support, suspended above the doorway and bearing his given name in letters boldly engraved.

Nina dismounted and led her horse to the nearest of the ornate hitchracks. This one sported a design that, seen up close, took her breath away. It was carved with a series of leaping dolphins. The sculptor had captured the sea creatures' every graceful vault, spin, and whirl, breathing life into inert stone.

She crouched beside her horse, her nose practically touching the design as she took it all in. Her fingers were tracing the dolphin shapes when a deep male voice startled Nina upright.

"Know what those are, madam?" the voice asked.

She shot to her feet, to see before her a middle-aged man with a full beard and thick graying hair. He looked nothing like Nina expected. But there was an attitude in his bearing that told her he was kin. He held himself proudly straight-backed and self-assured, the picture of confidence—

—Until his jaw dropped and he took a step back, gaping at her.

"By the Powers!" he swore. "What manner of sorcery is this? How come you by that face?"

Nina rubbed her cheek, momentarily flummoxed by her brother's accusatory tone. She sometimes forgot how closely she resembled Theil Verek of Ruain. Many might mistake the two for twins rather than sire and offspring.

Nina stood staring at Legary, seeking words, trying to quell the wave of mirth that rose unbidden inside her. Her baby brother looked so shocked, so deeply unnerved—and elderly beyond reason—that she should not be finding the moment comical. But she did. Nina burst out laughing.

"On my oath," she gasped, half breathless with her amusement, "I wear this celebrated face by virtue of my birth. I am Lord Verek's eldest daughter. You are that man's youngest son, so I am told, though it's little of him that I see in you, Master Stonecrafter," Nina added, getting her laughter under control and fixing upon her brother a mock-critical gaze.

Legary could not seem to shut his mouth. He went on gaping at her for several heartbeats. Then he burst out, "But it's all of him that I see in *you!*" Legary rubbed his eyes as if doubting what they showed him. "Breath and blood!" he swore. "You're the spitting image."

Nina shrugged. "This face has brought me trouble from time to time, I must confess. But upon occasion it has opened doors and made me welcome." She touched her chin and smiled. "Which do I find here, brother? Will you send me on my way, or will you invite me in? I ask to sit with you long enough to deliver what news I bring from our distant homeland." In afterthought, she added, "Dalton says hello, by the bye."

Legary responded by spreading his arms wide, closing the distance between them and enveloping Nina in a tight embrace. He'd almost hugged the air from her lungs by the time he released her. Grinning, he spun around to his shop door and slammed it shut so hard that the slate over the doorway wobbled drunkenly.

"Come to the house with me," Legary said, and took Nina's hand as if they were children going out to play. "Meet my wife and let her clean up that mess on your forehead. What happened there? Your horse slam you into a tree or something?"

Nina raised her free hand and felt the hard ridge of blood that had dried around the bite-wound on her brow. The wound was shallow. It did not hurt, and she'd forced from her mind yesterday's puzzling and unpleasant encounter with the leech-thing. But she would be glad to have a knowledgeable healer take a look at it. Legary's wife, she had been told, was a skilled wisewoman.

Legary escorted Nina to a substantial stone house down at the end of a side street that led off from the main square. A well-kept border of myrtle trees screened the house from the lane, so that Nina got no clear look at the building until her brother took her around to the front gate. That structure was massive, its ornamental stonework supported by tall, richly carved gateposts. The house itself was even more lavishly decorated with Legary's artistry. Horses galloped across the front of the building, vines climbed the cornerstones, birds flocked around the chimneys.

Every engraving was so precise, each line and curve so perfect, Nina's senses refused to believe the underlying material was rock. It seemed alive. She stepped through the gate and followed a garden path that skirted a front corner of the house. Stooping to lay her hands on the intricately chiseled foundation stone, she fingered the leaves out-lined there, and ran her fingertips along the etched, viny stem. Her touch confirmed what her vision rejected: this was art imitating life, but with fidelity of such a high order, it must confuse the very Powers of creation.

She turned to grin at Legary, who had followed her a short way down the path. "You are indeed a *wysard*, my brother," she exclaimed. "You've wrought magic in stone."

Legary dipped his head, acknowledging the compliment. But his smile slipped noticeably.

Nina wondered at this but had no chance to pursue it. The front door opened, and out stepped a gracefully built, light-haired woman of middle years.

"Who do we have here?" the woman asked, a flash of surprise in her face as she glanced from Legary to Nina. But then: "Oh!" the woman exclaimed before either of them could answer her. "That's a nasty looking scrape on your brow, young woman. Come straight in," she ordered, beckoning Nina to the door. "I'll get my kit."

There followed a time of introductions, delivered while Legary's reassuringly competent, no-nonsense wife—Willow, by name—cleaned the wound on Nina's forehead and rubbed a foul-smelling ointment into the abraded flesh. "Sorry about the stink," Willow muttered as she encased the upper part of Nina's head in clean linen. "But a bite from a *harudin*-worm needs strong medicine. No messing about with *harudins*. Those creatures can carry disease."

"They're also said to be messengers," Legary put in, handing his wife a damp towel for her to wipe her hands. "The oldsters claim they're bringing word 'from the beyond' when they latch onto you. Only when the message is delivered will they drop off."

Oh, great, Nina thought. *I peeled that thing off me before it was done saying whatever it had to say.* She shook her head, wishing anew that her appeal to the Powers had elicited a more clear and definite response. Why send a "messenger" that could bring germs of sickness to the recipient? Nina still had no idea whether the Powers had blessed or cursed her with the "kiss" of that leech.

"I must see to my horse," Nina said, rising from the kitchen table where Willow had tended her wound. "Brother, will you show me where I may house the animal? Is there a reputable place in town?"

Legary waved her back to her seat. "Your horse will join mine in the comfort of my own stables—just out this door and across the garden." He gestured at the back way from the bright and airy kitchen. "I'll fetch your animal while you endure further torment." Legary grinned. "I would wager this house that Willow isn't done with you yet."

He was correct. The woman rummaged again through her stock of herbal remedies and produced the makings of a strong, black, odiferous tea that, as it brewed, filled the air with scents both familiar and unknown. Nina inquired about the ingredients, her curiosity aroused for personal as well as professional reasons. If she was meant to drink the stuff, she preferred to know what was in it. She'd want to know how to make it, too, to add to her own collection of cures if the concoction proved effective.

"It's my private blend," Willow informed her with a guarded look while holding the teapot near an open window, fanning the fumes out into the garden. "Only dung flies and dogs seem to like the smell. There's nothing better, though, for clearing the blood of worm poison." The woman shot Nina a somber glance. "A *harudin* bite that's promptly cleaned and salved gives no trouble, most times. But you've gone more than a day without proper treatment, and maybe you've given disease a chance to take hold." Willow shook her head disapprovingly. "Though you may dislike the taste—and the side effects—you'll need to drink this." She handed Nina a large, steaming cup.

"'Side effects'?" Nina asked, resisting the urge to hold her nose.

"They're hard to explain," Willow hedged. "Or to predict. The effects vary. Some patients experience pleasant sensations." She shrugged. "You will start to feel strange after two or three sips, but keep going and choke it all down. Then just relax and go where it takes you. The 'journey' generally doesn't last more than an hour or two."

"How intriguing," Nina muttered, secretly wondering if her brother's wife was trying to drug her. She couldn't deny, however, that she'd been careless about the leech-thing, both in allowing it to bite her and in not thoroughly cleaning and medicating the wound afterward. She'd done nothing except wipe her forehead on the sleeve of her shirt.

How many times, Nina thought, *have I asked a patient to place their trust in me and in the cures I offer?* Now the table was turned. This wisewoman of Granger was asking for Nina's trust.

She gave it. Nina swallowed every drop, then allowed Willow to lead her to a sofa in the main living space at the front of the house.

Even before she had plopped down on a fat cushion, Nina was drifting in a potent hallucination. The room around her swelled to vast proportions. Only when she found herself slipping between the threads of a woven pillowcase, then descending inside the cushion that the fabric covered, did Nina grasp that the room was not expanding. Instead, she was shrinking—dwindling to the size of a dust mite.

For a little while—or perhaps an eternity, for time had no meaning where she now wandered—Nina explored the cushion's interior. She scaled the individual barbs of the feathers that filled it, climbing them as though they were tree branches. Here and there where the barbs stuck together, secured by the exquisitely tiny hooks with which Nature had endowed them, Nina had to turn sideways to push her way through. Her miniature self, she discovered, had surprising strength: she shouldered aside the stiff barbs as easily as her full-sized self would have parted a bead curtain.

Where broken feather-shafts crossed her path, Nina peeked inside them, studying the darkness that filled the long, hollow passageways. In a world of conventional size, those hollow lengths would hold ink for writing. But for such a tiny mite as Nina, the quills gaped like mineshafts, slanting away into lightless, echoing tunnels. Finding that she still had a voice, she shouted into a particularly cavernous tunnel, and heard the echo return from a great distance.

Other sounds reverberated from the tunnel, too, reaching Nina as the echo died away. Listening at the mouth of the quill shaft, she heard water dripping, and then a splash such as a fish would make when it leapt from a pond.

The water sounds were music to her. Nina had tired of the dry, stiff, barbed world of a feather-stuffed cushion. Besides, she was thirsty. The tea she'd drunk—the potion that had sent her on this journey—had left her mouth dust-caked.

With a bold step, Nina penetrated the darkness of the quill's hollow shaft. In moments, she was enveloped in its inkiness: she could not see her tiny hand in front of her minuscule face. But she hurried onward, her fingertips brushing the walls of the shaft to help her keep her bearings in the utter blackness.

Gradually, there came a change in the nature of the material under her fingers. Instead of the stiff, hornlike substance of a feather shaft, Nina encountered rock. She seemed now to grope along a subterranean tunnel punching its way through stone. Even the smell was different here. Rather than the dusty dryness of old feathers, the air was damp and redolent with moss and fish.

The air? No. As Nina emerged from the dark, stony tunnel, she found herself in water. Not splashing through water or wading it, but swimming it, living in it. She was no longer a dust mite: she had become a pond creature. Her arms were fins; her legs made flippers. Gills replaced her lungs. Nina swam as easily as any fish. She darted hither and thither through the water, exulting in her new shape and the freedom it gave her. She was now what she had been called since her infancy: a water nymph.

Moreover, Nina had grown in size—not restored to her normal dimensions by any means, but big enough to intimidate her fellow pond creatures. She could see them clearly in the depths of her new abode, for every creature glowed, flashed, or twinkled with luminescent color. There were clear greens, brilliant reds, electric blues. Curious to know what her own coloration might be, Nina bent to study her flippers—discovering as she did so that she still had a waist and could bend her body in the middle.

She found her limbs sparkling as if encrusted with precious jewels. Her flesh flickered emerald green, sapphire blue, ruby red, and every shimmering, fiery hue that was ever reflected from the depths of an opal.

"How beautiful!" Nina exclaimed. Or tried to exclaim, but she heard her voice as only a grunt such as the noise some fish made when they ground their teeth together. Intrigued, she tried other vocalizations, exploring the range of underwater sounds that she could produce in her nymphlike form. They were limited, it seemed, to grunts, purrs, and hums, with a few groans resembling the long-distance communications of great whales.

So engrossed was Nina in trying out her much-altered voice, while admiring her spectacular coloration, she almost got eaten. Warned barely in time by a swirl in the water, she looked up to see a black shadow looming over her. Nothing was visible within that shadow except a mouth: a mouth round, huge, ringed with white teeth—and bearing down on her.

Instinct saved her. Nina somersaulted backward, bringing her leg-flippers up in a kick that caught the predator's midsection. The creature emitted an earsplitting shriek and went tumbling. Its internal illumination—which it had dimmed during its attack—now flicked on as if the blow had set it alight. No longer a formless blob of toothy shadow, the creature was now outlined in a ghoulish shade of green. As it flopped away from her end over end, Nina identified it: She'd nearly been devoured by the same sort of leech that had latched onto her forehead and given her a nasty nip with those sharp little teeth, back when she was full-size.

"How'd you like that, huh?" she shouted, or grunted. Nina shook a front fin at the creature, exultant in her revenge on the species that had occasioned this weird, drug-induced journey.

The kick of her leg-flippers, along with the vigorous fanning of her arm-fin, shot Nina a considerable distance through the water. She could not begin to guess where she might now find the tunnel back to the feather pillow where—she hoped—her full-size self lay drowsing. She was drifting in now-calm water, pondering the problem of how to return to reality, when a sudden current caught her from below and pulled her into a rocky crevasse.

This cleft was very different from the quill-shaft tunnel she had followed to the water. This crack was jagged, not smooth, and it seemed to run straight down, as best Nina could judge in the deepening darkness within it. Above her, the waters continued to luminesce, glowing with colorful creatures. None of those bright things accompanied Nina, however, on her downward plunge. Their light was lost in the distance by the time a new radiance became visible below her.

The new light strengthened as Nina fell toward it. It glinted off the walls of the crevasse and illuminated starfish, crabs, oysters and anemones, all making a home in the rocks.

At last the crevasse opened, widening into a great, well-lit chamber, and the current ceased to pull Nina along. She found herself floating in a magnificent underwater cave. Stalactites hung from the high ceiling, glimmering like chandeliers. Jellyfish drifted along the cave's walls, emitting pulses of color: cerulean blue, viridian green, periwinkle purple. An octopus scooted across the sandy floor. As it reached a series of stone ledges that stair-stepped upward out of the sand, the octopus seemed to light a fire in its belly: the creature glowed red.

Nina watched, fascinated, as the eight-limbed creature made its way up the stacked ledges, climbing agilely, swiftly, until it reached a platform carved in solid rock. The raised area resembled a throne. This great cave with its chandeliers and brightly arrayed courtiers might be the audience chamber of an underwater deity. Every creature in it, including the drifting jellyfish and Nina herself, seemed to await the arrival of one who ruled the depths.

Nina studied the throne of rock, seeking the brilliant fire-octopus that had scuttled along the throne's base and then disappeared behind it, as if going to attend upon the deity. She caught no flash of its red, but instead saw a familiar, silky shimmer. The glow from a passing jellyfish picked out a changeable palette of colors—a deep green with flickers of purple and violet. Nina could not mistake it. There at the base of the throne lay a scrap of the strangely variable fabric in which she had wrapped her colossal friend Grog.

She gasped—

—and drew in air, not water. Nina again had lungs rather than gills. She was panting, and too stunned for a moment to understand that she had returned to her sister-in-law's front parlor.

Willow was there, seated beside the sofa upon which Nina lay sprawled. The woman was holding Nina's hand and frowning. The frown relaxed as Nina forced her eyes to focus and meet Willow's gaze.

"Drisha!" Nina swore, husky-voiced, her tongue feeling swollen in her dry mouth.

"It's all right now," Willow murmured. "You're back safe. Drink this." The woman held a cup of cool liquid to Nina's lips.

Nina sat up, taking the cup in both hands to gulp down the berry-flavored drink and relieve her parched throat. Wordlessly, she held the cup out for a refill, which Willow supplied from a pitcher on the side table.

"Some of my patients have an easy hour," the woman remarked as she poured. "They have told me of lying back in the grass on a summer's night, looking up at the stars. Others have feasted at a king's table, or visited distant friends and relatives." The frown returned to Willow's face. "I'm thinking that you, Lady Karenina of Ruain, had a somewhat more challenging time."

"I'll say!" Nina exclaimed. She put down the cup and rubbed her eyes, not yet fully anchored in the here and now. "That was remarkably strange. And so real! By the end of it, I wasn't sure what—or where— my true existence might be."

"I'm relieved that you're back and in your right senses," Willow said. "Only after you had drunk the tea did I stop to consider that I'd never before dosed a *wysard* with it." The woman sat back in her chair, as if to gain distance in case Nina reacted angrily to this disclosure. "I began to be concerned when you thrashed about and shouted in a language unknown to me. Your vision seemed to carry danger."

Vision? Nina wondered. *Or true visitation?* She checked her arms and legs for vestiges of fin and flipper, but found her four limbs shaped as they should be for a land-based life.

"I was more wonderstruck than alarmed," she said, returning her gaze to Willow. "But I did have one moment of terror when I nearly got eaten." Nina described her encounter with the leech and how her solidly landed kick had felt like revenge on every member of that creature's race.

Willow clicked her tongue. "That was the moment, I'll wager, when the *harudin's* venom left your veins. You broke out in a drenching sweat. I smelled the poison oozing from your pores."

"Oh," Nina muttered, embarrassed that she'd been sweating on Willow's good sofa and stinking up the elegant front parlor of Legary's home. "Sorry."

"Not at all," Willow said. "That was the desired result." The woman gave a nod of satisfaction, then rose to her feet. "All danger is past, and now I expect you'll want a bath."

* * *

By the time Legary came in from stabling Nina's horse and attending to the close of the day's business in his shop, Nina was fully recovered. She'd scrubbed away the sweat and washed her hair in a deep stone tub, and been shown upstairs to a comfortable bedchamber with a balcony overlooking spacious gardens. Nina dressed in her last set of clean clothes, and went down to dinner.

She found it served in a formal dining room off the kitchen. Two crisply attired attendants stood at attention there, ready to step forward at a signal from Legary or Willow. The young squires whisked away empty dishes, refilled wine glasses, served dessert, and then melted away into the dusk of a summer evening, having never uttered a word.

"Such luxury!" Nina exclaimed when she was alone with Legary and his wife. "Keep on like this, brother, and you'll never be rid of me. I'll move in to your beautiful house and impose on your hospitality forever."

Willow paused in the act of sampling an almond custard. She glanced at Legary, leading Nina to fear that the woman had mistaken her jest for a serious proposal. Nina was starting to explain that she had every intention of moving on, of heading west to find Galen in the desert hills. But Willow waved her to silence before she had even begun clearing things up.

"That's an excellent idea, and one I'd meant to put forward," the woman said, training her gaze on Nina. "Gary needs someone in his life who might reasonably outlive him. It takes a toll, burying as many wives as your brother has." Willow tilted her head, the look in her eyes intense. "You would be a comfort to him—a constant presence who would not go the way of all mortal flesh, who would not be forced by death to abandon him."

Nina could not say who was more nonplussed by Willow's remarks: herself, or Legary. The stonecrafter shifted uncomfortably in his chair, mouthing words at his wife that Nina took to be, *"Not now."*

Struggling to shape her own discomfiture into some semblance of an appropriate response, Nina was lost for a moment in sheer bemusement at having heard her brother called "Gary." Never had either of his parents referred to their youngest son by that shortened form of his name. Nina suspected that Theil Verek, especially, would find it unseemly, almost sacrilegious. For Legary the Younger was the namesake of the master *wysard* who had once held sovereignty in Ruain. The elder Legary had been Theil's beloved grandfather and his revered teacher. Some of those who had known both *wysards*—the old lord, and the young stonemason who descended from him—had been inclined to think that the younger Legary was the old lord re-embodied.

Now Nina couldn't help regarding "Gary" in a new light. He was without doubt a master *wysard* himself: master of his own domain. But he'd lost his youthful looks—to outward appearance he was a man in his late forties or fifties, bearded and starting to go gray. And his moniker, *Gary*, was a common name such as might be worn by any ordinary male on her old world of Earth.

"Let's drink our wine in the garden," he said, breaking a lengthening silence. "It's a beautiful evening. Not hot like it will be." He shot his wife a meaningful look. "Should our sister endure even one of our southern summers, she'll be keen to sail back to the cool north as quickly as Dalton can get her there."

Willow looked impatient at the change of subject, but she made no protest. She rose from the dining table and waved Legary and Nina through the kitchen and out the back door.

"I'll join you later," the woman said. "After I set these girls to work." Two young women were hanging on the back gate, awaiting Willow's signal. When she beckoned to them, the pair dashed inside, clanging the gate shut behind them. They disappeared within the kitchen as Nina and Legary left it. Immediately there arose the clatter of industrious table-clearing and dishwashing.

"Over here," Legary said, directing Nina to a stone-topped table screened by tall, flowering shrubs. "We'll be spared the worst of that racket, back behind these sweet myrtles."

When they were settled with their wine glasses, wrapped in the richly fragrant air of the garden at twilight, Nina waited for Legary to choose the subject of conversation. Would he return to his wife's comment about "burying wives"?

He did not. Instead, Legary sought an account of her travels with Dalton.

"I'm assuming that's how you got here," he said, smiling at Nina. "But put me right if I've guessed incorrectly. Perhaps you magicked your way to my door, oh great legendary goddess."

Nina cut him a glance. "Legendary? I fear the stories that have reached your ears may have been exaggerated. From the coast of our father's lands, I sailed to Easthaven in the conventional way, simply a passenger aboard the ship that Dalton captained." Remembering that exhilarating voyage, Nina was moved to boast about her then-intact wizardly powers. "I will admit to magicking a little mischief along the way, however."

She described, in increasingly gleeful detail, the rogue waves and sudden whirlpools that she had conjured up and thrown against her middle brother. Speaking of her antics now, to this youngest of her male siblings, Nina knew she sounded ridiculously childish and even a little petty. She'd summoned her powers of water-magic merely to tease and test her brother the weather-mage. But what fun she'd had at the time, pulling the wool over Dalton's otherwise acute magian senses.

"He never caught on!" Nina chortled. "When we reached Easthaven, Dalton walked me into town to meet his mistress." She clucked her tongue, recalling her surprise at seeing that side of his personal life. "Then he took me to a horse-dealer. Once I had my steed in hand, Dalton bid me farewell and waved me on my way." She grinned. "I almost felt sorry for him, that he'd endured such a stormy voyage bringing me to the southern terminus of his ventures in the sea trade. He never knew what I'd done to him." She shrugged, smiling at Legary. "Perhaps the poor boy figured it out on his return journey north. He must have had calmer sailing back to Ruain."

As Nina finished her tale, silence settled over the garden, broken only by the chirps of crickets. Legary stared at her across the table where they still sat alone. Willow had not come outside to join them.

After a moment, "Gary" picked up his wine and took a sip, continuing to contemplate Nina over the rim of his glass. Then he put it down and leaned toward her, bringing his bearded face into the dim light that seeped from a window behind them.

"My dear deluded sister," Legary said at last. He broke into a lop-sided grin. "I'll wager this house and all its furnishings that Dalton knew *exactly* what you were doing to him and his ship." Legary chuckled. "That's why he put you ashore at the first opportunity. Easthaven is far from the 'southern terminus' of his regular route along our coast. That honor is held by a place called Seawood, a port lying due east of Granger." Legary waved in that direction. "Seawood is not a week's ride from here." He cocked his head as if doing mental arithmetic. "But Easthaven? Do you honestly mean to tell me that you rode all the way here from that distant hive of villainy?" His grin widened. "My dear hoodwinked sister! How long did it take you? And how many scoundrels did you fight off along the way?"

Nina sat absorbing this, her wine forgotten. She didn't know whether to be outraged by Dalton's subterfuge, or delighted that her sea-captain brother was not, in fact, a gullible innocent. She remained poised between those two inclinations until Legary's next words tipped the balance in Dalton's favor.

"Another thing," Legary said, a little slyness showing in his grin now. "Our seafaring brother keeps a mistress in every port of call. In Tilda, you met one of his more respectable paramours. At least Tilda has a job and works for her bread."

Legary leaned back, out of the light, denying Nina a clear view of his expression as he added, "Most of Dalton's other lovers are what might be termed 'kept women.' Every time he sails into port and tumbles into their beds, he gifts them with considerable sums—enough to keep them in fine style until he comes 'round to them again." Legary chuckled. "I cannot doubt, that once Dalton put you off his ship in East-haven, he sailed on southward, enjoying the company of his women in every harbor town until he pulled in at Seawood, and there turned back. Had you come ashore at the true terminus of his long and leisurely voyage, you would have saved yourself a difficult ride through rough country."

With a light laugh that mingled admiration and amusement, Legary rose from the table. He reached to help Nina to her feet. Then he drew her into a tight embrace.

"I am pleased, legendary sister of mine, that you made that journey safely," he muttered as he held her close. "In all the many years of my dwelling here in Granger, you are the first and only member of my birth family to darken my door."

Chapter Nine

That night after much wine and conversation, Nina slept the sleep of physical and emotional contentedness. She awoke refreshed, and early enough to find her brother just finishing his breakfast. He was rushing to get to his shop.

"I've a commission to finish," Legary explained as he headed for the door. "The work is promised today. If I am to deliver it on time, my shop will be all rumpus and bustle, filled with noise and stone dust. You'd never be heard over the hammering and chiseling," he added with a shake of his head when Nina expressed a desire to talk more with him. The two had a great deal to catch up on. "Visit with Willow today, I pray you," he said. "We'll speak again this evening, sister."

When he was out the gate and gone, Nina settled a little warily to her own breakfast, eating it in the kitchen while Willow sat with her at the table. The woman nursed a cup of tea. After a few pleasantries and perfunctory attempts at small talk, Nina broached the subject she suspected was foremost in Willow's thoughts.

"Last evening," she said, meeting the forthright gaze of her sister-in-law's brown eyes, "you alluded, I believe, to the fact that *wysards* typically outlive those of non-magian birth. Is that what you meant about Legary burying his wives? He is not, I take it, a serial murderer?"

Willow's eyebrows shot up. "Quite the opposite," she replied. "Your brother is a serial romantic. Time and again he has married for love. Then he has suffered as his bride grows old, loses her teeth—sometimes her mind—and inevitably dies, leaving him alone once more." Willow shook her head. "Every woman in this southland knows who Gary is. They know he'll never age—not in the way a mortal ages, anyway. Every woman warns her daughter and her granddaughters to set their sights lower, to content themselves with marrying their own kind." Willow sighed, and leaned back in her chair.

"But do *any* of us listen to our foremothers?" she burst out after a moment. "No, never! *I* didn't listen. I pursued that handsome, wealthy man with every whit of charm and guile I possessed. Thus I became the latest of the several women who have been mistress of this grand house." Willow gestured at the stone edifice surrounding them.

"Do you regret marrying my brother?" Nina asked, moved to frankness by the note of bitterness in the woman's tone.

Willow snapped upright, sitting forward and reaching across the table to lay her hand on Nina's. "For myself, no—I have no regrets," she said. "I love Gary deeply. No woman could have a husband kinder or more attentive than he." Willow shook her head. "My sadness is for Gary. When we married, I was young and beautiful. Now I'm a woman past my prime, and I know he will not set me aside, but he will watch me grow old and feeble. In time, he will bury me in the family plot, alongside my predecessors.

"It's cruel!" Willow exclaimed, and gripped Nina's hand. "He deserves better. He deserves a wife who will stay at his side, strong and loving and *ageless* for all the many years of his lifetime." Willow looked beseechingly into Nina's eyes. "I was wrong last night, to ask you to stay here with him, to be a comfort to him when the time comes and he must lay me in my grave. That was morbid of me."

The woman released Nina's hand and shifted in her chair to gaze at the back lane Legary had taken on his way to work. The tree-shaded lane, just visible through the open kitchen door, had been cloaked in early-morning shadows at the hour of Legary's departure. Now the sun's rays slanted down through the leafy limbs and picked out a swirl of dust as a breeze kicked up. Willow stood and went to shut the door against both the dust and the increasing warmth of the day. Spring was past; summer was building toward what Nina suspected might be scorching heat. Within the thick stone walls of Legary's house, however, a welcome coolness lingered.

Nina was still trying to shape a response, seeking words that would sound sensible as well as sympathetic, when Willow turned in the doorway and declared: "When you leave here, I want you to take your brother with you. Return him to his own people. Up north where the *wysards* live, he can find a wife who is as magical as he is. Please, Lady Karenina," the woman begged. "Promise you will take him back to his own kind."

Uproot him from the home he has made for himself here? Nina thought, shocked by Willow's request. Legary, after all, was a grown man, capable of making his own decisions about where he would live and with whom he would share his life.

But Willow's anguish over her husband's inevitable bereavement was obviously sincere, and Nina found it touching. Although feeling herself inadequate to the task, she resolved to comfort the woman as best she could. Nina rose from the table and went to wrap Willow in a hug. She kept it brief, sensing that the woman was not entirely comfortable with displays of tender regard offered by near strangers.

"First off," Nina said, stepping back and holding her sister-in-law at arm's length, "let's drop the 'Lady' title. I'm just Nina." She grinned. "And with your permission, I'll be addressing my baby brother as 'Gary' from now on. He was never called that by our parents, you know. Is it your pet name for him?"

Willow relaxed a little, responding to Nina's informality. The woman started to shake her head, then to nod, and ended up smiling. "It's what everyone calls him here," she said. "As a girl growing up in this town, I didn't understand why he had 'Legary' over his shop door. It was only when I married the man that I learned his full name. I saw it for the first time when he signed the magistrate's marriage record."

And I don't understand why Legary displays his true name in public, Nina thought. In the larger society of Ladrehdinian *wysards*, it had been common practice for long ages to hold their real names close, never revealing them to strangers. Nina was now "Lady Archer," compliments of the merchant Roddy. That itinerant fellow had admitted that he, too, went under an assumed name: his mother had not saddled him with the insulting label "Nimrod."

Pushing these considerations aside, Nina turned back to the kitchen table. She drew Willow with her. "I'm eager to hear about your wedding day," Nina said, smiling as she retook her seat and Willow poured a fresh cup of tea. "I know you were a beautiful bride, for you are today a strikingly handsome woman."

"Such flattery," Willow mumbled. She waved away the sentiment but looked pleased nonetheless.

Nina trained her gaze upon the woman. "I offer you no false praise. Yesterday, I stood before this house enthralled by the craftsmanship that went into making it. But the moment I saw you at its front door, I knew I was looking at the true beauty and treasure of my brother's life. He is a fortunate man, to be blessed with a lithe and lovely mate who is also a skilled wisewoman. I am indebted to you for the treatment that cleared the worm poison from my veins."

And sent me on the strangest trip I've ever taken, Nina added silently.

Willow seemed on the verge of tears now, but Nina didn't let up. She could speak with a certain authority, after all, about the wisdom—or folly—of marriage between a *wysard* and a mortal.

"Unlike my brother," Nina continued, "I have wed only once. My mate and I were young together. I was barely eighteen; he not a year older when we married." Nina smiled, remembering. "We had many happy years together, my husband and I. But eventually, inevitably, the man I loved grew old. He withered ... I watched him wither away, and the sorrow in my heart was a knife. The knife went deep on the day my husband died—that inescapable day when he went the way of all mortal flesh."

Nina paused, realizing that her time of bereavement was more sharply etched into her memory than were many other of her Earthly experiences. Her life on that ocean world was feeling increasingly distant. Ever since she'd recrossed the void to return to Ladrehdin, she'd found her memories fading. The events surrounding Makani's death, however, came to her now in sharp focus as Nina talked to her sister-in-law about a personal grief she had never discussed with anyone except her mother, the Lady Carin.

"I buried my husband at sea," Nina went on, locking gazes with Willow as she finished her story. "That was his dying wish. My husband was no magian being, but he and I were alike in many ways—bound by our shared love of the ocean. He had the sea in his blood, as do I."

Willow slowly nodded. "Gary told me you had married a mortal. He meant to reassure me, I think ... same as you're doing now." The woman gave Nina a wan smile. "But I can take no comfort from your words. The pain you felt when you lost your husband ... Gary has endured the same, time and again. He buries a wife, and a year or two later he marries anew, knowing the grief it will bring him." Willow passed a hand across her mouth. "Nina, I think you're wiser than your brother. You've saved yourself much pain, refusing to remarry, choosing instead a life of independence. I beg you: Share your wisdom with your brother. Show him that he need not repeat, endlessly, a cycle of grief. If he must marry—and evidently he must, for the man never stays single for long—then he ought to go north and find a lifelong mate, a woman of magic."

Nina sighed. With her story of Makani, she had not extricated herself from Willow's well-meant but unsound scheme to drive Legary out of his home and send him rootless into the great wide world. But there was time. Before she'd left Ruain, Nina had received commissions from her sister and her mother. Those women wanted portraits made of Legary and Nina together. Legary had not been seen in the north since he came of age, years ago, and he sailed away in search of new challenges and opportunities. His birth family was understandably curious to know what he looked like these days.

As Nina relayed to Willow her intentions for the desired portraits, the woman's face lit up. Willow seemed to forget her fixation on saving Legary from the grief of loss. Anxiety fell away from her. She grew animated with excitement.

"How wonderful!" Willow exclaimed. "I've long thought that Gary neglects his duties to his parents. He does not send them nearly as many letters as he ought. Now, to hear that portraits are wanted, and wanted so keenly that you have come all this way to arrange them: My heart is gladdened, sister." Willow grinned. "You must command Gary to drop his old-man's guise and sit for the painter in his true form. His noble parents will wish to see their son as he really is: young and vigorous, not aging and gray."

"Um," Nina faltered, not sure she understood. "Do you mean Legary's hair isn't really as salt-and-pepper as it looks?"

"That's deception!" Willow exclaimed. "It's wizardly deception. In truth, there's nary a gray streak in it. But Gary thinks he does me a kindness by 'aging' along with me." The woman emitted a huff of exasperation, or perhaps it was disgust. "He thinks he eases my way in society by appearing to be a man of my own years. Faugh! I married a magician who never ages! Why would I now prefer a gray-haired man with crow's-feet at his eyes?"

Nina grinned, and shrugged one shoulder.

"I sometimes think men have no idea what women want," she said. "Thank you for telling me about this act he's put on. I confess: Legary's appearance startled me. You know he's twenty years my junior—he wasn't born yet, when I left our parents' home. I was wondering how he could look so much older than I'd anticipated." Nina reached across the breakfast table to squeeze Willow's hand. "I'll speak to Gary about it, persuade him to drop his 'venerable' pretext while he sits for the portraits. When he's looking ravishingly handsome, perhaps you can make doe eyes at him and convince him you'd prefer a young man in your bed."

Willow was silent for a heartbeat, then burst out laughing. She laughed until tears ran down her face. Nina joined in the merriment, glad to see it, for the bout of laughter loosened the knot inside Willow. When at last the woman wiped her eyes and rose from the table, she seemed freed from worry.

"Now," Nina said, catching at the moment, "let's clear away this mess." She gestured at the remains of an hours'-old breakfast. "Then we must decide how to spend the day. I will be guided by you in all things, for you are at home in Granger, and I know nothing of this place. Where shall we start the tour, once we've tidied up?"

Nina began stacking dirty dishes, intent on making herself a welcome guest by shirking no part of the domestic chores. Running a house the size of this one must be nearly a fulltime occupation. Last night on her way to bed, Nina had glimpsed an entirely separate wing, opening off the same landing that fronted her own luxurious guest room. How many bedchambers, she wondered, did this mansion hold?

Willow waved her away from the table. "Put those down," the woman said, so sharply that Nina obeyed without question. She plunked the dishes back on the table, fearing she'd given offense.

But her hostess was smiling. "My noble sister," she said, "do you forget that I married a wealthy man? You'll not be a kitchen drudge here in my home. Nor shall I. I've a veritable army of maids to do the washing-up, and the cooking. Breakfast is the only meal that I prepare with my own hands, for it gives me an hour to chat with my husband before he goes to the work that consumes his days. For all the rest of the housekeeping, I get the girls in."

With that, Willow flung open the kitchen door and beckoned to the covey of young women who had flocked around the back gate. At her signal, the girls came flying, chattering among themselves.

These were no ordinary housemaids, Nina decided, standing back and watching the girls throw themselves into their tasks. They awaited no word of instruction from Willow, but formed themselves into teams of two and three, some of which tackled the kitchen cleanup while others spread through the building, vigorously dusting and straightening as they went. The young women were clearly at home in this place, on easy terms with their employer. Nina heard several of the girls bid Willow a cheerful "Good morrow," but few addressed her as "madam," and not a single one dropped a curtsy.

"What a lovely crew!" Nina exclaimed as she exited the kitchen at Willow's elbow. "Seldom have I seen servant girls go to their work so readily."

Willow inclined her head. "I do not view them as servants. They are my household staff, and I pay them as such. They earn good wages in my employ." The woman guided Nina down a side corridor, away from the hubbub of energetic tidying-up. She talked as they walked.

"I pay better than most of the merchants in town," Willow said. "But that's not the only reason these girls wish to work for me. I treat these young women with the respect they are owed. I'm not constantly looking over their shoulders, I do not order them around. They all know how to keep house. I leave them to get on with things as they see fit. More than that, these girls know they are safe here from men's leers and rude remarks." Willow sighed. "When they leave and head to their homes each day, they are likely to be ogled by every man in the street. For that seems to be the nature of men in the street. But here behind these stone walls, the girls can have a few hours' peace, out of men's sight."

"Like a convent," Nina murmured. "A distaff community shut off from those men who think that women are objects, toys, prey, or property."

"Quite so," Willow replied. "I expect that you, sister, have attracted a deal of unwanted male attention in your travels." The woman came to a stop in the corridor they had followed from the kitchen. She turned to study Nina. "You have the face and figure of an otherworldly goddess," she said, her tone matter-of-fact, in no way fawning. "With your raven hair and those dark eyes that strike sparks, you must turn every man's head."

Nina felt herself blushing. She seldom considered the effect she had on men.

"You are kind," she murmured. To hide her momentary flutter of self-consciousness, Nina told Willow about the three ruffians in Plainsboro and how she had thwarted the plans of those men.

"Marvelous!" the woman exclaimed. "I wish every girl was raised to handle weapons the way you handle them. Perhaps the men would think twice about putting their hands on us, if they thought themselves at risk of a sharp blade in the cullions."

With this, Willow unlatched the door to which she had brought Nina. It opened upon a well-lit, herbalist's workroom. The heady scent of dried flowers and crushed herbs transported Nina back to Ruain as she remembered her father's similarly well-stocked workspace. The sights and smells of Willow's private domain also recalled the cottage of Nina's great-aunt Megella. If she'd had any doubt, after yesterday's vanquishing of the leech poison, that Willow was a formidably capable wisewoman, Nina could harbor no reservations now. The shop of a professional apothecary would not be better stocked or organized than was Willow's workroom.

"Tomorrow," Willow said when Nina ceased exclaiming over the woman's vast collection of herbs and remedies, "I will take you on my rounds if that is your wish. I've a dozen patients in my care at present. But no case is so critical that they cannot spare me for a few hours. I prefer to spend today learning from you, my well-traveled sister, and also teaching you. You wished to know, did you not, how to make the potion that pulled the *harudin* poison from your veins?"

What followed were hours of intense concentration, of scholarly conversation and detailed note-taking as each woman shared her unique knowledge of medicinal plants and natural cures. Nina described the potent herbs of the north country, and touched on the exotic plants she had learned to use during her time as an Earth islander. Willow spoke with authority about the curative powers of every plant and mineral in her inventory. By day's end, Nina's head felt stuffed with new knowledge and insights.

Not all of those insights dealt with herbs. Nina learned that Legary had built the workroom especially for Willow, and to the woman's specifications. "Gary" had presented the sanctum to his new wife early in their marriage as a kind of courtship gift.

"You know how some male birds will collect bright flowers or colorful pebbles, to win favor with their mates?" Willow commented, giving Nina the history of the room where they worked. "Gary is like one of those birds. With each new wife, he adds on to this house. He constructs a special room for his latest bride—a place where none of her predecessors has ever set foot."

Feeling that the conversation was drifting back dangerously toward Willow's quest to spare Legary from heartache—and ruin his life in the process—Nina steered her hostess toward safer ground by requesting a tour of the mansion. From the ground-floor workroom they ascended to the bedchambers and explored the wing that Nina had noticed last night. Each upstairs room was spotlessly clean and well aired. Nevertheless, the entire wing felt abandoned, as though no one had slept there in decades.

"The children of Gary's first two marriages occupied these rooms," Willow explained. "His earliest families were huge." She pointed down the echoing hallway. "By wife number three, I think the man was beginning to comprehend how complicated his life might become if he continued to sire mobs of children. Would they not all want something from him? How was he to provide for them all? None would inherit this house, because he would outlive them. Several of his eldest children went to work in his shop, and the most talented were trained as full apprentices. Those, he sent out into the world as master stonemasons, able to provide for themselves.

"I believe," Willow continued, "that Gary found his daughters easiest to 'dispose of,' if you will forgive my choice of words. The girls married and left home. But the boys? Some grew resentful, so I have been told, when they realized that their father would not die and leave his estate to them. The stories that have come down from those years speak of angry quarrels and family turmoil." Willow rubbed her lower lip. "Any woman of this present age who wishes to become Gary's latest bride must enter into the marriage contract knowing that she will bear him only a single child, or two at most." Willow smiled. "That suited me. I had no wish to become a brood mare. Gary and I have one daughter. As a child, Amber delighted us. As a woman, she has made us proud. She owns a shipping business on the coast at Seawood."

Thus speaking, Willow took Nina down to the parlor to view a miniature portrait of her grown daughter. Though the image was small, Nina could see the family resemblance. In Amber's features were hints of Lady Carin as well as Willow.

Nina marveled to realize that she was this young woman's aunt. Moreover, there had been previous generations of her nieces and nephews, all of them growing up in this same house, all unknown to her during the years when she'd lived across the void. For a moment,

Nina had an almost frightening sense of how much time had passed while she'd been away from this world of Ladrehdin.

But her mind could not hold the impression for long. Those who traveled the void, as Nina and her mother had traveled it, lost the ability to keep track of time in a strictly linear fashion. Since returning to Ladrehdin, Nina had found it best to avoid dwelling on temporal mysteries that lay beyond the rational realm.

That evening, Legary came home satisfied with his day's work, for he had delivered the promised statuary. After dinner, he and Nina went to the garden for drinks, but Willow again excused herself. The woman seemed determined to give the siblings ample time to talk, free of her company. Perhaps she thought Nina could best press the case for "Gary" getting a magian wife, if Willow were absent from that conversation.

Nina, however, had topics of her own to discuss with Legary—beginning with her assumed name of Nerissa Archer. Here in a land of strangers, Nina preferred that her real name not be bandied about as Legary's was.

She'd not opened her mouth to speak of it, though, before Legary was thumping the table, heaping sudden abuse upon their brother Dalton.

"Yesterday," Legary said, turning to Nina, "I was glib about Dalton putting you off his ship in Easthaven. But now that I've had time to reflect, my anger has risen." Legary frowned, and thumped the table again. "To treat you with such disrespect, you who are the firstborn and the greatest among us! That cur will answer for his conduct, when next I see the fellow in Seawood." Legary shook his fist in an eastwardly direction. "By the Powers, sister! You might have been killed, traveling the length of that treacherous road by yourself."

"I was not alone!" Nina exclaimed, startled to realize that she had not yet told her brother about Roddy, or most especially about Grog. Legary knew them both: Roddy had called the stonemason a friend as well as a supplier of goods. "On the second day of my ride," Nina related as she reached across to stop Legary from venting further anger on the garden table, "I fell in with the merchant Roddy—Nimrod, that is—and that man's bodyguard. Those two were my constant companions from northeast of Plainsboro all the way to Winfield."

Briefly, Nina sketched the highlights of her time with the odd pair. She omitted a great deal from the early days of their journey, for it seemed unfair to both Grog and Legary that she had gone this long without giving an account of the giant's disappearance. She rushed into that story now, describing the chasm that had yawned open with so little warning, it swallowed a youth of Winfield. Nina told of Grog rescuing the young man, and then throwing himself into the abyss.

"He went willingly," she said. "I saw no fear or hesitation. Grog was eager, excited—like someone who had longed for home and finally found his way back there." Nina tilted her head, filled anew with wonder as she recalled the sparkle in the giant's eyes and the spring in his step. "I thought he must perish, lost in the bowels of the world. But Roddy believes our big friend has gone where he belongs."

"What an extraordinary tale!" Legary exclaimed, staring at Nina in the deepening dusk. "It must be the talk of Granger by now. Everyone here has seen the giant who rides with the merchant Nimrod." Legary sat back, rubbing his forehead as though he had trouble absorbing what Nina related. "If my shop door hadn't been closed and locked against interruption for the better part of three days while I finished the work I'd promised, I would have heard every sort of rumor by now." Legary reached for his wine glass and tipped it to Nina in a small toast. "I'm grateful to have the story at firsthand from a reliable witness before the tale grows twisted."

Nina nodded. "It's sure to be retold—and embellished—for generations. What ancient legend of Ladrehdin could top it?" She sipped her wine, silent for a moment, contemplating what she had seen and surmised regarding Grog's return to the underworld. Then Nina leaned forward in her chair, shaping a question for her brother.

"Did Roddy ever tell you how he perceived Grog?" she asked. "To me, the giant resembled a great whale. But Roddy said Grog was a rock troll, his legs columns of stone and his shoulders like blocks of granite."

Nina shifted to better glimpse her brother's face in the dim light from the window behind them. "What did *you* see in the giant?"

"A mudpuppy," Legary replied. "One of those huge salamanders that people call waterdogs." He scratched his chin, studying Nina. "Grog's big ears stood out like great feathery gills. I often wondered how he could breathe in our dry, southern summers. To me, Grog looked like he belonged at the bottom of a murky pond."

Slowly, Nina nodded. "If you crossed a whale with a rock troll, mightn't you get a gigantic mudpuppy?" she murmured, more to herself than to Legary. Then: "Is Grog a shapeshifter, do you think? Might he come from a race of deep-dwelling transmogrifiers?"

"A strange notion!" Legary muttered. "What makes you think it?"

Nina took another sip of wine, gathering her thoughts, sorting and sifting. Carefully, she laid out her arguments: Grog's form was so changeable, everyone who looked upon him saw something different. He had been found at the edge of a harbor, looking out to sea as though his rightful home lay in or upon the ocean. Yet the fellow had come willingly inland when Roddy offered him the hand of friendship. Grog had seemed only resigned, however, never happy with a life spent traveling up and down the same road, subsisting mostly on raw liver and brined beef.

"Liver and brine," Nina said, ticking them off on her fingers. "Liver is rife with iron. Brine is salt. Where else do we find iron and salt?" She answered her own question: "The ocean is salty, of course, but think also of mineral salts that come out of the ground: phosphorus, sulphur, and the like. I'm sure a stonemason must know a great deal about the iron and the salts that are found in rocks."

Nina looked searchingly at her brother. Legary appeared puzzled. But he nodded, and gestured for Nina to continue.

"If you ever saw Grog eat," she said, "then you know he couldn't get enough. He never seemed satisfied." Nina tapped the table for emphasis. "What if he swallowed great quantities of raw liver and brined beef as poor substitutes for *rock itself*? What if the poor fellow craved iron and minerals, and he had to eat the only foods in this upper world that even came close to giving him what he needed?"

Nina leaned back, aware that her argument had taken a ridiculous-sounding turn. But she was remembering the man of stone who'd leapt into the chasm, Grog's chiseled-from-rock appearance in that final moment. She told Legary how unaffected Grog had been by the chasm's suffocating fumes and blistering acids. She repeated Roddy's contention that the rupture in the bedrock was a portal: a doorway through which the out-of-place giant had found his way back to his proper realm.

Nina talked also of deep ocean rifts, phenomena she had learned about during her sojourn on volcanic islands in a vast alien ocean. She speculated that Grog could have oozed like lava through a similar rift in Ladrehdin's Eastern Sea. Finding himself no longer underground but deep in an ocean trench, the shapeshifter adopted a whale-like body and swam to the Easthaven harbor. There, Grog shifted again into a form suited for life on land: he took the guise that Roddy perceived as a rock troll, but many others saw as a giant bull.

"Being a sea creature myself," Nina said, drawing all of this to a close, "I glimpsed Grog's former whale shape. And you brother, stonemason that you are, but also the son of a water-sylph: you detected within him a blending of the land with the water. Did you not say he appeared to you like a mudpuppy? Does not water-soaked soil make mud?"

By this point, Legary had drained and refilled his wine glass thrice. He was leaned well back in his chair, cloaked in the shadows of the garden under a starry night sky. For a time after Nina concluded her discourse on Grog's fundamental nature, Legary said nothing. But then he burst out laughing.

"Sister!" he exclaimed. "You have filled my head with a more fantastical tale than ever I've read or heard." Legary plunked down his glass and pushed himself upright, rather unsteadily from all the wine. "Expect no sensible reply from me tonight," he said. "You must give me a day to consider all that you have put forward. In my wearied brain, I have formed an idea that may throw a narrow shaft of light upon these deep matters. At present, however, I am in no condition to lay that idea before you. I bid you good-night!"

* * *

Breakfast next day was a rushed affair, for Willow was keen to check on her dozen patients. Nina tagged along, much as she had accompanied Aunt Megella during her childhood studies of herb-lore. As the women walked together from house to house, meandering along Granger's narrow lanes and out toward the town's fringes, Willow did not renew her theme of ousting Legary from hearth and home. The woman only reminded Nina that she must persuade "Gary" to drop the pretense of advancing years so that his true visage might be captured by a painter of portraits.

Upon their return through town after visiting the last of Willow's patients, the two women dropped by Legary's shop and found the door open. Willow sent Nina inside while she continued homeward.

"Stay awhile, and see the genius of your brother's work," Willow said. "I've the shopping to do, and a dinner menu to plan." She smiled. "Thank you for making the rounds with me today, sister. I was glad of your sage advice, one healer to another."

The women parted with a slightly awkward hug, and Nina stepped inside what proved to be a pleasingly clean and orderly workshop. Colorful slabs of stone leaned against the walls, waiting to be carved into lintels, pillars, even chimneys. On one half-finished chimney pot, tree branches twined in a complex pattern climbing toward a canopy of leaves, the effect so lifelike that Nina expected the leaves to flutter in the breezes from the shop's open windows.

Beneath those windows, two young people were at work, bent over the ornate designs they were carving. A blond-haired lad was chiseling an ironstone pedestal into the form of a rearing horse. At another table, a dark-eyed lass of about sixteen had a pointed instrument in her hand, which she applied to a brick-red cladding stone to pick out the individual scales in the wings of a fiercely snarling dragon.

The apprentices—for such they were—seemed sure of Nina's identity. They asked no questions, only directed her through to the back of the shop and to a wide door that opened upon a secluded courtyard.

Flowering shrubs lined the yard's high stone walls. Trees flanked one corner, shading a table and chairs tucked aside in a private alcove.

Legary was there, seated at the table and frowning over his ledgers. He worked a counting frame, sliding its colored beads back and forth, evidently not liking the answers they gave him.

"Something not adding up?" Nina asked as she approached the table.

He grunted in reply, and barely looked up as he waved her to the seat opposite. "I've lost track," he muttered, trailing off as he focused on the problem at hand.

Nina sat quietly, watching as Legary flung beads this way and that, his fingers moving with the nimble speed of one who had done such calculations many times before. On the table was a pot of tea with a tray of cups, so Nina served herself and let her thoughts wander while she waited for her brother to finish.

"Ah!" he exclaimed at last, slamming home a row of the wooden beads with such force, Nina feared they would splinter. "Found it." Legary took up a quill pen, dipped its point in ink, and made two notations in his account books. He totted up a column of figures, studied the resulting sum, and almost crowed with satisfaction.

"I thought so." He leaned back in his chair and grinned at Nina. "That merchant friend of yours underpaid for the last order he placed with me." Legary stroked his beard. "I'll be settling that account the moment he pulls into town. Nimrod's in Winfield, you say?"

Nina nodded. "That's where I left him. He said he might be there a while. Business would be brisk, he thought, on account of ... what happened with Grog." Feeling that she had worn out the subject of Grog, Nina shifted to a topic inspired by her present surroundings.

"I tried out those whistling stone bullets of yours," she said. "Up in Plainsboro, Roddy maneuvered me into putting on a show with them. I had everybody in town watching me knock apart hay bales." She described the sling-work exhibitions she had staged, and the resulting clamor for the munitions that Roddy sold from the back of his wagon. "Those people cleaned him out," she said. "I expect he'll be wanting more from you."

Legary chuckled. "I've a barrelful of those things sitting in the shop, gathering dust. You'll have all you want, and Nimrod all he can haul." Legary threw his cold tea over his shoulder, splashing the flowerbed behind him. From the pot he poured a cup of fresh. "I'm curious: Why do you call him 'Roddy'? I've known the fellow for years and never heard any name but Nimrod."

Nina clucked her tongue. "That's a poor label to hang on anyone who does not deserve it. 'Fool, idiot, chump.' That's what the word means to me, and I could not bring myself to address the merchant so disrespectfully." She shrugged. "Whether 'Roddy' or 'Nimrod,' he admits that both are false identities. But he didn't tell me his true name." Nina cocked her head, remembering the merchant's casual refusal to divulge it. "In that regard, the man is strangely like a *wysard*.

"Which reminds me," she rushed on, realizing that she was into her third day with Legary and Willow and she still hadn't told her hosts how she wished to be known. "When amongst strangers, Roddy called me 'Lady Archer'—inspired, I suppose, by my bow hunting. I have grown accustomed to that as my public title." With a fingernail, Nina tapped her teacup. "If it's not too late—if I'm not already known in these precincts—then I would ask that you and Willow use my assumed name when others are near."

Legary nodded. "It shall be so. I've had no occasion to mention you by name to anyone in this town thus far. Beyond my apprentices and Willow's flock of workers, few know that my sister is visiting for the summer. But word will get around. As it does, I'll be sure the gossips have only your preferred title."

"But everyone in this land knows *your* real name," Nina said, still fidgeting with her cup. "You're bold enough to have it inscribed over your shop door." She shook her head. "Our old tutor Welwyn pounded it into me: Magian folk who go among strangers had best guard our identities. Were you not so taught?"

"I was." Legary shrugged. "But all those years ago when I came south, such precautions seemed unnecessary. Back then, I was the only *wysard* south of Ruain—except for Galen, of course, and his isolated pocket of Gift-touched hillfolk. But they're way over in the Ore

Hills, far west of here." Legary gave a vague wave in the direction that Nina meant to travel before summer was too far advanced.

She paused, considering, then nodded. "Truth be told, I did the same thing in that distant place where I spent so many years. No rival *wysards* ever appeared in my island home across the void. None arose to challenge or threaten me. No one there had the knowledge, the power, or the evil intent to turn a *wysard*'s name against its owner. In the absence of such, I felt no need to adopt a false name."

"Happily, the lack of evil intent is a universal trait in the new, young *wysards* who now drift, from time to time, into this south country," Legary commented. "Our sister Vivienne—and old Welwyn—took care to teach their apprentices the ways of Archamon."

"You've seen the results even here?" Nina asked. "You're telling me that magian folk are again living openly in these grasslands, as they did before those terrible Wizards Wars?"

"I know of none who have come to stay," Legary said. "None but myself have put down roots here. But *wysards* do pass through, most of them seeking their own apprentices. Even a dairy maid may become a candidate if she can coax milk from a dry cow. Here in the south, the bar is not set high." Legary tipped his head, regarding Nina thoughtfully as he stroked his beard. "Do you know, sister ... I've had my suspicions about our friend the merchant. Nimrod has made me wonder, upon occasion, if he is not a *wysard* in disguise."

"Roddy?" Nina exclaimed. "Magian? What in the world gives you that idea?"

Legary smiled. "In your travels with him, did you notice that he always has his pick of the best campsites, all along that road through dry scrub and prairie? Other travelers will quarrel—sometimes violently—over the few stopping places that offer a little muddy water for themselves and their horses. But Nimrod somehow finds fresh springwater, pleasant ponds, and green grass, ready at hand each evening when he's minded to pull in for the night. He never needs to contend with his fellow wayfarers for those choice watering holes."

Slowly, Nina nodded. "I *was* a little surprised that we camped so comfortably every night. But I thought it was because he knew the road so well. He's been up and down it so many times, he must know every inch of that route."

Legary shrugged. "I've traveled that road myself, clear to Easthaven and back. I've ridden it in company with other merchants and artisans, and occasionally I have made the trip with Nimrod." He grinned. "I assure you, sister, that traveling with a man of 'Roddy's' talents makes for a far more pleasant journey. And a safer one. It's my opinion that Nimrod knew exactly who—and what—you are, 'Lady Archer,' before you ever saw him. He sensed the magic in you, perceiving it like a reflection of his own gifts. He deliberately placed himself and his bodyguard in your path." Legary chuckled. "Though of course a *wysard* of Nimrod's abilities needs no bodyguard. His own powers are protection enough."

Nina became aware that her mouth was hanging open. She shut it, then parted her lips to sip her now cold tea. A hazy memory or impression rose in her mind—something about Roddy's easy laugh, and the echo in his speech of someone she had once known well.

Legary gave her no time to think on it further. The stonemason was fiddling with the beads in his counting frame, clacking them together in an absentminded way as he went on speaking.

"I also suspect," he said, "that Nimrod took Grog as a sort of apprentice." Tilting his head, he added, "Perhaps 'apprentice' is not the right word. In light of what you have told me about the big fellow, I'm now inclined to think that Grog is a magical being in his own right. Perhaps Nimrod sensed the giant's power, same as he sensed yours." Legary grinned. "The pull of that power must have been strong, to induce the merchant to approach Grog in the first place. Any man's natural instinct would have been to turn tail and race away from such an imposing, alien creature. But the way I heard the story, Nimrod walked straight up and opened his arms to the colossus."

"That's what he told me," Nina said. She paused, then added, "You laughed so hard last night, brother, when I gave you my thoughts on Grog's nature, that I supposed you had rejected every word. Do you now say my ideas have merit?"

Legary stopped twiddling the beads. He leaned across to take Nina's hand.

"Forgive my laughter," he said, smiling. "I had no other way to greet such an astonishing tale as you laid forth. But all day I've turned it over in my mind, and I find that it accords with what I myself have seen and known of that odd, unspeaking giant." Legary released Nina's hand and tapped the stone of the tabletop where they sat. "Have we not been taught that our honored mother, Lady Carin of Ruain, renewed the wellspring of magic in this world? We who live in the sunlit, blue-sky realms of Ladrehdin have seen a reawakening of the Power. Even now, we're seeing it spread from the wizardly strongholds of the far north, all the way down to the Southern Seas."

Legary pointed at the flagstones under his and Nina's feet. "If you and Nimrod are correct in thinking that Grog comes from the underworld, then perhaps he and his 'people' have felt that same reawakening. Perhaps they were locked in stony silence and immobility until the revival of this world's deepest magic freed them in a kind of subterranean rebirth."

"And that's how Grog got lost!" Nina exclaimed. She nodded vigorous approval of her brother's speculations. "Dazed by his reawakening—as surely he must have been—Grog roamed in underground realms that we can only imagine. I picture him exploring the roots of mountains and the deep caves that brim with cool water—those sunless places made bright by creatures which glow with their own inner light." Nina recalled the luminescent fish and jellies that she had seen in her drug-induced vision.

"But then he roamed too far," Legary prompted as Nina paused. "He got lost down there. Eventually he found a crack—a rift—and followed it, hoping it would lead him to his people."

Nina took up the thought. "Instead, he emerged in this upper realm and found himself obliged to adopt first one shape and then another—doing what he must to even exist up here."

Legary stroked his beard again. "The rumors about Grog's disappearance—the tall tales that were bound to spread far beyond Winfield—are now reaching me here at the shop. People are calling the giant a demon of the deep. Or else he's the king of the underworld, depending on the gossip's former view of Grog. Those who knew him as an inhumanly strong but gentle creature are now saying he's a god. They think he has reclaimed his gem-encrusted throne in the glittering halls of Netherworld."

Nina smiled. "I think they're right. Do you know, brother, I believe I visited the giant's throne room when I swallowed Willow's remedy for leech bite." She pushed back her chair, preparing to rise. "But I will tell you that story later. The afternoon wears on, and I need to visit my horse lest the creature forget what I look like. I've not been around to see Trav since you stabled him." She paused, perched on the edge of her seat. "Before I go, however, I must deliver a message from your wife."

Briefly, Nina outlined the plan for the portraits of herself and Legary that had been commissioned by the ladies Vivienne and Carin. She presented the plan as an edict, not a request: Legary *would* make himself available for however many sessions a painter might need to produce the desired artworks. Furthermore, Legary would drop his middle-aged guise and make himself presentable.

"The beard must go," Nina declared. "And get rid of the gray hair." She clucked her tongue. "Willow doesn't like it. She told me you had conjured this silly illusion, aging yourself, trying to pretend you were a man of her own mortal years. Drisha's knuckles, little brother!" Nina exclaimed. "What woman wants to be bedded by a graybeard when she's got a young buck for a husband? Be yourself and please your wife."

Legary flushed to the gray roots of his hair. But then he grinned. His grin widened until he burst out laughing.

Nina left him doubled over with mirth. As she walked back through Legary's shop, she saw the apprentices pause in their work. The two young people stared toward the private courtyard, their eyes widening at the gleeful noises their master was making.

Satisfied that "Gary" now knew all that was expected of him, Nina threaded her way between blocks of stone, some of them elaborately sculpted and some still awaiting the artist's hand. Passing beneath the sign that proclaimed the stonemason's identity to all who wandered by, Nina stepped into the street and took the side lane to the home that the nearly ageless *wysard* shared with his much-loved but only too mortal wife.

Chapter Ten

Two weeks into her visit, Nina had a comfortable but busy daily routine. Mornings were given over to the healing arts, with Nina often accompanying Willow on her rounds, though other times staying behind in the wisewoman's well-stocked workroom, preparing remedies prescribed by one or the other of them. Willow had put it around town that her houseguest was a "consulting physician" from the exotic East. The intrigued locals—many who were only curious, alongside the genuinely ailing—flocked to the two women to buy all manner of potions, powders, teas, and ointments.

Legary arranged the work in his shop to give himself two or three unencumbered hours each afternoon, during which time he sat for a portrait with Nina. He'd mounted only token resistance to the portrait idea, and none at all to Willow's request that he drop the illusion of age. The face that Legary presented to the painter—and to his wife— was unlined now: strong, handsome, and clean-shaven. If the townsfolk thought it odd that Legary suddenly looked decades younger, they kept their surprise to themselves.

The painter, an artist renowned throughout the southland, was brought in from Seawood and made at home in Granger's best lodging house. The man refused an invitation to stay with Legary and Willow, although he could have been accommodated easily in the empty wing of the couple's mansion.

"If I look too long upon the faces of my subjects," the painter protested, "I cease to see them. Familiarity breeds blind boredom. No, no!" the man exclaimed, waving away the offer of hospitality and averting his gaze, as though he feared to catch even a casual glimpse of Legary or Nina. Consequently, they never saw the painter except when the man came to Legary's shop at the appointed hour each afternoon, to take up his brushes and commit to canvas a breathtakingly realistic likeness of the siblings.

So deep was the painter's concentration during these sessions, Nina and Legary felt comfortable speaking of private family matters, assured that the artist was too lost in his craft to hear their quiet conversations. Occasionally the man would shout at them: "Hold your pose! Be still!" But never did he say, "Stop talking." His every sense coalesced in the one faculty: that of seeing. Nina concluded that no sound could penetrate the man's awareness—nothing short of a volcano erupting at his feet.

She took advantage of these sessions, therefore, to deliver news from home—her ancestral home in Ruain—but also to speak of her other world and her other life across the void. Nina told Legary how distant that place seemed to her now, as though the epoch of its existence had been wiped away as soon as she'd left the islands.

She came close to admitting that she'd lost not only her memories, but also her magian powers. But a teasing comment from Legary, a passing quip about his sister the sea goddess, made Nina hold her tongue. Would he look upon her with pity, even contempt, if he knew that his elder sister, the once-powerful firstborn daughter of House Verek, was no longer truly magian?

* * *

On a cloudy but not cool evening in the third week of Nina's visit, she sat down to dinner with her hosts, the meal to be served—as was customary in that house—by two neatly dressed young men. The attendants poured the wine and went through into the kitchen to fetch the steaming dishes that had been prepared by Willow's household staff.

That meal never made it to the dining room table. From the back door into the garden came a tremendous noise of shouting and wailing. All three diners—Legary, Willow, and Nina—sprang to their feet and rushed toward the sounds of trouble.

"Come quickly, Mistress!" cried a girl of about fifteen who appeared barely able to choke out the words. Tears streamed down her face. "It's Bevvy. She's bad hurt. Her mother come home to find her near dead." The girl burst into sobs. "Violated she's been, and beat senseless by the brute."

"Drisha!" Willow swore, then punctuated that mild oath with stronger language. She turned to a slightly more composed young woman who had entered the kitchen on the heels of the weeping girl. Nina recognized both of them. They were among the housekeeping horde who gathered at the back gate each morning to await Willow's signal and commence cleaning.

"Rose," Willow ordered the composed girl, "fetch my kit. You know where I keep it."

Rose nodded. The girl pushed past all those who stood in the kitchen, where the serving lads had joined the circle which was centered around the distraught fifteen-year-old. Rose slipped into the corridor that led to Willow's workroom. As the girl disappeared down it, the wisewoman turned to Legary and Nina.

"No time to saddle a horse," she said. "I'll get there quicker walking." Willow laid a hand on Nina's arm. "Will you come with me, sister?"

"We'll all go," Legary growled.

He grabbed an arm of each serving lad, pulled the two boys out of the circle, and thrust them through the back door, out into the warm summer evening. "Saddle my horse," he barked. "I'll escort the women on foot to the Widow Halden's, but you are to bring my horse quick as you can. Know you the way?"

The boys nodded, both of them tight-lipped and somber. As they started for the back gate and the stables beyond, Nina called to them:

"Saddle my horse as well. The roan gelding. You know that animal, and my gear?"

The lads, hesitating at the gate, shot looks at Legary as if seeking his permission to comply. Nina repressed the urge to rain abuse upon them, and instead met Legary's own questioning look.

"If you mean to ride in search of the rapist," she snapped, "then I'm going with you. Give me a moment to collect my weapons."

Not waiting for Legary's reply, or to see that the boys obeyed her, Nina raced upstairs to her bedchamber. With sure and practiced movements, she strapped on her throwing knife and her rapier in its hip-slung scabbard. Armed for the first time since riding into Granger and being made welcome in her brother's home, Nina leapt down the stairs and into the kitchen. She was cursing under her breath lest her slight delay had prompted Willow and Legary to go on without her.

But both were there, readying themselves for whatever the night might bring. The stonemason had slipped a knife into his own belt, and the wisewoman was shouldering the bag of remedies that she kept ready for moments of urgent need.

"Let's go," Willow said, her voice tight. She led the way, making for the tree-lined lane that Legary generally took to work each morning. Willow, however, turned in the opposite direction, moving with such quick steps that Nina had to break into a trot from time to time to match the woman's pace.

Their destination was a farmhouse, an isolated abode beyond the town's south-lying districts. *Just the kind of place where a jackal might prey on a girl he finds alone and unprotected,* Nina thought, feeling her rage build. *By Drisha and the Powers, I will not rest until that cur is brought to justice.*

At the farmhouse door, Legary stayed on the porch while Nina followed Willow inside. They found the victim in a back bedroom. Her mother was bathing the girl's face with a damp cloth. The flickering of two candles picked out bruises on every inch of exposed skin from the girl's face to her ankles. The room was warm: the girl called Bevvy lay on her bed uncovered by a blanket, and only barely covered by the tunic that had been mostly torn from her body.

The girl moaned, not fully conscious but awake enough to feel the pain of her injuries. Besides the bruises, there were dark smears of blood on Bevvy's face and on her thighs. One arm lay on a pillow beside her, resting at an odd angle, obviously broken or badly dislocated at shoulder or elbow.

"Need more light," Willow muttered. The wisewoman unshouldered her kit and set the bag on a table near the bed. Murmuring about candles, Willow started rummaging through the bag's contents.

"Here," Nina said without thinking. Extending her right hand palm up, she conjured a witchlight orb. She set the globe of cool light on the table, and summoned another six witchlights to arrange on the bed around the brutalized child.

Truly only a child, Nina thought with bitter fury as she studied the girl in the clear, shadowless glow of the magical orbs. Bevvy could not have been more than fourteen. Her attacker had treated her like a piece of meat, leaving her beaten and broken.

"First, a soporific," Willow said, speaking crisply now and taking charge of the room. She waved the girl's mother away from the bed and into the kitchen. "Boil water," she ordered. "Lots of it."

Willow turned to Nina, who had stationed herself at the doorway between bedchamber and kitchen, out of the wisewoman's way but ready to assist. "I dare not touch the child without first deadening her senses," Willow said, the look in her eyes resolute but tinged with anguish. "I will cause her excruciating pain elsewise, feeling for broken bones and for bleeding deep in the girl's vitals. I dread even lifting her enough to get a drop of *ashawort* down her." The wisewoman dipped into her bag as she named the same powerful painkilling herb that Nina would have reached for with any patient so badly injured as this.

"I'll help you," Nina said. She stepped to the other side of the bed. "But before you put her under, let me see if the child can name her attacker. She's barely conscious, but perhaps she can whisper in my ear."

"She already has," said the girl's mother as the woman reentered the room carrying a handleless cup and a steaming kettle. "In my ear, I mean: she's named her attacker. When I came home and found Bevvy in this state, she told me: It's that scoundrel who stopped by here yesterday—him wanting directions to Granger, or so he pretended." The woman cursed hotly. "A lie, for anybody standing on our porch need only look over his shoulder to see the edge of town and the path that goes there.

"That fellow reeked of strong liquor," the woman added. "I fancy he'd already found the lowest tavern in town, and he'd come prowling out to these parts looking for anything he could steal." As the woman set the cup down and filled it with boiling water, she looked at her broken child. "He found a treasure worth taking, all right," she muttered.

"What does that man look like?" Nina demanded, eager to identify her quarry and get on his trail. "Can you describe him?"

The woman nodded. "No taller than me," she said, proceeding to sketch the man in such detail that Nina would know him on sight. "Dirty hair the color of straw, down past his shoulders. Dirty clothes, dark—black or maybe brown, stained with old sweat. A long scar on his face, here." She put a fingertip to the corner of her left eye and traced a line down to her jaw. "He carried an old sword in a beat-up scabbard. Plain, cheap, no trimming or etching."

Nina was starting to praise the woman's powers of observation, when an agonized moan from the girl brought all three women to her. They reached for Bevvy, wanting to give comfort but hardly knowing how to safely touch her bloodied frame. Willow grabbed a cushion and made ready to slide it under the girl's shoulders as Nina helped Bevvy's mother raise her just enough that the girl could swallow a deadening agent without choking on it.

That every movement sent waves of agony through the child was clear from her screams. But when they had her securely propped and Bevvy had drunk a cup of *ashawort* tea, the girl managed to whisper a single intelligible word before slipping into merciful unconsciousness.

"Hood," she rasped.

"Hood?" Nina straightened from the bedside, and turned to the girl's mother with eyebrow raised.

"He must have put a hood over her head," the woman muttered, sagging as she leaned against the bedroom wall for support. The woman had stood remarkably strong, Nina thought, through all of this. But now her anguish was almost taking her feet from under her. "Bevvy couldn't tell me much," the woman added, her voice soft as she brushed the hair from the child's face. "But why else would he have left her alive? If he thought she'd seen his face, if he feared she could betray him to the law, he would have killed her."

Nina nodded. It made sense. The jackal had probably surprised Bevvy, taking her from behind with such violence that he'd wrenched her shoulder from its socket. He'd flung a hood over her head, thinking she'd never identify him if she could not see him.

But by how many other ways, Nina thought, grimly, *would a woman know her rapist?* By the stink of him, the cheap liquor on his breath? By the odor of his stale sweat? Or by his voice? Bevvy had heard the cur ask for directions to the town that lay a short ride down a country lane. She would know and remember that voice when, later, it would curse and taunt her as its owner defiled her.

Nina's gaze raked the girl's motionless form. The soporific had taken full effect; Willow was probing deeply now for shattered bones and internal bleeding. If Nina had been called upon to treat this child, she would have adopted this same approach, first addressing the immediate threats to life. Only then would come the gentle spreading of the girl's legs, allowing the healer to wash the blood and gore from the private realms of womanhood, and search those intimate regions, within and without, for rips, tears ... even cuts made deliberately with the point of a knife, if the rapist had been particularly depraved.

As she watched Willow begin that delicate examination, Nina wondered whether this girl's body could ever heal sufficiently to permit the bearing of children, some day in the future. Or if Bevvy could endure the touch of any man ever again, even a loving husband. Assuming, that is, that the girl survived what had been done to her.

All three women winced as Willow spread the girl's legs, revealing, by the cool light of Nina's conjurations, the appalling extent of the damage. Involuntarily Nina shifted her gaze, only a fraction, but enough to direct her focus away from the horror and onto a wispy thread or straw that appeared to be stuck to the girl's inner thigh—glued in place by the child's shed blood.

"Wait!" Nina cried as Willow made to remove the blood with a dampened cloth. She pushed aside the wisewoman's hand and leaned close for a careful look. *Not straw*, Nina thought, raising up. With her forefinger she pointed out the damning evidence to the two women who stood with her, one on either side of the bed. *Not straw, not thread. Hairs. Long, yellow hairs.*

"Look at this, both of you," she directed Willow and Bevvy's mother. "Witness with me. Here is the proof that this child has truthfully named the jackal who did this to her. It's that cur's hair, left behind to condemn him in any court of law."

"So it is, Lady," murmured Bevvy's mother as Nina painstakingly picked the hairs out of the sticky smear of blood and ejaculate that held them. "He cannot now deny it." The woman shook her fist in the direction of Granger where, presumably, the jackal had gone to celebrate his crime and congratulate himself on leaving no witness. But the blood-caked hairs bore mute testimony to every outrage that he had committed on this girl's body.

"Keep these safe," Nina said as she handed the hairs to Willow. "Have you an empty tin in your kit? Some way to guard against damage or loss?" Nina paused as Willow carefully took custody of the evidence. Then, fingering the hilt of her rapier, she added, "I intend to kill that jackal. If the law objects to the justice I deal out, I will need this proof to defend myself."

"The law will not object," Willow murmured. The wisewoman secured the hairs within a roll of clean linen that she tucked deep in her bag. She turned to Nina. "Go," Willow said, gesturing at the door. "I will do all that must be done here. It falls to you and your brother to track down that fiend. A man who is capable of this"—Willow indicated the mutilated loins of the unconscious girl—"must be stopped before he can do it again."

Nina nodded. She sprinted from the room and through the kitchen, and banged open the farmhouse's front door.

Legary was there in the dark night, waiting for her, no longer hovering beside the door but standing at the foot of the porch steps. He held the reins of his horse and Nina's mount. The two lads who had been pressed into service, to saddle both horses and bring them here, waited off to the side. They shifted their feet and spoke together in low voices, watching as Nina took Legary by the arm and drew him out of the boys' earshot. They need not hear the particulars that she meant to convey to the stonemason. Not even Legary should know all of it: Nina would not violate the privacy of the young rape victim by describing all the damage she had seen in Bevvy's mangled flesh. But she gave enough detail to provoke blistering curses from her brother.

"Drisha damn the man to *farsinchia!*" Legary swore. "How do we find him?"

"The girl's mother says to seek him in the lowest, meanest tavern in town," Nina replied. "She gave me a good description of the cur. I will know him if I see him."

Legary nodded. "The Dog and Rat is the worst cesspit in Granger. We'll head there." He handed her Traveller's reins, and mounted his own horse as she swung into her saddle.

"You boys!" Legary barked at the lads who stood waiting. "Remain here on watch. A badly injured girl lies in this house, attended by the Widow Halden and by my cherished wife. Let no harm come to any within! Give me your word that you'll guard the women until my return."

"We swear it!" cried the boys in unison. One grabbed a pitchfork that lay propped against the porch, and with it jabbed the air for emphasis. "Anybody comes near, he'll get *this.*"

Nodding his approval, Legary reined his horse around. He and Nina took the lane to Granger at a dead run, the stonemason in the lead, trusting to his knowledge of local byways to safely cover the distance at speed on this cloudy, moonless night. They brought their horses to sliding stops at the door of the run-down tavern Legary had named, the Dog and Rat.

Nina was off her horse and through that door before Legary had tossed his reins over the hitch-rack.

"Wait!" he yelled.

She ignored him. She'd already spotted her quarry. A man with long, straw-colored hair sat drinking at the bar. His back was to the door, giving Nina a clear view of the sacklike hood that he'd stuffed between his dirty brown tunic and the stained cowhide belt encircling his waist.

Her rapier hissed a warning as she unsheathed it. Not all of the tavern's patrons had noticed her yet; the place was ill-lit, smoky dark. But those who had observed her rapid entrance, and who now saw her standing weapon in hand behind the greasy-haired man at the bar, got up from their tables and melted into the room's shadows. They sensed what was coming, even if the jackal did not. He went on drinking like a man with no cares and nothing on his conscience.

Nina reached with the tip of her weapon to hook the sack out from under the man's belt. Skewering it, she sent the hood flying. From the corner of one eye, she saw an aging barmaid catch the thing, then wrinkle her nose and throw the hood down on a table that was littered with empty mugs and beer glasses.

The light tap of a swordpoint brought the jackal to his feet. His body jerked, a spasm of surprise as he half fell off his stool. Fumbling to draw his plain, poor weapon, the man whirled to face the threat.

Anticipating his move, Nina had backed off two paces. She would not immediately engage this ale-soaked, filthy mongrel. Nor would she grant him a quick death. He—and everyone within earshot—must first hear her accusations. All must know her reasons for slaying him.

"Did you think yourself safe, with that hood over the girl's head?" Nina jerked her chin at the sack that lay on the dirty table. "Did you believe she could not name her attacker?"

The jackal steadied himself against the bar at his back. His look of surprise gave way to a snarl, and then to a leering grin that split his coarse, cruel features as he ran his gaze over Nina.

"You wanting the same, whore?" he sneered. "Come out to the alley with me and get a taste of *this*." He made a lewd motion with his hips. "You got a big enough mouth for it, you cheeky trull, standing there with a sword and playing like you know how to use it."

Nina ignored his taunts. She raised her voice to reach every corner of the now-silent room.

"This man," she said, pointing at the jackal, "has raped a girl of fourteen years. He left her butchered and broken. Mistress Willow is with the child now, attempting to save her life." As a low murmur coursed through the onlookers, Nina gestured at the hood on the table. "In his cowardice and depravity, he thought to blind the girl and stop her giving testimony against him. But he left behind unassailable evidence: *this.*"

With a lightning-quick lunge, Nina sliced away a length of the jackal's hair before he knew she'd moved. Her blade sent the hank sailing through the air to land beside the hood.

"Before all assembled here," Nina declared, shouting above the crescendo of surprise that rippled through the crowd, "I bear witness against this craven defiler of an innocent child. My eyes have seen the strands of this man's hair made fast upon the body of his victim— affixed to her torn flesh by the blood he spilled from her loins. The Widow Halden and Mistress Willow have seen the same and will so testify."

The rumble from the onlookers held more anger now than surprise. Most of the tavern's patrons were on their feet, and a movement deep in the crowd warned that they were threatening to surge forward and deliver their own brand of mob justice.

Nina raised her sword high and put out her other hand, waving the crowd back and calling for silence.

"If the girl dies," Nina spoke into the sudden hush that her gestures invoked, "this man will hang for murder. But I mean to have satisfaction from him here and now, for what he did to her."

The onlookers broke into cheers and applause, egging her on, eager for the promised swordfight.

The jackal glanced left and right, checking for a way out or perhaps for allies. He found neither. The crowd was against him. As they ringed the combatants, they cut off any possible avenue of escape. Surrender or attack were his only options.

Nina wondered afterward what she would have done, had the man chosen to drop his weapon and throw himself on her mercy. She doubted it would have made an iota of difference. Her rage burned too deep. She'd seen too clearly what this fiend had done to a young woman's body.

The man swung his blade at her. Nina dodged with graceful ease. She closed with a single step, and in a blur of speed she drove her weapon into the jackal's groin. Her blade not only removed the man's genitals, it severed the chief blood vessel of the upper thigh, the major artery that the medics of Nina's old world called "femoral."

A pity, she thought as blood spurted. *I'd wanted him to die slowly.*

But at least he would die in pain. He was screaming.

As Nina watched him collapse into the brimming pool of his blood, she reflected on the many witnesses who were hearing this man's howls of agony, and all who would long remember the sound of it. But only the jackal had heard Bevvy's screams. Had she shrieked with such terror and pain?

Nina wiped the blood from her blade and sheathed the weapon. She looked around, finally remembering that she had not arrived here alone. Where had Legary been during all of this?

She spotted him just inside the tavern's door. His face wore a noncommittal look, as though he strived with conscious intent to betray no reaction to what Nina had done. Slowly, she raised her hands in a gesture that might be read as surrender or deference, and walked to meet her brother.

"Am I to answer to the law?" she asked, speaking up to be heard over the hubbub at her back. A few of the tavern's patrons stood staring at Nina, slack-jawed. But most had crowded toward the bar behind her, emerging from the room's smoky shadows to witness the jackal's death throes. The onlookers spat curses at him. Then a cheer arose, marking the moment of the man's final breath, Nina supposed. For the cheer was followed by a sharp shout of: "Get that carrion out of here!"

Nina turned back to Legary.

"I suppose I must go before the sheriff," she said. "If this town has one."

"It does," Legary murmured. "Pray, wait for me here."

Nina nodded, and watched him make his way through the crowd. People were jostling for better views of the emasculated corpse that was being hauled out to the back alleyway. But Legary ignored the limp, lifeless figure. He made for the dirty table where lay a hank of the jackal's hair and the hood the rapist had flung over Bevvy's head. Legary picked up every strand of pale hair and folded them within the dark hood. He rolled the latter and slipped it under his belt.

"Securing the evidence," Nina said when he rejoined her at the tavern's entrance. She smiled her thanks. "Well done. I may need every scrap of evidence, if there's to be a trial."

"You will not stand trial," Legary muttered. "Ride with me back to the Widow Halden's."

"Of course."

Nina was half out the door when she saw a man barreling toward her and Legary, shoving the crowd out of his way. She'd noticed the fellow earlier, behind the bar pouring drinks. Her assumption—that the rat-faced man owned this filthy establishment—was confirmed when he skidded to a halt in front of her.

"Lady Archer!" the fellow exclaimed, bobbing his chinless head at her. "Splendid swordwork. Simply splendid. A privilege to behold."

"Sorry for the mess," Nina snapped, in no mood to be complimented by a rodent for besting an utterly unworthy opponent. "I will arrange for its ... purgation." Such language as was seldom used outside the sickroom came naturally to Nina's mind in this instance, for a "vigorous evacuation of the bowels" seemed an apt metaphor for the jackal's demise. Some of Bevvy's friends, Nina thought, would embrace the chance to dip their fingers into the shed blood of the girl's rapist. Willow's cleaning crew would go at the "purging" with gusto, if Nina were to ask those young women to rid this tavern of any remaining trace of the jackal's existence.

But the innkeeper declined. "Not necessary, my lady," the rat exclaimed. "Humbled I am by your gracious offer, but my own girls will tidy it up."

He turned to Legary. "I knew that fellow were a bad 'un," he said with an unctuous smile, nervously wringing his clawed hands. "I disliked the cur the minute he came in. But the fellow paid for what he drunk. What could I do? I had no cause to think him a violator of innocent maidens."

Such a show of outraged principles! Nina thought, eyeing the rat narrowly. *Half the men gambling and drinking in this cesspit would violate innocent maids without a twinge of conscience, if they thought they could get away with it.* But perhaps those curs would remember, in future, the justice Nina had meted out tonight to one rapist.

The beady-eyed innkeeper cut her a look as if reading Nina's disgust in the way she glared at him. The eldest daughter of Theil Verek could summon to her countenance all the menace of her sire's famously penetrating gaze. No mere mortal—certainly not this rodent—could long endure the black look she gave him.

The fellow blanched. With a gasp catching in his throat, he turned back to Legary.

"Sir," the rodent said, trying to sound brisk and confident despite his nerves, "I trust the matter is concluded. I've no word to say against Lady Archer for any violence committed here tonight. Your esteemed relation has my deepest thanks for ridding my establishment of vermin. In return, you will not be holding me to account for seeming to, er, harbor a criminal beneath my roof?" The rat—this tavern's in-house vermin, in Nina's view—held out his hand and smiled his oily smile. "Shall we shake on it ... m'lord sheriff?"

Nina whirled to stare at her brother. Legary did not return her gaze, only laid his hand on her shoulder and steered her toward the door.

The high sheriff of Granger did not take the innkeeper's outstretched hand. Legary ignored the rat, except to repeat the assurances that both he and Willow had earlier given Nina:

"The law does not object. There will be no inquiry and no trial."

Chapter Eleven

A change came over the town in the days following Nina's slaying of the rapist. Most of the women went out of their way to congratulate her, praise her, hug and kiss her. They wore their gratitude with straight-backed pride, as if Nina had elevated the self-esteem of every female in Granger. Women of all ages went about their daily tasks with their heads high, and ready with stares to ice the blood of any male who dared affront them.

The townsmen, in contrast, were like dogs with their tails between their legs. Nina had taken to wearing her rapier when she went out. The men of Granger, catching sight of her striding along the street with her weapon at her hip, invariably crossed to the other side. More than once, Nina glimpsed a masculine hand move swiftly to shield its owner's crotch, as if every male in sight feared to lose his "family jewels," as Nina had heard the organs called during her years beyond the void.

She smiled, grimly glad that her ruthlessness toward the rapist had brought the women an interval of peace. Perhaps, too, she had encouraged the men to reflect on their attitudes toward the opposite sex. To realize—some of them for the first time—that women were not objects.

Clearly though, it was time to make her plans for saying good-bye to Legary and Willow. Nina would leave Granger, and soon. She had done all she could to help Willow nurse the child, Bevvy, back to physical health. The girl would live. Whether she would heal from the mental and emotional damage seemed doubtful, however. As soon as Bevvy could crawl out of bed, she'd fled the room where the jackal had ravaged her. She moved into her mother's bedchamber and into the widow's bed as if she were a child of two. Bevvy spoke little and ate little, and showed no interest when her friends came to visit.

Nina had nothing to offer beyond the kindness and the patience that were extended to the girl by every female in her circle. The Widow Halden and her daughter were well looked-after, with neighbors seeing that their kitchen was abundantly stocked, their farmhouse and outbuildings in good repair, and their animals tended. For Bevvy's continued care, Willow would provide, as she had done in the weeks following the rape. The wisewoman had organized an army of women to sit with the girl, change her dressings, and apply healing ointments. Nina could ride away from Granger secure in the knowledge that she owed the girl nothing more than the justice she had dispensed.

What, however, might Nina still owe Legary? A change had seized her brother too, somewhat akin to the nervousness that gripped most of Granger's male population. But Nina could not believe that Legary now feared her.

No—the alteration in the stonemason's manner seemed to spring from a feeling of wonderment that bordered on reverence. Legary took to treating her like she was his sovereign instead of his sister. They continued meeting at his shop almost every afternoon, to sit for the painter's final touches to the paired portraits that were wanted by Vivienne and Carin. But their talks during these sessions were not so easy and relaxed as they had been. They did not speak so freely now, of family and personal matters.

Nina missed the comfortable familiarity of their former sibling relationship. She wondered: Was her brother diminished because he had stood in the tavern's doorway and watched while she slew the rapist? Had she unintentionally robbed him of his status in Granger, as not only the town's most illustrious artisan, but also its chief officer of the law?

It was on their final day with the painter that Nina glimpsed the true reason for her brother's newly deferential attitude toward her. The portraits were finished, approved, and admired by all in the shop. Then the painter agreed, just this once, to accompany his sitters to Legary's home, and there supervise the packing of the works, preparing them for transport by wagon to Seawood. From there, the paintings would go by ship northbound to Ruain. The artist would not accompany the portraits to the deep-water docks at Seawood. That responsibility fell to none other than Roddy, who had ended his lengthy business in Winfield and come at last to Granger.

The merchant did not arrive alone. He'd replaced his lost bodyguard, the enigmatic Grog, with a new attendant whose identity left Nina gaping. At the merchant's side rode the boy of fourteen who had received from Nina instruction in slinging—and who had stirred her suspicions by proposing to make his own stone-throwing weapon from the tongue of his dead father's boot.

"How in the world?" Nina greeted the merchant as he reined his wagon to a halt in front of Legary's shop. "When last I saw that boy, he and his family were bound for Easthaven. I thought you had tarried remarkably long in Winfield. But now I perceive that you've been up that Drisha-forsaken road again, all the way to the coast and back down once more."

Roddy shook his head. "Not so, my lady." The doggish merchant grinned at her. "Though you are correct that I was ensconced in Winfield rather a long time. It is there that I met the boy." Roddy's grin widened. "Behold the work of your most accomplished pupil. Jon here has met the test." Roddy threw aside a tarp and revealed a fresh antelope carcass stowed in his wagon. "Call your brother, if you please, to help me unload this meat. Let's get it on the fire so that we may feast tonight, and tell each other our stories."

That, they did. Roddy, Nina, and Legary sat that afternoon in the back garden of the stonemason's house while the boy called Jon helped Legary's lads-of-all-work cook the meat in an outdoor pit. The boys lined the hollow with cobblestones heated in a blazing fire, then threw in buckets of beetroot and parsnips. Atop the vegetables went slabs of the antelope layered with beef and pork, sealed under clean burdock leaves. The smoky aroma of the roasting dinner made Nina's mouth water, and recalled her time on the road with the merchant.

"I'm bursting to know," she said, turning to Roddy. "How have you come to Granger in company with that boy? When last I saw either of you, you were miles and weeks apart."

Roddy scratched behind his ear. "In fact, my lady, Jon was not so far behind us during the whole of our southbound journey. It seems he did reach Easthaven, late on that day when you watched him leave the camp you and his family shared. But disaster befell the clan before the stroke of that midnight."

On the evening of their arrival, the merchant related, as the family wandered the streets of a strange city, ruffians fell upon the fatherless brood. Three men stole their wagon and horses, and they took Jon's mother, the silent Isobel. The villains would have made off with Jon's sisters as well, except the boy flew at them with a knife in each hand, cursing the men. The girls were screaming, kicking and biting their would-be abductors.

So great a noise did the children make, patrons spilled into the streets from every disreputable establishment within earshot, curious to know the commotion's source. The ruffians, seeing themselves outnumbered, threw Isobel from the stolen wagon and attempted to race away. But the horses of Isobel's team took fright at the mayhem. They bolted, careening the wagon up onto a wooden sidewalk and crashing it against a tavern wall.

By the light of many lanterns that night, brought into the street to survey the damage, it was discovered that one villain lay dead, crushed between the wagon and the wall. The other two men tried limping away, but they didn't get far on account of one's fractured ankle and the other's shattered collarbone. One of the horses had a broken leg and was put down on the spot. The other animal disappeared down a back alleyway, taken by an opportunistic onlooker.

Jon was powerless to prevent the theft, for he sat in the street cradling Isobel's head, weeping for the loss of his mother. The unspeaking woman had uttered no sound during any of this: not when the ruffians seized her, nor when they grabbed for her daughters, nor when they threw her from the wagon and broke her neck.

"I wonder," Roddy said, nearing the end of his tale, "whether Jon ever in his life heard the sound of his mother's voice." The merchant shook his head. "Was the woman always mute? Or had she crooned lullabies to her children in their infancies ... before fate dealt her the blows that rendered her silent."

In the aftermath of the family disaster, Jon did his best for his siblings. He tried to keep them together, but the law—and well-meaning busybodies—intervened to separate them. Sympathetic townsfolk undertook to foster the youngest girls, while the older ones were taken in as housemaids. An Easthaven fishmonger offered Jon an "apprenticeship" that was close kin to bondage. The boy fled the job and the town within a week.

Jon had nothing, Roddy related. The family's few items of value went to the tavern's owner to pay for the damage their wagon and team had done to the man's wall. Nothing was left for a decent burial. Isobel got an unmarked pauper's grave on the outskirts of Easthaven. Jon visited the fresh grave to bid his mother a final farewell. Then he walked out of town with only the clothes on his back ... and the sling he had made with leather from his father's boot.

"That sling—and your instruction—saved him," Roddy said, giving Nina a wry smile. "As Jon walked that long road, he practiced, remembering all that you had taught him. Soon he was killing enough rabbits to avoid starvation. Along the way he fell in with travelers, trading the fresh meat he could supply them for a place in any southbound wagon. By the time he reached Plainsboro, Jon was bagging big game—antelope mostly, but he claims to have downed a wild pig." The merchant grinned. "When it became known in Plainsboro that another skilled slinger had come to town, the locals demanded he give lessons. He charged a fair sum—enough to buy a horse."

Roddy gestured toward the young man who was happily roughhousing, beyond the back gate, with the two lads who minded Legary's stables by day and attended the sheriff's dining table at night. "The old nag barely got him to Winfield, but arrive he did ... only a fortnight after you and I parted company in that town, my lady. The boy came quickly to my attention. He needed work; I needed a bodyguard—and someone to bring in fresh meat." Roddy grinned. "From time to time, Drisha does smile on our worldly enterprises."

The merchant paused. Softly then, he added, "Jon assures me, by the bye, that his father's drowning was accidental—the result of inebriation."

Nina nodded, satisfied at last. "A remarkable turn of fate," she murmured, marveling to learn this recent history of a youth she had never thought to see again. Her estimation of the lad was redeemed by Roddy's account. The boy was resourceful and hard-working. He might make for himself a good future—if Roddy did not turn him into an avaricious wheeler-dealer.

The merchant roared with laughter when Nina voiced this observation as they stood up from the garden table to go indoors, to enjoy the slow-roasted feast that was being brought in from the backyard pit. Still grinning, Roddy held Nina's chair in the dining room, Legary saw Willow to her seat at the table, and soon the four of them were deep in conversation. They talked of the finished portraits and Roddy's commission to deliver the works into "Damon's" hands when next the philandering captain sailed into Seawood. That city on the southeast coast had not often been on Roddy's itinerary, but the merchant had long considered expanding into those regions. He welcomed the chance to go there with Legary's blessing—and with samples of the stonemason's artistry.

"There's wealth to be made in shipping," Roddy observed, "and wealthy folk crave fine things. I'm thinking to make room in my wagon for one or two of those fancy pedestals that Master Legary turns out." The merchant arched a bushy eyebrow at Nina. "There'd be a mite more profit in them, don't you know, than in a barrel of whistling sling-bullets."

"Which reminds me," Nina remarked, turning to her brother. "If you've more of those things, I want sackfuls to take with me in a few days, when I head west to call on Galen. One slinger armed with those can sound like a multitude."

"In a few days?" Roddy echoed, his brows knotting together. "By Drisha's twenty rib bones! You can't mean to brave the western desert so soon ... or as one slinger alone? *No one* ventures into the badlands at this time of year."

Nina shrugged. "Then I suppose I will venture by myself. Whether I go alone or in company, it's time to be on my way."

The merchant stared at Nina. He no longer grinned. With a fierce scowl, he rounded on Legary.

"I never thought to hear such madness spoken beneath your roof, Master Mason," Roddy boomed, sounding not only angry, but shocked. "You know as well as I: a desert crossing in the heat of summer is deadly folly. You must forbid it, if you would not have your sister's bones bleaching in the sun of that unforgiving wilderness."

In answer, Legary leveled his gaze at the merchant. A hardness crept into the stonemason's look, and for an instant Nina saw their father in his eyes. Something of Lord Verek's unyielding glower sparked in his youngest son's gaze, like the glancing strike of steel on flint, and was gone just as quickly.

But Roddy had seen it too. The merchant looked down at the table and muttered, "Your pardon, sir, if I have given offense."

A brief silence fell upon the gathering, broken when Legary took a sip of wine and put his glass down sharply.

"I thank you for your concern, Master Merchant," Legary said, gazing at Roddy with fixed regard and studiously avoiding Nina's glance. "My honored sister knows she is welcome to stay beneath my roof until cooler weather arrives—or forevermore, if she chooses. The lady journeys, however, when and where she will. It's no man's place to say otherwise. But she'll not travel the desert alone. Corlis is back in Granger."

"Corlis!" Roddy exclaimed. "I wouldn't have thought—"

The merchant broke off mid-sentence, as if reconsidering the wisdom of airing his thoughts on the individual so named. He sat studying Legary. Then Roddy turned to Nina.

"You are the most fearless woman I have encountered in this life," he said with a visibly strained smile. "But if there's anyone in the south who can guide you across that soulless desert in high summer, then it's Corlis."

* * *

"Who in the kingdom of Greatrakes is Corlis?" Nina demanded later that evening, when dinner was done and Roddy had gone with his young bodyguard to claim a space in Granger's market square. "And when were you planning on telling me that you'd procured me a guide? I don't mean to sound ungrateful, but I generally like to choose for myself the company I keep."

"A wise policy," Legary muttered as they settled at the garden table.

It was full dark now, the evening far advanced. Nina conjured a witchlight orb so that she might study her brother's reactions as she questioned him. On the night of the rape, she had summoned many magical lights to aid Willow's work. Nina had done that wizardry without thinking about it. Afterward, she was pleased—and deeply relieved—to realize that she could still make that small magic. Her greater powers had deserted her: perhaps she was no longer a true *wysard*. But still she had witchlight at her command.

The glowing orb showed Legary fidgeting, picking up his wine glass and putting it down without drinking.

"What is it, brother?" Nina studied her younger sibling. "Who is Corlis, and why do you deem it necessary that he go with me?"

Legary fingered his glass again, then seemed to remember there was drinkable wine in it. He took a long swallow. Staring beyond the reach of the witchlight, he searched for words in the garden's dark corners.

"In truth," he said at last, "I do not know who Corlis is or where the man comes from. He first showed up in Granger about seven years ago, leading a party of merchants who carried gold and silver. They'd come from the mines of the desert hills that Galen calls home. Among the exquisite pieces they showed me, several bore Galen's hallmark. The merchants had bought the best of his work, they said, and were on their way to sell the treasures to the wealthiest of east coast citizens." The witchlight picked out Legary's wry smile. "Our friend Nimrod is correct: Seawood is a prosperous town, home to a great deal of money and to people who enjoy spending it. I myself have received a number of well-paid commissions from the dignitaries of that place."

"What has kept Roddy from going there weekly?" Nina exclaimed. "The man possesses such a nose for profit, I am amazed he hasn't put himself at the heart of the town's commerce."

Legary shrugged. "Perhaps he stayed away on Grog's account. My impression of Seawood is that it would not welcome a giant mud-puppy into its filigreed, lace-curtain society."

"I suppose not," Nina said, nodding understanding as she tried to picture the leviathan sipping tea from a painted porcelain cup. "But now Roddy has Jon at his side. He may plan to make himself and the boy presentable enough for high society." She grinned at the thought of the merchant turning his puppy-dog eyes to the coast of the rising sun and the riches it held.

"But tell me more about Corlis," Nina went on, returning to the subject of her guide, or escort, or whatever he was meant to be. "The mention of the man's name seemed to surprise Roddy. And clearly the fellow makes you nervous, brother. Though I cannot tell whether he makes you uneasy *because* you're my brother, or because you are the sheriff of Granger."

"It's a little of both," Legary muttered, again staring into the darkness. "I know nothing of the man's character. No ill word has reached me about him, but that may be because he's never in town long enough to make trouble." Legary shook his head, looking perplexed. "The inn-keepers tell me he pays generously for his drinks and meals. He always drinks alone, they say, and speaks no word to any man or woman except to ask for food and ale. He allows no one to sit at his table or engage him in conversation. The barmen observe that he tips well, and no woman can complain of his behavior. He does not so much as glance at any maid who pours his drink or brings his dinner. I've even asked the sporting girls if he engages their services."

Legary looked a tad uncomfortable discussing such matters with his sister, but on he soldiered. "The girls deny it—though many have openly invited his attentions. They seem to think him handsome. They know he has money, too, from the way he spends on food, drink, and supplies when he's in town."

"How intriguing!" Nina exclaimed. She grinned at her brother's discomfort. "The more you tell me, the more acceptable I find your mysterious nomad. Though I might have preferred to choose my own guide, I can't deny the fellow interests me. He sounds like a storybook character."

"It is my considered belief, honored sister," Legary said, locking gazes with her now and revealing a seriousness far removed from Nina's levity, "that you will lose your way and die in the desert if you do not go with Corlis. The merchants trust him to bring them safely through the barren sands. In late spring he completed one such journey, delivering to Seawood his party and their goods without harm or loss to any man. Now he is returned to Granger, preparing to ride back westward."

"When?" Nina asked.

"All is arranged: I spoke with him this morning. He leaves in three days' time to escort you to Galen's home." Legary took Nina's hand and squeezed her fingers. "I do not wish you to go. Even with Corlis as your guide, the journey will be hazardous. And it unsettles me, that I know so little of the man." He bit his lip, and frowned. "But Corlis knows Galen," he added. "Though I have never met a man so tight-lipped as he, I've gotten enough out of him to be assured that he does know our brother."

Legary tipped his head, studying Nina. "If I had not seen the magical speed of your swordplay that night in the Dog and Rat, never could I reconcile myself to entrusting you to a man of such unfathomed character. You will not need to fight the fellow off, I hope. I am confident, however, that you can do so ... should his conduct prove ungentlemanly."

How much of the appalling detail about Bevvy's intimate injuries did Willow end up giving him? Nina wondered. She couldn't doubt that this outpouring of brotherly worry had its origins in the brutal rape of that child. What was done to her had sickened Legary, as it had many in town.

Nina smiled reassurance, touched by her brother's concern. "I pray you be easy," she murmured, meeting Legary's gaze. "Our mother long ago taught me: If my life or my body is threatened, I do not stay my hand."

Legary nodded. With a last squeeze of Nina's fingers, he sat back in his chair and gestured at the witchlight. "I thank you for the Ercil's fire," he said. "Long it's been since I've enjoyed an orb's pleasant glow."

"Why don't you make them for Willow?" Nina shot him a questioning look. "That night in the room with Bevvy, I acted without thinking that I might startle the girl's mother. Willow needed light, and before I knew what I was doing, I'd made half a dozen orbs. The Widow Halden said nothing—she was too distressed, I think, to even notice them. But afterward, Willow mentioned that you no longer summon Ercil's fire, and she wishes you would. She misses the glow, too. Why have you stopped?"

Legary sat back deeper in his chair, hidden in shadow. For a long moment, he did not speak. His answer, when it came, was a whisper in the darkness.

"I have stopped because I have lost the gift. Ercil's fire no longer answers my summons."

"What?" Nina leaned toward him, confused. "I remember our mother struggling with it, early in her studies. But hers was a special case. To a native-born *wysard* of Ladrehdin, witchlight is instinctive, I'd always thought."

Legary heaved a sigh. "I haven't known how to tell you ... I've been of two minds about whether I *should* tell you." His words floated out of the gloom beyond the reach of Ercil's light. "But with your departure so near, I am compelled to acknowledge the full extent of my wizardly impoverishment. Witchlight is the least of it."

Rocking forward in his chair, Legary brought his face into the light, and Nina saw anguish in his eyes. "Perhaps after you left home years ago, you heard the story of the ruthless tyrant who threatened this entire region from Granger to the Southern Seas."

"Yes!" Nina exclaimed. "Your role in that tale is legendary. Our mother told me of the army you raised. You bespelled stones and sent them like soldiers to crush the oppressor's forces."

Legary sighed again. "That episode has indeed passed into legend, far removed now from the living memory of any mortal being. Generations of the ungifted have come and gone since those days. Vivid, however, are my own memories of what it felt like to have such power at my command, to exert mastery over the bedrock of the world."

Nina's breath caught. She drew back a little, her spine stiffening. "But now, brother?" she breathed in a whisper. "What of your powers now?"

Legary snorted, a sound of self-contempt.

"I sit before you," he said, "only a hollow shell of what I once was. No longer do the stones answer my summons. I cannot raise them from the quarries, but must employ rock-cutters to do the heavy work of extracting each boulder and delivering it to my shop. And there, to ply my trade, I must chiefly use the mundane tools of the stonemason's craft—a mallet and a chisel." He wagged a finger in the air. "At the height of my powers, I could carve stone with the tip of my finger. But now I must devote hours of backbreaking labor to such artistry as I once accomplished in moments. What little magic I have left goes into the rarest, finest works that are commissioned by the most demanding—and the wealthiest—of my patrons." Legary scoffed. "It's quite the prostitute I have become."

Nina sat stunned. Legary, too? Her brother had also suffered the loss of his greatest magian power? She was on the verge of confessing her own wizardly impairment, of unburdening herself of the secret she had held since leaving the sea at Easthaven. But too many questions rose in her mind. They crowded out her impulse to make a clean breast of it.

"You are not powerless!" she exclaimed, reaching for Legary's hand. "The magic of your Gift shines in every work you create. I have seen it in your shop and in the walls of this house. Also," she rushed on, interrupting Legary's attempted protest, "everyone in this town has seen you age yourself and then reclaim your youth."

"Illusion!" he exclaimed, pulling his hand free and waving away her words. "A crude illusion. Not true wizardry." Legary shook his head and grimaced. "Simple and few are the tricks that are left in my bag. The Powers have taken my real gift from me."

"How? Why?"

"Why?" Legary echoed. "To ask that, is to question the Elementals themselves." He threw out an arm in a gesture that encompassed the whole of creation. But then he paused, and leaned into the witchlight to rivet Nina with his gaze.

"I cannot speak for the Elementals," he whispered, "but I will share with you my conjectures, for I would not see you suffer a loss such as I have endured. It may be, sister, that I am now punished for having squandered my gift in prideful ways. Going back to my boyhood, I used my powers wastefully. I scarred Ruain with countless pits, raising slabs of rock and leaving behind a devastated landscape, for no reason other than I could. It was desperation, I believe, that made our father send me to Dalton on the coast."

"Where you built docks and breakwaters that serve to this day!" Nina protested. "You did not waste your gift, you used it well."

"Under supervision," Legary countered. "As long as Dalton was there, ordering me around, I built in purposeful ways. But too head-strong to be long controlled, I sailed south at my first opportunity. And every place I came ashore, I heaped up stones. Such magnificent edifices I raised, each of them a monument to my arrogant, wizardly pride!"

Legary threw back his head and emitted a mirthless hoot of laughter. "The irony now is that several of the grand houses in Seawood—where my wealthier patrons live—are structures that I conjured into being long ago, when my extravagance knew no bounds. It is my fate, I now think, to maintain and embellish those buildings forevermore. Each time that I deliver some new ornamentation to an already ostentatious mansion, I am reminded of my youthful, foolish pride."

Nina sat quietly, absorbing Legary's words, applying them to her own situation. Slowly, she reached for the witchlight and twirled the orb in her fingers.

"A punishment," she murmured, staring into the light. "For misusing your gift."

"That is my belief. It's the conclusion I have drawn from lengthy meditation on the matter." Legary sat back. "I had not thought to tell you all of this. I do not wish to burden you with my troubles. But it's been on my mind since you spoke to me of the 'tricks' you played on Dalton in the course of your southern sailing. How you conjured whirlpools and waves to tease him."

Abruptly, Legary rocked forward again into the light. "Take care, sister," he warned, his voice uncharacteristically sharp. "Do not misuse your gift. Offer no insult to the Elementals, and above all do not test the patience of the Powers."

Nina shot him a glance. She was on the verge of blurting, "Too late!" when Legary startled her by pounding the table in a sudden show of approbation.

"How it delights me to see you fully possessed of your own great powers!" he exclaimed, grinning at her with almost manic enthusiasm. "The speed of your sword-thrust that night in the Dog and Rat—it thrills me to picture it. To speak truth, though, I saw not so much as a blur. The weapon was in your hand, you began your attack—and then the jackal was on the floor, his blood spurting." Legary shook his head wonderingly. "All the town speaks of it still, with a great many 'witnesses' claiming they saw every move. But they lie. For no mortal eyes could have followed the sweep of your blade. Faster than lightning it was!"

Feeling that this praise came dangerously close to the "wizardly arrogance" Legary had warned her about, Nina muttered something self-deprecating. Her brother waved aside her words.

"I saw magic!" he insisted. "A display of unfettered Power." He laughed. "Having witnessed such strength, I *can* watch you ride away with Corlis—confident that you'll best him in any contest of arms." Legary scooped up his wine glass and drained its few remaining drops. "But I think it need never come to that," he added, gesturing with the empty goblet. "Will not my sister the sea goddess simply conjure a wave and drown any desert rat who dares to offend her?"

Two days passed in a flurry of preparation. Nina sorted her clothes, choosing only those suitable for a desert trek. Her wardrobe had expanded during her time in Granger. It now held many garments that she could not take with her. Observing that Nina and Bevvy were nearly the same size, Willow claimed Nina's castoffs for her patient, thinking that fine clothes might draw the girl from her shell of silence. Nina relinquished the garments willingly, though secretly doubting they would do much to heal the child's wounded soul.

Getting Traveller ready for the journey took most of Nina's remaining time and attention. In consultation with a farrier who was trusted by both Legary and Roddy, she had the horse fitted with good shoes for desert walking. Mindful of the strong sun and desiccated air she would soon face, Nina oiled every inch of her tack and gear, not leaving the job to Legary's stableboys.

Late in the evening of the second day, she bid farewell to Roddy and to the surprising lad named Jon. They would be off in the morning, too, but in the opposite direction, heading east to the port at Seawood. Roddy vowed to stay in that city until Dalton dropped anchor in its harbor. No one seemed able to predict exactly when the seafarer known as Damon might once again venture this far south. Sometimes he sailed only as far as Easthaven, then turned around and disappeared once more, leaving the locals to speculate—wildly, in many quarters—as to the fair-haired captain's true origins and identity.

"I'll not spill the beans," Roddy promised, laughing his doggish laugh as Nina and Legary took their leave of him. "You have my word that I'll mind my tongue—and guard your portraits as though they were my children. However long it takes, I'll be in Seawood until I may personally deliver the paintings into the two hands of your mysterious brother."

"While he waits, he'll sniff out every pocket of money in the city and ingratiate himself with those who control it, I do not doubt," Nina muttered in an aside to Legary as they left the merchant to his own preparations and strolled back toward the stonemason's house. "I expect our friend will return to Granger richer than he left it."

"Thus it is so with Nimrod, in all seasons and chances," Legary replied, his lips crooked in a wry smile.

"I'm sorry I didn't get as far as Seawood on this trip," Nina added when they stood together by the back gate, taking in the serenity of a starlit summer's evening. Both were reluctant to go indoors and say good-night, for early in the morning they would part, with little expectation of seeing each other again for many years ... maybe ever.

But *wysards* live long. Perhaps she would come this way again someday, Nina thought. After all, she was a born traveler like her mother before her. Lord Verek had often remarked on the great journeys Lady Carin had made to distant worlds. Nina had also crossed the void, and she had done it at an age even younger than Carin's first passage through that weird nothingness. Wayfaring was in Nina's blood. Perhaps she *would* return to Granger and reunite with her baby brother, someday.

She looked up at Legary. "I'm sorry I didn't get a chance to meet your daughter," Nina said. "I understand my niece is quite the success."

"What?" Legary's smile faded as he stared at her.

Sensing a misstep, Nina proceeded cautiously. "Um," she muttered, "your daughter at Seawood. Willow mentioned her ... Said she owned a shipping business there on the coast?"

Legary continued staring. Slowly then, and sadly, he shook his head.

"Our daughter Amber has been dead for years," he murmured. "She and her husband once made their home in Seawood, that much is true. But while still a young woman she lost her man in an accident at sea." Legary heaved a sigh. "Not long afterward, Amber contracted a fever. To this day, Willow blames herself for not reaching our daughter in time to save her ... and save her unborn child, our grandson. I've told Willow time and again, that she's not responsible—the fever took Amber too quickly. Nothing could have been done. But Willow has never forgiven herself."

"I'm sorry!" Nina exclaimed, aghast that she had opened this old wound in her brother's heart. The tightness in his voice communicated more than his words.

Legary shook his head. "It was long ago. And though you may think me a monster for saying it, I have grown resigned to seeing my children die. All of them have—all my children from my previous marriages are gone. So are most of my grandchildren and some of *their* children."

He braced against the gatepost as though needing its support to bear up under the weight of so much loss. "Such is the price paid by a *wysard* who marries a mortal and begets mortal children," Legary muttered, looking up at the stars and raising both hands as if in supplication. "I've been through it many times now. But our Amber was Willow's only child. Her grief has not faded. It remains a hard stone in her heart."

Nina sought comforting words but found none. Though she, too, had loved and married a mortal, and had raised a huge family with that man, she'd quit the world of those faraway offspring before even the eldest had reached their final years.

Which of us is the true monster? Nina wondered, comparing Legary's steadfastness with her flight. *He stays and sees them die. I run so that I am spared.*

"Oh!" she exclaimed, struck by a sudden realization. "All that about Willow wanting me to take you out of Granger ... you were to go with me and find yourself a wizardly wife up north. Willow has been silent on the subject lately, but I recall she was keen to get you out of here so you won't have to watch her grow old and die." Nina reached for Legary's arm. "That's her own grief talking, isn't it."

He nodded. "Amber's death taught her what it feels like when the loss of someone you love cleaves your heart in two. Only those who have been through it can know the soul-deep pain of it." Legary paused, then softly continued. "Willow was young when she and I married. She'd never experienced a profoundly heartbreaking loss, until Amber died."

"But now, having felt such pain," Nina murmured, "she thinks to spare *you* from ever feeling it again, by driving you away. What love! You are a fortunate man, brother, to have a wife who would give you up rather than see you hurt again."

In the starlight, Nina saw Legary smile.

"Now you know why I will never leave the woman," he said. "The love she has for me is equaled only by mine for her. Willow is my wife until death do us part."

Part 2
The Nomad

Chapter Twelve

Despite what the sporting girls of Granger might think, Corlis was not handsome, Nina decided. But the tall, sinewy, silent man was decidedly intriguing.

Her guide through the desert reflected much of that land's subdued coloration, and seemingly all of its grit. Under his slouchy, buff-leather hat, he had sandy hair cropped short. On the morning they rode out together he was clean-shaven, but as the days passed his mustache and beard grew thick and wiry, showing darker than the hair under his hat. His eyes, looking out in a narrowed gaze from a weathered face, seemed perpetually to squint against the sun. Nina couldn't make out what color they were. Mostly they stayed hidden by his hat's low brim. Catching an occasional glimpse, however, she found that they, too, seemed to reflect the landscape around them: sometimes sagebrush green, other times flinty gray.

His horse, black-skinned under a smooth white coat, was of a desert breed Nina had never seen before. She admired the animal's elegantly arched neck and the proud set of its head, from which large, dark eyes regarded her with an alert curiosity that seemed wholly lacking in its rider.

Which was not to say that Corlis lacked alertness. Though apparently devoid of any interest whatsoever in his traveling companion, he was ceaselessly alert to the surrounding emptiness. He scanned ahead for who-knew-what threat, and threw frequent glances at the two pack animals that followed him on a long lead. Those horses, like his own mount, were agile, compact animals, their lean muscling making Nina's solidly built roan look heavy in comparison.

Corlis had offered no complaint or criticism, however, when Nina presented herself on the morning of their departure from Granger, riding her muscular, well-conditioned mount. The man had swung down from his saddle, picked up and examined each of Traveller's specially reshod feet, and run his shadowed gaze over Nina's gear, eyeing her bulging saddlebags and bedroll, and her bow in its scabbard. With a brusque nod that could have signified approval or only acquiescence, Corlis had remounted and headed west out of town, his packhorses stringing out behind him. Not once had he looked Nina eye-to-eye or spoken to her. He seemed not to care whether she came with him or stayed behind. So pronounced was his indifference, it bordered on insolence.

Staring after the man who had taken gold from both herself and Legary to see her safely across the barrens, Nina called to mind a useful maxim she had learned during her time on Earth: "Begin as you mean to go on."

Heeding that saying, she urged Traveller to a trot, rode up abreast of Corlis, and fell in alongside him.

When that got no reaction, Nina took Trav into the lead, where she set an unhurried pace for the first day of their journey. Never once did Corlis call to her or ask that she either speed up or fall back. When she happened upon a spot of shade and reined Traveller in for a brief rest, Corlis did likewise with his animals. On that first day, having heard no word pass the man's lips, Nina said nothing to him either. She did not deign to consult him on a single matter, but decided for herself when to pause and for how long, and where they would take their midday meal. Alerted to the presence of water by a startlingly lush thicket of stunted willows off the side of the sandy trail, she led her "guide" into green shadows at the edge of a seeping spring. Again Corlis offered no comment, but dismounted and brought his horses up beside Trav to drink of the cool, clear water.

While the animals grazed, their riders ate bread and cheese from their own separate stores. Nina had no idea what food, or how much, the pack animals might carry. Their canvas bundles gave no clue to the provisions that Corlis had purchased, presumably with some part of his very generous fee. The packs were not opened that first day, nor for many days thereafter. Nina and Corlis ate only what they carried in their personal gear. And unlike her previous company for her long ride last spring, there was no sharing and no conversation.

As the sun dropped westward and Nina saw no likely campsite clear to the horizon, she fell back, relinquishing the lead to Corlis but putting Trav in lockstep beside him. She would bow to the man's superior knowledge of these featureless flats, but she would not retreat to the back of the line to eat his dust.

Maddeningly, Corlis seemed not to notice when Nina took up her post at his right hand. For a time, they rode on at exactly the pace Nina had set throughout the day. But gradually, Corlis began to veer away from the trail and away from Nina. Again with no word or glance her way, the man angled across a windswept stretch of bare rock, heading for no discernible landmark.

Nina veered with him, riding into desolation: this sunbaked land was an unbroken, treeless waste. Or so it appeared. But at the end of a hard-packed expanse of chalky ground, a ravine opened, slicing darkly through the late-afternoon incandescence. A faint path descended into that promise of coolness.

The path was too narrow for two horses abreast. Still ignoring Nina, Corlis started down it ahead of her, his nimble mount unhesitating. Both packhorses followed, surefooted as goats. Nina, however, dismounted. She would not risk injuring Trav on an unfamiliar descent, the steepness of which she could not judge from where she stood. The sun's low angle cast the ravine's depths into blackness.

She started down on foot, leading her horse and taking her time, giving her eyes a chance to adjust to the shadows after the glare of the desert. The path angled steeply enough that her boots skidded a time or two. Behind her, Traveller let out an occasional uneasy snort but he continued picking his way down, choosing his footing as carefully as

Nina felt for hers. She had time to wonder, as she made her slow descent, whether she would find Corlis at the bottom. Perhaps his neglect of her would extend to abandonment, and he'd be nowhere in sight when she finally made it down.

But he was there, stripping the pack animals of their loads. He'd already unsaddled his mount and tethered that horse to graze beside a tree-shaded pool that stretched the length of the ravine. Just enough late-day sunlight reflected from the sky above to show a current stirring the water. Nina could see no obvious inflow, but she suspected the current arose from another of the perennial springs that she had come to rely upon during her southern travels. If this desert was as generously dotted with seeps as the scrublands were around Plainsboro, then this height-of-summer crossing of the barrens might be less arduous than she'd been led to believe.

Then again, Legary had ascribed magical powers to Nimrod—"Roddy"—for the merchant's ability to find fresh water whenever he wanted it. Looking around at this damp, hidden sanctuary, Nina was half inclined to think the same of Corlis. He seemed every bit as secretive as the legendary *wysards* of old, and she doubted that many ordinary travelers could know of this place. It lay well off the main trail, and Corlis had taken care to approach it over ground that was too hard and denuded to show any trace of their passage.

Shrugging off her speculations, Nina led her horse to water, then stripped Trav of saddle and gear. She found him a good spot of grazing away from the animals Corlis was tending. Hidden there from her aloof guide, she crouched amid her bags and watched him make camp in the shadows at the pool's edge. Any other traveling companion would have had her willing help with the necessary tasks of evening. But if Corlis chose to ignore her existence, she would ignore his. After giving her horse a brisk rubdown and inspecting his feet, Nina made her own camp near the water, keeping a stone's throw apart from her guide. She built a small fire to heat water for tea and for a wash-up.

The latter was accomplished in privacy behind a jumble of boulders. Unwilling to risk an encounter with the unknown denizens of this oasis—such as night-roaming scorpions—Nina conjured Ercil's fire.

By the orb's steady glow, she inspected the hidden side of the boulder heap, checking that no poisonous vermin would interrupt her ablutions. If Corlis wondered at the light that seeped around the boulders' edges, let him think she carried a candle. Or let him think her a witch. Nina didn't particularly care.

Her evening meal was again bread and cheese, to which she added a single strip of dried meat from her personal stores. With Corlis showing no sign of parceling out any of the supplies he had packed, Nina thought it prudent to stretch her own provisions as far as she could. No extremity of hunger would have driven her, at this point, to ask the man for any morsel. His silence had run up against her stubbornness.

Let's see who can go the longest without uttering a word, she mentally challenged Corlis.

By the time she'd finished her meager meal and drunk a second cup of tea, twilight had yielded to full night, throwing the ravine into inky blackness. With nothing to do except open out her bedroll next to her little fire, and arrange her weapons at hand in case she needed them during the night, Nina shut her eyes and tried to sleep. The only sound near her was the soft gurgling of water, the oh-so-gentle movement of the pond's current.

The sound became hypnotic. Drawn into it, Nina began to float away, not carried into sleep but borne along on memories: memories of the water spellcraft she had formerly commanded. In her mind's eye she saw the great waves she had conjured while still a young child—her reckless magic-making bringing despair to her parents, those two *wysards* of Ruain who had wisely sought to impose limits on what had threatened to be, in Nina's case, a limitless, uncontrollable gift. She remembered the efforts of her old tutor, Master Welwyn, to impress upon her the essential wizardly virtue of self-restraint.

Nina was reaching back, far back to the days of her earliest training in the *art magick*, when another sound floated in, drifting above the faint gurgling of the pond.

For a moment she could not grasp what she was hearing. But the new sound swelled louder, loud enough to break her near-trance. Its tones scattered her thoughts of yesteryear and brought her eyes flying open.

Music. She was hearing music. Soft, sweet notes in the night.

Nina raised up on one elbow to see Corlis sitting at the pond's edge with a small musical instrument at his lips. The tune he played was gentle but not mournful. It seemed an ode to this hidden sanctuary— or a siren song for the creatures that, until then, had swum unseen in the water at his feet. As Nina watched, a fish leapt into the air, its scales glistening in the light of her guide's flickering campfire.

She was out of her bedroll in an instant, moving along the pond's bank to take up a position nearer Corlis—not to better hear the tune he played, but to be ready if another fish answered his musical summons. Nina, her knife in her hand, crouched atop a rock that gave her a view straight down into the water.

She was rewarded almost immediately by the approach of another large fish. This one did not leap, but swam slowly past her vantage point.

Her knife flashed: she had her prize. Out of the water on the end of Nina's blade came a much bigger and better supper than she had made on jerked meat and hard bread. Stifling the exclamation of triumph that rose to her lips, she held true to her vow to not break the silence ahead of Corlis. But perhaps with his music, he had already lost the mental wager Nina had made with him.

His tune had faltered at the moment Nina stabbed the fish—only slightly, but enough to say he'd noticed her. She did not glance at him, but took her catch to her private spot behind the boulders.

Corlis went on playing then, but his music now sounded almost like a lament. Its cheerlessness raised a question in Nina's mind: Had she committed sacrilege, shedding blood in this sanctuary?

Nina shrugged. Corlis would have seen the knife in her hand and must have guessed her intentions. He could have stopped her with a word, but he'd said nothing. If she'd done wrong, he was also culpable.

Hidden behind the boulders, Nina conjured witchlight and examined her catch. The fish was large and heavy, and of a type unfamiliar to her. But it looked and smelled clean and wholesome. With a quickness born of long practice—she'd consumed tons of fish during her island sojourn beyond the void—Nina soon had the silvery creature scaled, gutted, and ready for the fire. She extinguished the cool witch-light before returning to her campsite, happy to leave Corlis in the dark, as it were, about the source of the radiance. Her small, hot fire had burned to glowing embers by now—exactly right for baked fish.

The flesh proved to be delicious, juicy, delicately flavored. Nina ate until she could hold no more, and still there was fish left. She stirred her little fire and contemplated her leftovers. There was enough to make breakfast on, but her excellent catch needed eating at its freshest. She glanced over at Corlis, who still sent his music into the night, but softly now.

Not giving herself time to think about it, Nina rose to her feet and took her uneaten portion to the man's campsite. As she laid the fish on a flat rock near his fire, Corlis never looked at her, and Nina made no effort to catch his eye. On her way back to her own fire she paused, crouching on the pond's bank to wash the fish oils from her hands and mouth.

As she straightened, the music died away. Before Nina could stop herself, she'd sent a sideward glance toward the player. But Corlis didn't see. He'd set aside his small wind-instrument and was reaching for the cooked fish. Nina's last glimpse of him that night, before she turned her back and returned to her bedroll, found him taking a big bite. The light of his fire caught a trickle of juice dribbling down his beardless chin.

* * *

Always an early riser, Nina awoke before dawn. But Corlis was already up and doing—making his breakfast, to judge from the clatter of pans. Nina slipped out of her blankets and immediately began to shiver. Deep in this ravine beside the spring-fed pond, the air was frosty.

Her first task was to dig a jacket out of her tiny reserve of spare clothes, and button up against the cold. Then Nina rebuilt her fire and put water to heat. She was already regretting last night's generosity. That fish would have tasted fine this morning. Sighing, she turned again to her bags but took only a small, crusty bread roll from her stores. That would be enough to begin the day on, considering how she'd gorged last night on her lucky catch.

A disturbance in the air, not quite a whistling sound, alerted her to something rushing her way. Nina whirled, her knife unsheathed before she'd fully swung round to face the threat. But it was no threat: it was breakfast. A chunk of meat landed with an oily *splat* at the edge of Nina's campfire, barely missing her pan of boiling water.

She jerked her gaze toward Corlis, or toward his last known location. But the man was not at his fire. Searching for any movement in the still-dim ravine, Nina picked him out among his ghostly white horses, barely visible but turned away from her. It must have been he, however, who'd lobbed the meat in her direction. Unless it had fallen from the sky. Nina shook her head, doubting that desert eagles would be dropping hot salt pork into this ravine. For that was what the meat proved to be—a little charred on the outside but edible, and warm almost to the point of sizzling. She cut thick slices to fill her crusty roll.

As the day's ride began, Corlis set a quicker pace than yesterday. He was breaking camp and heading out almost before Nina could get her foot in the stirrup. Forced by the narrowness of the ravine to trail behind him and his packhorses, she followed as he picked a path along the pond's edge. Through a dense stand of desert willows, Corlis took them deeper into the cleft. The dawn that brightened the sky high above made little headway against the shadows cloaking the waterside. Nina could only trust that her horse would find safe footing as she trailed behind her guide.

After a time the willows thinned, the shadows lifted, and Nina detected an end to the pond that nearly filled the elongated floor of the ravine. They had reached the water's farthest point. Here Corlis paused, not dismounting but giving his three horses time to drink their fill. His animals took on water as though they expected never to see it again. Nina's roan, however, dipped his muzzle only briefly, seemingly satisfied with the long drink he had enjoyed before leaving camp not an hour before.

Nina swung out of her saddle and went to her knees at the water's edge, driven by her salty breakfast to imitate her guide's horses and slake her thirst while she could. The actions of Corlis and his bred-for-the-desert animals hinted that fresh water might be scarce the rest of this day. Nina dabbled her fingers in the pond at Traveller's feet, coaxing him, but the horse showed no interest. With furrowed brow, concerned that the roan's instincts for self-preservation might fail him in this unfamiliar place, she reluctantly remounted and followed as Corlis moved on.

He led them up a faint, moderately steep trail that climbed out of the ravine, but not all the way to the high plateau they had traversed yesterday. Instead, the trail dipped down again, taking them into and across a dry wash, up over the lip of it, and onward into a maze of gullies and gulches.

Nina was lost before noon.

Try as she would to mind her bearings in the maze of rock, sand, and spiny vegetation, she found no way to keep track of which canyon they followed or which cleft Corlis chose. At a great many places during the day, the way before them split in two. Steep-sided gullies appeared on either side, some of them impassably clogged with fallen boulders or desert plants that were so prickly and close-packed, no horse could push its way through. But in other places, one ravine would open off into a second defile, offering a shady cut through the rocks that might seem more inviting than the sun-blasted notch they were following. Sometimes Corlis would take that second opening. But at other times he kept straight, or as straight as was possible on this hemmed-in, winding way through a steep-walled labyrinth.

Nina kept close to her guide, uncomfortably aware that she was now fully dependent on Corlis to take her through the maze. And to find water in this desolation. No stream moistened the bottom of any cleft through which they rode. Occasional patches of vegetation would show more green than gray, hinting of roots that had found water underneath the sand. Surface water, however, was absent. As the midday sun beat down on horses and riders, Nina took worried note of Traveller's copious sweating and her own damp skin. Both of them were losing precious moisture, with no prospect in sight of replacing it.

Corlis pressed on through the shimmering heat, never varying his pace and never glancing over his shoulder to be sure Nina followed. Her head was beginning to swim, her straw hat doing little to protect her from the sun, when at last her guide reined up.

He'd brought them to no water that Nina could see, but there was shade: A ledge of rock, high and wide, jutted out from the vertical wall ahead of them, throwing the wall's footings into shadow. The darkness under the ledge appeared almost black, so great was its contrast with the glaring sun. The shaded space looked wide enough to accommodate all four horses, and the overhanging ledge stood so tall that both riders could have ducked beneath it while still mounted, without scraping their hats.

Corlis, however, dropped from his saddle before his horse reached the shadows, and Nina soon wished that she had followed his example. For at the back of the dark space, recessed deeply into the black wall beneath the ledge, water trickled. The flow was not great, but over time it had filled a series of depressions that stretched the length of the sheltered space, all along the base of the wall.

The four horses smelled or saw the water before Nina did. Traveller joined in the general rush, practically jolting her out of her saddle as he sped for the nearest water-filled depression. One of the packhorses came at him, its teeth bared, nipping at the roan's shoulder in a vain attempt to force its rival aside. Nina's horse was bigger and heavier than the compact desert animal. Trav knocked the packhorse out of his way as Nina snapped the end of her reins across the animal's laid-back ears. With a squeal of frustrated rage, the smaller beast veered off, to vie with competitors its own size for a place at the overflowing troughs.

Such was the frenzy of the thirsty foursome as they crowded their way to the water, Nina found dismounting a hazardous proposition. But so was staying in the saddle, with the ledge hanging low enough over her head to dash out her brains, should Traveller choose to rear and use his hooves in fending off his rivals.

The other horses, however, seemed to have accepted the new pecking order. As the animals settled to the serious business of slaking their thirst, Nina observed that Traveller had won a prime spot, almost directly under the trickle that dripped so slowly, it would need hours to replenish what the animals were taking. The horse Corlis rode stood next to Trav, drinking from the same wide depression. The pack animals, though shunted somewhat aside, were finding their fair share of the precious water in the endmost troughs, near the edge of this sheltered grotto.

Cautiously, Nina slipped from Traveller's back and squeezed her way out of the herd. Once in the clear, she looked for Corlis, wondering if the man had been standing there watching, laughing as she fought to stay in the saddle and not get crushed or brained. But he was nowhere to be seen.

In that moment, Nina's heart was in her throat. Alone, she would never find her way back to the cool ravine with the fish-filled pond. The trickle of water in this stony grotto might sustain the life of one person, but not four horses. If something had happened to Corlis, Nina would be forced to slaughter at least two of the animals, that being a kinder fate than allowing all of them to die of thirst.

Nina came close to embarrassing herself. She'd opened her mouth, ready to scream his name. But Corlis saved her the humiliation. He came into view, approaching down the center of the canyon, lugging leather buckets that brimmed with what appeared to be melons no larger than apples.

Corlis walked straight to the depressions at the foot of the wall. The horses had emptied those natural troughs of nearly every drop, but now they watched eagerly as the man brought in his double load of emerald-green fruits. Corlis dumped the buckets into the low places from which the horses had drunk.

His three animals went at the melons as if starving. Traveller took a moment to sniff the unfamiliar fruits. But then he snatched a mouthful and crunched with enthusiasm, clearly enjoying the unexpected treat.

Curious, Nina edged up beside her horse, keeping clear of the other animals. The melons were going fast, but a quick grab at the pile under Traveller's nose secured her a half-eaten sample. Taking it out into the sunlight, Nina studied the fruit's smooth rind and the chunk of green flesh that clung to it. As cautious as Trav, she gave it a sniff, which was all it took to get her mouth watering. Whatever this thing was—such a melon as Nina had never seen before—she was now prepared to fight the horses for a bigger taste than the scrap in her hand afforded.

That became unnecessary. As Nina whirled and took a step back toward the grotto, eager to scoop up her own share before the horses took every bite, she discovered Corlis looking at her. He averted his gaze within half a second, but Nina was certain he had been watching her examine the fruit. For with a casual sideways toss, seemingly not looking where he was throwing, Corlis lobbed a whole melon her way.

Nina caught it one-handed, drew out her knife, and settled in the shade below the ledge to slice it in half. The fruit had no central pit or stone, only a cluster of small seeds that proved as tasty as hazelnuts. The flesh was mildly sweet, not cloying but citrusy and wonderfully cool. Nina realized, that since arriving in this place of rest and refreshment, she had not swallowed a drop of water, either from the leather bottle tied to her saddle or from the trickle that had watered the horses. But now, after consuming the fruit, she felt no need for water. The melon had quenched her thirst.

Damn the man, Nina thought, casting a frowning glance at Corlis, who also sat in the shade eating fruit. *Damn his unwillingness to speak.* Where had he found these melons? What were they? How did they grow in this desert? Nina the herbalist had a dozen questions for him, but she would not break her vow to keep silent for as long as he did.

The grotto was not their day's destination. After every scrap of melon was consumed, including the rinds which the horses particularly relished, they were on the move again. As Nina trailed her guide through yet another ravine, she watched for any spot of vegetation, any tuft of green among the sandy reds and grays of this land. But she glimpsed no melon patch, no solution to the mystery of those marvelously satisfying emerald fruits.

As she rode on, Nina realized she wasn't sweating like she had been earlier in the day. The sun was past its zenith now, which might contribute to a more comfortable ride. But the air was still hot, and so searingly dry that man and beast should feel parched within an hour of drinking. At no time, however, did Nina feel the urge to reach for her water bottle, though they rode into the evening, not pausing again until deep twilight found them on the banks of a shallow, water-filled depression.

The waterhole lay at a sort of crossroads where the ravine they were following intersected a slope-sided gully. Crystals of salt rimmed the pool, suggesting that the water was utterly undrinkable. The horses spurned it until Corlis dismounted and dug into his packs for what appeared to be a clump of grass, tightly wadded. He tossed the clump into the pool, then turned back to the horses and began stripping them of packs and gear.

Taking this to mean they had reached the end of their day's travel, Nina also swung down and unsaddled Traveller. She looked around for any suitable grazing for the animal, and settled on a patch of miltgrass amid low, spiky bushes. It wasn't much, but Trav went at it intently, tearing up mouthfuls as though too hungry to care what he ate. A glance across the salt-rimmed waterhole showed Corlis a little way down the side gully, tethering his three horses at intervals to give each a share of what little vegetation grew in this low spot.

Nina took advantage of the man's distance from camp to go behind a rock and relieve herself. Attending to her bodily needs had presented certain challenges thus far in their journey. She seemed almost never to be off her horse. But she was drinking so little, she had not often felt the call of nature these past hours.

Also while Corlis was distracted with his horses, Nina conjured Ercil's fire. By the orb's light, she rummaged in her gear for her tea mug. She also drew out a packet of dried marsalaine, a sweet herb that had the power to freshen stagnant water. At the shallow pool, Nina filled her mug and took a sip, needing to gauge just how bitter the water was, in order to know how much of her precious herb-stock would be required to render it drinkable.

But lo! The water was already fit for use. Not artesian-spring fresh by any means, but far less salty and caustic than might be expected, given the crust of minerals that ringed the pool.

Nina eyed the wadded-up grass Corlis had tossed in. Reaching from the waterhole's bank, she hooked a finger in the saturated, now swollen clump and dragged it toward her. She teased out two or three wet blades of grass and nibbled them.

Salty. So extraordinarily salty, Nina choked. She turned her head and spat, urgently needing to get the taste out of her mouth. She dipped a mugful of the treated water and gulped it down, then a second mug to stop her tongue from feeling like the skin was being peeled off.

"Strong stuff," Nina muttered at the clump, which no longer floated in the pool, but had settled to the pale, sandy bottom, heavy with the salts it had drawn from the water. "Stronger than my eastern herbs."

She straightened, and went to fetch her horse for a now acceptable drink. As she passed her pile of gear, Nina left her mug and the packet of marsalaine, but continued to cradle her witchlight orb. Full dark had descended, Corlis had made no fire as yet, and Nina was indisposed to wander by night in a desert that might present a great many venomous threats. From horseback that day, she had glimpsed a few reddish lizards, and a fast-moving streak that she'd supposed was a snake. Nina had also spotted a long-eared rabbit hopping away down a side canyon. She'd been sorely tempted to go after it, craving the fresh meat. But on no account would she risk becoming separated from her standoffish guide.

Nina spotted Corlis coming back down the gully, leading his own horse—leading the animal to water as she was doing with hers. But she and Traveller were nearer the pool, and they got there first. While Trav drank deeply of the freshened water, Nina filled a pan for tea and for a later face-washing.

Corlis paused beyond the reach of Nina's conjured witchlight. Too late, she realized she had absentmindedly settled the orb on her shoulder as she tended to Trav and dipped up water. Whatever Corlis might suppose the light to be, he now knew it was not a candle.

Oh well, Nina thought with a mental shrug. *If the man has questions, he can ask me ... if he ever finds his tongue.*

When Traveller had drunk his fill, Nina returned him to the sparse patch of miltgrass and set about making her camp. Fuel for a fire was almost nonexistent, but she scraped together enough dry vegetation for a flame so tiny, it barely warmed her water pan.

Corlis did better. Nina observed that his campfire, though not exactly roaring, was sufficient to heat whatever small chunk of meat comprised his supper. More salt pork, she supposed, since the man had taken exactly as much fresh game as Nina had on this journey: which was to say, none.

How long will this go on? Nina wondered as she made yet another meal on hard cheese and harder bread from her stores. *Does he think I'll beseech him for a taste of that pork? Never.* She'd graze along with Traveller before she'd stoop to begging.

Nina washed her face and hands and crawled into her bedroll. She lay watching her tiny fire dwindle. When it was burned to ash, she extinguished her witchlight as well.

Looking across to Corlis, who sat at his separate fire beyond the shallow pool, Nina watched the man wolf down his supper. Though it had the distinction of being a hot, cooked meal, his repast seemed as meager as hers had been.

Nina drifted into sleep thinking that the man looked lonely. *But it must be said,* she realized as her eyes closed upon a final wisp of awareness, *I am lonely, too.*

* * *

How many days it took to get through the desert canyonlands, Nina could not say. She lost all track, with every morning finding her wrapped up against the cold, then forced to shed her jacket shortly after sunrise, to sweat in the unbearable heat of each mindlessly monotonous day. Corlis led them from one barely adequate waterhole to the next, treating the worst of them with the clumpy grass that drew out the salt. Once, he produced more bucketsful of the thirst-quenching melons, again accomplishing the feat while Nina had her focus elsewhere.

Worries about finding Traveller enough to eat absorbed much of her attention. The three desert-bred horses seemed to do fine on the sparse grazing, but Trav was losing weight. His ribs weren't showing, but every evening as she gave the horse a thorough rubdown and checked him for sores or hot-spots, Nina fancied she could feel less muscle and more bone under her currycomb and brush.

She neared a breaking point, her concern for the animal almost driving her to speak to Corlis, to demand an accounting of the supplies that the two packhorses had carried all this way. Only a scant few of the bundles had yet been opened. Finally conceding, wordlessly, that both he and Nina had to eat, Corlis broke open a pack of jerked beef and dried beans. Nina found her portions waiting beside her gear one evening when she returned to her own modest fire, having answered nature's call out in the prickly brush. She fell on the beef as one starving for meat. The beans required an overnight soak before they would be edible, so she made her breakfast on them the next morning, and every morning thereafter.

But what of Traveller? Nina's worry for the horse drove her deep down side canyons on any evening that saw them make camp while a little brightness remained in the sky. On those occasions, she grabbed the two leather buckets Corlis had used for melons and filled them with whatever dry grass and fodder she could find.

Coming back to camp one twilight, picking her way through the deepening dusk, she set down the loaded buckets, preparing to conjure witchlight to see her safely back to the waterhole where she had left Traveller tethered and hungry. But Ercil's fire had to wait while Nina grabbed her knife. A small goat was bounding down the slope of the canyon, heading for that same waterhole. The creature never made it. Nina's strong throw found the animal's heart, dropping the goat in its tracks at the bottom of the gully.

With the carcass slung across her shoulders and a bucket in each hand, Nina staggered back to camp, finding her way by the flameless glow of the orb she had belatedly summoned. Out a ways from Corlis, she dropped both buckets and extinguished the witchlight, unwilling to display the magic too flagrantly. Leaving the buckets in the dark beyond the fire the man had built, Nina carried her goat to the water-hole and flung it down on the pond's salt-crusted rim, intending to butcher the carcass as soon as she had fed her horse.

But two surprises awaited her. The first was that Traveller was feasting on a pile of pellets like lumps of cake, redolent with the fragrance of barley malt and fresh grass. So mouthwatering was the aroma, Nina scooped up a pellet to sample. She tasted oats and other grains, seeds of pumpkin and sunflower, lightly sweetened with molasses. The held-in-reserve rations Corlis had produced for Trav more than made up for the lack of forage in this inhospitable desert.

Nina's second startlement came fast upon the first. She turned back to the waterhole, to find her kill almost ready for the spit. Corlis had butchered the goat. Into the animal's flesh he was rubbing salt, scooped from the pond's rim.

Beggar it all! Nina swore silently, standing with her hands on her hips and glaring at him. *That man will have to fight me for it, if he thinks to take the whole thing.*

Once the salting was done, however, Corlis reached again for his butchering knife. He quartered the carcass, and took two of the hunks to the fire he had built while Nina was off hunting in the side canyon. With practiced movements—this was clearly not the man's first goat-roast—he soon had the meat spitted and cooking over a more substantial fire than Nina would have thought possible in this treeless waste. Corlis had gathered enough thorny stems, dry sticks, and brushwood to build a fire big enough to accommodate not just one spit, but two.

Returning to collect the rest of the goat, he picked up the remaining pieces but did not take them directly to his fire. At the edge of the light it cast, Corlis stood holding the meat. From under the brim of the hat that almost never came off his head, the man fastened upon Nina the only frank, direct gaze he had fixed upon her in all the long days of their journeying. With a wordless jerk of his head, Corlis issued an invitation in which Nina also read a question:

Would she share her kill with him ... and share a fire with him tonight?

After a pause in which to consider what his invitation might signify, Nina gave him a short, abrupt nod of acceptance. Dropping her hands from her hips, she turned to the gear she had stripped from her horse. Nina fished out her favorite tea and only mug, chose the best from her remaining supply of cheese, and headed for the man's camp, pausing on the way to scoop water into a pan. At the fire with Corlis, she set the water to heat.

Not looking at him, she drew her knife intending to slice the cheese. But the blade bore traces of blood from the goat's heart. Back to the pond Nina went, to clean the weapon. Then on around to her saddle-bags, to find a clean scarf upon which to dry the blade.

By the time she returned to her companion's fire, Corlis had produced a mug of his own. More surprisingly, he'd come up with a pair of nicely turned wooden bowls.

Quite the formal affair, this meal is becoming, Nina thought, not sure whether to be pleased or wary. In the space of a single evening, Corlis had gone from ignoring her, to supplying her wants. He'd fed her horse, butchered her kill, seasoned the meat, and taken upon himself the job of cooking it. While Nina prepared the tea, Corlis turned both spits and tended the fire. The goat was small, and roasting it in quarters made for quick cooking. Soon the first two pieces were off the fire, the remaining hunks were sizzling, and Corlis was handing Nina a bowl that brimmed with hot, tender meat.

With her clean and polished knife, she sliced and shared out the cheese, then poured tea into the man's mug. In the firelight she sat back to enjoy one of the tastiest meals she had ever eaten under the stars. The salt from the mineral-laden pond had given the meat the perfect touch of seasoning, surprising Nina with its delicate flavor.

During all this time, no word was exchanged. The silence that hung over the meal was not what Nina would have called companionable, but neither was it tense or brittle. After she had consumed fully half of the goat, and Corlis had eaten his share, they sat on opposite sides of the fire, each sipping another cup of tea.

Sated and increasingly comfortable, Nina felt her eyes closing.

Uh-uh, she thought. *Do not fall asleep at this man's fire.* She had no idea where this unexpected turn of events might lead, but sharing a meal with Corlis felt like crossing a bridge. Things had changed between them: for the better, Nina hoped. But the consequences of this strange evening remained to be seen.

She roused from the overfed stupor that threatened to have her nodding off. With a great yawn, Nina forced her eyes open and got to her feet. Holding her tea mug in one hand and her battered old pan in the other, she stood looking at her dinner companion.

Corlis had stood up when Nina did—a gentlemanly courtesy she had not expected. Confused by nearly every event of the last two hours, she found herself dropping a curtsy before she even thought.

Mother of mercy! Nina mentally cursed herself. *What are you? Six years old, remembering your manners because Master Welwyn says a lady of Ruain should know the proprieties?*

Nina felt herself blush from collarbone to brow. Intensely grateful that the fire had burned low, she doubted Corlis would see the sudden flush that warmed her skin. But was that a smile on his face? Had the man actually *smiled* at her?

Fleeting his expression was, and now Corlis seemed intent on hiding it. In response to Nina's childish but oh-so-gracefully executed curtsy, the man doffed his slouchy hat and bowed to her.

Before he'd straightened his back, Nina had whirled and walked away. She resisted the urge to fan her hot face with the pan she held.

Back in her own domain—on the far side of the alkali pond where her gear was piled and her horse dozed—Nina busied herself with her evening wash-up. She worked in the dark, revealed to Corlis by neither fire nor witchlight. She took care to cast no glance at the opposite campsite where he had reseated himself beside his dying blaze. But Nina was willing to wager every penny of the man's substantial fee, that Corlis was over there listening to her bedtime rituals. She rushed to finish, crawled beneath her blankets ... and fell asleep with her hand on the hilt of her knife.

Chapter Thirteen

The deeper they pushed into the badlands, the hotter the sun on their heads. Corlis now broke each day into two sessions of travel that alternated with two periods of rest. Riding began in the very early dawn—what might be considered the middle of the night—and continued without pause until mid-to-late morning. Then they sheltered the horses and themselves in what shade could be found around whatever water, and slept during the harshest part of each day.

Mounting up again in late afternoon, they continued past sundown. The heat was so oppressive, it robbed them of appetite. Meals dwindled to one a day, taken in the night just before their midnight snooze. After eating, and rolling up in their blankets on separate sides of a single campfire for what amounted to only a nap, they were up and off again in the dark.

Thus the days passed in a blur of shimmering heat under a pewter sky, and bone-chilling nights lit by the stars. Her growing exhaustion almost had Nina nodding in the saddle. But as she greeted from horseback the cockcrow hour of each day, she slapped herself awake and pulled her bow from its scabbard. For early was the hour which proved best for taking what little game these ravines offered.

As a pink predawn light touched the canyon walls, the hiss of her arrow sounded loud in the silence, startling Corlis at the head of the train. He turned to see Nina off her horse, scrambling up a short slope to collect her kill—another small goat. Corlis came to help, his butchering knife in hand. Quickly and without speaking, he gutted the animal and slung it on a packhorse.

Though the man also carried a bow, he perplexed Nina by showing no interest in taking game. Corlis seemed content to live on dried meat and beans, supplemented by the thirst-quenching melons that he mysteriously produced from time to time. Perhaps, Nina thought, he begrudged the minutes it took to dress game, although Corlis did it so skillfully, the task delayed them little. She couldn't help noticing, however, that her guide ate appreciatively of whatever fresh meat she managed to bring down. Corlis always gave her a nod of thanks, though never a word of it, after their occasional midnight goat-roasts. Common courtesy was insufficient, Nina concluded, to force speech past the lips of this stubbornly silent man.

But where civility failed, pain succeeded. Nina at last heard the voice of her guide. Corlis erupted midmorn in a blistering string of oaths.

It happened while they were unloading the packhorses, preparing to take their heat-of-the-day rest. Nina was stripping the second animal of its burdens, while Corlis had charge of the leader in the string. Both packhorses were already drowsing on their feet, accustomed by now to getting the bulk of their rest at midday while using the shorter nighttime break to eke out a living on the desert's prickly vegetation. Nina was turning away from the second horse, her arms full of packs, when she glimpsed a small animal leap from a burrow under the hooves of the horse that Corlis was unloading.

The packhorse shied violently, snorting in high alarm as though a snake had struck at it. But Nina saw enough gray fur and round ears to identify the troublemaker as only a mouse. The little creature streaked away, disappearing into a side gully.

Nina dropped the packs she carried and lunged to catch the frightened horse before that animal could race down the ravine in the opposite direction. She secured the horse by its lead rope, booting a stone onto the rope's trailing end, for that was the only readily available means of tethering the animal. Under Nina's touch, the horse quieted, having been startled rudely awake but no longer feeling itself threatened.

Corlis, however, was the air-shattering opposite of quiet. Nina turned from the horse to attend to the man who was cussing a blue streak. He lay sprawled, not in the dirt but atop a mound of the most savage vegetation that Nina had seen growing in this merciless land. The clustered bushes bristled with four-inch spikes. Corlis had been knocked off his feet by the startled packhorse. He'd landed on his back amidst masses of thorns, crashing into them with enough force to sink the spikes deep into his flesh. As he attempted now to extricate himself, swearwords streamed from his lips. Impaled on all those thorns, Corlis could hardly move, but every twitch of a speared muscle was plainly torture.

"Be still!" Nina barked at him.

Her voice cut through his swearing and brought it to an end as if a sword had cleaved his tongue. Corlis ceased his struggles and stared at her as Nina planted herself at his feet. She leaned to take both of his hands in hers. By some miracle or maybe instinct, Corlis had kept his hands out of the thorns. The packs he'd been stripping from the horse's back had gone flying when the animal plunged sideward and slammed him into this predicament. Perhaps he'd grabbed for the frame of the horse's packsaddle, trying to keep his balance; and with his hands stretched thus in front of him, Corlis had avoided the error of using them to break his fall. Nina flinched to picture thorns driven straight through his palms, as they would have been, had he not kept his hands clear.

Whether spared by wit, instinct, or simple good luck, his calloused but undamaged hands were now firmly held in Nina's. She leaned back, preparing to haul the man straight toward her, up and out of the thorn patch.

"Brace your boots against mine," she ordered him. "I'll have to jerk hard to get you on your feet. Come with me as I lift you, and *don't* twist sideways. You'll only make it worse."

Corlis looked skeptical, as though doubting that Nina could yank him upright when he outweighed her. But Nina's slim shape hid a wiry strength. She'd been trained since childhood in the use of weapons, and her many years of drawing a bow had built the muscles of not only her shoulders and upper back, but also her legs and trunk. Nina proved her strength—and elicited from Corlis a pain-filled yelp of surprise—by jerking herself backward and hauling him upright in one hard pull.

He came to his feet bristling with almost more thorns than the bushes he'd left. When Nina had him up and standing, she released his hands and stepped behind Corlis to assess his injuries. The sheer number of them drew from her an involuntary "Drisha!" Thorns pierced the man from the back of his head to the seat of his pants and on down to the backs of his knees. Every piercing bled freely, with his slightest movement costing Corlis more blood. His clothes were stained from the nape of his neck to his boot-tops.

"I'll be a while getting those out of you," Nina said as she stepped around to face Corlis again. "Come into the shade and lean against the rocks." She led him into the shadows below a narrow stone shelf. "You won't be able to sit down until I've ..." *Plucked your butt,* she started to say, but decided that would sound too pert.

Also arguing against flippancy was the pain Corlis was in. Nina read it in the man's halting steps as she helped him escape the increasingly hot sun. It had climbed high during the morning's events, and its merciless glare nearly filled the pocket canyon where they had paused to rest. Nina's first concern was to get all of them—the horses, Corlis, and herself—out of that murderous sun.

"Stand here," she ordered him, "and keep still. If you move, you could break those thorns off under your skin, and then I'll have to dig for them. If I miss any and they work down deep inside you, down to your vitals, they could do real damage. Maybe kill you."

Nina studied her patient's profile. Corlis stood facing the canyon wall, bracing against it with both hands. The thorns that protruded from his neck prevented him turning his head to meet her gaze, and they made even a nod painfully impossible. But as Nina turned away to see to the horses and collect her medicine kit, Corlis surprised her with half a dozen words. They were clearly voiced in a pleasing baritone, though he spoke out of the side of his mouth as he faced the wall in front of him.

"Return quickly, lady. I'm on fire."

The man's voice had a curious effect on Nina's heart. The organ leapt in her chest and sent her pulse racing.

Only because it's been so long since I've heard the sound of human speech, Nina scolded herself.

But she couldn't deny how agreeable was the sound of this particular male voice falling upon her ears. Nina had begun to wonder whether Corlis was ashamed of the way he talked, and had kept silent from embarrassment. What she heard in those few words, however, presented no cause for shame. The man's voice was rich and melodic. Nina detected a tightness in it, a product of the pain he was in. But warmth was there as well, in defiance of that pain ... warmth like an undertone that hummed below the man's words and made Nina's heart skip a beat.

In haste, she turned away, making no reply except a muttered, "I'll bring water."

Within a few steps, Nina had command of herself again, and knew her priorities. First: the horses, to be tethered in separate patches of shade with saddles and whatever packs they still carried. Nina would not take time now to strip them of their loads. But she dug out the clumpy grass that Corlis used to sweeten bitter water. Opening off from the pocket where they had halted was a hollowed-out space, more a niche than a grotto, protected by the canyon's steep walls and overhanging ledges. In the shade of that hidden hollow, a salt-rimmed depression held a small pool, the only available water for the horses. Nina tossed in a wad of sweetgrass and left it to its work.

With the animals out of the sun and their water seen to, Nina's attention swung back to the thorn-impaled Corlis. From his saddle she took his canteen, and relieved her own horse of her waterskin, medicine bag, tea mug, and pan. Rushing to her patient, Nina found the man standing as she had left him, leaning braced against stone walls in a narrow ribbon of shade. But now his arms quivered, and as Nina rejoined him, Corlis swayed. The motion was slight, and he steadied immediately. In Nina, however, alarm rose.

"Perdition!" she swore, digging in her medicine kit for the close-fitting, kidskin gloves that had been Willow's parting gift to her. "Do those thorns carry poison?"

"Plenty enough," Corlis replied, his voice sounding stronger than he looked. "Get stuck by two or three and you'll get the sweats."

"You've got a damned sight more than three," Nina growled as she pulled on her gloves. "I'll start at your neck, then do the back of your head ... and work down from there. Tell me if you need me to stop."

Methodically, she began yanking out thorns. The pain, she couldn't doubt, was excruciating. Corlis bore it well, with nothing like a whimper escaping him, but with many sharply indrawn breaths and much cursing between gritted teeth. Nina scanned each extracted thorn to be sure it had come out all the way to its tip. The thorns, fortunately, showed themselves to be sturdy, not prone to breakage. Moreover, the skin of each four-inch spear was smooth, with tiny holes along their lengths but no barbs—Nina could jerk them out without shredding her patient's flesh. Even so, every wound bled freely as she removed each thorn. By the time she had worked her way down to the waistband of her patient's trousers, blood mixed with sweat was dripping into the man's boots.

Nina paused there, long enough to stir a painkilling powder into a mug of water.

"Drink this," she said, reaching around Corlis to hand it to him. "I'm nearly done. Then you can get off your feet."

During the bloody minutes of thorn-plucking, Corlis had stopped himself swaying by leaning his forehead as well as both hands against the rock wall he faced. But as he turned slightly to take the mug from Nina, his left shoulder banged against the wall and he nearly went down. Nina grabbed him and propped him up while he drank thirstily from the mug that he had managed not to drop. When he'd emptied it, he did drop it and resumed his former stance, face to the wall and backside to Nina.

She finished yanking thorns from the seat of his pants and the backs of his thighs. When all were out, she helped him down, not to a sitting position—his butt was too damaged for that—but curled on his side in the dirt.

"Rest now," she said as she peeled off her bloodied gloves. "I must wash the wounds, but I want hot water for that."

Collecting all the brushwood needed for a decent fire took long enough that the sun had moved noticeably westward by the time Nina gathered the fuel and sparked a flame. In what was now a broader and deeper patch of shade, she filled her pan from her waterskin and set it to heat. Beside Corlis she knelt, and began undoing the ties of his blood-soaked shirt.

Her touch stirred him to speech. Without opening his eyes, Corlis muttered, "Got to water the horses."

"I'll do it," Nina said, "after I've washed your back. We must get your shirt off before it's stuck to your wounds."

When she had the garment loose in front, Nina eased Corlis onto his stomach and peeled his shirt off, tugging it from under his waistband and over his shoulders. The disrobing cost him an effort. Corlis lay in the dirt panting with pain by the time Nina dipped a cloth in warm water and laid it on the man's bare back. He gasped at the sudden sting. But then he gave a moan of relief, brought on by the deadener Nina had stirred into the water.

"Sleep," she told him. "I'll see to the horses, then fix a little supper."

Leaving him face down in the dirt, Nina went first to Traveller and led the horse to the tucked-away pool. Trav drank eagerly of the sweetened water, and at such length Nina had time to collect the sacks and bags that had been scattered in all directions when the packhorse knocked Corlis into poisonous thorns. From one bag, she took dried beans and set them to soak. Another sack yielded the jerked beef that would be supper unless something edible walked into camp and invited Nina to shoot it. Between tending the horses and doctoring Corlis, she wouldn't manage even a brief hunt before nightfall.

When Traveller had slaked his thirst, she tethered him to browse dry jagwort and knotgrass, and poured him a pile of the rich feed that was keeping him going on this journey. The desert horses of Corlis could survive on what this harsh land offered, but the roan from the east of

Ladrehdin would be starving, if not for the feed that Corlis had packed along—in exactly the right amount, Nina suspected, to see the horse through. She doubted that a nugget would remain by the time they reached the Ore Hills. From observing her guide and his strict adherence to a timetable, Nina had come to believe that Corlis knew precisely how much he could dole out from their provisions, at every campsite and rest stop, without exhausting their supplies.

Which made today's events doubly unfortunate. The many wounds Corlis had suffered—particularly to his rump—must take days to heal sufficiently for him to ride again. And what of the poison the thorns had injected deep in his flesh? Nina had no way of judging the poison's severity or how Corlis might react to it. They might be stuck in this pocket canyon for days. Glumly, Nina shook her head as she went to water the horse that Corlis rode.

While the animal drank, Nina fished her guide's hat out of the thorn bushes. It had left the man's head when he fell, and now bristled with spines. Patiently, she yanked them out, occupying herself with that task between turns of leading each horse to the secluded waterhole. The approach to the pool was too narrow to permit the passage of more than one animal at a time, so watering all four took Nina from her patient for nearly an hour. The sun was westering lower when they'd all slaked their thirst, and she had tethered each horse in its individual patch to graze what it could.

Returning to Corlis, Nina stirred up the fire and put more water to heat—pans of it this time, filling every cooking vessel from her own gear and from the equipment Corlis had packed. The man was fast asleep now, lulled by the painkiller she had given him. Gently, she removed the cloth that cooled his bare back. Less gently, she cleaned his wounds with a disinfecting soap from her medical kit. Nina knew from personal experience how sharply it would sting even a minor scrape. Worked into such a multitude of punctures as Corlis had collected, the disinfectant must burn like the fires of *farsinchia*. Even so, Corlis did not stir.

Assured that he was firmly in the painkiller's grip, she reached around to loosen the man's trousers and tug them down. His rump, bared to Nina's inspection, looked like a pincushion—a bloody and extremely tender pincushion, it had been pierced so deeply by so many finger-length thorns. "Drisha's bollocks," Nina swore under her breath as she dipped a fresh cloth in the pan of warm, soapy water and continued scrubbing.

His trousers proved a hindrance as Nina attempted to reach his lowermost injuries, the punctures on the backs of his thighs. Sighing, she put down her cloth and repositioned herself at her patient's feet. With difficulty, for Corlis seemed to favor snug-fitting footwear, Nina got his boots off him. Then she stripped him of trousers and undergarments, leaving the unconscious man lying naked in the dirt.

With no clothing to get in the way of an all-over scrubdown, Nina gave him one. On his wounds, she used the strong disinfectant, but elsewhere she lathered his sweaty body with a mild, elderflower-scented soap. As she bathed Corlis, Nina strove mightily to fill her thoughts with the valid concerns of the healer, and nothing else. She checked the man over for any old injuries or physical conditions that might benefit from the attentions of a skilled wisewoman.

What Nina found, however—despite her attempts to ignore such details—was a man in his prime: leanly built but well-muscled, his strong and unmissably masculine body pleasingly formed. Her patient's skin was leathery where sunlight could reach it, but it showed smoother in the places normally covered by clothes. Nina detected a half-dozen old scars on Corlis, all of them long healed. One on the man's upper arm appeared to be from the cut of a sword or a large knife. His side bore evidence of a goring. The puckered skin on one ankle, covering what looked to be a missing chunk of flesh, led Nina to suspect the death-dealing bite of a venomous snake. She could imagine the stoic Corlis carving up his own flesh, ridding himself of venom before it spread to his vital organs.

Her examination complete, Nina rolled Corlis facedown once more. Into his pincushion rump, she rubbed a jellied ointment that would numb the pain—an uncommon and hard-to-obtain deadener that must be used frugally, since her kit contained only a single small jar. With a little of the boiled water she'd set aside to cool, Nina made a paste of dried bulrush and ground-up calamine to dab on the man's back. The poultice should draw out the poison and dry the secretions from his wounds. Then she left Corlis to rest.

As for herself, Nina was dead on her feet. For hours she had been rushing around: tending horses, doctoring Corlis, gathering brush-wood, making camp. Now she had the linens from her medical kit to wash out, and with them her patient's clothes. Nina had seen no evidence that Corlis carried a spare shirt, much less an extra pair of trousers. She couldn't let him don the same bloodstained clothes she'd stripped off him. They might carry traces of thorn poison that he could absorb through his skin. With a tired sigh, Nina set herself to do the washing-up.

By the time she'd finished, her feet were dragging. Even so, her huntress instincts detected the small game that ventured into their campsite. An ashy-furred rabbit was making its hesitant way, keeping under cover along the base of one stony wall.

Stealthily, Nina drew her knife. She stood motionless, poised to make the throw at the instant she had a clear target. But as she waited, a second rabbit came into view, hopping slowly through the same sparse cover. Neither creature escaped her. Nina threw hard and fast, and dropped the second rabbit in its tracks. The one in the lead, succumbing to confused panic, broke cover and ran straight at Nina. It fell to a stone that she scooped from the ground and slung with deadly accuracy.

"Supper!" Nina crowed as she collected her kills. The prospect of fresh meat did much to invigorate her. Even so, as she contemplated the work that lay ahead, of gutting and skinning the rabbits, putting them to cook, and disposing of the entrails at enough distance to keep from drawing predators into their camp, Nina felt the need for a pick-me-up. From her kit of medicines, she chose a stimulant powder, taking care to dissolve only a few grains in a cup of water.

Tiny though the dose was, the drug sent Nina soaring. In the space of minutes, she had both skinny rabbits roasting on the fire and had buried the viscera well down a side canyon, in a hole dug by hand far deeper than was necessary. She summoned a constellation of witchlights and scattered the orbs around their campsite, brightening the pocket canyon to such a degree that she never noticed when twilight's last glow gave way to full night.

In the grip of manic liveliness, Nina stripped as naked as Corlis, and crouched over a steaming pot of water to scrub the dirt and sweat from the clothes she'd removed. After spreading her laundered garments alongside his to dry in the parched air, she returned to the campfire with a bundle of fresh attire that she'd fished from her saddlebags. But now Nina felt too hot and sticky to even think of getting dressed.

Still naked, she hunkered in the light of Ercil's fire to wolf down both roasted rabbits. With them, Nina ate a bowl of beans, not minding that they hadn't soaked long enough. She chewed the tough lentils into a starchy paste, washed down with cups of mint tea.

Sated but wide awake, Nina warmed more water from the pool and bathed herself as thoroughly as she'd washed Corlis. With elderflower soap, lathering until she frothed from ears to toes, Nina filled the air with the honey-and-citrus scent of a flower that would never grow in this place.

Well scrubbed and twice rinsed, Nina stood in the witchlight glow with arms outstretched, letting the desert dry every inch of her. After so much sand and sweat, it felt divine to be this clean. Experienced wayfarer that she was, Nina knew how to keep herself tidy on the road when tub baths were few and far between. This journey, however, had challenged her resourcefulness in the matter of personal grooming. She could almost feel grateful to the packhorse for knocking Corlis on his butt and giving her this opportunity to feel like a civilized woman instead of a grubby barbarian.

"Breath and blood!" Nina swore then, her voice loud in the empty night as she took note of the goosebumps that were rising all over her body. After sunset in these badlands, temperatures dropped fast. Nina had been so full of feverish activity all evening, she was only now feeling the marked chill in the air. But Corlis! She had left the man lying naked, too far from the campfire to catch a ray of its warmth.

Racing to undo her bedroll, Nina threw all her blankets over the violently shivering form of her neglected patient. Collecting his bedding as well, she spread the coarsest of his blankets on the ground beside Corlis, covered that with a softer one, and flung the rest over him. From the bundle of clean garments that she had earlier pulled from her bags, Nina donned spotless underclothes and a lightweight shirt.

Not taking time to do up the shirt's ties, she threw herself down next to Corlis and reached for him under his mounded blankets. Firmly, not caring whether she started his wounds bleeding again, she rolled him toward her, off the cold ground and onto the double layer of bedding that she'd spread alongside him.

Corlis groaned as Nina turned and tugged his naked body, as she pulled him into the warmth of her arms and wrapped herself around him to share with him her body heat. The man was shivering so hard, his teeth chattered. But still, he did not wake.

Was Corlis so unaccustomed to painkillers, that even the modest dose Nina had administered was enough to knock him out for the several hours that he'd lain unconscious? Or was it the thorn poison permeating his body that robbed Corlis of his senses? Huddled with him under the piled blankets, Nina felt blood ooze from his wounds. By morning, her fresh new clothes, blood-spotted, would tell a tale she would rather her patient not know. But as a healer, she must do what she could to care for him.

Besides, Nina thought as she held the man's body and tried to chafe warmth into his clammy skin, Corlis was her only way out of these canyonlands. Without him to guide her through the maze of ravines, she would wander lost until she died and left her bones to bleach in the desert sun, as Roddy had warned.

* * *

Nina dreamed. In her dreams she returned to the ocean world, and to the island home she had shared with her mortal husband. She dreamed of lying with Makani on the coral-sand beach, the two of them twined together on a blanket, making love under the stars. They'd married young, teenagers when they wed, both vigorous, strong in body and appetite. Theirs had been a passionate marriage. Nina dreamed of her husband's touch, how he had caressed her, had cupped her breasts with the gentle strength of his hard hands ... his palms calloused from gripping the reins ...

Not reins, interjected a wisp of foggy awareness. Makani was no horseman. He was a sailor and fisher, his hands hardened from a lifetime of handling the rigging of his small boat. *It was the rigging rope*, Nina's dreamy mind insisted, a touch of urgency rising within her. *Not the reins.*

The pounding of her heart woke her. Nina's eyes flew open to behold a glaring sun that immediately made her squint. As she turned her head away from its harsh light, she saw blankets: a mound of bedding, jumbled together and thrown aside. She'd fallen asleep under those covers last night with her arms around Corlis, warming him with her body. Now she lay unblanketed—and scantily clothed. As Nina sat up, her thin shirt slipped from her shoulders, leaving her breasts uncovered.

She sprang to her feet. Her gaze darting everywhere, Nina looked for Corlis as she tugged her shirt into place and hastily did up the ties that she had neglected to fasten last night.

The man was nowhere to be seen, and the only horse in sight was Nina's Traveller. The roan remained tethered where she had left him yesterday. Of the three pale horses owned by Corlis, however, Nina detected no sign.

"Drisha's knuckles," she muttered as she collected Trav and led him to the waterhole. "What in the name of mercy happened last night while I was deep in dreams and dead to this world?" Her heavy sleep was a consequence of her own actions, Nina could not deny. She'd worked herself past the point of exhaustion, the powerful stimulant from her kit inducing a drug-fueled frenzy. When the drug wore off, her comedown had been hard and deep. The sun today, risen high in the sky and blasting like a furnace, testified that Nina had slept very late.

The absence of Corlis told its own story, but one that Nina could not easily interpret. While she'd slept, the man had slipped from her arms, thrown back the blankets, and found strength enough to get on his feet and disappear from camp.

But what else had he done?

While her horse drank, Nina went behind a rock and examined her underclothes for signs of intimacy. She breathed easier to find her linens as pristine as when she had donned them after her bath. Things had not gone so far. Yet Nina could not shake the feeling that the calloused hand cupping her bare breast had *not* been that of her lost, dreamed-of husband.

Though her underthings showed nothing but cleanest white, Nina's fresh new shirt was heavily stained from the closeness with which she had held the bleeding Corlis during his violent bouts of shivering.

Shaking her head at the ruin of a garment she'd worn for less than a day, Nina returned to her horse and walked with the animal, seeking any available shade. The sun at its zenith beat down so directly, the canyon's steep walls offered little shelter. A thin shadow under a rocky ledge was the best Nina could do for her horse, for the moment. Before she expanded the search through the maze of gullies, she had to change her bloodstained clothing for the older apparel she'd washed last night. Her laundered garments, badly frayed from her travels, waited where Nina had left them to dry. The clothes she had scrubbed out for Corlis were gone from those same snags and stumps.

Nina finished her change of costume barely in time to guard her privacy. As she pulled her old shirt over her head, Corlis came around a corner. On foot, he approached from the brushy side canyon where Nina had tethered the man's horses last night.

A rush of panic gripped her. Were the horses gone? Had Corlis forced himself from his sickbed to go looking for them? Had the animals broken their tethers and strayed, or been downed by predators?

Nina hastened to meet Corlis, her fears on her lips and dread like a knot in her stomach. Without those three desert horses, she—and this man with whom she had shared a bed—must perish before escaping these badlands.

"Whoa!" Corlis greeted her, looking surprised and perhaps amused as Nina ran toward him. "What's your hurry? No sense getting in a stir till evening. Too hot now."

Nina skidded to a halt in front of him. "Your horses!" she gasped. "Are they safe?"

"They're fine."

From under the brim of his slouchy hat, Corlis eyed her. Something in the man's gaze made Nina think him a bit crestfallen. In a flash, she understood: He had supposed it was himself, not his horses, that had aroused Nina's concern.

"And you?" she hurried to add. For in truth, she was gravely concerned about him. He could not be as fully recovered as he appeared. "How's your back?"

"Sore," Corlis replied with a grimace. "So's my butt. You got any more of that pain medicine?" Before Nina could answer, he clarified: "Not the stuff I drank—put me out like a light. I mean that jelly you slicked on my bare backside." Corlis grinned. "That's good medicine. Keep a man in the saddle."

Nina refused to blush. As a healer, she saw her patients in every stage of dress and undress, and she put her hands on any part of the patient's anatomy that needed her touch. Though this man was on his feet again, he was still her patient, still under her care. With him she must adopt the role of expert herbalist—the proud, skilled, appropriately aloof wisewoman who had tended his wounds. In that role, Nina refused to blush.

But as she faced away from Corlis to search her kit for the precious jar of deadener, Nina couldn't subdue the part of her that was *not* the detached, aloof healer. That part, womanly to its core and far from wise, warmed with remembering the masculine anatomy she had touched and held last night.

"Here," she mumbled, coming up with the jar and holding it out to Corlis without meeting his gaze. "Use it sparingly. That's all I have."

To her dismay, the man started to drop his trousers.

"Beggar it!" Nina swore, taking a step back. "What are you doing? Go behind a rock."

"Why?" Corlis asked, puzzlement in his voice as he paused his disrobing. He looked at her, his eyes shadowed by his hat brim. "Lady, you've seen everything I've got."

"That's different!" Nina blurted, sounding like a child—like the same silly six-year-old who had ended a goat-roast with a wildly inappropriate curtsy. Her next words did nothing to salvage the situation. "You didn't know. You were asleep."

Corlis scratched the unkempt growth of beard on his chin. "Not all night, I wasn't," he muttered. "But have it your way. I'll find a rock."

As the man turned and walked off, disappearing around a corner and taking the jelly jar with him, Nina dived again into her medicine kit. Her scramble yesterday, to counter poisoned wounds inflicted by a plant she had never come across before, had left her kit a disordered jumble. Nina dumped its contents on a blanket and set about reorganizing her supplies ... attempting all the while to recover her cool professional demeanor. This would be a long and very awkward afternoon if she kept letting Corlis throw her into a state of confused, juvenile embarrassment.

You did not sleep with that man, Nina told herself, her movements sharp as she repacked her medical stocks. *You gave him only what you would give any patient in his condition.*

From the corner of one eye, she watched Corlis reapproach. Nina did not look up until he stood over her and held out the jar of deadener. With the quickest glance then, a glance that went no farther than the jar, she took it and dropped it into her bag. From the kit's now tidy interior, Nina removed clean linen and the calamine-bulrush mixture with which she had poulticed the man's wounds yesterday. Rising from her crouch, she made herself face him, determined to show nothing except a healer's concern for her patient.

"Are your wounds inflamed?" she asked. "Pull up your shirt and let me see."

"Want me to go behind the rock?" Corlis said, smirking at her.

It was no good: Nina's facade of professional composure fled fast and far. "Stop it," she grated, powerless to prevent herself turning red. "Drisha's teeth, man! I can't have you dying in a poisoned fever before we're out of this wasteland. Pull up your damned shirt and show me your back!"

Corlis obeyed, but slowly and still smiling. With his gaze locked onto Nina's flushed face, the man tugged his shirt out of his waistband and lifted it to reveal, first, his chiseled abdomen and muscular chest. So near to Nina did he stand, she felt the heat that radiated from his torso—a striking contrast to the clamminess of the man's skin last night. Turning away from her by slow degrees, Corlis gradually presented his back to Nina, freeing her from his amused and deliberately provocative gaze.

Only then did Nina realize she had stopped breathing.

With a faintly audible gasp, she got her lungs working again. For a moment, however, Nina could not bring herself to touch the man's back, though clearly his wounds demanded attention. Most of the punctures had swelled, all were crusted with dried gore, and many oozed colorless serum and a little fresh blood.

"Sit down," Nina ordered, adopting her sternest healer's voice, taking refuge in her most unyielding bedside manner. "In the shade. This will take time."

"Bad, is it?" Corlis asked as he gingerly seated himself in the shadows below a ledge.

"Bad enough that you should rest today," Nina replied as she sat on the ground behind him. "You oughtn't to be on your feet at all, this soon." With fresh water, she moistened the clean linen and bathed the man's back. "I think you went into shock from thorn poison last night. You were shivering like a cat on ice, your teeth chattering."

"I couldn't get warm until way up in the night," Corlis said, then paused. Under Nina's touch, he arched his bare back much as a cat would respond to being petted. In a lowered voice, he added, "Mighty fine of you to help me out with that ... all last night."

Again Nina blushed, grateful that Corlis was looking the other way, his gaze directed toward the indifferent rock. She gave him no reply except to scrub less gently at the crust of blood on a particularly swollen wound.

"Ow!" Corlis protested. "Not so hard."

"It might be infected. Might need the pus squeezed out." Not giving him a chance to brace himself, Nina squeezed.

Corlis yelped. "Damnation, lady! Warn me next time. That hurts."

The wound produced only an ooze of fresh blood, reassuring Nina, for the moment, that infection had not set in. "No pus," she told her patient. "I'll fix you a cup of painkiller. You need to sleep."

Corlis half swung around toward her, prompting Nina to put a firm hand on his shoulder blade to keep him facing forward. "Be still," she snapped.

"I want none of your knockout stuff," he snapped back, speaking over his shoulder. "No time for sleeping. We'll ride out soon, when the sun's a little lower."

Nina scoffed. "If you think your back hurts, just wait 'til you try sitting in a saddle."

"I'm sitting now, aren't I?" Corlis retorted with what was, Nina had to admit, an unassailable fact. "That jelly of yours works a charm. I'll take all of it you can spare me. But I'll not again swallow whatever you gave me to drink yesterday. It puts me under, and we've been here too long already. Gotta move."

This also was a point Nina had to concede. "I suppose the horses are running out of anything to eat. Is that where you went before I woke up? To find something for your animals?"

Corlis started to nod, but the clotted wounds on the nape of his neck stopped him. "I staked them way back in that side canyon," he muttered, "in a patch of dry browse they've probably already finished off. If not for those thrice-damned thorns, we'd have left here yesterday. As it is, we've stripped this place ... and drained its water."

In the midst of laying a chamomile compress on the most swollen of her patient's wounds, Nina cast a shamefaced glance at the several water-filled pots she had left sitting around their cold campfire. One still held soapsuds from last night, from her drugged frenzy of washing-up.

"I understand," she said with a guilty sigh as she tied the cool compress in place. "From earliest childhood, I was taught to respect the natural world and never take too much from it ... or waste the gifts it bestows upon us."

A lesson I seem to have forgotten along the way, Nina admitted silently. *To my shame and to my cost.*

"Take an hour to rest," she urged Corlis as she tugged the man's shirt down over the compress. "I'll pack up and see to my horse."

Nina rose to her feet. She whirled away from Corlis and busied herself with emptying the water pots, determined to make the best use of every drop, treating each as if it were sacred. Which, in the desert, it was. From the cleanest pot, Nina refilled her waterskin and her guide's canteen. In a leather bucket, she set beans soaking for their next meal. The bucket would ride horseback with the rest of their supplies. Thus reminded that she had not eaten today since waking from strange dreams at noon, Nina chewed on jerked beef as she went about breaking camp.

Corlis shifted around to lean a shoulder against the nearly vertical wall of rock that shaded him. In the shadows below the ledge, the man's hat hid his eyes. Even so, Nina felt his gaze follow her as she emptied pans and gathered her gear. To take herself out of his line of sight, she grabbed the pot of sudsy wash-water and lugged it to the meager patch of vegetation that her horse had cropped nearly to its roots.

"Forgive me," she murmured as she poured the dirty water over the shrub's severely lopped stems. "From this poor offering, may new life spring."

Moving with the silence of a temple acolyte, Nina stacked the pot with the other gear and slanted a glance across at her patient. Corlis had his hat over his face now. Slumped in the shadows, he seemed asleep.

Careful not to disturb him, Nina went to give her horse one last drink from the canyon's secluded waterhole.

"If you're the praying sort," she murmured in Trav's ear as she walked beside him, "then pray that we'll find enough water to keep us all alive until we're clear of this Drisha-forsaken place."

Whether the conventional, lip-service deity of Ladrehdin had any interest in this merciless land of sand and sun, Nina trusted that the Powers held sway here, as they did everywhere. The Elementals made their presence known in these badlands with undisguised ferocity. Fire, air, and stone were all around, in scorching sun, lung-searing wind, and towering rock. Water manifested more subtly here, gathered in small, secret pools, hidden in the rocks and protected from the sun.

Corlis had demonstrated an uncanny ability to find those hidden pools, including the one Trav now drank from. Creature of water though Nina was—or as she had been, before her fall from grace—she wondered whether the water of this desert would reveal itself to her, should infection enter her patient's wounds and thence his blood ... leaving Nina to wander these canyons alone.

As Traveller took a long drink from the severely depleted pool in the shadowy grotto, Nina went to her knees at the pool's edge. Bowing low, touching her forehead to the cool water, she sent up a plea.

"Powers that rule everywhere," she murmured, "never-failing Powers of Eternity, I beg your forgiveness for having wasted the gifts you bestowed so abundantly upon me. I beg to be shown how I may make amends." Nina paused, then added, "If it be your will that I thirst in this desert, then without complaint shall I accept my punishment. I beseech you, however, to spare the horses and the man Corlis. So lightly does that nomad move through these desert canyons, he leaves barely a trace of his passage and partakes of only as much as the land can spare. Punish him not, I entreat you, for lingering too long in this place of refuge. Our delay here was forced by circumstance."

Why she said all of this, Nina wasn't sure. The Powers must know everything that had happened here. The silence in the grotto, however, a silence broken only by the sound of water dripping slowly from some unseen source, urged Nina to seek leniency for Corlis. The man had no share in the blame for stripping this place of scarce water and sparse vegetation. The mishap with the thorns was not his fault, and neither was Nina's recklessness with the water. That was all on her.

Her obeisance done, Nina straightened and got to her feet. She collected her horse and returned to the campsite, to find that Corlis had disappeared again. He was gone to gather his own horses, she supposed. Nina took advantage of the man's absence to grab up the blankets they had shared last night. Quickly she separated hers from his and neatly rolled the bedding, ready for tying onto their respective saddles.

By the time Corlis came back leading his horses, Nina had all her personal gear strapped onto Traveller's back. The man took his animals to drink, one by one, at the dwindling source in the grotto. Together then, Corlis and Nina loaded the packhorses with their equally dwindling supplies. Nina couldn't help noticing how Corlis weighed each bag in his hand before he secured it in place.

"While you slept yesterday," she informed him, "I killed rabbits for my supper. Of the beans I ate little, and I took no beef at all until a few minutes ago. My horse got his usual ration of feed yesterday, but none thus far today."

Corlis threw an inquiring look over the back of one packhorse, where his hands were busy tying up the load. In answer to his unvoiced question, Nina explained her reason for offering this inventory.

"I have seen how sparing you are with our food and supplies, how you've portioned them out at exactly the moment of need and not an instant too soon, nor a morsel too much. Lest you suspect that I took more than my share after knocking you out last night, I promise that was not the case. Profligate I may have been with the water. But with our supplies I was careful."

Corlis tipped his head and smiled. "Find me tightfisted, do you? Economy is necessary in the desert. Close upon the heels of waste, death will walk." Done with the pack animal, Corlis made to swing his saddle onto the back of his riding horse. The move wiped the smile from his lips as it forced from his throat a cry of pain.

"Let me do it," Nina exclaimed, rushing to the man's side. "You'll open your wounds and bleed again. Here," she said as she thrust his bedroll at him. "Make yourself a pillow while I load the rest of your gear. Your rump will need cushioning."

With a nod of acknowledgment, Corlis stepped out of Nina's way. As she readied his horse, he loosened the rolled bedding enough to flatten the blankets and make a pad. Nina held it in place as Corlis mounted and eased his butt onto the cushion.

"That'll help," he conceded, looking down at Nina. "You have my thanks, lady. You're an angel of mercy ... a quality I had not expected in a witch."

"A *what?*" Nina gaped at him. "What did you call me?"

"No offense meant." Corlis raised one hand in a placating gesture. "But can you have doubted that I know who and what you are? Before we left Granger, I had my ear to the ground for any word of you. I heard what you did to that mongrel who raped the girl, how you cut him down with a lightning stroke. People say you're an avenging goddess and one of the Immortals. That last, I got from your brother. I know what *he* is, and he told me you were like him, only greater than him. More powerful."

As Nina stared, Corlis touched his hat brim in respectful salute.

"Lady," he went on, astonishing Nina with every word, "you're not the first *wysard* I've met, nor the first I have guided through this desert. Your kind have been coming through for a while now." Corlis studied her. "But of them all, you're the most terrifying. The others have mostly been youngsters, new to wizardry, still testing their wings. You, though? You're even older than the sheriff, and I know how long that fellow's been around. And I know he's in awe of his sister. He said you can kill with a thought. You'll summon a flood to bury a man, same as he called the stones to crush an army, way back before I was born."

"You've heard that story?" Nina asked, her voice faint in her ears. "It's only a legend now, one that hardly anyone believes."

"I believe it," Corlis said. "I've seen your brother grow old and then make himself young again. I've seen the life he breathes into cold stone, and I've seen those magical lights that you make. I got a close look this morning, for you'd left three burning all night. When I woke and found you asleep beside me, I tried touching the light that hung over our bed. In my hand, it did not burn long. But I saw enough to know it for magic. I've seen other sorcery, too, from those other *wysards* I've taken through these canyons."

Nina could only stand blinking at him, mind whirling from these revelations. When she made no reply, Corlis lifted his reins and urged his horse to a slow walk. "Mount up, lady. We must go. The sun's dropping."

Woodenly, Nina obeyed. A thousand questions filled her thoughts as she gathered Traveller's reins and swung onto the roan's back. Was it fear of her—fear of the witch who had slain the rapist—that had tied the tongue of Corlis at the start of their journey? Drisha knew, once the man got to talking, he said much that was worth hearing. Wizardry was clearly becoming more accepted in the south country, if this nomad so willingly made his services available to the gifted ones—those he called Nina's kind. But why had Corlis agreed to be Nina's guide if he thought her a vengeful man-killer?

Legary must have paid him a fortune to take me on, Nina thought. To judge by the man's initial reticence around her, Corlis had feared even to glance Nina's way. Since last night, however, her guide's conduct had shifted from awestruck respect to cheeky familiarity.

He has become overly *familiar,* Nina thought, chewing her bottom lip. If Corlis gave her cause to make him fear her again, she would have to do it with blade alone. For Nina could no longer conjure a wall of water against him or any man.

"Do you know," Nina called to Corlis from her accustomed place at the back of the packtrain, "I had wagered with myself that you would not speak to me this entire trip. Imagine my surprise to discover that you *can* talk."

The wounds in his back prevented Corlis from twisting in his saddle to toss a reply over his shoulder. Instead, in the last few feet of width before the canyon tapered to a narrow ravine, the man reined his horse around so he could address Nina directly.

"The old legends teach us," he said, peering at Nina from under the brim of his hat, "that a mortal never speaks to a goddess unless she first speaks to him. I thought it best and safest to keep my mouth shut and my gaze averted. Your brother the sheriff had warned me in the strictest terms that you are not a woman to be trifled with." Corlis gave her an impudent grin. "But lady, you undressed me and crawled into bed with me, and wrapped yourself around my naked body. That gives me to think you aren't so terrifying after all. A goddess you may be, but firstly you're a woman."

Chapter Fourteen

They rode until long after dark, Corlis finding his way by moon-light through an ever-branching maze of ravines. As he had every day of this journey, he brought them to another life-sustaining waterhole.

As he dropped stiffly from his saddle, Nina grabbed the blankets which had cushioned his wounds only slightly during their long hours of riding. The man's jaunty bravado of earlier in the day had deserted him. Corlis was gasping with pain.

Nina conjured Ercil's fire and worked by its light to make camp. She spread his blankets on a patch of sand and ordered the man to lie down while she built a fire against the chill of the night. Corlis made little protest. Though mumbling about watering the horses, he stayed where he was, curled on his side under a blanket.

"I'll tend the animals," Nina murmured. "But you first. Sit up." Gently, she helped him do so. "Get your shirt off. And your trousers."

This time, Corlis had nothing cheeky to say as Nina undressed him and rolled him onto his stomach. By witchlight's glow, she cleaned each thorn puncture from the back of his head to his thighs. The shallower wounds were closing, already beginning to heal. Some of the deeper punctures, however, showed signs of inflammation. The skin around them was swollen and hot. A cool compress, followed by several minutes' exposure to the chilly air, did little to draw out the fever.

Frowning over her patient, Nina opened the small jar of deadener and dabbed the unguent down the man's back, down to the curve of his butt. As she worked, Corlis moaned. At first, the sound communicated only pain. But as the numbing properties took hold, his moans began to seem more those of a man who enjoyed a woman's touch. From her years of attending at bedsides, Nina knew that the motions of her healer's hands could put ideas into the heads of some patients, even those barely conscious.

She finished quickly and put away the precious ointment—she had to make it last. If Corlis could not swallow a painkiller without it knocking him down for a day, then the jellied unguent was the only palliative Nina could give him.

Even without a sedating drink, the man had ceased his moans and slipped into sleep, too exhausted to feel hunger. Nina spread his blankets over his naked form, then went to water the horses and find them something to eat. She left all four animals saddled and mostly loaded. Midnight was past, and if Corlis kept to the pattern he had earlier established, they would be up and on their way long before dawn.

She made an unsatisfactory supper on beans alone. She'd already had her share of jerked beef for that day. In any case, Nina could hardly stomach the stuff anymore. After extinguishing the witchlights and banking the fire, she set herself to watch for any game that might venture to drink at the waterhole. Nina would not refuse even a sand cat at this point. But all remained silent until the wee hours ... when a whisper in her ear and a hand on her shoulder brought her out of sleep.

"Time to go, lady," Corlis murmured. "Let's ride while the moon shows the way."

* * *

Over the next days and nights, Nina learned just how carefully her guide had timed this part of their journey. He'd planned every step to coincide with the full moon and its waxing and waning phases.

"It's tricky through here," Corlis admitted. "I need the moonlight to be sure of our path. Can't afford to get lost in these ravines. In summer, very few of them hold water."

So the pattern was reset, and even more rigidly adhered to than before his mishap with the thorns. Ride out in the middle of the night. Continue until late morning. Sleep through the hottest part of each day. Saddle up again in late afternoon, ride long past sundown, devote the midnight hours to a light meal and a quick snooze.

The pattern was grueling for the able-bodied. For Corlis, battling the pain and swelling of his wounds, it was torment. Every morning and night, Nina helped him out of his saddle, dabbed him with deadener, and forced him to rest while she tended the horses. Every shot she had at a desert rabbit, she took, but she fed most of the rarely obtained meat to her patient. Corlis needed it more than she did.

As the days passed in a fog of pain for him, and for Nina a haze of fatigue and worry, she grew to miss the sound of the man's voice. Corlis had ceased to chivvy her about her habit of undressing him. Only seldom did he speak at all. The man needed every ounce of his strength to sit in the saddle and pick his way through the canyon maze. Unfailingly he led them to water, but at such cost to himself, Nina began to harbor doubts that Corlis would live to bring her out of these badlands.

She considered giving him the mind-altering tea that Willow had used to clear the leech poison from Nina's blood. But the memory of Willow's words stopped her. "I am glad to have you back and in your right senses," the wisewoman had said. Corlis had shown a marked sensitivity to the painkilling drink Nina had given him while she yanked thorns from his backside. A modest dose had rendered him insensible for hours. Then when he woke, he had been chatty, impudent, and half euphoric, rising from his sickbed and tending his horses as though the deep punctures in his back were minor nuisances. Half a day later, he'd almost fallen out of his saddle, panting with pain, his drug-induced euphoria gone.

Given his unexpected reaction to a painkiller Nina had administered with confidence, she hesitated to dose the man with a powerful hallucinogenic she'd tested only once, and that on herself. Her strange experience with the tea suggested it would drive him from his right mind. Willow's palpable relief about Nina's restored mental state made her wonder whether Corlis could return from whatever bizarre journey the drug might send him on. No, she couldn't risk it.

Hardly a testament to my powers as a healer, Nina berated herself as she rejected the tea and rationed the deadener, forced by the dwindling state of her stock to use the unguent on only his gravest wounds. None of those hot, red, swollen lumps would produce pus, making Nina suspect a deep-seated infection that lay beyond the reach of any treatment, short of carving it out with a knife.

"It's necessary," she told him. "You must allow me to cut open and drain those tumors."

Wearily, Corlis shook his head. "Not yet," he mumbled, barely awake. "Two days. In two days' time, we stop. Then carve me up."

Those days were agony for the man, but at the end of them Nina felt her hopes rise. Corlis had brought them to a shady, well-watered place, a rock shelter that was almost a cave tucked back in a canyon, hidden from the sun by not only a protruding ledge but also tall trees. A spring-fed pool below the cave provided reliable water for a vastly more luxuriant growth of vegetation than Nina had seen since this journey began. Straight-trunked, leafy trees shaded the shrubs and berry bushes that grew on the pool's banks. Away down the canyon beyond the fringe of trees, a trickle of springwater sustained a lush ribbon of meadow. The meadow was colorful with jade-green grass and fragrant with the only desert flowers that Nina had encountered besides sandburs and withered cactus blooms.

"It's beautiful!" she exclaimed as she swung out of her saddle. "Plenty of fresh water, and wood for a decent fire. Get your clothes off. I'm cutting those lumps out of you."

Nina turned the horses loose, not taking time to unload or even tether them. Thirst and hunger would anchor the animals to this green oasis; they needed no other restraints against straying. From the packhorses she took only the cooking gear, and from Traveller only her saddlebags and medical kit.

"Drink this," Nina ordered her guide. "Don't argue." She handed Corlis a cup of the sedative that had put him under on the day he tumbled into thorns. It was the pain relief the man had needed but refused ever since, for fear of sleeping away the precious moonlit nights. "I've given you a double dose," she told him. "Drink it, then get on your stomach and sleep. By the time you wake up, I will know what's in those fevered lumps on your backside."

What the swellings held, to Nina's astonishment, was worms. As she cut into the reddest, most bulging knot on the man's rump, masses of maggoty worms erupted from the incision. The grubs were small and white, and packed in so tightly she wondered how they'd not suffocated each other.

As she dug the maggots out of that wound and others on Corlis's back, Nina flung the worms into the nearby campfire. But the roasting, sizzling creatures made such a stink, she began throwing them instead into a pot of boiling water. The steam that rose then from the cooking grubs carried surprisingly meaty notes. The aroma might have made Nina's mouth water, if her stomach hadn't been turned by the wriggly masses of maggots bursting from Corlis's flesh.

"What in the name of mercy *are* these things?" Nina murmured to her unconscious patient. "I was worrying about infection, but this is an *infestation*."

For more than an hour she worked, removing every worm and flushing every puncture they had nested in. Each colony of worms had enclosed itself in a sack of tissue, a tough membrane that Nina first thought was made—or parasitized—from the flesh of Corlis. But after scooping the maggots out and washing worm-slime from inside each sack, Nina found she could pull the empty "nest" out, each coming clear as a fully intact membrane. From every swollen wound, the deflated maggot-sack slipped with a wet *pop*. Evidently the worms had spun or secreted for themselves a protective covering, an impermeable membrane that might explain the failure of Nina's disinfectants to reach and eradicate the nests.

If no medicine could get in, however, toxins had leached out from every sack, poisoning their host's blood. For days, Corlis had ridden in a fogged torment, consumed by the pain of the infestation, hardly able to eat—only sticking in his saddle and picking his way through the badlands by force of will.

"But you are purged now," Nina murmured to him. "Tomorrow, I'll give you mint tea and springwater until your teeth float, to wash from your blood the last taint of worm-rot. I'll build your strength on fresh goat meat." For unmistakable were the signs, all around the pool, that desert goats came regularly to this lush oasis.

Nina was ready for them. Before dusk fell, she'd established a comfortable camp in the shallow cave above the pool. Her patient's evacuated wounds were clean and packed with disinfectants. Corlis lay asleep under layers of blankets. Robbed of his senses by the double sedation, the man had twitched no muscle while Nina sliced into his buttocks and back and scooped maggots from his flesh. When he woke, he would be acutely tender in all those places. But with the removal of the wriggling masses and their seeping poison, the puncture wounds the worms had infested should heal quickly.

Hunting proved excellent in the meadow and on the banks of the pool. Just before sunset, Nina dropped two goats with perfect kill-shots. By the light of Ercil's fire, she butchered and roasted the small carcasses. So starved for fresh meat was she, Nina ate a whole goat. Only her promise to Corlis, to surfeit him with meat, kept her from consuming much of the second animal as well.

Self-sacrifice, however, proved unnecessary. Nina woke in the pre-dawn to discover a herd of goats grazing in the meadow alongside the horses. Her quick bowshot brought down a straggler as it clambered through a rockfall on its way to water. When she went to collect her kill, the other goats hardly noticed her. They seemed unaccustomed to two-legged hunters, and only moved away slightly at her approach.

Reassured that she could step into the meadow's edge without frightening away this bounty of meat on the hoof, Nina searched among the flowers and grasses for plants that might produce edible roots. She pulled up only a handful, but even a nibble on a fresh, sweet tuber would be a treat after the monotonous trail diet of dried beef and beans.

Back at camp, she found Corlis still sleeping. Encouragingly, however, the man had rolled from his stomach onto his side. His sleep seemed now to be the deep and essential rest, not of drug-induced unconsciousness, but of a body and mind given over to the needs of healing.

She left him to it. With a mug of her favorite tea in hand, Nina walked down to sit on a shady boulder at the pool's edge. Finally she could allow herself to relax and enjoy this respite from brutal sun and nagging thirst. There was enough water, game, and grazing in this place to sustain whatever length of convalescence Corlis might require.

Nina sat musing on the man who had become more to her than a guide. In spite of herself, she cared for him in a way that was very different from the healer's deep but necessarily detached concern for a patient. Caution murmured to her, however, about the dangers of opening her heart to this man.

"Remember your brother and his wife," Nina whispered to herself. "Remember the grief of inevitable loss. The love between a *wysard* and a mortal must end in pain."

She need not take the lesson only from the example of Legary and Willow, of course. Nina's Earthly husband had been of the short-lived, non-magian world. She had watched that man grow old and feeble, she'd held him when he died, and she had committed his mortal remains to the ocean they'd both loved. Nina and Makani, as young newlyweds oblivious to everything except their passions, had vowed to love and cherish each other lifelong, "until death do us part." Both of them had honored those vows. Even when the passing years had sapped Makani of his vigor, while Nina seemed never to age beyond twenty-five, she had remained true to him—true until his death, and beyond it. Never in her adopted realm, nor since returning to this world of her birth, had Nina been with another man.

"Is it time?" she asked herself. "And must it be love?"

The bold remarks Corlis had tossed her way, in the brief hours after the man found his tongue until he fell too ill for such impudence, had suggested only lust on his part. But what else could there be between a desert nomad and a wayfaring *wysard?* At the end of this journey, they would and must go their separate ways. Nina would continue her grand scheme of visiting family; Corlis would recross the desert, paid handsomely by some ambitious merchant or foolish wanderer seeking safe passage. Only the most foolish of wanderers, Nina must now admit, would ignore the advice of those who had warned against testing this pitiless land in the heat of summer.

In truth, she had been apprehensive from the start about crossing a desert without benefit of water magic. She'd hurried away from Granger out of shame: mortified by the loss of her powers, and even more distressed by Legary praising her supposed strengths. She should have told him what had happened to her. Especially after he revealed his own wizardly downfall, Nina should have confessed. Instead, she'd run, stubbornly defying every entreaty by Legary and Roddy to wait for better weather. She'd run to the desert ... and now she was thinking of falling into the arms of a man who could be nothing to her.

Lost in her reverie ... drifting into increasingly vivid daydreams of bedding Corlis not as her patient, but as her lover ... Nina didn't hear—over the sound of her raised pulse—what approached from behind. She sat on her water-washed boulder, oblivious to danger, unaware of her patient making his slow, silent way down from the cave above the pool. It was a testament to her old tutor, the wizardly Master Welwyn who had taught all of his apprentices to maintain self-control in the face of the unexpected, that she didn't jump out of her skin when Corlis barked at her: "Don't move!"

Nina obeyed, for in those two words was an urgency which spoke of peril. Attuned now to her surroundings, her daydreams shattered, she listened to the soft sounds of the man's approach. She heard the caution in his movements, the care Corlis took with every step as he drew near.

"It's a snake," he hissed from a little way behind her and to one side. "Deadly. When I say to, *get off that rock.* Toward the bank, *not* into the water."

Nina didn't nod, but gave a barely audible whisper: "I understand."

She heard Corlis take one more step as if to brace himself.

"Go!" he yelled.

Nina flung herself sideways. She landed on the bank well away from the water. Like the practiced fighter she was, she rolled and came to her feet. With her gaze locked on the sleek, black, furiously struggling creature that Corlis had pinned down with a forked stick, Nina started to grab for her knife. Unwilling, however, to throw it and possibly lose the weapon in the water, she reached instead for the quiver of arrows that awaited her on the bank. She had propped the quiver there, alongside her bow, in anticipation of another easy goat hunt.

With one fluid motion, Nina drew out an arrow and stabbed it through the eye of the snake that was even then wriggling out from under the stick that held it. Her arrow's razor tip penetrated the creature's skull and flaked stone off the boulder under it—the boulder where she had sat fantasizing.

"Beggar all!" she swore, hardly knowing whether to be more startled by the snake or by Corlis standing there open-eyed and buck naked. "Seldom am I caught so unawares. How long have you been awake?"

"Not long," he muttered. "Just in time to look down and see your death approaching. Nothing survives a bite from a whiptail viper. This pool is full of them."

"And I was so looking forward to a swim," Nina murmured.

Corlis shook his head. "Bad idea. So is washing goat carcasses here." He nodded at the shady pool. "This time of year, the vipers mostly sleep. Let 'em taste blood in the water, though, and they come out looking for more. Looking for something to kill."

Nina shuddered. "Snakes in the Garden of Eden."

"Eden?" Corlis echoed. "Where's that?"

"Just a lost place in an old story, a deceptively pretty place like this garden in the desert," Nina began to explain, but broke off as she reached to steady Corlis. He had started to toss aside his snake-pinning stick, but then found himself needing it for support as he swayed on his feet.

"Back to bed," Nina ordered. "Lean on me."

The climb to the cave left Corlis sweating and his muscles trembling. Even so, as Nina eased his naked body down to the blankets, the man put his hand on her breast. Through her thin shirt, he squeezed gently.

Nina looked him in the eye as she peeled his hand off her and thrust it aside.

"Not yet," she said, straightening to look down at him. With her hands on her hips, she declared firmly, "You're still my patient."

"But when I'm well?"

As Nina met the frank gaze of the man's gray eyes, her unguarded daydreams about him swam before her. She swept them aside and shrugged one shoulder.

"No promises. I haven't made up my mind about you."

He grinned with his old brazenness. "Don't they say 'one good turn deserves another'? I saved your life just now."

Nina scoffed. "What exactly do you think I've been doing since that day you took on a buttload of thorns—and worms."

"Worms?" The grin vanished from the man's face.

"Maggots," Nina said. From a far corner of the cave, she brought Corlis the pan of cooked grubs. She hadn't yet disposed of the multitudinous little creatures, wanting first to have Corlis see them and tell her, if he could, what they were.

"I scooped a potful of these out of your back and rump," she said, stooping to show him. "I had thought it was thorn poison making you sick, but it was worm-rot." In graphic detail, Nina described the maggoty eruptions from her patient's swollen wounds. "Another day in the saddle, and the worms might have eaten through to your guts." She made a face. "For the 'good turn' you did for me today, I'd say you've been repaid."

"Sandfly maggots!" Corlis exclaimed. "The old men of the desert speak of them, but until now I had never seen one. Only ever saw a horse they'd killed." With his thumbnail, he scraped at his lower lip. "Lady, you've got me wondering." Corlis ceased his study of the cooked worms and looked up at Nina. "Are you an angel of mercy ... or of misfortune?"

Nina arched her eyebrow. "What do you mean by that?"

Corlis cocked his head, regarding her. "Never before in all my trips through this desert," he said, "have I had the bad luck to fall in a thorn patch. And never in my life—until now—have I taken on sandfly maggots. Am I lucky that you've been here to keep me alive? Or did all of this happen on account of me taking a water-witch into this desert? Maybe the old dry bones of this place are letting me know they don't want you here."

Down in the trees around the pool, a bird burst into song—one of the few Nina had heard in the desert. She turned her head to listen. Then she looked back at Corlis.

"I suspect," she murmured, holding the man's gaze, "that only time can answer your questions ... and mine."

Chapter Fifteen

The time for answers came not many days later.

Much sooner than Nina would have liked, they abandoned the snake-infested pool, Corlis deeming the vipers an even greater threat to the horses than to themselves. They lingered only long enough to gorge on roast goat and get many cups of mint and ginger tea down the recuperating patient. With his fevered wounds drained, the worm poison flushed from his body, and every thorn puncture healing, Corlis was soon fit to get them back on the trail.

Continuing west, they rode through a series of ravines, each shallower than the last. A final gully—a mere depression with a trickle of water at its bottom—would bring them out of the canyonlands altogether, Corlis said. Beyond the gully's low rim, the featureless flats of the high desert stretched to the horizon.

"From here, we ride at night, and we ride fast," Corlis said as he dropped from his saddle. "There's no shade and no water out there for miles." He gestured at the tiny trickle that flowed through the gully, the little stream from which all four horses were thirstily drinking. "Get all you can, while you can."

Nina heeded his advice. On her hands and knees, she joined the horses and drank until her belly sloshed. Then she topped up her waterskin and filled both of the leather buckets the packhorses carried. The heavy drain by the riders and their animals depleted the trickle, leaving only mud in the bottom of the gully.

At sunset, they began the hardest ride of Nina's life. Across a packed crust of sand and chalk, Corlis pushed them relentlessly. He allowed no rest. His three white horses seemed in their element here. Eagerly they ran, their manes flowing, hooves barely touching the ground. Like escaped prisoners they were, fleeing the confinement of the canyons.

Nina on Traveller could not keep up. The roan from the eastern seaboard was perfectly suited for long-distance journeying—Trav could cover many miles every day, but at a far more leisurely and rational pace than this mad dash. As she fell farther and farther behind, Corlis was forced to restrain his animals, much against their will. More than once that long night, Nina lost sight of her guide, and only found him in the starlit desolation by following the sound of his cursing and his horses' angry neighing.

At last, she and Traveller could take no more. "Hold up!" Nina gasped as she located Corlis and his band of sprinters. "I must rest."

Not waiting for the man's assent, she slid from her saddle and grabbed a bucket off the nearest prancing packhorse. During this nightmare ride, the bucket had lost most of the water she'd stowed in it. What little was left, Nina gave to Traveller, topped up with a generous measure from her waterskin.

"How much farther?" Nina panted when she caught her breath enough to speak.

"Miles," Corlis said. "There's water ahead. Let's get to it before the sun rises and bakes our brains."

Of the rest of that night, Nina could later remember little. Details were lost in the haze of her weariness and in anxiety for her horse. Nina feared Traveller would drop dead under her. His breathing was loud and labored, his flanks lathered, his muzzle flecked with foam.

Forgive me, Nina sent the thought to him, her fingers twined in his mane. *Never would I have come on this foolish, selfish journey if I'd known what would be demanded of you, Trav.*

The sun was well up, its heat growing intolerable before Nina spotted their destination. Ahead were trees growing out of the sands in a cluster that spoke of water at their roots.

"Thank the Powers," she breathed.

Nina reined Traveller to a walk, and then to a halt. Dropping from her saddle, she took down her waterskin and the now-empty bucket she'd confiscated from the packhorse. Taking only two swallows for herself, she poured the rest into the bucket for Trav.

"Just a little farther," she murmured as the roan slaked his desperate thirst. "Then we'll be in the shade and you can rest." Once they reached that oasis, Nina silently vowed, nothing and no one would drive her from it until Traveller was fully recovered.

Not remounting, she led the horse the rest of the way at a slow walk, sweating under a furnace-hot sun. Nina cried aloud in relief when they reached the first of the trees and passed through into a wide grove. So thick was the foliage, she expected to find a deep pond, perhaps a lake, at the center of the cluster.

What she saw instead of water, however, was Corlis down on his hands and knees, digging frantically in damp sand. His horses also pawed up the ground, searching for the moisture that must have only recently departed from this place. Centered under the trees was a large, low basin: formerly a lakebed but now drained of water, although still dark with dampness. Below those wet sands, tree roots must find all the moisture they needed. But of drinkable water, Nina saw none.

"Damnation, lady," Corlis exclaimed as Nina walked up leading Traveller. "There's *always* water here." The man ceased his scrabbling in the sand. He rocked back on his heels and looked up at her, his expression despairing. "I'd say the old dry bones of this desert have spoken."

"But perhaps they will not have the last word," Nina murmured.

She stripped her saddle and gear off Trav and removed his bridle. "Rub him down for me, will you?" Nina handed Corlis a rag from her saddlebags. "Then please wait for me here. For what I'm about to do, I want to be alone."

Corlis shot her a questioning look, but said nothing as Nina walked off.

She headed for the farthest edge of what had plainly been a substantial body of water until its recent, inexplicable draining. About halfway across the lakebed's damp sands, a line of trees shaded a fingerlike ridge of higher ground, screening off the low-lying basin beyond. That deep, sandy bowl gave Nina the privacy she wanted. Under cover of the trees, she disrobed and left her sweat-soaked clothes on the ridgetop. Naked, she slid down into the bowl and fell on her knees. With her eyes closed and her hands raised in supplication, Nina threw herself on the mercy of the Powers.

"I have been arrogant," she confessed. "I have forgotten the training of my youth. The Powers belong, fully and eternally, to the Elementals who rule the natural realms—the realms from which the *wysards* of Ladrehdin draw our strength. The Powers must never be misused, wasted, or taken for granted ... or played with like toys.

"For my prideful conduct," she went on in a whisper, "I beg your forgiveness. I come before you filled with remorse for having so often squandered the gifts you gave me. What a foolish daughter I have been to you! From the mother and the father who gave me life, I learned that we who call ourselves *wysards* owe, to you, all that we are. Every magician of Ladrehdin, even the greatest among the Ancients, must be to you a mere child, an infant lacking in knowledge and understanding." Nina bowed low, touching her forehead to the sand. "I have been to you a self-serving and thoughtless child. I beg you will pardon me for disregarding the lessons of my youth."

She paused, remembering her talks with Legary and how he had admitted that he had been punished for abusing and misusing his own wizardly gifts. On impulse, she sent up an extra plea on his behalf.

"If I may ask your further indulgence," Nina said, bent so low that her lips touched the moist sand, "my beloved youngest brother, Legary the stonemason, acknowledges that he also is at fault. He regrets the profligate waste of his gifts and the boastful way he expended them, years ago in the days of his youthful pride."

Nina fell silent, looking inward ... feeling her way, as it seemed, back through time. Her thoughts drifted to the childhood home she had shared, not with Legary, but with her brother Galen, the fire-master. Nina saw herself as the girl of six who had summoned a wave from a pool of magic, and then ridden that wave across the void, to wash up on the shores of a distant world. Vast, her strength had been in those long-ago days. Water would rise at her most casual command.

Though now, through the lens of hard experience, Nina saw that no wizardry could or should be casual. Each summoning of the Power drew from the wellsprings of the Elemental Ones: fire, air, stone, and water. Every act of magic depended upon their willingness, their goodwill, their generosity—or whatever the right word was, for bestowing upon their servants such supreme favor.

It was with this renewed understanding, and with profound humility, that Nina sought once more to summon water—not with the negligence of her youth, and certainly not in the reckless way she had conjured waves when she sailed with Dalton from Ruain. Her attempt, at this time and in this place, arose from deep and immediate need. In the back of her mind, Nina could see Corlis and the horses thirsting on the banks of the waterless lake. She could picture their bones whitening under the sun, like the piles of old bones they had passed last night ... the skeletons that loomed out of the dark, appearing at intervals during their race to this place of shelter.

Nina pushed aside those images of death, to keep the focus of her mind's eye on a distant river of water she had begun to sense deep below her—deep in the underworld beneath these desert sands. Riveting her magian senses upon it, Nina detected not only the strong, fast flow of that buried river, but also an upwelling, like a flume or a channel that branched from the river's main course and bent upward through bedrock, bending toward but not reaching the basin in which she kneeled.

"Mother of Waters," Nina whispered to that hidden river, "I pray you will grant your servant but a small portion of your life-giving powers. Rise to me here, if you so will it, and fill this bowl under the trees so that my companion and I, and the faithful animals who give us their trust, may live to pay you homage."

With her mind and her magian senses—the latter feeling rough, Nina had touched them so little in recent months—she reached for the flume that branched off from the central course of the underground river. With a ribbon of her water-magic flung around it like a rope, she caught the channel and tugged upward.

At that instant, a finned leviathan swam into Nina's view, fighting its way upstream against the swift flow of the main river. With a powerful stroke of its tail flukes, the whale propelled itself into the buried channel that Nina was pulling toward her. So great was the leviathan's leap upward, it brought the channel gushing to the surface. Nina was knocked aside as a mighty geyser erupted from the sands beneath her. A column of cold water shot upward, spouting high above the trees and raining down with the thunder of a cloudburst.

In moments, Nina was swimming, so quickly did the lake basin fill with water from the captured flume. What was more, she did not swim alone. The leviathan was at her side, only now the creature seemed more a huge salamander than a whale.

"Grog!" Nina cried. She wrapped her arms around the shapeshifting friend she had thought lost to her forever. The identity of the gigantic salamander could not be doubted. Around his throat, worn like a neckerchief, was a scrap of the cloth from which Nina had fashioned for Grog a fresh new tunic. In her saddlebags, she still carried the piece that he had left at the edge of the new-made lake outside Winfield, scene of his disappearance.

"Thank you, my friend," Nina mumbled. She pressed her face against Grog's smooth, greenish-brown skin. "Thank you for coming to me here. I know you cannot stay. Your home lies below, in the world of the shining deep. I saw it in my vision, the kingly throne room with your glowing courtiers."

Grog twisted to lock his large blue eyes onto Nina's face. He gazed at her, his look wistful. With the webbed fingers of one hand, he caressed her bare skin. Nina had forgotten she was naked. But in the presence of this primordial being, this magical creature of the underworld, it mattered not at all. Grog nodded to her then, a gesture more graceful than the stiff-bodied bows he had barely managed when he wore the poorly fitted guise of a hulking surface-dweller.

Whipping away from her, Grog dove for the bottom of the basin, a bottom that now lay under many feet of water. Having abundantly refilled the lakebed, the freshwater geyser had ceased to flow. A depression remained in the sand, however, showing the way back to the channel, back to the underground river and thence to the mysterious netherworld that was Grog's native home. With a few strokes of his webbed hands and a flick of his powerful tail, Grog disappeared into the sand.

Nina saw him off. Then she popped to the surface, realizing with a vague feeling of surprise that she was *not* actually a fish, and she did need to breathe.

She came up to find Corlis staring at her from atop the ridge where she had left her clothes. He stood under trees that grew near the waterline and shaded both the ridge and the refilled lake basin. From the crown of his hat to his boots, the man was dripping wet. Nina surmised that Corlis had been caught in the downpour produced by the supernatural geyser.

"By the sun above!" he swore as she raised her head above water. "Lady, I feared you had drowned."

She smiled. "I assure you, sir: *I* can swim."

Corlis nodded, looking dazed but thoughtful. "Seems likely, for a water witch. And a goddess of mercy who brings a flood to the desert. I've got my answer about you." He tipped his soggy hat back on his head. "You still making up your mind about me, lady?"

Nina remained treading water in the deepest part of the lake, hiding her nakedness from him. But then she swam closer. In the shallows she stood up, and raised both hands to smooth her long, raven hair back from her face.

"Can *you* swim, man of the desert?" she asked.

"No, la-lady," Corlis stammered. "I can't." He whipped off his hat and raked her with his gaze.

"Then get your clothes off, man, and let me teach you."

They never made it into the deepest part of the conjured lake. Corlis resisted full submersion—not so much because he feared the water, Nina thought, but from the brief glimpse he'd had of the creature that had swum with her before disappearing into the lakebed. Witches,

Corlis reasoned, were said to have familiars. He was fully prepared to believe that the familiar of a water-witch might take the form of a gigantic mudpuppy.

"Best leave the fellow undisturbed," he said.

The man did submit willingly to the all-over bath that Nina gave him with the last of the elderflower soap she had brought from Granger. He allowed her to shave from his face the beard and mustache that had grown bristly during their time in the desert.

Both of them washed clean and glistening wet from head to toe, they lay together then under the trees. Their first coupling was fierce and raw in the way they both seemed to need.

But after the rush and heat of that initial joining, Corlis proved to be a more generous lover than Nina had expected. He took his time with her, exploring her body with his hands and mouth, offering a gentle nibble here and a vigorous tonguing elsewhere. Into shudders of pleasure he carried her, such pleasures as she had almost forgotten were possible. Twined in passion's embraces, they lost themselves in lovemaking all that day, until hunger of another sort wedged them apart to gather wood and build a fire.

"What's left to eat?" Nina inquired as she hefted the empty sack of dried beef.

"Only beans," Corlis said from the side of his mouth as he chewed on a last strip of the jerky. "About seven days' worth."

"That's all?" Nina swallowed the bite of beef that she had gnawed from her own share. Slowly, she shaped her next question. "How far is it from here to the Ore Hills?"

Corlis sighed. He spit out the jerky and gazed at her from across the fire. In its light, his eyes had regained their indeterminate color. The eyes Nina had been looking into all day, however, had shown themselves to be a deep gray-green, and changeable with his mood. The greater his state of arousal, the darker they became. For most of that day under the trees beside the lake, they'd been charcoal.

"Four days," he mumbled, breaking a short silence that said more than his words.

Nina sat back, sipping her tea and contemplating the end of a journey that she now wished to prolong—possibly to forever. For a moment she cradled her tea mug. Deliberately then, with studied movements, she set the mug aside and slipped off the shirt she had donned, the only garment she'd bothered to pull over her nakedness when they sat down to eat.

"That gives us three days here," she murmured as she opened her arms to him. "Let's make the most of every minute."

Their remaining time together passed in sensation rather than thought. Ruled by desires that deepened hourly, they ate only occasionally and slept in snatches, wrapped in each other's arms and repeatedly waking to caresses and new pleasures.

The magic of this place permeated Nina's senses. She felt the Elementals all around her: in the sparkling sand of the lakeshore, the cool air under the trees, the heat of the sun and the campfire's glow. Most especially, she felt the Powers of water and fire: the water she had drawn to this place, and the carnal fires that inflamed her passions. They swept over her in waves of force, uplifting her, giving to her intimacies with Corlis a sensuality that no mortal could hope to experience—no mortal, that is, who had not lain with a *wysard*.

Their coupling left the man lost for words. Seldom did Corlis gasp out anything intelligible, but at times Nina heard him call her "goddess" or "witch." That was as it should be. She wanted the man to fully appreciate that she was more than the wayfaring woman he had been paid to guide through the desert. For reasons she didn't completely understand or acknowledge, Nina wanted Corlis to remember her, and to remember every hour they shared by the magical lake.

At midmorning of the third day, as they lay entwined on a blanket, sated for the moment, Nina stroked her fingers across the man's bare backside. She explored the pockmarks that her purging of the worm-infested wounds had left in his rump.

"You'll always have these, I think," she whispered. "Over time, the scars may fill in slightly, but I fear you will never lose these reminders of sandfly maggots."

Corlis raised his head from resting it upon Nina's naked breast.

"It's not maggots I'll be reminded of, lady," he murmured, looking at her with eyes shading from gray to charcoal. "I'll be remembering the touch of your hands ... how they eased my pain when the thorns laid me low ... and how tight their grip is when you wrap yourself around me." He gave an appreciative click of his tongue as he grinned at her.

Nina smiled. "Then give yourself to me again, man of the desert. But be warned: I might go so far as to bruise you this time."

"May you do so, lady ... and may the marks of your fingers never fade from my flesh."

Corlis came to her with a vigor that invited Nina's tightest grip. He moaned as she pulled him hard to her, their bodies joined and mounting together in exquisite, ever-rising urgency. At the moment of shared release, he gave a great shuddering cry. In the sounds of his pleasure there was no pain, only the ecstasy that a goddess could bestow upon a mortal who had earned her favor.

* * *

The hour of their departure from the lake found them saddled up at dusk. Another hard night's riding would be required, Corlis said, to bring them again to shade and water.

All four horses were ready. The animals had gotten more rest than their owners in recent days. Traveller and his herdmates had lazed away the time, grazing under the trees, cropping the lush grass that had sprung up in a green meadow around the magical lake. Nina had no more fears for Trav, no more worries that this desert trek would demand too much of him. The roan seemed to take strength from the same forces that Nina felt swirling all around her. Astride the animal she rode out, this time keeping pace with the swift sprinters that Corlis rode and led.

Sunrise of the new day found them dropping down into another shallow ravine, the first of what proved to be a series of gullies that were similar in character, but not in size, to the wide canyonlands they had previously crossed. They would need only four days, Corlis said, to wend their way through this much smaller maze. When they emerged at its western rim, a brief climb would take them into the Ore Hills. There, Corlis would deliver Nina to the home of Galen.

"Will you stay in the hills for a time after that?" Nina asked, and immediately regretted her question. It was better for them both that their liaison should end when this journey did. They had no future together, nomad and *wysard*.

Let him go, Nina thought. *Pay him the rest of his fee and let him go.*

Corlis did not answer, except to brush back a strand of Nina's hair that had worked loose from her raven-dark braid and fallen upon her cheek.

"No, lady," he murmured then. "Directly we gain the Ore Hills, I head south. I'll travel far down the spine of the mountains."

Nina did not ask what business would take Corlis on southward into lands she knew nothing of. Perhaps he had a party of merchants or other itinerants waiting to hire him. It mattered only that she had his answer: When he had delivered her safely, as he'd promised to do, he would be on his way.

She reached to stir the pot of beans. Corlis reached at the same time, not to stir but to remove the bubbling pot from the fire.

"They'll keep," he muttered as he took the spoon from Nina's hand. "Lie with me, lady."

That night and every night until the end of their journey, their love-making was gentle, and so deeply intimate that Nina both feared and welcomed the emotions this temporary lover aroused in her. It seemed so long now since death had taken her husband, that man of a distant world. Since that day, she had worn her widowhood like a shield, a protection against ever again feeling the heart-deep pain of loss. With Corlis, that shield had cracked. Nina's heart would ache when this man was gone.

But that means your heart remains alive, murmured a voice from her depths. *Wysards live long. Perhaps you will give your heart away again ... someday.*

* * *

The hour of parting had come. They stood together outside the shop of Galen, master metalsmith of the Ore Hills. Nina pulled Corlis aside, into an alleyway that ran alongside the shop. It wouldn't do either of their reputations any favors if Galen's noble sister were seen kissing the drifter who wore the public mantle of aloof, taciturn loner.

"Well, sir," Nina said when they broke apart. "I believe I owe you the second half of your fee. Was that not your arrangement with Legary? Half up front, for the buying of supplies, and the remainder to be paid upon my safe delivery to Galen's doorstep."

Corlis took a step back from her and planted his hands on his hips. "Lady, you wound me!" he exclaimed, but with a look more amused than offended. "How can you think that I would take gold from you? I would have died in that Drisha-forsaken desert if not for you and your witchery."

"I think you would not have *been* in that desert, not at this time of the year anyway, if it wasn't for me and my obstinate insistence on traveling," Nina rejoined. "Legary tried to stop me. He said no sane person would attempt the journey at the height of summer."

Corlis nodded. "Your brother is correct. Obviously, I am not sane. Only a madman would hazard the badlands in the dry season." With a raised finger he tipped up the brim of his slouchy hat, the better to see Nina in the shadowy alley. "May Drisha strike me dead," he swore, "if I ever try it again. I only did it this time because the sheriff paid me a fortune ... and because he said you were a water-*wysard* who could conjure up a lake anytime, anywhere."

"Oh!" Nina exclaimed, unable to stop her hand from flying to her mouth. Had Corlis been relying from the start, on powers that she had not been sure of ever recovering? "I didn't realize," she began, then trailed off. Looking into his eyes, she burst out: "What a disappointment I must have been to you! All those days of desperate struggle to find water for the horses and ourselves. Were you thinking every hour that I would simply snap my fingers and lo! water would appear?"

Corlis rubbed his chin. "Crazy I am, lady," he muttered, "but not crazy enough to go into the desert without my own ways of finding water. To say truth, I never expected a thimbleful from you." He rocked back on the heel of one boot, then forward again as he added, "But in the end—right near the end—you called up a whole huge lake. A lake of pure magic. That's something I'll never forget, my lady," Corlis softly murmured, locking his gaze on Nina's face, drinking her in with his gray-green eyes.

"Nor will I forget," she whispered.

She struggled to find the words for everything else she wanted to say to him. Words failed her, however. There seemed only one final thing to do: she dropped him a graceful curtsy, a gesture of both esteem and farewell.

Corlis whipped his hat from his head. He bowed low, and came up holding his hat to his chest as though to protect his heart.

"Good-bye, lady," he murmured. "You have been many things to me. But not for a moment, my goddess, have you been a disappointment."

Part 3
The Outcast

Chapter Sixteen

G alen was not in his shop.

His apprentices directed Nina up the hill to a three-story lodge built of rock and surrounded by surprisingly green and shady grounds. The desert butted right up to the Ore Hills, but these slopes climbed high enough above the sunbaked flats to escape the worst of the summer heat. The same sorts of spiny brush and shrubby grass that Nina had seen in the canyons also grew in these hills, appearing in manicured beds to either side of the narrow street she walked up. But pine trees shaded these slopes, and up here water was more abundant. As Nina climbed, weighed down by her weapons, her saddlebags, and a satchel with the last of her clothes, she heard water trickling behind garden walls. A simple fountain of stacked rock came into view as she turned the corner of a retaining wall and approached the hillside home of this brother she hadn't seen since she was thirteen and Galen not a year younger.

No one answered her knock at the door. Raised voices, however, drifted to Nina from somewhere in the back.

She dumped her burdens on the front porch and made her way around. Guided by the voices, she came to a break in the stone wall that surrounded Galen's private grounds. Set into the wall was a gate, its iron bars wrought in fantastical designs. Nina picked out frilled lizards, winged dragons, and hooded snakes writhing skyward amidst a lacework of vines and trumpet flowers.

Through the close-set ironwork, she glimpsed her brother. He stood at the rearmost part of the grounds, speaking with an individual who lingered just outside a back gate that was more plainly made than the ornate showpiece through which Nina spied him.

His back-garden visitor was a woman, as tall as Galen and notable for her ramrod-straight posture and the long brown tresses that drifted from under her sunhat. The woman wore what Nina took to be the costume of these hills. During her walk from Galen's shop, she had seen similar clothes on the women she'd passed in the steep street: baggy trousers that reached just below the knees, and loose-fitting tunics with sleeves down to the elbow, covering only the upper arms. Fashioned of pale and lightweight fabrics, this was desert clothing—garments made to be cool and practical in the heat of these southwestern hills. Nina resolved to dress herself in the local costume before riding out from this place.

First, however, she must make her arrival known to her brother. But Galen stood so deep in conversation with his visitor that Nina hesitated to call to him. She found herself listening instead—as Galen was listening, with close attention, to his brown-haired visitor. The woman at the back gate seemed to be doing almost all of the talking, and she did not sound happy.

"You *must* take her," the woman snapped, her voice loud enough to carry to Nina's ears. "She's yours. I cannot keep her longer."

"But—" Galen began, and was immediately interrupted.

"I *cannot*," the woman emphasized. "I can do nothing for her. For what she has become, she falls now to your charge."

The woman stood eye-to-eye with Galen, fixing him with a gaze so flinty, Nina wasn't surprised when Galen backed down. He attempted to say no more, only gave a nod that communicated resignation as well as agreement. As the woman whipped around and made to leave, Galen started to follow her out the back gate.

"Brother!" Nina shouted at him, unwilling to further postpone their reunion, regardless of the drama she seemed to be interrupting. "I have been months getting here, by sea and by sand. Will you not welcome me to your home?"

Galen almost tripped over his own feet, so abruptly did he stop and spin around. To keep himself upright, he grabbed the back gate and balanced on its rail. His gaze arrowed to some part of the garden that Nina could not see through the bars of ornamental ironwork that shut her out.

"Over here by the dragons!" she called, and waved.

When he looked and saw her, he gasped. So loud was his intake of breath, Nina heard him over the soft murmur of the water fountain. Its gentle music filled the garden now that Galen's angry-sounding visitor had turned and stalked away.

He didn't cry Nina's name or exclaim aloud in any way other than the gasp. Galen only stood staring at her through the metal bars. Then his gaze shifted back to the unseeable part of the garden.

"Sheyla," he murmured, almost too softly for Nina to hear. "My honored sister stands at yon gate. Will you admit her, and extend to my blood kin the courtesy of our home?"

"I will admit your *sister*, sir, for I know nothing against *her*," came the sharply voiced reply from a new player on the scene, someone Nina had not yet glimpsed. "Others of your 'blood kin,' however, I shall *never* welcome within these walls."

What have I stumbled into? Nina had time to wonder in the brief silence that fell upon the garden, a silence broken by rapidly approaching footsteps. The steps paused on the garden side of Nina's gate. From somewhere just out of her view came a *clank*, a sound suggesting the lifting or removal of a latch or pin. The ornamental gate swung open, and Nina found herself face-to-face with a woman very different from Galen's back-door visitor.

This lady was older, and her hair was lighter. She wore it piled on her head like a crown of blonde gold streaked with pewter silver. In her build, she was heavier than the slender woman who had stood speaking to Galen. Her backbone, however, was just as straight, and both her manner and her apparel were more elegant. This lady wore a sky-blue tunic over a full skirt in sandstone red. Heavy upon her neck, waist, both wrists, and several fingers were adornments of gold, silver, and copper. So intricate were their designs, so masterful the craftsmanship, Nina could not doubt that each fabulous piece came from the hands of Galen, the metalsmith-*wysard*.

He still stood on the far side of the garden, halfway out the back gate as though anxious to follow the woman who had addressed him there in unyielding tones. Nina took a step toward Galen but then paused. Common courtesy demanded that she pay her respects to the gold-bedecked, bangle-wearing lady who had let her in.

That woman, however, had already disappeared. Her rapidly departing footsteps carried her into the deepest shade of the garden, directly behind the house. Nina heard the click of hard-soled shoes ascending a short flight of stairs like the steps of a back porch. Then a door slammed, so loudly that the noise echoed off the garden's trees. Nina saw Galen wince.

Trouble on the home front, she surmised. From the fury conveyed by that slammed door, Nina would have wagered every coin in her purse that the woman under all the gold was Galen's mortal wife. With *her,* undoubtedly, he shared this hillside lodge. But the slimmer, younger, flinty-eyed woman standing firm at the back gate? If that one was Galen's mistress, then he had trouble on both fronts. For the wearer of the eminently practical trousers had seemed every bit as angry as the wearer of the gold—and that flinty, trousered woman had had a great deal more to say to Galen.

With a mental shrug, knowing she'd get the story out of him when Galen was ready to tell it, Nina launched into a sprint across the garden. Reaching Galen at the back gate, she threw herself into his open arms and hugged this brother from her childhood, the only one of her siblings who had been known to her from birth. The two of them had been born so close together, they might well have been thought twins if not for their remarkably dissimilar looks. Galen the red-headed boy had matured into a powerfully built man whose great shock of hair glinted a little darker now, like copper in the sun. *Like our mother's beautiful hair,* Nina thought as she tousled it.

"Thank the Powers," Galen murmured, stepping back to meet Nina's gaze. "They've sent you just in time."

Sent me? Nina wondered, startled by this suggestion that a force outside herself had guided her steps. Aloud, however, she asked only, "Just in time for what?"

Galen's answer was a short shake of his head and a troubled smile. "Come with me. You're exactly what she needs."

He took Nina's hand as if they were children again and he was the little brother in need of his big sister. Together they climbed a steep path that led up higher into the hills behind Galen's house. Well ahead of them went the flinty woman. Nina caught only glimpses of Galen's visitor as the woman ascended, weaving her way through dense stands of pines.

Galen's lodge and garden were entirely out of view by the time they reached the top of that stiff climb. The woman stood waiting for them, off to the side of the rocky path. She was half hidden behind a pile of boulders from which an old tree grew, its branches gnarled and wind-twisted. The woman said nothing, only pointed at a cave that yawned darkly in the hillside.

Galen gave her a brief nod of acknowledgment, a gesture that communicated familiarity with this place. He approached the cave mouth but he did not enter the darkness beyond. Instead he crouched just outside the opening, and called softly into the shadowy depths.

"Jacca," he said, his voice gentle. "It's Galen the goldsmith. I've brought my sister to help you. Lady Nina is a powerful worker of water magic. She'll make you safe."

So much for wizardly secrecy, Nina thought, irritated that Galen would not only reveal her name, but would speak of her magian nature so boldly, and before multiple witnesses.

For the woman behind the boulders was not the only person to hear his words. Out from the cave's depths stumbled a child, a girl of about eight. Her wide green eyes declared her ancestry: this girl had Galen's eyes. With him she shared the same shade of emerald that had passed through the generations from Lady Kate of Earth to Lady Carin of Ruain, and from Carin to her eldest son, the master smith of these hills.

But if the color was the first thing to catch Nina's attention, the fear in the child's eyes ran a close second. The girl appeared terrified. Also, she was burned. The child's hair was singed, her clothes bore scorch marks, and on her bare arms blisters rose from patches of red and peeling skin.

"You poor thing!" Nina exclaimed, her irritation forgotten in her concern for the girl's injuries. "That must hurt. I'll give you something to make it better." She reached automatically for her medicine kit before remembering that she had dropped it with the rest of her bags on Galen's front porch.

She started to order him to go down and fetch it. But then the girl screamed—and burst into flames. Or more precisely, flames shot from the child's fingertips.

In frantic terror, the girl flapped her hands as though to beat out the fires. But her gestures served only to fling the flames from her fingertips onto the legs of her short trousers—and a little way beyond as well, across the slight space between the girl and the still-crouching Galen. Smoke rose as fire caught in his shirtsleeve.

"Mercy upon us!" Nina exclaimed.

Without conscious thought, she raised a hand and summoned water. A wave materialized at the mouth of the cave. With a loud sound of surf chafing against rock, it broke upon Galen and the girl, dousing the fires and soaking them both.

Nina stepped back to avoid a similar wetting as the wave rolled toward her. With another gesture as unplanned as the first, she motioned for the wave to subside. Showing it the palm of her hand, she patted it down as though calling for silence.

The wave obeyed. Every drop fell to the ground and soaked the chalky soil, leaving a damp expanse in front of the cave.

"Thank the Powers!" Galen exclaimed again, breaking the sudden quiet that had blanketed the hillside in the wake of Nina's conjuration. "You need no longer fear your fire-magic, Jacca," he said, holding out his arms to the child. "Lady Nina will make you safe."

O ho! Nina thought as understanding dawned. *What we have here is a powerful young adept, untrained and shamefully unprepared to use the gifts the Elementals have bestowed upon her.* Nina would have rounded on her brother, to give Galen a tongue-lashing for having failed to school his daughter in the most rudimentary of the wizardly arts: that being the exercise of self-control.

But first, she must treat the injuries the child had inflicted upon her own skin, all her burns and blisters.

"Galen," Nina snapped, making no effort to hide her displeasure at her brother's neglect of this girl. "In the hope of being invited into your home, I left my medicines and bags at your front door. Go down and fetch my belongings. Bring food as well. I've eaten nothing since breakfast, and I have found that fixing other people's mistakes can be hungry work."

As Galen rose from his crouch and squelched downhill, water dripping from his hair, his face wore a hangdog expression that told Nina she had guessed correctly. The girl who had flown into his arms, seeking the safety of his embrace the moment both of them were soaking wet and in no danger of spontaneous combustion, was Galen's out-of-wedlock child.

And the girl's mother? Nina turned to see the flinty woman still hovering in the background. All of that woman's previous anger had drained from her face. Now she appeared nervous and irresolute as she stood half concealed behind the boulders.

"The child needs dry clothes," Nina addressed the woman. "Can you bring her some?"

The woman nodded. But instead of retreating to follow Galen down the hillside, she came out from behind the piled rocks. Hesitantly, the woman skirted past Nina and joined the girl at the mouth of the cave.

"Jacca darling," she muttered, reaching as if to touch the girl's singed hair but then withdrawing her hand and fingering her own brown tresses instead. "Please fetch out the pack we brought here from your room. Bring it into the sun. We'll get you dried off out here. It's too cold in that cave, all wet like you are."

"Yes, mama," the girl murmured, again confirming Nina's suspicions.

The child called Jacca disappeared into the shadows. In moments she was back, dragging an oblong sack that reminded Nina of the duffel bags that had been ubiquitous in her old home across the void. When Jacca cleared the cave's mouth, her mother took hold of the bag and helped the child haul it into a patch of sun. Jacca stood back as the woman undid the sack's tie-cords and got it open. She pulled out a child-sized wardrobe of neatly folded garments, all of them sewn from the same bleached, lightweight fabrics that formed the basic costume of these hills. As the woman shook them out, Nina glimpsed streaks of brighter color and made out fanciful designs worked in embroidery.

"Here's one of your favorite shirts," the woman said as she held up a tunic adorned with a delicate bluebird. "Would you like to put it on?"

Jacca shook her head. "No, mama," the child whispered. "I don't want to burn it."

The woman burst into tears. She dropped the tunic atop the pile she had removed from the sack. The bag's heavy fabric kept the clothes out of the dampness where Nina's magical wave had soaked the soil. The woman, however, collapsed into that wet patch and sat there sobbing, her cries thrown back from the cave, its echoes serving to intensify the sounds of heart-wrenching sorrow.

Jacca took a step toward the woman, but then pulled up short. The confusion in the girl's face revealed more to Nina than words could have. She stepped forward to offer a solution to the child's dilemma.

"Hug your mother, Jacca," Nina said in the no-nonsense voice she adopted at the bedsides of patients whose road to recovery needed a healer's firm guidance. "You're still too wet to burn. But just to be sure," she added, bending to scoop up the clean clothes and the sack that had held them, "I will soak you both if I see, hear, or smell the slightest hint of fire. Only first let me move your things out of the way."

To her blunt and practical manner, the girl and her mother responded as Nina had hoped. The woman stopped wailing. Jacca rushed into her arms, and the pair of them clung to each other with desperate need. Nina stood by, watching and listening for any flicker or crackle of flame. The embrace of mother and child lasted long enough for the sun to dip lower in the west and bring the pair into the shadow of the hillside above them. Jacca, though wrapped in her mother's arms, began to shiver in her wet clothes.

Releasing her, the woman stood up out of the damp chalk. "Step into the sunlight, child," she said, brushing in an absentminded way at the smudged seat of her trousers. "Let's get you warm and dry before you catch cold." She started to lift the girl's scorched, bedraggled tunic over the child's head. But Jacca protested.

"Not in front of Master Galen's sister!" the girl pleaded with the self-conscious awkwardness of a bashful youngster. "I'll go in the cave to change my clothes."

"No need for that, not on my account," Nina said. She smiled at the child from over the heaped garments she still held. "I am a healer—a woman knowledgeable in herbs and remedies. Over the years I have seen many people naked, from newborn babes to withered old men."

I've seen vigorous young men naked, too, interjected a thought, bringing with it the mental picture of a stripped-bare Corlis. Nina shoved the memory aside.

"But of course, a maiden must have her privacy," she continued, directing to Jacca a nod both respectful and understanding. "I shall turn my back." As she spoke, she did so. "I will keep your clean clothes up off the ground until your mother can take them from me. Will that be satisfactory?"

From behind Nina came a moment of silence, as though Jacca was not much accustomed to having her feelings consulted or respected. But then: "Yes, water-lady," the girl piped in what Nina supposed was her most formal and proper voice—the tones in which a young gentle-woman might address a local lord or magistrate. "That will be most satisfactory. I thank you for your courtesy."

Nina couldn't help smiling at the child's gravity of expression. But since she was now facing the other way, she had no worries that Jacca would see and misconstrue her amusement. She was still smiling when the girl's mother came to take fresh clothes from the pile Nina held.

"Thank you," the woman mumbled, directly meeting Nina's gaze for the first time. "For the water and … everything. Jacca's been afraid to touch me." The woman paused and cast her eyes downward. "Shamed though I am to admit it," she whispered, "the child terrifies me. I thought she would burn down the house with her and me in it."

Questions filled Nina's mind, too many to ask with a naked little girl waiting for her mother to bring clothes. Obliged to set aside her wider curiosity for the time being, to deal with matters immediately at hand, Nina muttered under her breath, "How long has this been going on?"

"A week, or a bit more," the woman whispered. "At first, it was only sparks at her fingertips. But then the sparks became flames. She burned herself and her clothes. She set fire to her hair." The woman raised her head, and in her brown eyes Nina saw despair. "When the curtains blazed up, I barely managed to beat out the fire before the whole house caught. That's when I brought her here. It's cool and damp in that cave."

Nina nodded. "I understand. Power in its raw state, uncontrolled and untrained, can be terrifying and overwhelming—both for the young adept and for the people who love her."

"Yes!" the woman exclaimed, forgetting to whisper. "Lady of the water, I love my child." She looked beseechingly into Nina's eyes. "That is why I must give her up. And you must take her. If Galen will not, I mean."

Nina started to reply that the girl's father must naturally be relied upon to do his duty.

But has he not neglected the child shamefully to this point, and perhaps even disowned her? countered her inner questioner. Nina was not certain that Jacca even knew her true parentage. Galen, upon arriving at the cave and calling to the frightened child within, had named himself "goldsmith," not "father." And then there was the girl's reference to Nina as "Master Galen's" sister.

"May I please get dressed now?" came Jacca's embarrassed little voice from the direction of the cave. "The water-lady's brother might return with her things."

"Quite right," Nina said, crisply speaking over her shoulder to the girl but keeping her gaze on Jacca's mother, and her thoughts on Galen's misconduct. "It's not very far from the goldsmith's house to this cave, is it. I'm sure he'll be back soon, and he'll bring my kit of medicines. Then I can put something cool and soothing on your blisters, Jacca. You're being very brave, but I know they must hurt."

"Yes, water-lady," Jacca mumbled. "They do hurt. I'm stupid to have burned myself like that."

Nina half whirled around, but caught herself before invading this shy girl's privacy.

"Never say that about yourself, Jacca," she snapped, tossing the reprimand sideways while thrusting her armload of clothes at the girl's mother. "You are not 'stupid.' You have a marvelous Gift—a power of magic. A power that no one has taught you how to control."

Another pause ensued while Jacca's mother took clothes to the girl, and while Jacca absorbed Nina's words. Then came the tentative little voice again: "Will you teach me, water-lady?"

"I will," Nina said. Vigorously she nodded so that the child would see. "And Master Galen will help me. You know, do you not, that the goldsmith has a power of fire much like your own?"

"He's so strong! I have seen him melt rocks," the girl replied, speaking this time at Nina's elbow.

She looked down to see Jacca dressed in a fresh tunic and short trousers. So plain were the clothes, many a girl would have disappeared within them, rendered invisible by such colorless attire. But on this child, the simple garments set off her startling green eyes and lustrous hair. One side of Jacca's head was singed. On the other side, though, her hair grew thick in rich shades of brown, copper-streaked in the sun.

Nina smiled at the girl. "Master Galen is a powerful summoner of fire. I am of the opposite element. I am, as you've styled me, a 'water lady.' When Galen and I were children together, he set fires and I raised floods." Nina grinned. "We drove our parents to distraction. So despairing were they of ever teaching us self-discipline, they handed us over to a master magician who had the trick of making us do right ... without seeming to 'make' us do anything." Nina turned her head to gaze northward.

"Looking back," she added with a click of her tongue, "I don't believe we ever figured out how our old tutor tamed us. But by the time he'd released us from our years of apprenticeship, we knew how to use our powers. More importantly, we knew when *not* to use them, and how to keep them in check."

"Teach me!" Jacca exclaimed. "I beg you, water-lady! Make me your apprentice."

Nina reached down to smooth the unburned side of the child's hair. "Already you are my pupil, Jacca: I have instructed you to never call yourself stupid. Beyond that," Nina added, "you must be apprenticed, and soon, to a master *wysard* who will take formal responsibility for your training. But that is not my choice to make. Your parents must decide on the terms of your apprenticeship. They will choose the master to whom you will go, and for how many years."

Had it been up to Jacca and her mother, Nina would have gained an apprentice then and there. Both clamored for her to take the child on.

She struggled to explain why she could not, finding it difficult to present reasonable arguments while skirting the central issue of parental approval. If Jacca did not know that she was Galen's daughter, then Nina couldn't come right out and say: "Child, it is to your father, Galen the goldsmith-*wysard* of the Ore Hills, to whom you should be apprenticed. But if he will not agree to that, then Galen and your mother must decide, together, what is to be done with you."

To Nina's relief, the entreaties of mother and child were interrupted by the return of the unacknowledged father. Galen came noisily up the path from his garden, being loud on purpose, Nina thought, to give warning to any girl or woman who wished not to be seen. Jacca's mother heard him, and took the hint to slip away. In her light-colored clothes, she flitted through the forest of pine trees like a pale wraith, heading off the trail and away from the cave.

Galen came into view a short way down the hillside, leading a donkey that was laden with all the sturdy beast could carry. *He means for me to camp up here*, Nina thought, scowling at the load of supplies Galen was bringing. *Don't I even get a tub bath or a decent bed after enduring the desert to see him?*

Such concerns seemed selfish, though, in the face of Jacca's far more serious discomforts. With scarcely a word of greeting for her brother, only a disapproving frown tossed his way, Nina grabbed her medicine kit off the donkey's back. She turned from Galen and busied herself salving Jacca's burns. To the girl's inflamed blisters, she applied lavender oil and the last dollop of the precious deadener that had seen Corlis through his ordeal of thorns and worms.

Rounding on her brother with the now empty jar, Nina snapped at him: "I need more of this. The name's on the label. Every apothecary and wisewoman will have heard of it, but not all will have it—not this far into the hinterlands, I wouldn't think. You may have to search." She narrowed her eyes at Galen in a way that meant: *Do not come back without it, brother. You owe me.*

Galen only nodded. He stuffed the jar in his pocket and wordlessly returned to making camp. The donkey had hauled canvas and poles for a tent, which Galen set up facing the cave. He left a cozily comfortable space between the cave's mouth and the tent's opening. Within that space, centered on the packed soil of the footpath, he built a fire-lay but did not light it. The sun was still up and the hillside too warm for a fire at present, although Nina did not doubt that a deep chill would descend upon these heights at dusk.

Lastly, Galen unloaded food enough for six. For their supper, he had brought roasted chicken, braisers of steamed vegetables, and a bag of fresh greens. Nina was nibbling the greens before he'd finished arranging the bounty around the cold fire. Her desert diet of jerky and beans had her craving the crisp salad, the crunchy raw radish, the peppery taste of watercress.

"This is good," she said, relenting in her exasperation with him. "Please thank your wife for me."

Galen let out a low grunt of denial. "I got this at the inn up the street from the stables. While the boys were loading it all on the donkey, I checked on your horse," he added. "That's a fine-looking roan."

"Traveller's his name," Nina said, warming as always to praise of her horse. "He made it across the badlands almost as well as those small white horses that seem bred for the desert. You know the ones I mean, that pale breed Corlis favors."

Galen nodded. "They were there, a few stalls away from your roan. Even those animals need a day or two to recover from the desert. Your horse must have the strength of a *savitar*, to have carried you through those canyons in summer."

From where he crouched at the cold fire, laying out plates and utensils alongside the pans of food, Galen glanced up at Nina. Even after so many years apart, she could read him as clearly as when they were children together. *You also must have a dragon's strength*, his glance said, *to have survived that journey. Or did you simply conjure water the whole way, and float across the desert?*

Nina smiled at him, resolving to keep her affairs secret until Galen made a clean breast of his own. "I had a good guide," was all she'd admit to, for now. "Corlis knows that desert like the back of his hand."

"Master Corlis is nice," interjected Jacca as she emerged from the tent, the interior of which she had been inspecting since Galen tied down its canvas. "He gave me blue feathers one time, from a pretty bird he caught in the desert."

How revealing, Nina thought, intrigued that the nomad who cultivated a public aura of tightlipped standoffishness would show kindness to a lonely child. For Nina was increasingly convinced that Jacca *was* alone. At sight of Galen, the girl's mother had dashed off without a word. And Jacca's father was pretending to be only the neighborly village goldsmith who had brought his sister the water-witch to help the girl in her time of trouble.

All of this must get sorted, and soon, Nina thought, but kept her determination to herself for this evening.

"I'm glad Master Corlis has been kind to you," she said, turning to the girl who now crouched beside her. Jacca was nearly eye level with the pans of food, studying them intently. "People say Corlis doesn't talk much," Nina added. "But he and I passed many an hour in ... conversation ... during our journey here."

Galen nearly popped his neck, so sharply did he glance at her from where he was laying out the meal. Both of his rust-colored eyebrows shot up, disappearing under the waves of hair that fell over his fore-head.

"'Tis true, brother," Nina said with a grin, falling so naturally into her old habit of teasing Galen, it seemed no time had passed since their childhoods. Except the secret she was teasing him about: *that* was of a more adult nature. "Corlis *can* talk. To be sure, he started off swearing, but he did end up speaking with me. And in a most gentlemanly and pleasing fashion, I might add."

Galen eyed her, his head atilt. Slowly, he nodded. "The man's only human, after all," he muttered, cryptically.

"May we eat now?" Jacca chimed in. "I'm hungry."

"So am I," Nina said. Resolutely she pushed Corlis from her mind as she settled cross-legged beside the girl. "The chicken will be fine as it is, cold. But I like my vegetables hot. Will you warm them for us, Jacca, with your finger-fires?"

"*Me?*" the girl cried, looking aghast. "Oh, lady! Please don't make me. I'm scared."

Nina put her arm around the girl's shoulders. "No one will make you do anything, child." She gave Jacca a reassuring squeeze. "There's nothing for you to be afraid of. I'm right here. I'll drench you, if need be.

"But I've got a better idea," she added, looking across at Galen. "Brother dear, I see you have brought us two teapots. That was well considered. With two, Jacca can have the tea she prefers, and I can drink my own favorite." *Or make the child a sleeping tonic,* Nina silently vowed, *if Jacca's nerves get away with her tonight.* "But Galen," she continued aloud, "before we heat water for tea, please fill the pots cold and bring them here. Set them on either side of Jacca, one at her left hand, the other at her right."

Galen caught on immediately, as Nina knew he would. From a cask of water his sturdy donkey had hauled up the trail, he filled the two pots and arranged them as requested. Then he returned to his side of the unlit fire and crouched there, his hands held casually in front of him, but ready for whatever might happen next.

"Now then, Jacca," Nina said, turning to the girl. "Please look upon this as a lesson. You did ask me to teach you, did you not?"

"Yes, water-lady," the girl replied in a small, nervous voice.

"That is good," Nina said, smiling at her. "As one of your teachers, I shall do my best to train you the way I was trained." She glanced across at Galen. "My brother may remember, as I do, that our old tutor insisted we practice our powers in small ways. He said an apprentice must learn to work small before we can confidently work big. Does that sound reasonable to you, Jacca?"

"Yes, water-lady," the girl repeated, still uneasy.

"Then that's all you need to do." Nina continued lightly hugging the child's shoulders. "Just reach out and make a very *little* fire, right at your fingertips. Touch the fire to the vegetables until they start to smell delicious. That will be your sign that you've heated them enough. When you're done with your fires, simply dip your fingers into the water pots. Will you give it a try, so that we may eat this fine supper Master Galen has brought us?"

For a moment, Jacca remained still as a stone. Slowly then, tentatively, the girl nodded. Her hands shook as she stretched them toward the vegetables. When tiny flickers of flame appeared at her fingertips, she gasped.

"Excellent!" exclaimed Nina and Galen with one voice. The smith was watching the proceedings as closely as Nina. But after that one word, Galen held his tongue, leaving further encouragement to the "water lady" who was arguably less qualified than he, to be teaching the child the magic of water's diametrically opposite element.

"Now touch the pans," Nina murmured, leaning close to Jacca's ear. "Touch them ever so lightly, and then don't move until we see how well they're heating."

The girl's bare and blistered arms were beginning to quiver—mostly from nerves, Nina thought, but partly from the strain of stretching. Nina started to reach out a hand, to pull the pans closer and relieve some of the tension in the child's muscles.

But then she recoiled, an involuntary reflex of self-preservation, as the flickers of fire at Jacca's fingertips exploded into roaring blowtorches. Flames hit the vegetable pans with the force of hammers, knocking their contents skyward and melting the iron from which the braisers had been fashioned.

Galen's reflexes proved quicker than Nina's. Before she had recovered sufficiently to summon a single drop of water, he'd killed the flames with a snap of his fingers. He had even acted in time to prevent the molten metal from splattering. The iron of the pans lay on the ground in neatly formed clumps, looking like the cast ingots that were the raw materials of the metalworker's art.

"Well done, Galen!" Nina exclaimed, or started to. But before anything else, she had to quiet the hysterical child who was sobbing into her shoulder.

"It's all right, Jacca," Nina said in her most soothing tones. "You did nothing wrong. Nobody got hurt. Master Galen will fix the pans. Dry your tears, child, and help me gather the vegetables. We only need to wash the dirt off, and they'll be fine to eat."

It took an extensive search. The force of Jacca's spellwork had blasted roots and tubers over the top of the tent and up into the rocks above the cave. Nina and Galen turned the quest for vegetables into a treasure hunt. Soon they were laughing as they had when they were children roughhousing together in hidden-thing hunts at home, roaming the grounds of the manor house in Ruain. Their merry high spirits infected Jacca. The child quit sobbing and joined gleefully in the search.

When they had enough for a meal, and their serving plates were piled high with recovered foodstuffs, Galen unobtrusively reheated the food with a quick, two-fingered wave. Small though his gesture was, Jacca caught it, impressing Nina with her ability to recognize a magical working.

"I saw that," the girl said. "How did you *do* it?" She held her hand over her plate. "Everything's warm now, but I don't understand how you can *do* it without making fire and burning things the way I do."

Galen looked thoughtful, then shrugged. "I'm not really sure how I do it, truth be told. I just think about what I want to happen ... and it happens. It's been that way since I was a child. Fire and flames, or just their heat without the blaze—when I want them, they come to me. Or they go where I wish them to go."

"Yes!" Nina exclaimed, studying first her brother, then Jacca. "It's the same with me, child. When I want water, I don't worry about *how* to summon it. I just know that I want it. I wish for it, and it comes."

Thank the ever-merciful Powers that I can truthfully say that again, Nina thought with a swift mental obeisance to the Elementals. She remained acutely aware that only within the past week had her gift for water-magic been restored to her.

"Perhaps Master Galen has answered your question without realizing it," Nina went on, speaking to Jacca. "The magic of summoning comes down to 'wanting.' Maybe you have been thinking too much about your fears, Jacca, when you would do better to concentrate on your wants."

Nina leaned back, rolling the idea around in her head. "That's your lesson for this evening, child. The next time the flames spring up at your fingertips, do not give in to fear. Think only of what you want to happen. Do you wish to heat your supper? Boil water? Kindle a campfire? Or do you only want the flames to die away? Whatever it is, focus on what you *want*. Direct your fire as you wish it to go. Does this make sense to you, girl? Will you try to make it so?"

Jacca was looking at her wide-eyed, as though startled by the concept that she might, herself, control her flare-ups through the simple expedient of *wanting*. Slowly, the child nodded. "Yes, water-lady. I will try."

Nina hugged her again. "That's all any of us can do. Now I suggest we taste this sumptuous repast that Master Galen has hauled up the hill for us. There's plenty here," she said, turning to her brother. "Will you stay and eat?"

Galen rubbed the back of his neck, looking rueful. "Nay, sister, I dare not. My wife was in a temper when last I saw her. I'd best go down to dinner with my lady." He paused, then added, "She and I must talk together, I believe."

Nina stifled a snort. There was nothing amusing about the situation, but still she couldn't help the grim little smile that touched her lips as she replied: "Yes, brother dear. I believe you and your wife have much to discuss."

Chapter Seventeen

J acca was too keyed up for sleep. After they'd washed and put away their supper dishes, and buried the picked-clean bones of the roasted chicken, the girl wanted to show Nina her "bedroom" in the cave. The sun was fully below the western hills now, turning the cave's mouth into a yawning pit of blackness. As she stood within it, Nina conjured a witchlight orb, summoning Ercil's fire with no conscious thought, only the wish to have it.

"Oh!" Jacca exclaimed. She took a step back, but then edged up so close that her nose nearly touched the orb. "I've seen Master Galen make lights like this. They're pretty! Can you teach me how?"

Nina nodded. "I expect so. It's not difficult magic. Though I have known of one legendary *wysard* who, for the longest time, could not get the hang of it." Nina smiled, remembering how Lady Carin had confessed to her, back in Ruain at their reunion, that she'd only recently mastered the trick. "Here, take it," Nina added, rolling the orb from her hand into Jacca's. "Feel how delicate it is. And how cool. It is a kind of fire, but it burns without heat."

"That's what I want," Jacca muttered. "If I must make fire, I want it to be cool."

"Remember what we talked about with Master Galen?" Nina asked as she called to her hand a second orb. "Keep foremost in your thoughts what you *want* instead of what you fear."

Jacca nodded, too absorbed in her study of the witchlight to offer any other reply. The girl led the way into the cave, which proved to be shallower than it appeared from the outside. Around a slight corner, they came to a room of sorts, a rocky chamber that had been fitted out for sleeping. On a ledge of stone was a straw pallet heaped with blankets. Along one wall sat a water barrel smaller than the cask Galen's donkey had hauled. A drinking cup waited atop the barrel, and scattered around were candles and an oil lamp. It seemed that Jacca's mother had tried to give the girl some basic comforts while hiding her away in this cold, dark cave.

Nina shivered. "It's freezing in here, Jacca. Grab your blankets and let's go to the tent. We'll sleep warmer under canvas."

Jacca hesitated. "But rock won't burn. What if I set fire to the tent?"

"You're forgetting, child," Nina said patiently. "Remember this evening's lesson: You're to think of your wants, not your fears. *I* will be sleeping in the tent, all cozy under fluffy blankets. You are very welcome, if you *want* to join me there."

Again came a pause, but then Jacca nodded. "Thank you, water-lady. I *want* to be warm, but to make only cold fire like this." The child gave the witchlight back to Nina. From the sleeping ledge, she scooped up an armload of blankets, and with them an object that resembled a four-legged pillow. Jacca followed Nina out of the cave.

In short order, they had their tent comfortably arranged. Galen had provided them with a finer tent than Nina had seen in all her travels. The roomy shelter had an oilcloth floor to keep out the dirt. Tucked into one corner were two bulky rolls of bedding, which opened out into sleeping pallets that were stuffed not with straw, but with feathers that fluffed up luxuriously when Nina gave the pallets two brisk shakes. The bedding even included cushions. For the first time in more weeks than she could count, Nina would not be pillowing her head on her saddlebags, though she'd brought them and her medical kit into the tent with her. Discreetly, pretending to unpack only such items as a hairbrush and a face towel, Nina set out burn ointment and fresh gauze, in case Jacca's fears overwhelmed her tonight.

The girl almost squealed with delight at the fluffiness of the feather pallets, but she rejected the included cushion in favor of her own. The pillow with legs that Jacca had brought from the cave was a stuffed toy shaped like a tortoise. The cloth plates of its "shell" were cleverly embroidered in shades of brown and tan mimicking nature's own designs. The high, domed shell made a comfy pillow for Jacca's singed head, but it was a stumpy front leg of the tortoise that the girl wanted Nina to see.

"The claws spread apart," Jacca said, demonstrating. "See? They open up wide, and down inside the leg it's hollow like a box. That's where I keep my favorite things."

From out of the hollow leg, the girl pulled three blue feathers—the kindhearted gift from Corlis, Nina surmised. What appeared next, however, was a treasure of far greater monetary value. Jacca hooked her finger deep in the soft box of embroidered fabric, and tugged into the witchlight a bracelet crafted of gold and silver, adorned with brilliant gemstones in fiery shades of red.

Drisha's bones! Nina started to swear. But mindful of the girl's tender years, she softened the oath to one that she'd used in her own girlhood. "Sweet mercy! How extraordinarily beautiful. What a lucky girl you are, to have such treasures." Nina intentionally used the plural, to include the feathers along with the gold and gems. For she would not disparage a gift that was given charitably by a man she esteemed.

Jacca touched a finger first to one, and then to the other of her riches. "Master Galen gave me the bracelet," she murmured, "and Master Corlis said I could wear the feathers in my hair." The girl sighed, then shook her head sadly. "But I daren't let my sisters see them. They'd take them from me. I have to keep them hidden in my turtle. You won't tell, will you, water-lady?" Jacca glanced up at Nina with sudden worry in her bright green eyes.

"I would never tell!" Nina vowed. "Your secret is safe with me."

"Thank you, water-lady," Jacca mumbled. "I knew I could trust you."

"You can. But what of your sisters? Are they not kind to you? How many do you have?"

"Two," Jacca replied, frowning. "They are older than me, and they order me around. If I find a pretty rock or even a pinecone in the forest, they steal it from me if I take it home."

"That's not nice of them," Nina muttered. "Does your mother know how they treat you?"

Jacca shook her head. "Mama would stop them if she knew. But I have to stay quiet, because if I say anything against my sisters, they go crying to our father. Then I'm in trouble."

Nina paused, needing a moment to curb the anger that was exploding in her heart. Galen had much to answer for. By failing to acknowledge this child as his daughter, he'd left the girl living in fear, surrounded by abusers in an abusive home.

"What kind of trouble comes to you?" Nina asked when she could trust herself to speak without displaying fury. "Does your ... uh, does your 'father' strike you?"

"No, he never hits me," Jacca said. "Mostly he ignores me." The girl shrugged. "But if my sisters complain about me, he sends me to sleep with the horses. I never mind that. The horses are warm, and the hay is soft." A gentle smile touched the child's lips. But then her eyes got wide, and she exclaimed: "How awful it would be, if I set the hay on fire and killed the horses! I must never sleep in their barn again."

"Tah, child!" Nina countered, sounding like her great-aunt Megella, the northern wisewoman who frequently voiced a similarly sharp note of exasperation. "It's your wants you must dwell on, not your fears. Don't be worrying about fire in the hay."

"Oh," Jacca muttered. "I keep forgetting." The child touched her bandaged arms. "It's just that my blisters are hurting again. They make me afraid of myself."

Nina studied the girl's sad little face and saw the fear in her eyes.

"I'm sorry I'm out of the medicine that dulls the pain," she murmured. "I hope my brother will soon find more." Nina lifted her medicine kit onto the soft pallet where she sat with Jacca. "I do have a painkiller you can drink. It's likely to make you very sleepy. If you down a cup of it, you won't wake up all night, and maybe not until midday tomorrow. By then, if Master Galen's search is successful, I may have more of the good jelly for your blisters." From her kit of herbal reme-dies, Nina withdrew the packet of soporific powder. "I'm afraid it doesn't taste very good, but maybe you'd like to try it."

"Yes, please!" Jacca exclaimed, her eyes shining in the witchlight that brightened their tent's interior. "I can't make fire when I'm sleeping. At least, I don't think I can." The child touched the singed half of her head, and frowned. "But maybe that's what happened to my hair. What if I fall asleep, and you fall asleep, and I set us both on fire?"

Swallowing another sharp *Tah*, Nina thumbed open the packet of painkiller. "That's one of those 'what ifs' that you shouldn't think about," she said. "Besides, child, I'm made of water. If I smell smoke in the night, I'll call up a wave and drench us both. Take your medicine now, and sleep soundly. We'll start fresh tomorrow. Together—you, me, and Master Galen—we will discover how to master your fears and bank your fires."

* * *

Jacca slept until noon and beyond, allowing Nina ample time for a private talk with the girl's mother. That woman—who gave her name as Taji—appeared at sunrise with a breakfast feast. She kindled the campfire that Galen had laid but not lit last night. With an economy of effort which spoke of long practice in preparing meals over an open fire, Taji soon had sausages sizzling, eggs frying, and bread toasting.

Nina expected the mouthwatering aromas to rouse Jacca from her drug-induced slumber. But the child slept on, unmoving except for the slow rise and fall of her chest as she breathed the cool air of dawn. Both women sat just outside the tent's opening, keeping watch, alert to signs of returning awareness as they broke bread together and talked about the child.

Other than a "Thank you for breakfast," Nina dispensed with civili-ties. She launched into her questions: Did Taji know that Jacca's sisters stole from her? Did she approve of her husband sending the child to sleep in the stable, when it was the other girls who had done wrong? And most pressing of all: Why was a young adept living with her mortal mother instead of being apprenticed to her magian father? What excuse could either parent offer, for having so neglected the child's wizardly training that Jacca was now burning her own flesh with her uncontrolled magian fires?

Taji answered every question that Nina put to her, but with such a paucity of words as would rival the reputation Corlis cultivated for flinty reticence. From what little the woman said, however, Nina learned that Taji had not told Galen of the daughter their liaison had produced, some eight years ago. Instead, the woman had chosen to pretend that the man to whom she was married had fathered her youngest child, as he had fathered the older girls in the family, as well as the couple's two sons.

But shortly after Jacca left the crib, Taji admitted, her husband Maynor began to ignore the little girl. He never spoke to Jacca except to reprimand her. He had never laid a hand on the child—Taji would have left him and taken Jacca with her, she claimed, had Maynor ever physically harmed the girl. Yet the woman had allowed the emotional abuse to continue—the neglect, the lack of fatherly affection, the mistreatment by her siblings.

"Surely Galen must have known!" Nina interjected. "All this time, he must have known. That child has his eyes. They are unmistakable."

Taji chewed her lip.

"It's her beautiful green eyes that gave me away," the woman muttered. "If Jacca had been brown-eyed like me—like my other children—Maynor might never have suspected. Even at this late date, for the sake of his honor and our four legitimate children, he might have chosen to go on pretending that Jacca was his." Taji shook her head. "But now the girl has fire at her fingertips. Drisha's mercy upon me! Jacca is showing the world who her father is." She drew a long breath and sighed it out. "I had hoped the girl would inherit nothing from Galen. I wanted a normal child, not a creature from the realm of wizards and their magic and their dreadful immortality."

We're not really immortal, Nina thought, picturing the long line of *wysards* who had lived and died, mostly in secrecy through all the centuries that predated this present age of the Power's restoration. *But perhaps she's not entirely wrong. There is something dreadful about outliving the mortals you love.*

"Your husband's reputation," Nina said, throwing off the muse and locking gazes with Taji. "That is your pitiful reason for hiding the truth from Jacca?"

The woman winced. But then she straightened her shoulders.

"I have protected Maynor as best I can," she said, her voice regaining the hard edge that Nina had earlier heard in it. "For his part, Galen has shielded his wife. Not until yesterday did Mistress Sheyla know—for a certainty—that Jacca is Galen's. Though obviously the woman might have guessed, as my husband did guess."

"As might anyone who ever glimpsed the child's eyes!" Nina exclaimed. "I don't doubt that every soul in the Ore Hills knows who Jacca really is. Only the child herself has been forced to suffer the consequences of the lie her parents tell, and the lie both of you live. Drisha's ballocks, woman!" Nina swore at Taji. "Jacca should have been apprenticed to Galen as a two-year-old, or certainly as soon as her gifts began to manifest."

"I told you," Taji snapped. "Jacca began setting fires only a few days ago. Before that, she was a perfectly ordinary child. Too quiet at times, which made it easy for Maynor to ignore her, and her sisters to tease her. But until the fires started, I had no reason to suspect that she had inherited Galen's 'gifts,' as you call them. I've another name for them. I did not want this curse to befall her—to ruin her life and my own."

"*Ruin* her life!" Nina exclaimed. "By the Powers, woman. That child now has a chance to become who she really is—to *know* who she is. Jacca will live under the shadow of her mother's lie no longer. By the oath of my House, I swear it: Jacca will be properly apprenticed to a master *wysard* who will train her in the ways and the lore of magic, according to the child's own gifts."

"That is all I ask of you, Lady of the Water," Taji murmured. "Do you not recall my words to you yesterday? Take the child, I said. Take her from these hills and make her your apprentice. Or deliver her into the hands of others like yourself, who can be to the girl what I never can."

Taji stood, knocking tea dregs from her mug. "I shall not return to this place," she said. "Nothing more will I bring you, and no further words will I speak to you ... or to Jacca. I renounce the child. She is warlock's spawn, and nothing to me."

"Another lie," Nina muttered, holding the woman's gaze. "You love that girl. She showed me the stuffed turtle you made her."

Taji's face crumpled. She burst out crying.

"How cruel you are!" the woman sobbed. "Yes, I love the child. I've loved her from the crib, and I'll love her till I die." Taji buried her face in her hands, weeping so hard and so loudly that the noise must wake Jacca, or so Nina thought. Yet the child slept on, oblivious to her mother's pain—and to the fact that Nina had just sworn, by the high and unbreakable oath of House Verek, to be the girl's guardian.

Nina reached out, wanting to take Taji into her arms and offer comfort. But the woman twisted away and darted aside into the forest. Just before she disappeared, becoming again a pale wraith vanishing amidst pine trees, Taji called back over her shoulder:

"I loved Galen, too. I want you to know that. I might still love him ... except that I can't grow old with him."

Then she was gone, away in the trees and not by the path, leaving Nina no certain way to track her down this unfamiliar hillside. But in any case, she had no reason to follow the woman. Taji had renounced the child. Jacca was Nina's now.

"Not mine alone," Nina muttered as she ducked into the tent to feel the pulse of the still-unconscious girl. "It's far past time that Galen acknowledged this magian daughter of his."

* * *

While she waited for Jacca to awaken and for Galen to bring the unguent that would ease the pain of the girl's burns, Nina wrote Legary a letter. In it, she devoted few words to her badlands crossing, saying only that she had made the journey safely, and that Corlis had comported himself well, both as a guide and a gentleman. She acknowledged her youngest brother's generosity in funding the trip, and conceded that he had been correct about the rigors of desert travel in summer heat.

After those preliminaries, Nina undertook her real reason for writing: she needed to make confession. She told Legary what she had never admitted during their long talks together in Granger. Nina described the loss of her powers, how she had been unable to summon even the tiniest wave after leaving Dalton's ship at Easthaven. She spoke of her confusion, her sense of diminishment, and the shame of being thought a great worker of water-magic when she could not conjure a drop. Nina thanked Legary for his warning about the dangers of dissipating the Power in acts of ego—as she had done while aboard Dalton's ship, conjuring waves simply to flaunt her strength.

Skipping over everything that Legary did not need to know, Nina gave him the gist of events at the dried-up lake, how Corlis had despaired to find no water, only damp sand under the trees of that previously infallible oasis. She told of prostrating herself before the Powers, pleading for the lives of Corlis and the horses. Whatever punishment the Powers might have decreed for Nina, however severe the penalty they levied upon her, she would willingly have accepted, if only mercy might be shown to the mortal man and the four loyal animals who had done nothing to earn the disfavor of the Elementals.

"In that moment," Nina wrote, "I saw a river of water under the sand. As magic rose in my blood—a fresh new gift of the Power—I reached deep for that water. Within it, I found a magic greater than any I have known before: Grog came swimming up that river, his form like a great whale. He lunged from the depths and glided to me. For a few moments, only long enough to receive my welcome and my thanks, Grog left the underworld. He swam with me in the new lake that flooded the desert—its pristine waters a promise of life for all who congregated in the sand, whether mortal, mage, or beast."

Nina paused, remembering her delight at Grog's arrival, and the overwhelming feeling of gratitude that had engulfed her as fresh cold water flowed into the lake basin. In that moment she felt reborn, remade: reaccepted into the society of *wysards*.

Again putting pen to paper, Nina went on.

"I do not say that Grog is an Elemental," she wrote, "but I have come to think that he may be a messenger of the Powers, their representative ... or even, in a way, their embodiment. Is he not a creature of water, air, rock, and fire? When he reached me in the lake he was no longer a leviathan, but arose from the depths as a great salamander—a creature that breathes air, loves water, and burrows in the ground. Before that, at the chasm outside Winfield, I saw him become a man of stone and jump into the burning abyss, embracing that fiery underworld as his home."

Nina paused once more, her pen hovering over the letter as she ran through her memories of Grog.

"In the desert," she continued then, "he seemed to serve the Powers as their intermediary. When I begged the Elementals for mercy, when I asked for a bounty of water to refill the lakebed, it was Grog who came. Whether he *brought* the water to me, or 'merely' swam in upon that life-giving flood, I cannot know. But I feel that he is looking out for me. Perhaps all the years that I spent across the void estranged me, for a time, from the Powers of this world. Perhaps Grog has made himself my intercessor, acting on my behalf, pleading my case with the Elementals. I do not know.

"I write these things to you, Honored Brother," Nina concluded, "because I have shared my thoughts about Grog with no other living person. Not even the merchant Nimrod knows all that I have seen, felt, or surmised about his former bodyguard."

Again Nina's pen grew still. She tapped it on the paper as she considered whether to tell Legary that she had asked the Elementals to restore to him his own former powers—Legary's once-legendary command of stone, rock, and boulder. Her instincts argued against any mention of her entreaties on his behalf. She would not want to raise his hopes, in case the Elementals chose not to restore his gifts as fully as Nina's own had been renewed at the desert lake.

Perhaps I can do no more for Legary, she thought as she put her pen aside and rolled the finished letter. *Galen's daughter, however, begins her wizardly journey with a clean slate. I must teach Jacca the lesson that every child of House Verek has learned for millennia—the lesson in humility that only a few of us have ever forgotten.*

In a whisper, Nina repeated the words like a catechism: "The Power belongs to the Elementals." To abuse it was wizardly arrogance ... such arrogance as goes before a fall.

That was the great lesson she would instill in Jacca, in every fiber of the girl's being.

"I'm hungry," came a drowsy little voice from the tent. "May I have a crust of bread?"

"You'll have all the bread you want, child." Nina smiled at the tousled head that appeared in the tent's opening. "There's cheese, too. And sausages. Wash your face and hands, then help me heat things up."

Jacca stumbled to her feet and headed for the water cask that Galen had set under trees at the edge of their campsite. A brisk scrubbing with the barrel's cold contents enlivened the girl. She returned to the cooking fire looking more awake.

"That was a wonderfully long sleep you had," Nina commented as she sliced bread. "How do you feel?"

Jacca crouched above the pan of cold sausage and took a moment to consider her answer, her head atilt as though in puzzlement. "I feel different," she finally said. "Like I'm happy inside. And I'm brave, in here." She laid her hand over her heart.

"How excellent!" Nina exclaimed, beaming approval at the girl. "A braveheart must have double sausages. Heat up that pan, won't you, while I make tea."

Nina expected the child to recoil at the idea of pan-warming. But Jacca gave the sausages a moment of fixed study, then looked across at Nina.

"Will you give me a ball of cool light, water-lady?" the girl asked. "I think I need it."

But not for illumination, Nina thought as she conjured Ercil's fire in the full light of midday. She passed the orb to Jacca, and wondered: *What are you planning, child?*

The girl held the witchlight in both hands, staring into it as if the orb were a crystal ball that could tell the future. Gently then, Jacca released the orb, leaving it to hang in midair in front of her eyes.

How did you know it would float there? Nina wondered. *Did you simply wish for it to do so? You're a clever one, little niece.*

Nina watched intently as the girl stretched her hands toward the pan of cold meat. From Jacca's fingertips, flames sprouted—compact fires like the glow of candle wicks.

Over the soft fizzing of the flames, Nina became aware of Galen stomping up the hillside. As before, he made much unnecessary noise, announcing his approach to this enclave of females.

Slowly, without shifting her gaze from Jacca's ten flickering fires, Nina raised her hand, signaling Galen to stop where he was. She hid her movements from Jacca to avoid breaking the girl's concentration. With her hand poised above the child's head, however, Nina was ready to summon water in case the fire-magic of this young adept exploded as it had yesterday, white-hot and able to melt iron.

But the girl's small flames did not burst their bounds. Jacca touched them to the pan, and the congealed grease began to drip. The sausages sizzled and filled the air with the promise of a delicious late breakfast for the girl, with a second helping for Nina.

Having accomplished the heating without incident, Jacca pulled back, withdrawing her hands but not extinguishing the fires at her fingertips. The flames continued to flicker brightly as she held her hands in front of her, one to either side of the suspended orb of witchlight.

"Oh!" the girl exclaimed. "I meant to get water first. I forgot."

"Here you go," said Galen as he came up from where he had halted at Nina's signal. He plunked a pot of water down beside Jacca. "Cool your digits in there."

The girl plunged first one hand, then the other. Her fires hissed as she doused them, and steam rose to touch the witchlight. The orb went out, leaving no trace of itself.

"Oh no!" Jacca cried, staring with wide-eyed startlement at the now empty air. "I didn't mean to hurt the pretty light."

"You didn't hurt it," Nina said. As she lowered her hand behind the girl's back, she smiled reassurance at Jacca. "It will return whenever you need it. But tell us, for I'm sure Master Galen is as curious as I am: What did you need the light *for*? There's plenty of sun today."

Jacca shook her head. "It wasn't for seeing. It was for cooling. I asked the cool light to make my fires be not so hot."

Over the girl's head, Nina locked gazes with Galen. *Is he thinking what I am?* she wondered. *Is Jacca's fire-magic too hot to handle unless she first ices it down?*

"I think you might have a rival in the art of ore-smelting," Nina muttered.

Galen arched an eyebrow at her. Then he grinned, but said nothing.

Nina's comment made no impression on Jacca. "This is good," the girl mumbled around a mouthful of reheated sausage. "May I have the bread now, please?"

The girl ate with a good appetite after her long sleep and her brief but intense session of magic-making. While Jacca filled up on foodstuffs that were left over from last night's supper and today's breakfast, Galen unloaded fresh supplies from the donkey he had again led up the hillside. From a woven bag, he delivered to Nina a full jar of the pain-numbing jelly she had ordered him to find. He also gave her the story of its procurement.

"Nobody in the village had it," he said. "But the old apothecary sent me to an even more ancient woman who lives down in a canyon at the desert's edge. The old lady charged me a fortune for that little jar," Galen complained as he nodded at the container Nina held. "But she said she would give half the money back, and throw in a second jar for free, if I could tell her how to kill sandfly maggots before they killed a horse—or a man.

"It seems Corlis had more to say, this trip, than he usually does when he drifts through here," Galen added. "He's spread it around that sandflies are swarming in the desert. He claimed he picked up a few maggots but managed to dig them out before they poisoned him. The old lady said that was unlikely. But she was willing to pay, and pay well, if I could shed any light on his story."

Nina pursed her lips. "Your ancient herbalist is right to be skeptical," she muttered. "I saw no evidence of sandflies 'swarming' out there. But Corlis did pick up an infestation of the maggots—and he was not the one who dug them out. It was I who sliced him open and scooped a potful of worms out of his back and his rump."

Galen looked at her slack-jawed. "How in the name of ever-loving mercy did he come by them? I thought those pests were vanishingly rare, like the plagues of antiquity."

Nina shrugged. "If they are seldom seen now, it might mean they're active only in the hottest months, when people generally avoid the desert. I know only that Corlis fell backward into a thicket of thorns, and I had to yank the thorns out of him. In some of those spikes, I noticed tiny holes. My guess is that sandflies laid their eggs in the holes, and that's how Corlis got them, from the thorns that pierced him. In his flesh, those eggs hatched, and worms grew. The man was in bad shape by the time he finally let me take a knife to him and cut open the swollen nests of maggots that covered his back."

"Drisha!" Galen exclaimed. He gestured at Nina's pen still lying on her stack of letter paper. "Write this down and I'll take it to the old lady. Write it out twice, if you would, for the apothecary to have a copy. If we do get sandflies swarming out of the desert and into these hills, folks will need the remedy. The old stories contend that the maggots, once they're under your skin, are always fatal."

"An exaggeration," Nina muttered as she reached for her pen. "To dig them out, all one needs is a sharp knife and a strong stomach. But your local healers might wish to know what I used on the wounds to relieve pain and ward off infection. I will put down everything I did for Corlis."

Without going into intimate details or naming names, Nina thought as she settled under a shady tree and began listing the treatments and medicines she had applied. *No others need to know the story of the man's worm-infested backside. I must make Galen swear that he will not embarrass Corlis by bandying it about.*

Galen, however, had moved off and was helping Jacca clear away the pans and dishes of her late-day breakfast. Nina, as she wrote, kept an ear on them. The pair of fire-makers were soon practicing their art together, using pots of water as targets, but reserving two pans for Jacca to dip her hands. The girl seemed increasingly confident about summoning flames to her fingertips. She couldn't yet extinguish her fires without quenching them and raising steam, but she was not flapping her hands in panic, spreading fire everywhere as she had been only yesterday.

The child is a quick study, Nina thought as she paused her writing to watch Jacca bring a pot of water to a boil. The girl's technique involved a levitating orb of witchlight, same as for the sausages. The orb floated between Jacca's outstretched hands, evidently chilling the young adept's magic to temperatures the child could control.

"Make a fresh pot of tea with that, won't you?" Nina called across to where Jacca crouched beside Galen, both of them intent on the girl's spellwork.

"Drisha's bones!" Galen exclaimed as the pot went flying. It streaked over the ground and slammed into a tree opposite. Boiling water splashed high, wilting every leaf it touched.

"I'm sorry!" Nina and Jacca cried together.

The girl plunged her fiery hands into her pots of quench-water. "I didn't mean to do that," Jacca mumbled, looking crestfallen at this latest miscarriage of her magic.

"Nor did I!" Nina exclaimed as she sprang to her feet. "That was my fault, child, and none of yours. I distracted you. For my carelessness, I beg your pardon."

Jacca gazed at Nina with wide, startled eyes, making her wonder if this was the first time any adult had ever apologized to the child.

If it's the first time, it won't be the last, Nina thought, reaching to wrap her arms around Jacca. *I will not rest until I hear your father apologize for lying to you all these years.*

"I'm hot, water-lady," Jacca mumbled, extricating herself from Nina's embrace. "I want to go in my cave now. It's so cool in there, and Mama said I should always go in the cave when I get too hot."

At this mention of the girl's mother, Nina hesitated, wondering if she should tell Jacca that Taji had come while the child slept. But she elected to be silent on the subject of that absent woman. If Taji held to her promise to never return to this place, then it seemed possible that Jacca would not see her mother again.

"The cave's a good idea, child," Nina said. She stepped back and waved Jacca into her retreat. "While you cool off, Master Galen and I will sort through what he's brought us. We've got too much of some things, and not enough of others."

The cataloging of supplies gave Nina a chance to tell Galen about Taji's sunrise visit, and how the woman had renounced Jacca. Nina admitted that in the heat of the moment, in her anger at Taji, she had made herself the girl's guardian, rather foolishly swearing to it by the high oath of House Verek.

"But I am guardian only," Nina insisted, catching Galen's arm. "I did not take the girl for my apprentice. You *must* claim her, both as her father and as her teacher."

Galen shook his head. He looked miserable and ashamed, but also resolute as he laid his hand atop Nina's where she held his arm. "Honored Sister, I cannot," he muttered. "Any open admission that Jacca is my daughter would upend families and ruin lives. I fear Taji's husband would cast her from their home, leaving four children motherless and herself adrift."

Nina sniffed. "Taji was your mistress once. Why not again? Drisha knows you're wealthy enough to keep a woman on the side. What's to stop you building her a villa in the hills above your lodge?"

"What's to stop me? Sheyla," Galen replied, emphatically.

"Who? What?" Nina asked, momentarily confused. Then she remembered. "Oh, your wife. Are you *that* afraid of her?"

She'd said it half in jest. But Galen frowned and stepped back. He pulled his arm from Nina's grasp.

"My wife is a lady who deserves your respect, and my own," he snapped. "Years ago, I dishonored my marriage vows. I lay with another woman. But I swear to you, sister: Until Taji came to me yesterday and told me that Jacca was the child of our dalliance, I did not know it."

"You *must* have known!" Nina flared at him. "Who else around here could have given Jacca her big green eyes?"

Galen sighed. He rubbed the back of his neck as if to ease a sprain.

"What I may have suspected has no bearing on the matter," he muttered, sounding defensive. "I did not *know*. Taji chose silence and secrecy. Her silence ended only yesterday when she appeared at my home." Galen shot Nina an imploring look. "As the Powers would have it, Taji arrived at my back gate bare moments before the solution to the problem came knocking on my front door—in the form of my dearest noble sister, legendary conjurer of waves and goddess of distant seas."

"Tah!" Nina snapped, the old familiar note of exasperation leaping forth. "Brother, I ought to punch you for that. Jacca is *not* a problem." She glowered at him. "And don't be thinking that you will evade your responsibilities by dumping them on me. Jacca is *your* daughter, and she has inherited *your* gifts. It falls to you and to no one else, to train her."

"I cannot," Galen repeated, scowling fiercely. He planted both feet and folded his arms. "Now that Jacca's powers have manifested in unmistakable fashion, she *cannot* remain in the Ore Hills, where people know her only as an ordinary child—Maynor's youngest girl. You must take her from here, Nina, and you must do it quickly."

When Nina made no reply, only set her own feet and put her hands on her hips, Galen twisted away. He raised one hand to scratch his chin, then his ear.

He was still scratching when he turned back to her. "Now is the right time for you to leave," he said, a touch of desperation in his tone. "Taji has packed off her other daughters on their summer visit to their grandmother. That old widow lives to the north, up in the mountains where it stays cooler. Maynor and the boys are away hunting wild boar. There's no knowing how long they will be gone. But," Galen added, trying and failing to stare Nina down, "I can lead you from these hills by a path seldom traveled. You and Jacca can be on your way as early as tomorrow—with none here the wiser."

Nina kicked him. Just as if they were seven and six again, she took a quick step and booted Galen hard on his shin.

"Ow!" he cried, hopping on one leg. "That hurt."

"Good," she snapped, a decided note of warning in her voice. "Know this, little brother: I will hurt you far worse if you *ever* again suggest that the eldest daughter of House Verek should go slinking out of town like a beaten thief. And dragging my niece with me like so much baggage. How dare you!"

Nina was furious, angrier than she would have thought possible at this favorite brother, the boy she'd grown up with. In this moment, it was as though she didn't know Galen. She gulped deep breaths, fighting off the urge to make good on her threat. She had crossed a desert, enduring heat, thirst, hunger and exhaustion to reunite with him. Now he wanted only to be rid of her, barely a day after clapping eyes on her and seeing the woman she was, instead of the little girl he remembered.

"Lady Karenina," Galen mumbled, looking contrite and appropriately alarmed, "I beg your pardon—"

She cut him off with a gesture of dismissal.

"Be assured," Nina growled, leveling her gaze at him, "I will leave these hills when I am ready, and not a moment before. My horse requires rest. The journey here was difficult for him, and for me. He must have time to recover, and he needs reshoeing. The grit of those desert sands wears down iron in a most shocking manner. If you do not wish me to present myself at the stables, to personally attend to the matter, then you must see to it. You are to hire the best farrier. My horse is a valuable animal. If, upon reclaiming him, I perceive that he has been in any way neglected or mistreated, you shall answer for it. Do you understand me?"

"Yes, Honored Sister," Galen mumbled, and gave Nina a half bow, his manner as serious as hers. "How else may I serve you?"

"You may start by taking my filthy clothes to be washed. I trust there's a laundress hereabouts?"

Again he nodded to her, but Nina gave him no chance to say more. From atop the supplies they were meant to be sorting but had neglected in favor of arguing, she grabbed a canvas bag and upended it, dumping its contents on the ground.

"Tea," she muttered as she crouched to rummage in the heap. "Acceptable, I suppose, though not my favorite. But honestly, Galen." She scowled up at him. "*Lye* soap? You expect me to use lye soap on a burned child? I might as well blister her anew." She threw the bar at him, so hard that he grimaced when he caught it. "Bring me elderflower. If none can be found, then get from the apothecary his most gentle soap."

Nina went on digging through the supplies, criticizing most, rejecting some, and demanding items that might prove difficult for Galen to obtain, if he meant to keep her presence secret.

"Besides getting my old clothes scrubbed, I need new ones." She stood and held out her arms in the faint hope that Galen could accurately judge her size. "I lugged few garments with me through the badlands, for I expected to avail myself of tailors and dressmakers here in your hills." Nina scowled at her brother. "If I am to have no recourse to those, I require that you supply their lack. Additionally," she concluded, "I want a hot bath. Find a suitable tub and haul it here."

"I know the best place to bathe," interjected the voice of Jacca.

Galen jerked around, so startled that he dropped the soap. Nina whirled, nearly losing her balance, tripping over the piled supplies.

Jacca stood only feet away. She was with Galen's donkey, scratching behind the animal's ears as it drowsed in deep shade alongside the downhill path.

"Child!" Nina exclaimed, trying to smile through her flush of agitation. How much had the girl heard? "You gave me a turn. I didn't see you there."

Jacca shuffled her feet, looking uncomfortable as she twisted a strand of her unburnt hair around one finger. Evidently she'd heard enough to trouble her.

"I fell asleep in the cave," the girl mumbled. "I woke up freezing, and heard voices. They sounded ... angry." Jacca glanced from Nina to Galen, then dropped her gaze. "I hope you're not mad at me."

"Not in the least, child!" Nina rushed to hug the girl. "I'm sorry if Master Galen and I scared you. But Jacca, you have brothers, same as me. You know what they're like, how awful they can be sometimes." Over the top of Jacca's head, Nina withered Galen with a look. "My brother and I were having a little spat, the way brothers and sisters do. It's nothing serious, and nothing for you to worry about. Everything will soon be just as it should."

"When you've had a bath?" Jacca asked, looking up from within Nina's embrace.

Nina laughed. "A steaming bath sets all to rights. But it feels like ages since I've had a long soak in a heated tub."

Jacca wriggled free and took Nina's hand. "I know where there's plenty of hot water. It comes out of the ground. I won't even need to warm it up for you."

"Oh, that's right," Galen exclaimed. "I haven't been up there in years, but I know what Jacca is talking about. There's a hot spring not a mile from this cave." He grinned at Nina, a little hesitantly as if he wasn't sure grinning was allowed. Her temper had awed him. "Let Jacca take you there," he suggested, "and see what you think of the place. If it won't do, I'll haul up a tub."

She grinned back, her anger on the ebb. "A hot spring sounds delightful. We'll go straight there after I've sacked up my dirty clothes for the laundress. Galen, while you're waiting to collect my things," she added, "load those up." She gestured at the ingots of metal which were all that remained of yesterday's hapless vegetable pans. "They're in the way. I stubbed my toe on them this morning."

Galen sprang to the task as if eager for the solace of metal, the material of his art and his livelihood. In metal, he took refuge from his troubles with women: Sheyla, Taji, Nina, Jacca.

Nina shook her head as she ducked inside the tent to pull grimy garments from her bags. She was remembering her talk with Dalton, months ago in Easthaven, when she had cautioned him against father-ing an out-of-wedlock child that he wasn't prepared to properly apprentice, should that child possess the Gift. She never would have anticipated that it would be diligent Galen, not the philandering "Captain Damon," who turned out to be the irresponsible one.

In privacy in the tent, Nina shed her clothes down to her underthings. Galen's obsession with secrecy, his desire to keep her and Jacca out of the public view, assured Nina that this cave and the surrounding pine forest were off the beaten track. The path up here from Galen's back gate suggested this place might be his private property. If he thought his sister and daughter were well hidden here, then Nina had no reservations about stripping to her smallclothes. They had plenty of blankets to ward off evening's chill, and by day a brilliant sun baked this hillside. The heat of these summer days practically begged that limbs be bared. Nina peeled off nearly everything, bundled her stained and ragged garments, and pushed the bundle through the tent's opening, calling to Galen to collect it.

"Get those notes I wrote, too," she shouted at him. "For the herbalist and your apothecary. See them under the tree?"

It took some time for Galen to load the ingots, sack up the supplies that Nina had rejected, and pack those onto the donkey along with her untidy wad of clothes. It seemed the beast had turned uncooperative. From inside the tent, she heard Galen's muffled curses and the stomping of his feet and the donkey's. At last, however, all grew quiet except for the twittering of birds in the pines.

Nina stuck her head out.

"All clear?" she asked the girl who stood guard outside.

"He's gone," Jacca said, grinning at her. "Let's go."

Chapter Eighteen

The hot spring was more than Nina could have wished for. It bubbled up in a circular pool that was deep enough for diving. It also had ledges comfortably spaced for sitting as the warm waters gurgled around them. Jacca was shy at first, about undressing in front of Nina. But seeing the "water lady" dive in gleefully and then surface with her underclothes clinging to every contour and curve, Jacca cast aside girlish modesty and stripped to her skin.

The girl proved to be a surprisingly strong swimmer for a child born in a region where waterholes like this must be scarce. To Nina's gentle inquiries, Jacca replied that she had often swum in this hot spring and had done so quite recently, but only with her mother, never her siblings. Those four had no knowledge of this place.

Taji is free to come here, Nina surmised, *but she may bring only the child of her lover.* The thought deepened Nina's suspicion that all the land surrounding the spring and the cave was Galen's private holding, and none would be admitted here except by his express permission. If Taji had that permission, then perhaps her liaison with Galen did not lie as far in the past as both of them would have Nina believe.

The next morning brought further evidence of a continuing connection between the two. Nina awoke before dawn, to find three sets of new clothes laid out on the rocks near the cave's mouth. She donned baggy trousers that were cut to the pattern of the local costume, and pulled on a soft tunic embroidered with colorful flowers.

That Taji had gifted her the garments, and had come during the night in defiance of the woman's pledge to stay away, was confirmed when Jacca woke and declared: "My mama made those. Nobody else sews flowers like she does. Aren't they pretty?"

"They're beautiful," Nina murmured. With her fingertip, she traced the delicate needlework. "As soon as we've breakfasted, I will write your mother a note of thanks."

The meal became an hour of fire-practice for Jacca. The child heated pans of eggs and sausages, and tried to toast bread. Even with a cool orb of witchlight tempering her fires, however, her magic proved too hot for that task. The bread burnt black.

"No matter," Nina said as she sliced a new loaf and made toast in the conventional way. "You're making wonderful progress. Any master *wysard* of this world would be proud to have you for an apprentice. Why don't we leave off with fire-magic for a while now, and try your hand at conjuring witchlight?"

This suggestion so enthused the girl, Jacca and Nina stayed at it past midday, until they were interrupted by the noisy arrival of Galen and his donkey. Galen had succeeded in his assigned tasks, to an extent beyond Nina's most hopeful expectations. He brought soaps in half a dozen luscious scents, her favorite elderflower among them. Nina's old clothes came back not only scrubbed clean, but neatly mended and crisply pressed. With them was a new set, cut and sewn like the pocketed trousers and the airy shirt she had worn for much of her ride across the desert.

Galen also brought news of her horse. "Traveller will be reshod today," he reported, "by the same farrier that Corlis employed for his horses before he left for the southern mountains. The animal eats well and is filling out nicely. The stablehands give him light exercise daily. Your horse will be ready when you are."

Nina turned her head aside, hiding the sudden dampness of her eyes. She put it down to relief over her beloved Trav, but it was Corlis she asked after.

"He's gone already?" she murmured, looking back at Galen. "Corlis, I mean. I had hoped to give the man a letter," she hastened to explain, "to take to Legary. I want our brother to know that I reached you safely."

Galen grinned in a way that made Nina want to smack him.

"Your man rode out after only a day's rest," he said, studying her. "Before he left, however, Corlis spent a good fortune in my shop. I've got the shrewdest woman in the Ore Hills working my front counter. That lady drives a harder bargain than I do when people come in to buy and sell. She told me Corlis cleaned me out of small, packable jewelry. He walked out the door loaded with silver brooches, copper bracelets, gold necklaces." Galen clicked his tongue, a sound of satisfaction. "He took a bagful of my blades, too, everything from surgeon's scalpels to hunting knives. My shopkeeper said he didn't haggle. He never said a word, just paid what she asked, bagged it up, and left."

"Where will he go to sell it? Not east to the coast?" Nina asked, avoiding any mention that the fortune Corlis had dropped into Galen's pocket came straight out of Legary's. She could not doubt that the nomad's generous fee for taking her across the desert had funded the man's spending spree in Galen's shop.

Galen shook his head. "The lands southward from here, away down the spine of the mountains, are rumored to throng with warlords and tribes of folk that we would regard as only half-civilized. The rumors are enough to keep most people well clear. But I've heard that Corlis has made inroads there. He goes down from time to time, to sell weapons to the warlords and jewelry to the tribes." Galen shrugged. "Maybe they like that he doesn't talk. His habitual silence might be what preserves him there. All I know is that the man disappears southward for a year or more. Eventually, he returns to these hills, loaded down with pure nuggets of precious metals." Galen smiled. "That's how the warlords pay him. I buy those nuggets from him and turn them into treasures that fetch a king's ransom."

"What a fine arrangement the two of you have," Nina replied, only half listening as she pondered the problem of getting her letter into Legary's hands. "But is there no one else who may travel east from here when the cooler months make a desert crossing easier?"

Galen eyed her. "After the way Corlis broke his customary silence to warn the whole village that sandflies are swarming out there, I doubt anyone from here will dare to set foot in those Drisha-damned canyonlands. If they are ever crossed again from *this* side, I expect it'll be by Corlis himself ... and that won't be for a year or more."

He lied about sandflies and worms to keep people away from our lake, Nina thought. *That oasis is only four days' ride from these hills. Corlis raised the specter of killer maggots because he didn't want anyone venturing into that hallowed, magical, private place.*

Her suppositions about the man's motives filled Nina with a strange mix of joy steeped in sorrow.

"By the way," Galen said, jolting her back to their conversation. "The old herbalist thanks you cordially for the list you wrote out, about maggot treatments. In return, she sends you all of this."

He untied a sack from the donkey's load and handed it to Nina. She found within it a plethora of remedies, everything from stomach powders to gels for cooling brain fevers.

"By the Powers!" Nina swore as she sifted through the bottles and bags, opening some to breathe the fragrances of exotic preparations she had read about but never before seen. "Your herbalist has mastered her craft. How I would love to sit and speak with her." Before Galen could do more than frown at the idea of Nina leaving her hiding place, she added: "I trust the lady is training an apprentice? What a tragedy it would be, to let the inevitable passing of an old woman deprive this world of the vast knowledge she possesses."

"She did have a girl with her when I delivered your note," Galen said. He looked relieved that Nina had not pressed for a personal visit with the herbalist. "But I shall make inquiries and search out a suitable candidate for her, if the woman hasn't one already."

Wordlessly, Nina nodded. She had her nose in a jar of pungent insect repellant, and her eye on Jacca. While the "water lady" stood speaking with Galen, the fiery girl had busied herself preparing a late luncheon for the three of them. Jacca now beckoned them over, declaring the meal ready to eat.

And mostly it was. Though one dish was blackened and another underdone, the main course of vegetable soup drew praise from Jacca's guests. Galen partook of it with such grateful enthusiasm, Nina suspected he wasn't getting home-cooked meals these days. Evidently Sheyla remained angry with her cheating husband.

After the meal, Galen picked up where Nina had left off, in attempting to teach the young adept how to summon witchlight.

"The difficulty," Nina explained to him, "lies in the flame that invariably springs to Jacca's palm, when what she wishes to conjure is the flameless light of Ercil's fire." Nina raised her two hands palms up, in a shrug communicating helplessness. "The tenacity of the flame defeats me, brother. I believe only a fire-master such as yourself may puzzle out a way to tamp it down."

Galen shot her a look that said he read the deeper message behind her "helplessness": Only a master of fire, Nina was saying, should be in charge of training a fire-summoning novice. He sighed, but then with a smile he turned to Jacca and began to talk her through the uncomplicated magic of the witchlight orbs she loved.

While they worked together, Nina propped against her favorite tree and penned her notes of thanks: one to the herbalist for the wealth of remedies, and a brief message for Jacca's mother, acknowledging receipt of the clothes and praising Taji's needlework. Nina lingered over that second note, wanting to tell Taji how far Jacca had already progressed in her magic in just these two days, but held back by a suspicion that the woman would not wish to know.

I wanted a normal child, Taji had said, *not a creature of magic.*

The memory of those angry words brought Nina's note-writing to a sharp end. She made no mention of Jacca.

You renounced the child, Nina silently addressed the girl's mother, projecting disapproval downhill in the direction she had seen Taji run. *Let it be so. She is yours no longer.*

"Look!" came Jacca's excited cry, breaking into Nina's thoughts.

"You did it!" shouted Galen in the same instant. "Full marks for you. That's a perfectly proper orb of witchlight you've got there."

Nina turned her head to see Jacca dancing circles around the tent. The girl brimmed with happiness as she tossed an orb of Ercil's fire from one hand to the other. Nina expected the orb to shatter into sparks, so boisterously did Jacca play with it. The light continued to shine, however, through the girl's fingers. Then it gleamed in midair, floating in front of her when Jacca settled down to attempt the next step in her training. Galen wanted her to try heating water without touching the kettle with her finger-fires.

"Like this," he said, demonstrating. One snap of his fingers brought the water to a rolling boil.

"Let me have that for a pot of tea," Nina called as she rose to her feet. At the water barrel, she filled a smaller pan. "Here's a fresh target for you." She set the cold pan on the ground and picked up the steaming kettle by its wooden handle. "Excellent work, Jacca." Nina paused to smooth the unburned side of the girl's hair. "Now you can conjure witchlight for yourself anytime you want it. I'm proud of you, child."

Jacca looked up with shining eyes. "Thank you, water-lady," the girl said brightly. "It's not your fault you couldn't teach me how to do it. Master Galen just sees my fire somehow, and he knows what I'm doing wrong."

"That's because he's got fire inside too," Nina hastened to reply. "The same way you do." She glanced at Galen over the girl's head, and saw a curious mixture of pride and despair in his eyes.

He is starting to understand, Nina thought. *He's realizing that he cannot pawn this child off on a worker of water magic. Jacca needs him to teach her who she* is.

"Don't let me interrupt your practice," Nina added. She moved off to brew her tea. "Let's see what you can do with fire that's invisible, with the heat of it alone and no flickering flame."

This next level of spellcraft did not come as easily to the girl as witchlight had. For the rest of the afternoon, Galen coaxed and Jacca sweated. The child dripped perspiration as she attempted to "snap" heat into the cold pan. It was as if her fires blazed up under her skin, demanding to become visible while she fought to project only their heat and none of their light.

The two of them might have continued the struggle past sundown, had Nina not intervened.

"That's enough for today," she said, stooping to reclaim the untouched pan of water. "Jacca, you're dripping wet. Let's get you toweled off. I wouldn't want you in your cave, soaked like you are. But when you're dry and you've changed your clothes, maybe you should cool off in there while I fix us a light supper."

Jacca agreed to this with a heaved sigh that sounded like sheer relief. As soon as the child was comfortably tucked in her cave, Nina rounded on Galen.

"Don't push her so hard," she hissed at him. "Remember how many years you were apprenticed to Master Welwyn. Ten, wasn't it? You didn't learn everything in a day, and neither will Jacca."

Galen rubbed his eyes with his palms. "I got carried away," he admitted. "Something clicked in Jacca when she summoned the witchlight. I felt it like a door opening. I wanted to see what else lay behind the door."

Nina put her hand on Galen's shoulder. "I understand," she murmured. "I glimpsed that door too, while she was trying so hard with me this morning. I expect, though, that I may never see within it as clearly as you will."

Before Galen could respond to this hint about his future, Nina shifted the subject.

"If I am to ride out of here soon," she said, "and I'm to take Jacca with me, then the girl must be mounted on a horse of her own. I will not ask my Traveller to carry us both, nor to pack the bags and satchels that two wayfaring females must have." Nina grinned slyly as she indicated the mound of supplies which had accumulated at their campsite in very little time. "We will take our clothes and our soaps, a big kit of medicines, and plenty of food. We must have a pack animal, brother. And the mount for Jacca must be strong enough to endure a journey of many miles, but of a size and temperament suitable for a child of eight. From where will you procure the horses that we require?"

Nina paused to enjoy the look of consternation on Galen's face. His look deepened to true anxiety when she drove home her point. "Does

Jacca even know how to ride?" she asked, smiling her sweetest smile. "Have you ever seen the girl on the back of a horse?"

"Drisha blind me," Galen softly swore. "No, I have not." He rubbed the back of his neck as if to ease a spasm. "I must make inquiries."

"Of the girl's mother, I presume. For who else could answer that question to your satisfaction? Here," Nina added as she stooped for the letters she'd penned while Galen tutored Jacca. "When you see Taji, give her this with my thanks for the garments that she brought here under cover of darkness last night."

Nina handed over her other message as well, for Galen to deliver to the herbalist. The letter to Legary, she withheld, hesitating as she twirled the tightly rolled pages between her fingers.

"You can see no way at this time," she asked, "to get my message to our brother in Granger? I believe Legary would wish to know that I didn't die in the desert."

Galen smiled. "He knows. I've told him you're here. I sent word the day you arrived."

"You did?" Nina exclaimed. "How?"

Galen shrugged. "Remember Welwyn's knack for using trees to carry messages, oftentimes over exceedingly long distances?"

"I always wondered how he did it," Nina replied, nodding. "I could never get him to tell."

"He wouldn't explain it to me, either," Galen said. "But after I'd settled in these hills, and our youngest brother made his own way south, I decided to devise my own kind of far-flung communication. I'm no miner but I've always been drawn to metals, whether they lie aboveground or below. I can sniff out the rich veins of ore like a pig smelling truffles." He grinned as he tapped his nose. "When I'm not in my shop, working metals, I'm generally deep in a mineshaft, finding them."

"Much as Legary goes down in the quarries, to oversee the cutting of the stone slabs that he uses in his work," Nina commented, catching a glimmer of understanding. "You both touch rock."

"More than that," Galen said. "Legary *lives* on rock. If you toured the cellars of his big house there in Granger, you saw the bedrock that underpins his mansion. The first time I tapped out a message to him, from deep in a gold mine in these hills, I think I scared his wife half to death. It seems the whole house trembled around her." Galen chuckled. "She ran to fetch Legary home. And though puzzled at first, he soon worked out what was happening. We have since discovered that the link is inconstant. It varies in ways we do not fully understand, coming and going almost like the phases of the moon, but it is not so predictable as the moon."

"Or as the ocean tides," Nina muttered.

"Of oceans, I know little," Galen said. "But in recent days I have watched the moon wax bright over these hills—portending an auspicious time for your continued travels. By your leave, Honored Sister," he said with a bow that was playful but also wary, "I will be away now to find the horses for your trip."

At this reminder of Galen's intention to be rid of her, a frown tugged at Nina's lips. But she forced a smile.

"You are dismissed, brother," she teased him with a queenly haughtiness that was not entirely feigned. "But tell me first: How did Legary greet the news of my safe arrival?"

"He said to tell you that all was well with him. With both him and Willow, all things were right."

"I'm pleased to hear that," Nina murmured. "I had hoped it would be so."

She rose on her toes to kiss Galen's cheek, and saw him off as he turned with his donkey to trudge downhill. Nina stooped then to rummage in the fresh supplies Galen had brought. Tonight's supper for a young fire-mage who had burned too bright, overheating in her zeal to master her spellcraft, would be made on cold meats, soft cheese, and a basket of ripe plums. Nina nibbled on a plum as she walked to the cave to call Jacca to the meal.

The Powers willing, she prayed, *this girl will need many weeks of lessons on horseback before we can even think of my taking her on a months-long ride northward. I need more time. I need time to convince Galen that Jacca belongs here, with him. Maynor's reputation—and Taji's, and my brother's own—be damned.*

* * *

Three days passed as Nina awaited the answer to her silent hopes. She and Jacca spent the time bathing in the hot spring and refining the girl's skill with cool witchlight and scorching finger-fires. Try as she might, Jacca could not project heat without also summoning flame. Her every attempt to withhold her fires ended with her soaked in sweat and hiding in her cave, needing the chill of that place to bring down her fever.

As she contemplated the girl's hot, perspiring face, Nina turned again to the old herbalist for advice on treating maladies of excess heat. She sent the woman a message through Galen, requesting every preparation the herbalist knew for breaking fevers and cooling a patient's blood. If it did become necessary for Jacca to leave this place and journey forth in the water-lady's care, despite Nina's wishes to the contrary, then Nina would have to control the child's overheating without benefit of an icy hillside cave.

The herbalist responded with recipes and a bag of ingredients for cucumber-cool lotions and cold compresses. "This is what she uses on victims of sunstroke and heat prostration," Galen said when he delivered the materials to Nina. "Such conditions are not rare, as you might imagine, here on the edge of the desert badlands."

The cucumber lotion brought quick relief to Jacca's burned skin. The girl's blisters had responded slowly to Nina's previous treatments, but the herbalist's lotion cleared them up almost overnight. Soon no sign remained of Jacca's early mishaps with her magian fires, except for the badly singed hair on one side of the girl's head.

"My knife is sharp, child," Nina said, smiling as she combed her fingers through Jacca's undamaged tresses. "I have skill in handling a blade. With your permission, I will shave the frizzed ends from the hair that is burnt, and trim the longer side so your head doesn't feel so lopsided."

The girl submitted willingly. As Nina bobbed Jacca's copper-streaked hair, she remembered how her own raven locks had been similarly cut before she embarked on the journey that would change her life. Nina had been only a little older than Jacca was now, when she'd crossed the void to a distant world and sought out the blood relatives who awaited her there.

Maybe it will be for the best, after all, Nina mused as she dressed the girl's hair. *Northward from here, in the lands where offshoots of House Verek have settled, I am bound to find the blood kin who will take this girl and train her well. Perhaps Galen is correct, that Jacca ought to be apprenticed to a fire-master other than him.*

She found herself arguing the exact opposite, however, when Galen climbed the hill three days after their discussion of the horse that Jacca must have to go wayfaring with Nina.

"She can ride!" Galen exclaimed as he topped the path and spotted Nina at the water barrel, where she crouched to rinse a teapot. "Jacca *can* ride, and well. Not only that, the girl has a horse of her own. Except now the animal belongs to me." Galen's grin was smug. "I have purchased the beast from Taji and stabled it with your Traveller so the two can get acquainted before you ride out together. I'm having the animal shod by the same expert farrier, and I have acquired a sturdy pack-horse for your supplies."

As Nina rose frowning, Galen continued his self-satisfied babble of news. He was almost crowing.

"The time has come, sister! All is ready. In the very early dawn—not tomorrow, but the day after—I will lead you down this hill and start you on the trail through the foothills. From the head of that trail, you'll see the way north."

Nina faced Galen with her hands on her hips.

"All your plans have fallen into place, have they?" She smiled grimly, riveting him with her dark gaze. "Everything is happening just as you would have it. But that leaves you only a day, brother—only tomorrow to prepare your own horse and settle your affairs for a lengthy absence from home. You're coming with us."

"What?" Galen exclaimed. He took a step back. "No, Nina. That's not necessary. You can easily follow the trail through the foothills."

"But I say that it *is* necessary," she snapped, giving no ground. "What would possess you to put your kinswoman on an unfamiliar road through wild country, sending her off alone with a young girl, denied the safety of an escort? Your father would be appalled to know you were capable of such ungentlemanly conduct."

Galen gaped. "An escort? For *you?*" he spluttered. "Since when have you needed one! You're fully capable of taking care of yourself, Nina, and I know it."

She shook her head. "Either you come with us, or I take Jacca by the hand and walk us down to your front door. If your wife will not admit us, I will have the girl throw her hottest fires upon that lovely gate in your wall, the one with the flowers and the dragon. In an instant, Jacca can reduce your metalcraft to a molten mass—same as you did, Galen, with your odd bits of scrap-iron when you were half her age."

"You wouldn't," Galen whispered.

Nina cocked an eyebrow at him. "I would and I will ... unless you ride north with us."

Galen ran his hands through his hair. "I can't be gone that long," he muttered as he shifted his weight from one foot to the other. "I have a shop to run ... and a marriage to mend."

"Tah!" Nina retorted, again summoning Aunt Meg's sharp note of impatience. "You have told me of your competent shopkeeper. That woman can mind the till in your absence. As for your marriage ..."

Nina paused, aware that she was stepping into tender territory. She reached around to catch the long braid of her hair and run it through her fingers, letting the silence stretch. Then she continued slowly, her tone softening.

"It has been my experience," she murmured, "that a woman's anger cools fastest when the object of that anger keeps out of sight. I believe the best thing you can do, brother, is to leave your lady alone for a while."

Galen ceased to rock on his feet. He glared at Nina, but his look held more resignation than anger. Finally, he threw up his hands and heaved a sigh.

"Ten days," he snapped. "It's a ten-day ride from here to the mountain crossroads. I will leave you there, and nothing you can say will prevent me from doing so. The road northeast is well marked from that point. Though perhaps it will not be so heavily traveled at this time of year as it will be in autumn, when the crops have ripened and people are busy trading what they have for what they need, to lay in supplies for the winter." Galen shrugged. "But whether you share the road with others or you make your way in solitude, I have no fears for you. Legary has told me what you're capable of."

Nina narrowed her eyes at him. "Are you talking about the cur who fell to my blade? I assure you: he had it coming," she muttered darkly.

Galen nodded. "Do not mistake me, sister. I stand before you in admiration, not judgment. That dog deserved his death." He rubbed the back of his neck. "I hope you do not meet with his kind on your journey home. But if you do, the scoundrel's fate is sealed. No man may offend a goddess and expect mercy from her. Legary told me that, and I believe him." Galen paused, a crooked grin on his face. "You'll get no more arguments from me, Nina ... not for the next ten days." He shuffled his feet like a fidgety youngster. "I don't want you mad at me, girl. You're scary when you're mad."

Unable to maintain her frown, Nina was forced to return Galen's grin, glad for this glimpse of the little boy she'd grown up with. But Galen was no longer that boy. Now he was a man, his adult life tangled in complexities of his own making.

She stepped forward and took Galen's hand.

"It's settled then," Nina murmured. "Return here before sunrise on the day you have set. Jacca and I will be ready. For ten days then, the three of us will ride together as the blood-kin we are."

Chapter Nineteen

To Nina's relief, Jacca needed no persuading. The girl accepted her statement that they were leaving. She did not question or resist, only sacked up her clothes and helped Nina organize supplies. Jacca showed a gift for logical practicality in deciding what foodstuffs and gear they could take and which must be left behind. The girl watched Nina tie blankets into compact saddle rolls, and without instruction secured her own covers in the same fashion.

From the cave that had been the child's refuge, Nina took the candles but left the barely used oil lamp. In that confined space, witchlight served better than smoky oil. Jacca had become proficient in conjuring the cool orbs. Two came at her summoning, and by their light the girl and Nina scoured the place for anything that Jacca might wish to keep. Other than the child's dented water mug, however, and her precious tortoise pillow, the cave yielded nothing to go in their packs.

But in the predawn darkness on the day of their departure, Nina watched the girl press herself against the cold stone inside the cave's mouth. "Thank you," Jacca whispered as she hugged the icy rocks. "Thank you for taking the heat from my body."

They were sitting on their packs picking out stars in the still-black sky, when Galen appeared on the path. In far greater silence than his usual heavy-footed approach, he led his donkey up to them. Few words were exchanged as they loaded the beast with the bulk of their supplies, then tied what was left onto their shoulders. Galen led the way down, followed by Jacca clutching her pillow, with Nina coming last to watch that nothing and no one fell by the wayside.

The back gate at Galen's house stood open to receive them. In single file they entered the spacious garden, passed silently through the grounds, and emerged onto the street through the dragon-gate near the lodge's front door.

The lane at this hour was a pale streak of chalk, barely visible and empty of movement. Standing off to the side were four horses hitched to an iron rail. Two of the animals nickered as Galen's party approached.

"Trav!" Nina whispered. She rushed forward to pat the roan's neck and comb her fingers through his mane. "I've missed you. Did you think I'd gone and left you behind?"

The roan gave her a soft nudge and whickered a greeting. Beside him, a horse that Nina did not know was stretching to the end of its tethers. The big animal dipped its head to the child who came running up at Nina's heels.

"Bobby!" Jacca cried, her voice considerably louder than a whisper.

Over the shoulder of a third animal—the packhorse to which he was transferring supplies from the donkey—Galen sent the child a stern "Shh!"

Jacca obeyed, falling silent. But as Nina stood back and studied the girl who was stroking the muzzle of a horse that appeared entirely too large for her, she was powerfully reminded of the warmblood that had been the stalwart companion of her own girlhood. That horse, a towering gray named "Ghost" after the spooky legends that Master Welwyn delighted in telling, had carried Nina on her earliest solo ride, cross-country to the eastern coast of her home province. As Nina stood poised to accompany another young adept on another life-changing ride, it seemed fated that a second gentle giant should enter the picture.

"Introduce me," Nina whispered as she stepped up beside Jacca and the girl's oversized, bobtailed mount. "Is he friendly? Will he let me help you up?"

Jacca nodded vigorously. "Bobby's the best," she whispered. "He never bites and he doesn't buck. But one time I saw him kick a dog that tried to nip him."

"Entirely justified," Nina murmured as she boosted the girl into the child-sized saddle. Forewarned, she kept clear of Bobby's rump as she secured Jacca's bedroll, tied the girl's soft tortoise in front of her, then draped the barrel-chested horse with whatever sacks and satchels would not fit on the pack animal. In minutes, she had her own gear loaded on Traveller, Galen was mounted on his saddle steed, and the donkey stood blissfully unburdened, tied to the hitchrail and dozing in the predawn.

"What about that little fellow?" Nina whispered as she swung up on Trav and reined alongside Galen. "Are you just leaving him here?"

"Someone will be along to collect him," Galen whispered back. "He's not mine, I've only been renting the beast. He'll be back in his stall by sunrise, and happy enough to be shut of me, I don't doubt."

Nina smiled as the donkey whuffled, a sound of definite agreement.

"Let's go," Galen muttered. With a tug on its lead rope to get the packhorse moving, he rode in front of Jacca and headed down the pale street, moving out at a brisk walk. Nina watched to be sure Jacca was as accomplished a horsewoman as Galen had seemed to think. The girl did not disappoint: She waited until the packhorse was past, and then guided her animal into the lane, but at a prudent distance from a creature whose temperament was as yet unknown to any of the three riders.

Satisfied, Nina brought up the rear, resigning herself to the necessity of eating chalky dust. Someone had to ride behind, to keep an eye on Jacca and watch for tumbling packs. Nina couldn't very well hand the job to Galen, since she had demanded that he be their guide.

With a twinge of disappointment, she looked back at her brother's hillside lodge, a house she'd seen nothing of except its back garden. Nina had expected to be invited into Galen's home, same as she'd been welcomed at Legary's. But she had never entered through his front door, and Galen's wife Sheyla had only grudgingly admitted her at the side gate.

Studying that garden entrance now, Nina saw movement in the dim light of early dawn. Someone stood framed between the ornate gateposts, peering down the road. The figure lingered briefly as if following the departure of three riders and their horses.

Then the person withdrew. The gate swung shut. A latch was driven home with a solid metallic *clink* that came clearly to Nina's ears. She fancied she also heard the quick taps of hard-soled shoes as the wearer climbed the steps of a back porch. A door slammed shut with a bang so loud, it reverberated in the silence of the morning.

From the donkey came a harsh bray of resentment at having been startled from its well-earned snooze.

* * *

"How did you take your leave of your wife?" Nina asked. "Where did you say you were going?"

"I told her the plain truth—I said I was escorting my sister on her homeward journey," Galen replied. "I told her I would go only as far as the crossroads."

Which will take us longer than any ten days to reach, Nina thought with secret determination as she settled back against a mountain laurel on the first evening of their ride through the foothills. "Did Mistress Sheyla not think it odd that I spent no night under her roof during my visit with my long-lost brother?" she asked, turning again to Galen.

He shrugged. "I believe she was relieved that you sought no hospitality from her. Sheyla would have found it difficult, I think, to engage in polite talk with you while seething at me."

"I heard the door slam behind us, early this morning. She's very angry, isn't she."

"Angrier than I've seen her in all the years of our marriage."

This conversation took place in a whisper, with Nina and Galen sitting as far from the sleeping Jacca as they could while keeping watch over the child. Speaking while riding had proved impossible with Galen in the lead, Nina at the rear, and the girl in between. Jacca had ridden all day without complaint. She had not asked for rest beyond the stops they'd made for a late breakfast, an afternoon tea break, and finally an evening camp under the trees beside the foothills trail. But the girl had dropped so stiffly from the back of her big Bobby, it was obvious the child was not accustomed to the pace Galen set.

"You must slow down," Nina muttered. "Jacca cannot stick in the saddle for as many hours a day as you and I can."

Galen sighed. "I'm afraid I didn't realize that until I saw her dismount this evening." He rubbed the back of his neck. "I'm sorry for putting the child through this. Drisha's teeth, Nina!" he swore with soft intensity as he turned to look at her, sorrow in his eyes. "I'm sorry for all of it. You endured much to come here, wanting only to visit me and talk over old times. Instead of a glad reunion—and a comfortable stay in my home—I stick you in a tent and burden you with my troubles."

"It was a very nice tent," Nina said, smiling at him and bent on raising Galen's spirits. "But too bulky to pack along, with everything else we're carrying. Be sure you fetch it down from the hillside when you get home. Don't leave it up there to rot."

"Humph," Galen grunted. "I may be sleeping in that tent when I get home."

Nina reached for the teapot to refill her mug and Galen's. "How did you and Sheyla meet?"

Her question brought a smile to Galen's mopey face.

"Sheyla came into the shop," he said, "wanting to sell me her mother's jewelry. Her mother had died, leaving debts owing and no way to pay them. Sheyla hoped I would buy back the only things of value that her mother had still possessed at the time of the woman's death."

"What do you mean, 'buy back'?" Nina asked. "Had you sold them to her in the first place?"

"No, not to the mother. But I *had* sold them to the woman's husband—that is, to the man who would become Sheyla's father. Years ago, he purchased gold and silver from me to give as a wedding gift to his new bride." Galen sighed. "Back then, the family had money. Sheyla's father was a successful mine owner, and he ran a gristmill on the side. But the man was a gambler. By the time he died, he'd lost so much on bad bets that Sheyla and her mother were living hand-to-mouth. Then when the mother died also, Sheyla was destitute."

"She came to you for help," Nina murmured. "How desperate she must have been, to sell off her only valuables. And how it must have grieved her, to part with her mother's jewelry."

Galen tipped his head. He smiled again.

"Sheyla and her gold were not parted for long," he said with a wink. "I bought the jewelry from her, and gave a princely sum for it. Then I asked her to dine with me. Sheyla was twenty at the time, slim, shapely, and beautiful."

Nina chuckled. "I believe I glimpsed some of the gold that you bought and then gave back. When Sheyla opened the gate for me, I could not help but admire your lady's fabulous ornamentation. You do magical work, favorite brother of mine. And," Nina hastened to add, "Mistress Sheyla wears it now, these many years on, like the regal beauty she is."

Galen sipped his tea, then reached to massage his neck. "I've told her she's still beautiful," he muttered. "But she doubts my sincerity. Like every mortal woman to whom I have been married, she resents that she grows old, and I do not."

Dreadful immortality, echoed Taji's words in Nina's memory.

"Legary confesses that similar strife has afflicted his marriages, down through the years," Nina murmured. "Forgive me if I ask an indelicate question, but it occurs to me to wonder: *Why* do you and Legary remarry, time and again, when you are fated to see your brides become wrinkled old women and leave you widowers?" Nina rubbed her cheek as she pondered. "I went through that with my mortal husband, and the pain of his death was almost more than I could bear. But contrast the three of us with Dalton. Our middle brother does not marry. He simply keeps a mistress in every port of call. And swaps old flames for new conquests, I suppose, when the fancy takes him."

Galen threw back his head and laughed. "Does he? I'd not heard that. Clever boy." He scratched his chin. "I guess a man can do that when he's rootless. At home, Dalton is constantly on the move, riding the length and breadth of Ruain. Then when he's at sea, he drops anchor only long enough to offload his cargo and refill his ship's hold."

"That's just enough time, it seems," Nina said, "to keep his various mistresses happy without wearing out his welcome."

"I see the appeal." Galen cocked his head, nodding. "But when you've made your home in a place you love, a place that *feels* like home, it's hard to stay ... disentangled." He had paused as if unsure of the word he wanted.

"To say truth," he continued after a moment, "I have resisted marriage. I've suggested that informal arrangements might better serve the interests of certain ladies in the Ore Hills. Drisha's knuckles, Nina!" he swore, turning to her again. "They all know what I am. Every girl here knows that I have been in these hills for generations now, and they know I do not age as mortals age. Yet the foolish young things will almost never consent to an 'unlicensed' liaison. They want marriage." He forced a smile. "It must be said that all of my marriages have begun in bliss, and they have continued most pleasurably for decades after the wedding night. You know how it is with *wysards*," he added, shooting her a roguish and slightly embarrassed grin. "Mortals cannot resist our elemental passions—that power of seduction we all seem to have."

To cover her sudden discomfiture, Nina laughed, then gulped her now-cold tea. Galen's remark had sent her thoughts flying to Corlis. She wondered: Was that all it had been with the nomad? Only the lust of a mortal man who was besotted by the sexual powers of a magian woman? There for a time beside the magical lake, Nina had felt something deeper between them. But maybe she had deluded herself.

Let him go, she thought angrily. *Succeed where Legary and Galen have failed, and disentangle yourself.*

"We should sleep," she muttered, flinging tea dregs from her mug. "It's late. We still have days ahead of us, brother, for talking over old times."

* * *

The first crisis with Jacca came at noon of the following day. The girl had said almost nothing since beginning her ride. But at midday, as she dropped limply from the back of her big horse, Jacca mumbled, "I'm too hot."

At sight of the girl's flushed skin, Nina led her to a patch of shade. "Would it help to release your fires?" she asked as she filled a pot with water. "Blast this into steam if you'd like."

Flames appeared at the girl's fingertips. She brought the water to a rolling boil. Then the pot went flying, skittering over the ground and bashing against a tree. Hot water splashed everywhere, almost scalding Galen.

Nina was ready with two more pans. "As you like, child," she murmured. "Dip your fingers, or make these boil. You are the best judge of what you need."

Jacca plunged her flaming hands into the pots. "I need my cave," she whispered. "I need to cool off."

"Oh, child," Nina murmured as she yanked her medicine kit off Traveller. "I'm sorry I cannot conjure a frosty cave for you. But we have the cool lotion that soothes your skin, and I will make a cold compress."

"Can you conjure ice?" Galen muttered, looking at Nina from his crouch at the girl's side. Jacca was lying down now, seeking relief in moist leaves under a crabapple tree. "For all your skill with water," Galen said, "I don't recall ever seeing you make ice."

"That's because it's quite difficult." Nina went to one knee to bathe Jacca's face and arms with cucumber lotion. "I have not done it more than twice in my life. It's Dalton we need. That weather-mage can conjure snow and ice at will." She frowned at the heat that radiated from Jacca's skin. "I will try, but it's a poor substitute for the girl's cave."

Nina closed her eyes and raised a plea to the Powers. *By your favor,* she prayed, *and for the sake of this burning child, give me the strength to confine a substance which craves to be free.*

With wrenching magical concentration, Nina bespelled the water in the two cooling pans. She did not know she had succeeded until a yelp from Galen brought her eyes open.

"Well done!" he cried as he tipped ice from one pan and laid on it Jacca's brow. "This will lower her fever."

Nina offered up silent gratitude as she cracked the ice in the other pan and spread the chunks over the girl's chest. She lifted Jacca's limp, flameless hands and folded them over the girl's heart, then laid on a cold compress to drive the icy chill deep into her blood.

"Thank you," Jacca murmured. She lay with her eyes closed, and soon drifted into sleep. The slow rise and fall of her chest suggested a deep, untroubled slumber. As Nina hovered, watchful, the fiery red faded from Jacca's skin. The ice on her forehead melted, freeing itself from bespelled containment, and dripped into the child's hair.

"Drisha blind me," Galen muttered. "That's something else I didn't consider, that I might endanger the girl by taking her from her cave."

Nina wiped her brow with the back of her hand. "But Jacca could not have stayed in that place forever. What you need to think about now, brother, is how to help the child abate her fires before they burn her up. With lotions and compresses—and conjured ice and waves of water if necessary—I can keep the girl cool. But I can only quench her, Galen, not train her," Nina emphasized. "I do not know how to help her tamp down the fires that seem poised to boil her blood. Can you not think back to your boyhood, to your earliest fiery impulses, and find in those memories some guidance to give this child?"

"It wasn't this way for me, Nina," Galen muttered. "From the time of their first arising, my fires obeyed me in all ways. They came when I called, and did what I wanted. I never burned myself—"

He broke off, and shot Nina a grin. "I take that back. I do remember singeing my hair and blistering my skin. It was the night you made me burn down the door that hid the springwater pool across from our parents' rooms. I summoned a fire so hot, it melted the door's hinges and that huge iron lock that was meant to keep you out of that pool."

Nina laughed. "Your spellwork that night was spectacular, little brother. Our parents and Master Welwyn marveled at what you had done."

"But they exclaimed louder and longer over your magical disappearance that evening," Galen said. "I got the story only later, in bits and pieces, because they sent me straight to bed that night. I'm convinced Welwyn worked dark magic to render me senseless. I remember setting fire to the door and seeing you conjure a great wave in the pool, but nothing after that." He clicked his tongue, a sound of admiration. "That was the start of your wayfaring, wasn't it, Nina."

She smiled. "My longest journeys began that evening, yes. Without you to remove the door that stood in my way, I might never have taken that first step."

While they talked, Nina and Galen moved softly around the sleeping child. They pulled bread and cheese from their packs and made their midday meal on the simple fare, sitting together in the shade of gum trees a few feet from the girl, careful not to wake her.

"Speaking of magical disappearances," Nina mumbled around a bite of bread, "how do you suppose Taji will explain the bobtail's absence from Maynor's stables, and the vanishing of Jacca from the family home?"

"She's concocted a story that Maynor will approve," Galen said, "for it preserves his honor and fattens his purse. Taji will say that she has apprenticed Jacca to a master weaver in the mountains beyond the abode of the girl's grandmother. The apprenticeship contract is for a span of twelve years, with no possibility of the girl returning to the Ore Hills until she is twenty. But of course, no one will expect to see her here ever again, for the girl will likely have found a husband by that age, and will make her home permanently in the distant mountains.

"As for Jacca's horse," Galen went on, picking cheese from his teeth with one fingernail, "Maynor will praise his wife for the hard bargain Taji drove. I paid her double what the animal is worth."

Nina rolled her eyes, grudgingly impressed by the web of falsehoods that Galen and Taji had woven together. "It's good that you are a rich man, Galen. This scheme of yours, to be rid of myself and your daughter, is costing you a fortune."

"You injure me, sister." Galen shot her a sulky look. "I do not wish to be 'rid' of you—of either of you. I just know that Jacca will have a better life with our kindred in the north. There, she'll live a life of greater acceptance than she could know in these hills, were her illegitimate birth to be openly acknowledged here."

So Galen's aware, Nina thought. *He's aware that every person who ever glimpsed Jacca's eyes and then met Galen face-to-face must know that he fathered the girl. It's only a polite fiction, maintained for the sake of saving face, that keeps him from claiming the child. Tah! Can he not see that his actions are cowardly?*

"We'd best be moving on," Galen muttered as he got to his feet and knocked bread crumbs from his shirt. "Will you wake the child?"

Though reluctant, Nina nodded. "I'll fix her something she can eat while she rides. Perhaps it will occupy her hands and keep her thoughts off those fires that smolder within her."

* * *

Through the afternoon's ride, Jacca nibbled on bread and cheese, eating with a birdlike appetite and making it last. As the sun dropped lower, she washed down the last bite with a pull from the water bottle that was hooked to her saddle horn. Nina watched the girl splash water, dampening her tunic.

Then Jacca extended her hand, palm up, and conjured witchlight, working the simple magic with confidence. She set the orb on her shoulder, nestled against her neck as though to cool the blood that pulsed there. She summoned a second orb and pressed it to her neck on the other side.

For most of their ride thus far, the tree-lined trail through the foot-hills had been narrow enough to keep Galen's party traveling single-file. Through here, however, the way widened, allowing Nina to ride up and check on the girl.

"You're doing wonderfully well, Jacca," Nina said, and smiled at her. "I know it can be hard, going horseback for miles when you're not used to it. Can you make it a little farther? I'm sure we'll stop and camp soon."

Jacca kept staring straight ahead, to avoid dislodging the witch-lights. "How much farther is it, water-lady?" the girl murmured. "To where we're going, I mean."

This was the first time the child had posed any question about the journey, about its purpose or its destination. Nina realized to her dismay that she did not have an answer ready for the girl.

"Um," she faltered, mentally cursing herself for not anticipating this entirely predictable moment. "Master Galen is leading us to where a main road drops down out of the mountains. It crosses this trail that we're taking through the foothills. I understand the crossroads is a major landmark hereabouts," she lamely concluded. "Worth visiting."

To Nina's surprise, Jacca smiled.

"I've been there before," the girl said. "That's the road up to my grandmother's house."

Beggar it all, Nina thought, dropping back as the trail narrowed again. *Now the child will be triply disappointed, if it transpires that she must continue relentlessly northward with me, and neither return home with her father nor climb the mountain road to her grandmother. Will she not see our actions as a cruel injustice?*

The role Nina had sworn to serve, as guardian to Jacca until the girl was formally apprenticed, weighed heavily on her that evening as they rode aside from the trail and made their nightly camp.

* * *

The second episode with Jacca's unbounded fires put Galen in the child's debt. As he went to tether the horses in a patch of wild rye, Jacca tagged along. At the sound of her scream, Galen whirled to see a seven-foot timber snake lunge at him from out of the grass.

Jacca fried it. Fire streaked from the girl's fingertips, flames so hot that the thick-bodied creature had shriveled to ash before Galen could do more than recoil.

"Well done!" he started to exclaim. But an inferno had exploded in the thick grass, a wall of fire that panicked all four horses. They nearly knocked Galen off his feet, plunging around him, hauling at their reins.

His curses and Jacca's shrieks brought Nina at a run. Conjuring with both hands, she summoned a double wave of water. The upsurge deluged all of them—Jacca, Galen, Nina, the horses, the burning grass and the obliterated snake.

They were still attempting to calm the animals and wring water from their clothes when a party of hunters came quickstep from the wooded hills above them. The hunters had heard the shouting and seen the flash of fire. Bursting from the woods were three heavily armed men, wild-eyed and questioning.

"What's going on here?" demanded a burly fellow who wore a fearsomely large knife on his belt. "You folks got trouble? But blind me!" he swore then, a look of recognition brightening his eyes. "Blind me if it ain't Master Galen. Your pardon, sir, but you shouldn't be trying to smelt ore in these woods. The pines are tinder dry up on the slopes and at mercy of your fires."

"Be easy, Roshan," Galen replied, smiling as he extended his hand to their visitor. "This blaze was none of my doing. Not directly, anyway. A log exploded in our campfire ... sparks caught in this tall grass. Luckily for us all, my sister extinguished the conflagration before it spread." He turned to Nina. "May I introduce the Lady—"

Galen broke off, for he'd only then realized that Nina had never told him what name she wished him to use, if he must refer to her in public. There had been no "public" since her arrival in the hills, only seclusion and secrecy.

"Archer," Nina supplied. "Nerissa Archer." She nodded at Roshan but she did not offer the man a handclasp as Galen had done. Acutely aware that Jacca was nowhere to be seen, she wanted these men gone as soon as possible.

"My brother has not been entirely honest with you," Nina said, shooting Galen a look that stilled his tongue. "We are engaged in a contest of ensorcellments. He makes fire, as I'm sure you have seen at his forge. I, however, am a summoner of water." To emphasize this point, she swung her long, jet-black hair over one shoulder and squeezed rivulets from it.

"A duel!" cried one of Roshan's companions. "They're fighting a duel."

"Might we stay and watch?" exclaimed the third man.

Nina's heart sank. She had expected the trio to take to their heels, terrified of being caught in the crossfire of a wizardly battle. She hadn't counted on the easy familiarity with magic that had long set the Ore Hills apart from other southern provinces. Magic was generally accepted here, due to these hills' proximity to the western mountains where *wysards* had traditionally taken refuge.

Galen stepped up with the solution.

"It's a private family matter," he muttered as he took Roshan's arm and drew the man aside. "Just a spat between siblings, you understand. But it's a squabble that we would prefer to settle, the two of us alone ... without an audience."

"Right you are!" Roshan exclaimed, grinning. "I've a sister myself. She used to pull my hair and tweak my nose. She gets the better of me even today, if I don't look sharp."

He turned to his companions. "Let's be on our way, boys, and leave Master Galen to his drubbing." The three men laughed heartily as they climbed upward through the pine trees and disappeared over a ridge.

"Thank you for getting rid of them," Nina whispered to Galen. "I need to find Jacca."

She scanned the wet, blackened patch of grass but saw no sign of the child. Beating the bushes back toward the foothills trail, Nina turned her up at last. Jacca was huddled deep in a berry thicket.

"You can come out now, child," Nina coaxed, reaching to help the girl untangle her clothes from the briars. "Sweet mercy! Look what you've done to your skin. You've torn it, there where your burns were nearly healed." Nina started to *tsk* as she led Jacca from the briar patch. But then she felt the girl tremble, and was moved to soothe rather than chastise her.

"It's all right, Jacca," Nina murmured. "You're safe. Those fellows meant us no harm. They're friends of Master Galen."

The girl clung to Nina, quivering. "Mama told me to hide if men come," she whispered. "I'm never to speak to men I don't know."

Nina gave a sort of mental sigh, then felt a flash of anger, but ended up only nodding. "Your mother was wise to tell you that," she said. "I'm afraid it's a sad truth, child, that some men are cruel. They will hurt women and girls, even girls your age, or not much older." Her thoughts flew to the brutalized young woman of Granger, the girl named Bevvy who had been savagely raped at fourteen.

"I will tell you something, child, that my own mother told me," Nina said, holding Jacca close. "Magian women have the power to slay any man who would harm us. We must never kill casually. But do not withhold your fires, Jacca, if your life or your body is threatened. Strike down an attacker the way you destroyed the snake. You killed that creature to protect Master Galen. Remember it, and likewise destroy a two-legged viper if you must do so to protect yourself. Do you understand me?"

Jacca nodded. The girl no longer trembled. "Thank you, water-lady. You make me brave. I will remember your words."

Nina gave her a gentle hug. "Now I must put medicine on your cuts and scratches." She reached aside for her kit. But then she let out a soft "Sweet mercy!" as she caught sight of the abrasions on Jacca's arms. They were glowing with a kind of phosphorescent light, as if the girl's fires were trying to leak out through her torn skin.

"Is that painful?" Nina pointed at a long, gleaming-white scratch. "Would you like deadener on it?"

Jacca shook her head. "It doesn't hurt. It stings, but that's from the berry bushes. The way it's letting my heat out, though—that feels good. I like it."

Drisha, Nina thought as she dabbed a soothing paste on the scratches, first testing the medication on a shallow abrasion that glowed only dimly. Assured that the paste would do no more than relieve the sting of the briars, without extinguishing the girl's glow, Nina treated each cut and scratch. She did not bandage the wounds, as normally she would have. Jacca wanted nothing to block the light that emanated from the openings in her skin.

I hope this doesn't give her ideas about cutting herself, Nina thought as she sat back and studied the gleaming streaks on the girl's arms. *Galen is going to have to figure this out, for I am at a loss with this child. What kind of fire-mage is she?*

Dusk had fallen by this time, and they'd not yet eaten their supper. As Nina rose to begin preparations, she discovered that Galen had moved their camp while she tended Jacca. The horses were now tethered on the downhill side of the trail, at some distance from the higher-up patch of burned grass where the viper had met its end. Galen was down that slope, laying and lighting their campfire.

"I thought it best," he said as Nina and Jacca joined him, "to get clear of that snaky place. Those creatures are known to nest in pairs. More than likely, its mate died with it, in the same fire. But I would not be comfortable sleeping up there tonight, just the same." He smiled at Jacca, seeming to notice nothing unusual in her glowing scratch marks. "Thank you for saving me from that monstrously big snake. I'm not certain that even Lady Nina's nostrums would have kept the life in me, had that creature sunk its fangs in my leg."

"You did well, Jacca," Nina added, realizing that the girl's swift spell-work had almost been overlooked in the commotion of the grassfire. "I am grateful to you for saving my brother. You summoned fire even more quickly than he could have."

"Indeed you did." Galen extended his hand to shake the girl's. "I stood there stupidly gawking at the creature, too surprised to move. Thank the Powers you were with me."

Jacca looked from one to the other of them, her brow crinkled with what seemed confusion. She wasn't much accustomed to hearing herself praised, Nina thought. But then the girl put Galen on the spot, whispering to him as she took his hand: "I wish I could always be with you, sir. We could take care of each other."

"Um, er," Galen stammered, his eyes widening as he groped for words that would not come. Finally, he managed a weak, "We'll see, child."

Nina stepped in. "Yes, we shall see," she said briskly. "It's many days yet to the crossroads. Now, let us eat our supper. If summoning fire makes you as hungry, Jacca, as I am after conjuring all that water, I would not say no even to fried timber-snake. I'm starving."

* * *

Nina and Galen sat together after the meal, reminiscing into the night after Jacca fell asleep. "When we were children, did we ever fight a duel for real?" she asked, looking at her brother. "I don't remember."

Galen snorted. "Of course we didn't. I would not duel with you, for I knew I'd lose."

Nina laughed. "That's for sure. Water quenches fire."

"A fact I understood, even as a baby," Galen muttered. "From the time of my first wobbly steps, I was aware that you were not only my elder, but my superior. Your magic has always been greater than mine."

"Not so!" Nina exclaimed, blinking at him in surprise. "I was teasing, Galen. Water and fire are opposites, but they're also equals. My element may quench yours, but does not fire reduce water to steam?"

He sighed, and massaged his neck. "You are forgetting, sister, that I see the power of water every day in my forge. I use your element to cool the metals of my smithcraft. When I hammer out a blade of steel, I must plunge that blade into a vat of water to temper and strengthen it." He gave her a crooked smile. "Even when my fires succeed in turning water to a burst of steam, that seemingly evanescent vapor has a fire's power to burn unprotected skin." He met Nina's gaze. "What I knew instinctively, in my childhood, has not been contradicted but only reinforced by the lessons I have learned in the years since. The magic of a fire-mage is inferior to the spellcraft of a water *wysard*."

Nina gaped at him, dumbfounded. Before she could form any kind of meaningful reply, Galen was bidding her good-night. He rolled up in his blankets beside the fire, leaving Nina to stare after him.

What can he mean? she wondered. While she was perfectly content to be the big sister in the family, to claim seniority and playfully patronize her younger siblings, Nina had never viewed her wizardry as superior to theirs. If any of her generation could be regarded as having mastery over the others, then it must be the youngest child of Lord Verek and Lady Carin. It was baby sister Vivienne, after all, who would someday inherit their father's lands and sovereignties.

But perhaps the error in Galen's logic will serve my purposes, Nina thought, suddenly inspired as she left off staring at him and leaned back against her tree. *I will leave him to stew on what he has said to me this evening. A reluctance may grow within him, a hesitation to leave his novice fire-mage in the care of a water-witch who could inadvertently suppress the girl's spellcraft.*

If Galen feared for the child's art, if he thought Nina might prevent the girl from reaching her full potential as a summoner of fire, then maybe he would honor the child's plainly stated wish and take her home with him, and be the father Jacca needed.

Nina turned in and slept peacefully, satisfied with the favorable direction that events had taken today.

Chapter Twenty

The next fiery incident with Jacca revealed a heretofore unsuspected side of the magical talents she had inherited from Galen. They were another five days along the trail through the foothills, and had stopped for midday refreshment when Jacca jumped down from a heap of boulders she'd been exploring.

"Something's in there," she said, turning to Galen.

He shot to his feet, his hand stretched toward the boulders as he dropped his bread roll and prepared to blast an unseen danger into oblivion.

"What is it?" he demanded. "Another viper?"

Jacca shook her head. "I don't mean there's something hiding under the boulders. I mean it's *inside* them, a little way into the rock. It's heavy and shiny."

Galen maintained his battle-ready pose with one hand, but he raised his other to scratch behind his ear. "I don't understand, child," he said. "Can you show me? But not too close—there could be a snake in there."

"It's not a snake. It doesn't have scales."

Offering no further explanation, Jacca flung up her hands and conjured fire. Nina, who stood to the side watching and listening, saw flames spring to the girl's fingertips. Then the flickering flames became elongated torches. Jacca directed all ten at the face of the lowermost boulder in the pile. Fire roared, stone split, and shards of granite hurtled through the air.

"Drisha!" Nina and Galen swore together. Both ducked, avoiding the flying fragments, and together they lunged for the girl. Nina meant to pull the child backward, away from the shattered boulders. Galen was intent on pressing Jacca to the ground, to shield her with his body.

Before either of them could achieve their purposes, Jacca had ceased her flame-throwing. Silence descended upon the wooded slopes amid thinning swirls of stone dust.

"By the Powers!" Galen exclaimed. He straightened from his crouch and gawked at a boulder that lay split in two. The rock glowed red-hot, and from out of the cracked stone came a stream of gold. The molten metal flowed like lava. Collecting at the base of the riven boulder, it formed a pool that, to Nina's admittedly untrained eye, appeared to be fine gold with only a few scattered impurities floating atop it.

"See?" Jacca stepped to Galen's side and looked at him. "It was clumped up inside the rocks, all shiny and pretty. Do you like it?"

"Like it!" Galen cried. "Girl, this is what I live for. You've discovered a pure vein in a place I never would have thought to look. Gold's not been found out this way before." He was scratching behind both ears now. "But never in my years in the hills have I heard of a vein this rich reaching the surface anywhere."

Jacca shrugged. "Maybe you just didn't know where to look."

"That's a fact!" Galen said, grinning at her. "But what I'm wondering: How did *you* know where to look?"

Again came the shrugged shoulder. "I just felt it when I climbed on the boulders. The tops of the rocks were rough, but down inside they were smooth ... and cool ... and kind of perfect."

"Uncommonly perfect," Galen said, still smiling. "But after the way it melted under your torch-fires, this mass will take a long time to cool enough that we can handle it." He stood rubbing his ears, eyeing the golden pool as if taking inventory on it. "For now, I think it's best if we cover it up. We'll hide it where it lies, and I'll come back later to dig it out and pack it home."

Galen crouched to be eye-to-eye with Jacca. "You have my thanks," he murmured. "I find myself ever more deeply indebted to you, young lady. First you save me from snakebite, and now you show me where a great treasure is to be found."

He stopped short of asking Jacca how he might repay the debt that he owed her. Nina was on the verge of posing that very question, when Jacca showed herself equal to the moment.

"Will you make me another bracelet, Master Galen, from the gold that I found for you?" the girl asked, sweet voiced and guileless.

Nina held her breath, awaiting Galen's answer. She let out a long sigh of approval when Galen, after a brief hesitation, murmured, "Yes, child. I will."

* * *

The final and defining episode with Jacca's fires came when they were within sight of the crossroads. From the foothills trail, Galen pointed out the soaring peaks that rose to the west in forested ranks. Between two summits, a cleft was visible, and within the cleft a winding road could be discerned.

"That's the main road through the high mountains," he said. "It heads north and angles west, and after many miles reaches Cardan."

"Cardan!" Nina exclaimed, looking where Galen pointed. "Isn't that where our Master Welwyn had his cabin in the woods?"

Galen nodded. "That yonder is the road he would have taken, when he'd finished with all the apprentices he could find on this side of the mountains. He came to visit me once when he was drifting through these parts, scouring this countryside for offshoots of House Verek or anyone else he could train." Galen laughed. "Despite all the trouble we gave him, the old fellow seemed never to tire of whipping young adepts into shape."

"I haven't seen Welwyn in years," Nina said. "When I returned from across the void, they told me at home that he had left Ruain and wandered down this way." She rubbed at her lower lip. "How long ago was it, that he came to see you?"

"I can't remember," Galen muttered after a pause. "I know I saw him, but I wasn't really sure it *was* him, at first. He looked different.

His hair was darker—not gray like I remembered—and he had a lot more of it." Galen chuckled. "He reminded me of a big hairy dog."

"A *what?*" Nina snapped her head around to stare at Galen. "A dog? Like ... like a friendly hound that wanted you to pet him?"

Galen stared back. "Exactly that. I had to stop myself from giving the fellow's head a pat." He arched an eyebrow at her. "I take it that you've seen him too?"

Nina raised both hands in confused uncertainty. "I traveled to Granger in company with an itinerant merchant who matches that description. But the man was called Nimrod—or 'Roddy'—and he looked nothing like Master Welwyn. He only knew who I was because he'd done business with Legary, and they were friendly enough that Legary had mentioned me to him." Nina shook her head, unconvinced. "Legary has known that man for years. If he was really Welwyn, our brother must have realized that. He would have told me. Legary thought Nimrod might have powers, but he never suggested the man was our old tutor."

Galen could only shrug. "Who's to say what tricks an ancient magician like Welwyn might have up his sleeve? The fellow was fond of old legends about *wysards* in antiquity hiding their true identities. If he has been around since Archamon wrote the *Book*, or nearly that long, then there's no telling how many names and guises that old conjurer has worn through the ages."

Was the truth staring me in the face? Nina wondered, thinking back to her time with the merchant. In his jolly self-confidence, Roddy *had* occasionally reminded her of Welwyn. The merchant had also uttered her tutor's old catchphrase. *Don't you know,* Roddy had said once or twice to emphasize a point.

While Nina stood chewing on all of this, skeptical but wonder-filled at the possibility, Galen gestured toward the crossroads. That landmark was visible, but still a half-hour's ride ahead of them.

"Let's stop here for the night," he said as he led his horse and the pack animal off the trail and into a fringe of trees. "There will likely be traffic up ahead. I want you well rested, sister, before you commence the next leg of your journey. You may find it less leisurely than this ride through the foothills has been." Galen shot a glance to where Nina was helping Jacca down from the girl's big horse.

Nina met his gaze, and wondered. *What does he mean by that? Does he foresee me traveling lightly from this point?* With hope in her heart, she smiled at Galen, and then at Jacca.

"Let's get you cooled off, child," she said, taking note of Jacca's flushed skin. "Give us witchlight, please. It's so dim under these trees, I can hardly see what's in my medicine bag."

With practiced ease, the girl summoned three shining orbs. Two of them, she pressed to her neck, comforted by their delicate chill as Nina used the light of the third to peer into her kit. The diminished state of the cucumber lotion made Nina frown. To fight the almost daily overheating that afflicted the girl's blood, she might soon be forced to rely solely on conjured ice and water. Galen had thus far failed to teach the girl an effective means of self-regulation.

"You've been quiet today," Nina murmured as she dabbed lotion on Jacca's hot skin, using it sparingly to make it last. "We've hardly heard a word from you. Has this long ride tired you out?"

Jacca looked up at her, and Nina saw sadness in the girl's green eyes. "I'm not tired," she whispered. "I wish we could go on riding together forever. Me and you and Master Galen." The girl hesitated before adding in a wretchedly tiny whisper: "But we're nearly at the crossroads."

Nina couldn't help the tears that sprang to her eyes. She enfolded Jacca in a hug.

"In living our lives," she murmured after a time, as she released the child and met her gaze, "we must sometimes part from the ones we love. Children grow up and leave home. People fall in love, and they may go away together to make a new home somewhere else." Nina stroked the healed side of Jacca's head, where the girl's copper streaks were especially pronounced as her hair grew back after its singeing. "Some people—myself among them—seem destined to roam. We leave behind our parents and siblings, and we go out into the world to see the wonders that it holds." She smiled. "In my lifetime, Jacca, I've had many partings, and always there is a sadness to them. But I have known joyful reunions as well—they make the centerpiece of my current travels." She tousled Jacca's cropped hair. "Not only have I reunited with the ones I love, I've found new loves along the way. Whatever may happen tomorrow at the crossroads, child, know that you will always have a place in my heart."

As Jacca flung herself, sobbing, into Nina's arms, Nina brought her lips to the child's ear and whispered, "Have faith in the future. I do. You *shall* be reunited with everyone you love—if not soon, then someday. Tomorrow at the crossroads, the next part of your life will begin. In years to come, you will learn what you need to know to make your life what *you* wish it to be. So dry your tears, child. The future is a great adventure, and you are just beginning."

Jacca, however, did not wait for the morrow to set her future course. She took matters in hand as soon as Galen had finished with the horses and come to the campfire for his supper.

"I know you're my father," the girl said, addressing Galen with direct simplicity as she sat beside him at the fire.

Galen nearly choked on a mouthful of vegetable stew. When he'd washed it down with a gulp of tea and cleared his throat sufficiently, he turned to the girl and asked, in a voice barely above a whisper: "Who told you that?"

"You did," Jacca replied. "You and the water-lady. You talked a lot when we were at the cave. Every time I went in to cool off, I heard you outside." The girl shrugged. "It seemed like you thought I couldn't hear you talking. But I could."

Nina had to laugh at herself and Galen. "You must think us great fools, Jacca," she said, chuckling. "I suppose we thought that if we couldn't see you, then you couldn't hear us. Why didn't you tell us you knew?"

"It's a secret," Jacca said, turning her innocent gaze upon Nina. "No one is supposed to know."

Galen made another choking sound. Nina, taking pity, refilled his tea mug.

He gulped half of it, then reached for Jacca's hand, bringing the girl's attention back to him.

"Years ago," he said to her, looking into the eyes that mirrored his own, "before you were born, your mother and I were together in a way that neither my wife nor your mother's husband would approve."

"I understand," Jacca said, sparing Galen the awkwardness of describing that liaison. "I'm so different from my mama's husband, I never thought of that man as my father, even when Mama said he was. I wanted *you* to be my father." Jacca gazed up at Galen. "When I went past your shop, one time when Mama took me to the apothecary, I looked in and saw you braiding threads of gold and silver. You were making something very beautiful. It sparkled in the magical light that floated over your head. I've wished ever since that you could be my papa. And now I know you are."

Galen glanced across at Nina. His eyes shone wetly in the combined light of Ercil's fire and crackling wood.

"Honored Sister," he muttered, "I fear your favorite brother *is* a fool."

"Beyond doubt!" Nina exclaimed, grinning at him. "But I've come to think that the living of life is for the getting of wisdom. Live long enough, brother, and you might eventually obtain your share of it."

He screwed up his face at her, as if they were six and five again and Nina's teasing had made him pout.

She reached for her packet of writing paper. "I'll draw up the apprenticeship contract ... now everything's settled."

Jacca, however, seemed to regard matters as entirely *unsettled.*

"I know none of you want me," the girl declared, withdrawing her hand from Galen's and primly interlacing her fingers in her lap. "My mother doesn't want me. She gave me to you, water-lady." Jacca glanced across at Nina. "But you don't want me because I burn with fire and you're made of water. I know you'll take me if you have to, but I'm not the kind of apprentice you want."

As Nina sat gaping at her, too dismayed to respond, the girl turned back to Galen. "You don't want me either, sir, because I'm supposed to be a secret and people mustn't know." Jacca sighed, and looked down at her hands. "I wish I wasn't a secret. I wish I could go home with you. But I know you'll give me to the water-lady, same as my mama did."

The girl glanced across at Nina and tried to smile. "I'll do my best for you, lady. I promise I will."

"Oh, Jacca!" Nina lunged to her feet and rounded the fire, her arms outstretched as she sought to embrace the child and banish the girl's doubts and misunderstandings.

But Galen, being closer, got there first. He gathered the child into his arms, holding her as she wept, pressing her face into his shoulder.

"You're wrong, Jacca," he said, loudly enough to make himself heard over her sobs. "You're wonderfully wrong. There is not a *wysard* in this world who wouldn't want you for an apprentice. You have a gift such as I have not seen in any other young adept. I'd fight any magician of Ladrehdin for the right to train you. I'd even fight my sister—knowing I'd lose." As he said this, Galen shot Nina a wry smile.

She cocked an eyebrow at him and put her hands on her hips, ready to argue, but at a more opportune time.

"But more than that," Galen continued, speaking softly as the girl's sobs began to subside, "I will fight to be your father, Jacca—the way I should have done all along. Tomorrow, we turn back, you and I. I'm taking you home to live with me."

The child raised her tear-streaked face to peer into Galen's eyes. "Then I won't be a secret anymore?" she whispered.

Galen laughed. "We'll stand in the door of my shop, and I will speak the truth to anyone who passes: This green-eyed girl is my beloved daughter. Moreover, this fiery young adept is the greatest apprentice I have ever undertaken to train. Every soul in the Ore Hills—and far beyond—will know it before I'm through. But when we stop keeping secrets," he added, "troubles will likely come to people we love. Your mother's husband might ask her to leave their home."

"That will be all right," Jacca said as she dried her sniffles on her shirtsleeve. "Mama can live with us."

"Yes ... she can, if she wishes to," Galen muttered, a wistfulness creeping into his look. "But not in the house you saw—the lodge on the lane where we mounted our horses that morning. The lodge belongs to my wife, Mistress Sheyla. You and I—and maybe your mother—will live in another house that I own."

"Sweet mercy, Galen," Nina interjected. "How much of the Ore Hills is your private domain? How many houses have you?"

Galen tilted his head, and his eyes lost focus as he totted up numbers on a mental slate board.

"At this moment," he finally replied, his gaze clearing as he looked at Nina, "I can't say exactly. Each new wife has had her own house ... and I've had several wives. I'm certain, however, that I still own three lodges in the hills. Sheyla can keep what she has, Jacca and I will take the house nearer my shop ... and Taji may have the third dwelling, if that better suits her."

Nina was about to suggest that Galen should adopt their brother Legary's practice of building on a new room for each new bride, rather than incur what must be a substantial expense to give each her own new home. But her attention swung abruptly to Jacca.

The girl was glowing. With happiness, certainly. But more than that: A gleam of white fire was showing through the child's skin, the way it had shone through Jacca's berry-patch scratches. Only the fire wasn't gleaming from a few shallow cuts in the girl's skin. It was enveloping her from head to toe—and Galen with her.

Nina flung up her hands, preparing to summon waves of water to douse a magian blaze so hot, it brought the sweat popping on Galen's forehead. But he raised his own hand palm outward, signaling Nina to pause her conjuring. Otherwise, Galen did not move. He made no attempt to escape the inclosing fire, although it seemed to Nina that his hair and clothes were beginning to smoke.

Galen's gaze fastened on Jacca's, and a haze rippled between them like the heat-shimmers Nina had seen in the desert. The ripples seemed almost to be water, except Nina knew her element could not exist in the heat that radiated from the bodies of Jacca and Galen. This was wizardry beyond Nina's. She was seeing fire-magic of a kind seldom if ever witnessed by those who were not dedicated to that primordial force.

"Galen!" Nina shouted, unable to contain her anxiety. "You're burning up!"

His gaze remained locked with Jacca's a moment longer. Then he dropped his outstretched hand and clenched his eyes shut. At this signal, Nina conjured a double wave that dashed upon their steaming bodies with strength enough to flatten them. Both Galen and Jacca lay sprawled in the litter of pine needles that covered the woodland floor.

Nina swooped upon them, dreading lest she find life-threatening burns from their potent wizardry, or broken bones from the force of her own. But neither was injured. Jacca sat up, wiping water from her face and giggling. She glowed now with the brightness of a child's joy. Galen, as he climbed to his feet, wore a huge smile.

"I saw it!" he exclaimed. "Remember the door that clicked open in Jacca when she first summoned witchlight? I saw behind that door, Nina. It's extraordinary, the magic in this girl. I cannot explain what I saw, except to say it was the purest reflection of elemental fire that I have ever been privileged to glimpse. The Powers must hold this child close to their bosoms."

Do the Powers have bosoms? she started to say, but decided it might be blasphemous. She opted for a more practical question.

"That's wonderful, Galen, but did you also see how to help Jacca manage all that blazing elemental fire? Once the three of us part company, you won't have me to quench the inferno if it gets out of hand. Do you know what to do for her now?"

"I do," he said. "Jacca showed me. Or maybe it was the Powers working through her. Regardless, I now understand the furnace behind that door. I can teach my daughter to channel her gift in ways that do no harm, only good."

Nina embraced them both. "I'll get my pen," she whispered, "and draft the apprenticeship contract that seals you to each other."

* * *

The rest of that evening and the early hours of the new day were devoted to sorting and allocating supplies. Galen wanted Nina to take the packhorse, but she declined on the grounds that she didn't need another equine mouth to feed. From her time in the desert, the difficulties of finding fodder for multiple horses remained fresh in Nina's mind.

"Besides," she said, "you will need the pack animal to carry Jacca's gold, if you can't resist hacking off a chunk to take home as you're passing back by that windfall."

Galen smiled, but shook his head. "We're not going that way, we're taking the mountain road back," he said with a glance at Jacca. "It loops up to a valley where my daughter's grandmother lives. Jacca was denied her usual summer visit with that beldame, and I mean to make it up to her. Would you like that, girl?"

"Oh, yes!" Jacca cried, clapping her hands and dancing with joy. "I was sad when Mama sent my sisters to her but I had to go to the cave. I love Gramma. She's kind to me. She's got magic, too."

Galen nodded and scratched his ear. "I've met the old lady a few times, and I've seen her talent with a dowsing rod. She's found valuable ores and gemstones. It seems Jacca's gift comes from both sides— mother's bloodline as well as father's. The old lady has always been civil to me. I don't know what Taji might have told her, but the woman's wits are keen. She has known our 'secret' for years, I expect."

"Will she support you taking Jacca as your apprentice?" Nina asked. "It is customary, as you well know, for the contract to bear the signatures of two witnesses. If you do not wish to grab a wayfarer off the highroad yonder"—she pointed to the crossing ahead of them—"and make that stranger our second witness, then I must charge you with obtaining the grandmother's consent. If that woman will sign in Taji's stead, then I will consider my duties concluded as Jacca's sworn but temporary guardian."

Galen stood thoughtful, then nodded. "I believe the old lady will gladly sign. I'm also foreseeing that Jacca and I may arrive to find Taji at her mother's house ahead of us. If Taji has come to collect Jacca's sisters, then we can thrash everything out at one sitting." He grinned. "Are you certain, Lady Archer, that you do not wish to take part in that 'family council'?"

Nina shook her head, emphatically.

"I leave it to you, brother. Know that you ride to the battle with my sincere wishes for a victorious outcome." She paused, then added, "However much Taji may protest when she sees you again, she must choose in the end to do what's right for the child—as you have."

Nina stooped for the apprenticeship contract that lay on the flat rock where three binding signatures had been affixed. From Jacca, she had expected a childish scrawl. But the girl knew her letters: her name was more legible than the scribbles of either Galen or Karenina, as Nina had signed in full on the witness line.

As she rolled up the contract and absentmindedly tied it with a bit of twine, Nina glanced from Galen to Jacca. "I have something to say to each of you," she said in a tone so serious, both gave her their immediate attention. "I'll start with you, Jacca. From your father, you will learn the Creed of Archamon. Every *wysard* of Ladrehdin subscribes to it. Basically, it says that wizardly power belongs to the Elementals and must never be wasted or misused. Magian folk use the Power with the permission of its true owners. Never forget that, Jacca."

Nina paused, holding the child's gaze.

"Not long ago," she quietly continued, "I committed the error of squandering the Power in reckless and unseemly ways. I made magic for no reason except to flatter my ego. My spellwork was an arrogant attempt to impress another *wysard* with my magnificent skills." Nina chuckled wryly. "As it turned out, that other *wysard* was singularly *un-impressed*—so much so, that he put me off his ship and bade me begone.

"That was far from the worst of my punishment, however," she went on. "For abusing the Power, I had it stripped from me. Only recently has it returned. I am thankful every day that the Elementals heard my pleas, accepted my apologies, and restored my gifts. Now I make it a point daily to express to them my gratitude. I thank them for the water I drink and the air I breathe, the fire that cooks my food, and the rock upon which I find firm footing."

Nina laid her hand on the girl's shoulder. "What I would have you take from this, Jacca, is that you must follow the example of your father. Since boyhood, Master Galen has been diligent and useful in the practice of his craft. While still wet behind the ears, he was molding hinges and buckets and pot hangers, and giving them to anyone who needed them. Galen has never boasted of his skill, but all who have seen his works know that none can match his artistry. Walk in your father's shoes, not your aunt's, and you will never earn the disfavor of the Powers, the way I did."

"Yes, water-lady," Jacca murmured, then shyly amended, "Aunt Nina, I mean."

Nina smiled, and bent to kiss the child's forehead. Straightening, she turned to Galen.

"My advice to you, brother, may sound odd, but I have good reason to offer it: Do not dig too deep in your search for precious ores. Another realm lies below us, and I have met its messenger. That realm deserves our respect. It deserves to be left undisturbed. Do not dig so deep that you commit the crime of trespass.

"Here," Nina added, and handed Galen the letter she had intended for Legary. "Read this when you get home. Some of it may make no sense to you, but it will bear out what I have said. Perhaps someday you can speak personally with Legary about this matter. He also has met an emissary from the underworld, though he did not know it at the time. Legary can give you more of my thoughts than are contained here." She tapped the letter in Galen's hand.

He accepted it with a short, formal bow. "I thank you, Honored Sister, for your counsel. Be assured that we will be guided by it, both my daughter and myself. Now," he added, "allow me to present you with a parting gift of my own."

From his saddlebags, Galen took a small, drawstring jewelry pouch and pressed it into Nina's hands. "I made this for you long ago," he said almost shyly. "I hope you like it."

Nina gripped the pouch, feeling the pendant within it and fighting back a sudden wave of emotion. This made it real: they really were saying good-bye again, as they had when Nina, at not quite thirteen, had crossed to a distant world and left her beloved little brother behind. In Galen's gift, there seemed a kind of finality to this second parting. At the crossroads up ahead, he would circle back to his home in the hills, and take Jacca with him. Nina would rein her horse in the opposite direction, toward Ruain. She had to wonder: Would she ever see either of them again?

Wysards live long, whispered a quiet voice of consolation. *'Ever' is a long time.*

"Thank you, brother," Nina murmured as she pulled the pouch open and saw the gleam of sunlight on ocean waves. Galen had crafted the waves from blue steel topped in whitecaps of polished silver. The waves broke against a rocky shore formed of gold nuggets. Nina slid the necklace into her hand and felt the substantial weight of the pendant on its silver chain. This solid chunk of precious metals displayed little of the delicacy that Galen had woven into the gem-studded bracelet he'd made for Jacca. But there was power in this piece, as if Galen had flooded silver and steel with the unstoppable force of waves crashing against bedrock.

"It's crude," he said, sounding apologetic. "It's one of the first pieces I made in my youth, after I'd advanced from copper and ironwork and my teacher allowed me to take up the finer crafts of the goldsmith. I can do better now," he added with a modest grin. "But I took for my inspiration your water-magic, and I always meant for you to have this ... if you would want such a clumsy thing, that is."

"Clumsy!" Nina exclaimed. "Galen, it's exquisite. I'll treasure it." She blinked back tears. "I'll wear it as a talisman of the heart and a reminder of our magical childhood together." She flung her arms around him and embraced him as tightly as he hugged her. Then Nina knelt to let Jacca clasp the chain around her neck. When she had it secure and Jacca had admired the pendant, running her fingers over its leaping waves and textured nuggets, Nina gave the child a hug and a last quick kiss.

The three of them stood together then, looking at each other in silence. To spare herself another of the long good-byes that had concluded each leg of her southlands journey thus far, Nina brought her hands together in a brisk clap and declared, "That's it, then. You have your contract. Your path is set, as is mine. Let's mount up and ride, family."

No further words passed between them as they covered the short distance remaining to the crossroads. But there they paused again, as Nina rode close to whisper a final question to Galen.

"What will Maynor's temper be, when you make public your affair with his wife? Might the man challenge you to a duel?"

Galen shrugged. "He might. But excellent swordsman though Maynor is, he can't win. I will snap my fingers and melt his blade."

Nina grinned. "Don't repeat this to Legary or Dalton. They needn't know it. I love those boys too. But Galen, you really are my favorite brother. May you burn bright forever, fire-mage."

Part 4
The Wolf

Chapter Twenty-One

From the crossroads, Nina rode northeastward through a series of rolling hills that were grassy at their summits and thinly wooded in the valleys. Grazing abounded for her horse, and for her own sustenance Nina had her pick of game. She brought down antelope, rabbits, ducks, and the occasional small pig. Most days she had a surplus to share with her fellow wayfarers.

She stayed with none of them very long, and seldom engaged in conversation other than talk of the weather and the harvests. Summer was fading from this land. Fields were ripening, and a noticeable autumn chill began to touch the nights. Nina traded her straw hat and airy shirt for a felted cap and a long-sleeved tunic. In a modest roadside market, she paid an old woman a double price for a thickly woven blanket that replaced two of hers which had worn thin.

Occasionally Nina camped with individuals who might be itinerant *wysards*. Around them hung an aura, a projection of confidence without arrogance. They never hinted about what they were, and Nina never asked. Her years of study with Master Welwyn had ingrained too deeply her respect for wizardly privacy.

Her cautious interactions with these individuals made Nina wonder, however: How was she to know her relatives, if and when she encountered them along this road? She had set out from Ruain not only to spend time with her brothers Dalton, Legary, and Galen, but also to meet her sister Vivienne's descendants. Many of Vivie's line had settled in these regions between the Ore Hills in the southwest and the high, hidden province of Ruain to the northeast. Only now in this late stage of her journeying had it occurred to Nina that she might not recognize her own blood kin, if they adhered to centuries of magian tradition and kept secret their true identities.

She did not know, therefore, if the warning came from a magical source or only a concerned fellow traveler. But early one morning as Nina broke camp, saddling Traveller and preparing to leave the sheltered valley where she had spent the night, a woman from a nearby campsite came to speak with her. Nina had exchanged pleasantries with her last evening, as both of them were pausing their separate journeys along a fast-flowing stream under trees whose leaves showed touches of autumn orange.

"I feel it is my duty, one female to another," the woman said, standing before Nina with her fingers interlaced and resting on her ample stomach. "Reports have come out of the Rum Ridges that outlaws are up there, preying on solitary travelers. If you continue as you are, lady, I fear you will fall victim to them. It's better that you turn back, and not risk yourself and your honor to those brigands."

Nina looked at her in surprise. "The Rum Ridges?" She paused in tightening Trav's cinch strap. "I fear the name means little to me. In these parts, I am a stranger."

The woman nodded. "That's clear from the horse you ride and the weapons you carry." She lifted one hand from her paunch to gesture at Nina's rapier and belted knife. "The Ridges lie east of here, madam. If you continue in that direction, you cannot avoid them. This road approaches very near, but it does not climb or cross the broken country. Instead, the way turns northward and follows along in the dark shadow of those ridges." Nina's informant frowned. "It is a dangerous route for any traveler when the wicked men come down from their hideouts and prey on decent folk, as they are wont to do from time to time. You'll not be wishing to go that way, lady."

Nina stood wondering what options she had if this was the main road and it was now unsafe. She asked the woman, "Is there another route? My destination lies northeastward, and I was given to understand that this is the most direct way."

The woman tilted her head. "I fear, lady, that you have ridden miles astray. The ridge road can be quickest, that is true. But it is considered passable only when the brigands go marauding elsewhere and leave these regions in peace. Your safest course now is to turn around and ride to the foothills. There, you may pick up a bridleway that bends north, skirting the mountains." The woman sighed in sympathy. "Though it be a long ride from here to the hills, you will find it a surer course for reaching your destination alive."

Nina drew a long, slow breath, turning over in her mind the days and the miles that had passed since she'd bidden farewell to Galen and Jacca at the crossroads. Finally she gave the woman a nod.

"I thank you for your warning. I shall consider carefully what my course must be."

The woman eyed her as though expecting a more effusive or indebted response from Nina. But with a brief motion that suggested a washing of her hands, the woman gave Nina a short "Good morrow" and turned away, to return to her own campfire and to the husband and children who awaited her.

Nina loosened her weapons in their sheaths, and checked the slingstones in her belt pouch. She still had plenty of the whistling bullets Legary had crafted. Nina smiled as she recalled the effect those projectiles could create. They would make one slinger sound like a horde.

She mounted Trav and continued eastward.

* * *

The Rum Ridges rose on the horizon ahead, visible long before Nina reached them. They were nowhere near as high or as majestic as the mountains that now lay out of view behind her, those snowy peaks of western Ladrehdin that had sheltered *wysards* through the ages. In the broken country she rode toward, Nina saw nothing majestic. The ridges were rubble-strewn and scrubby. Both sides of the road she had traveled to this point were lined with sizable trees, their foliage thick, the leaves turning red and gold as autumn advanced. Ahead on the ridge slopes, however, Nina saw only wind-twisted ironwoods and tangled thickets of acacia.

She was still a mile or more from the base of those slopes when she confirmed a suspicion that had been growing upon her for two days: she was being followed. A wolf trailed her. The creature slipped through the trees on the north side of the road, keeping pace with her, well to one side and slightly behind. The wolf gave no impression of stalking her. Rather, it seemed to accompany her.

That it was no ordinary wolf seemed clear from Traveller's reaction. Several times the horse swung his head questioningly in the wolf's direction, his ears pricked with curiosity. But never did Trav show uneasiness. The horse seemed interested but in no way alarmed by the companion who had silently fallen in with them.

At the easternmost point of the road she followed, Nina reined up and sat studying the ridges that blocked further progress in that direction. They rose in uneven ranks to windswept heights topped by gnarled trees. A rider on a good horse could reach their modest summits in half a day, Nina thought, even in the absence of any trail leading upward.

She had no interest in attempting the climb. For at the base of those uninviting ridges, the road she was riding continued onward, making a sharp left turn and heading north.

"Finally," Nina muttered as she flicked Traveller's reins and took the turn. "It's been a long time coming, Trav. But now we face homeward. I confess, I'll be glad when my tour of the south country is finished. This land is not without its charms, but Ruain is more beautiful. Vastly more magical."

Nina kept an eye out for the wolf, wondering if the creature would slink away into hidden hollows in the ridges. Their ragged slopes seemed ideal for concealing four-legged predators as well as vermin of the two-legged kind.

But as she rode north, Nina again glimpsed the animal. The wolf had crossed the road and was trotting along in the shady verge which lay between her and the foot of the ridges. So narrow was that strip of land, being scarcely wide enough for two trees together, it gave the wolf hardly any cover. The creature moved alongside her in the open now, and for a mile or so it watched Nina as closely as she watched it. But gradually the wolf seemed to relax, as if satisfied that Nina would not take advantage of its exposed position to raise a weapon against it.

Once, however, the creature gave a yelp of alarm and fell back when Nina grabbed her knife and threw it into the half-wooded verge. She had glimpsed movement there, a startled hop in the underbrush just ahead of herself and the wolf. She reined up and dropped cautiously from the saddle, her rapier unsheathed as she parted a way through the brush and retrieved her kill. It was a rabbit, big enough to make supper on. Nina pulled her knife from its neck and carried the carcass one-handed, keeping her rapier ready in the other.

The wolf did not challenge her for the meat. Having recovered from its fright, the creature moved back into the open. But it stayed at a wary distance until Nina was remounted and moving again.

By late afternoon, the pattern had repeated twice more. Rabbits proved so plentiful in the narrow strip between road and ridge, Nina skewered another pair. Of these, however, she claimed only one. After recovering her knife from the last of her kills, she left the carcass where it lay, and walked back to her horse.

"That's yours," she said, remounted and twisting in her saddle to address the wolf that watched from off to the side. "I have not seen you eat since you joined me. Though the monks of Drisha may fast, I've never known a wolf to do it willingly." Nina gestured at the bloody carcass. "Sate yourself on that, with my compliments."

She lifted the reins and rode on at a slow walk, meaning for the wolf to understand that it could enjoy a meal without losing sight of her on this long stretch of straight road. To Nina's surprise, however, the creature did not tear into the meat she'd left for it. Delicately the wolf nosed the dead rabbit, then took the carcass in its mouth and came up alongside her again, keeping pace with her as it had done for miles.

Nina laughed. "Should I be flattered that you prefer me to a meal? Your choice strikes me as foolish. But then again," she reconsidered, "I suppose we must be stopping soon anyway. If these ridges are infested with brigands, a campfire after dark could draw them like a beacon. But I'll risk a smokeless flame in the light of day, and hope they don't catch the scent of roasting rabbit."

So saying, Nina covered only another mile before she angled off the road into its more thickly wooded western side, opposite the slopes that reddened in late-afternoon sun. With the efficiency of long practice, she stripped her gear from Traveller and tethered the horse to graze along a lazily flowing stream. Her two rabbits were soon skinned, gutted, and sizzling in their own fat over a small, clean-burning fire.

As she made a pot of tea, Nina looked around for the wolf. The creature sat on its haunches between her and the road, its rabbit lying un-eaten at its feet. The wolf licked its muzzle but curled its lip in an almost human expression of distaste, as though it had disliked getting blood in its mouth from carrying the dead rabbit.

"How fastidious you are!" Nina exclaimed, watching. "Do you not like your meat raw? Bring it here, and I will cook it."

Her suspicion that this was no common wolf became conviction when the creature promptly stood, took the carcass in its mouth, and brought it to within an arm's length of Nina at the fire. The wolf dropped the rabbit there and started to turn away. But then it paused, locking gazes with her in a way that no natural predator could long sustain without feeling threatened or challenged. In this creature's hazel eyes, however, Nina read no aggression, only a kind of hopeful sadness.

"What's wrong?" she asked. "Are you lonely? Is that why you're fol-lowing me?" She watched as the wolf resumed its post between her camp and the road. "I'm a little lonely myself," Nina admitted after a moment. "I haven't been on my own like this in months. Since it seems we both prefer company to solitude, let there be friendship between us. I will hunt and cook for us both ... and I will rely on you to warn me of marauders, for rumor suggests they're thick on this road."

In response, the wolf hunkered down with its attention on the ridges beyond the narrow roadside verge. Occasionally the creature flicked its ears toward Nina, following her movements as she butchered the wolf's rabbit and set it cooking with her own. The smell of the roasting meat made her mouth water, and set the wolf's nose twitching. The creature raised its head, sniffing at the tantalizing aroma but never ceasing its watchful study of the ridges opposite.

Nina pulled the cooked rabbit off the fire and let it cool before offering the wolf its portion. "Here you go," she said as she rose to her feet, taking care to speak to the creature and to approach within its line of sight so as not to startle it. Whatever this wolf was, and however well-disposed it might be toward her, she could not be sure it was entirely devoid of animal instincts. Best show it a proper respect and not crowd too close.

The wolf gave a yip of excitement as Nina tossed the meat, landing it in the leaves at the creature's feet. So avidly did the animal tear into the flesh, swallowing chunks at a gulp, Nina was moved to hand over a second rabbit as well. One of the fat creatures was sufficient for her supper, and clearly the wolf had not eaten lately.

Nina ran her gaze over her new companion, appraising it from its long muzzle to its black-tipped tail. The creature's thick fur of brown and tan looked healthy and gave no hint of protruding ribs. The wolf's eyes were bright and alert. Hunger, Nina concluded, was a recent experience and not a chronic state for this animal. But how could that be so, if it refused uncooked meat? Was this wolf unaccustomed to hunting for itself? Was it somebody's pampered pet, so domesticated that—until recently—it had eaten at its master's table?

"What happened?" Nina murmured. "Was your owner killed? Were the pair of you attacked on this road?"

The wolf looked at her, licking its muzzle, its ears twitching as it heard her questions. Then the creature raised its head and howled, sending a melancholy cry into the soft light of dusk.

Nina shivered. She retreated to her fire, which had burned to embers. Carefully she stamped out the last glowing coals and scattered the ashes, making certain that no spark remained. Then she gathered her gear, collected Traveller, and waded the shallow stream, leading her horse across to the opposite bank. The wolf stayed where it was, between the stream and the ridges, with its back to Nina and its attention on the heights that might hide danger.

In her slightly more secluded setting, Nina made no true camp, only dumped her gear and tethered her horse behind a coppice of trees. Within the coppice she unrolled her sleeping blankets, doubtful of getting much rest tonight but wanting her blankets for warmth. Summer was past, and the autumn nights had grown chilly.

As she arranged her covert under the trees, Nina took care with the placement of her weapons. Her knife and rapier, she kept near at hand. Her bow and quiver waited at the edge of the coppice, where she could stand behind a tree and shoot in any direction. Her sling with its pouch of stone bullets, Nina hung from a dead snag, out in the clear where no trees or brush would impede the whirl of that weapon.

Thus prepared to meet whatever the night might bring, she slid under her blankets, fully dressed and wearing her boots. For a time, Nina stared across at the wolf beyond the stream, watching the animal as it watched the ridges. As twilight faded, the creature's dark fur blended into the night. But still Nina could glimpse the paler hair of its muzzle and throat. Occasionally the animal would swing its head far enough toward her that Nina saw its eyes shine with a fiery white glow.

Like witchlight, she thought. *Like that animal has Ercil's fire in its eyes.*

Almost against her will, Nina relaxed into her blankets, leaving the wolf on watch as she slipped into a doze ...

... And was brought awake hours later by the muffled sound of a struggle.

Nina threw off her covers and grabbed her bow. Standing with an arrow on the string, she strained to see any movement in the night. The noise of the skirmish had died away. She could not tell from which direction it had come, only that the sound had been somewhat distant. Whatever was happening out there, it was not in her immediate vicinity.

Closing her eyes against the darkness, Nina listened, her every sense merged in that of hearing. At first, she caught only a breeze gusting in the treetops. Then the wind shifted, and carried upon it a low, menacing growl. Nina turned her head to better pick up the sound. It came from the ridges. She could not doubt that her wolf was up there. But as a breezy silence again enveloped the night, she had no inkling of the animal's movements, or what manner of threat it had encountered. Nina remained listening until the chill wind drove her back to her blankets.

The rest of the night passed sleepless but uneventful, and Nina was up hunting before sunrise, her bow ready for dawn visitors to the stream. She shot a wild pig and had it roasting on a spit before the wolf returned to the opposite streambank.

"Are you well this morning?" she asked as the creature sat on its haunches and sniffed the air, patiently awaiting its breakfast but almost drooling, Nina thought, at the prospect of hot pork. "Was that a fight I heard last night? If you've been injured, I urge you to let me treat the wound. I have medicines with me, and the skill to use them."

The wolf's response was to rub its face on its foreleg. Nina could not guess the meaning of the gesture. When she pulled the meat from the spit and stepped to her side of the stream, the wolf came up close on the farther side, giving Nina a good look at the animal's face. She saw no wounds there, nor anywhere on the creature's body when she flung the meat and the wolf turned away to gorge on it. Nina fed her companion almost the entire pig, keeping only a tenderloin for her own breakfast.

"Very well," she said when both had eaten. "In the absence of evidence to the contrary, I will assume that you were victorious last night, and you came away unscathed." She nodded to the creature, and smiled. "Allow me to extend my congratulations on your triumph."

This elicited a yip from the wolf, a glad sound that left Nina wondering just how much the creature understood of what she said. Many pet animals could respond appropriately to a person's tone of voice. This wolf, however, seemed to comprehend not simply tone or mood, but specific meaning. Deep in thought, her brows drawn together, Nina went to saddle Trav.

* * *

Five days passed as she continued northward under the brow of the Rum Ridges. At intervals along the road, Nina came to burned-out dwellings, nothing remaining of them except chimneys and stone foundations. A grass-grown clearing tempted her aside, to ride through the deserted lanes of what had been a small settlement. When a charred piece of wood caught her eye, Nina swung out of her saddle and picked it up from the ground. It was the carved and painted likeness of a songbird. Perhaps it had been a child's toy, or a keepsake treasured by some former resident of this place.

As she stood surveying the destruction around her, Nina wondered: Was this the work of marauders? Had the outlaws who holed up in the ridges plundered every homestead and hamlet along this road? Sighing, she wedged the burned but still beautiful little bird into the fork of a tree, then remounted and rode on.

Eager though she was to put this ruined and broken country behind her, Nina did not push Traveller. She held the horse to an easy pace with frequent pauses for rest. Her journey across the desert had taxed the eastern-bred roan. She had planned to remain in the Ore Hills long enough for herself and her horse to fully recover. Circumstances having conspired to upset those plans, she would not punish her big-hearted mount by asking too much of him on this penultimate leg of her journey.

"When and if we find my kinsfolk in these parts," Nina muttered to the horse, "I've every expectation of being pampered. I believe we've earned it, Trav—you and me both."

Idly, Nina glanced at the wolf who continued to trot along with her, threading its way through scattered trees in the roadside verge below the ridges. What would her relatives think, Nina wondered, if she arrived in their lands with a pet carnivore at her heels?

I suppose they've seen stranger things, she mused. *Being wysards, each and every one of them.*

For that was what Vivienne had said of her descendants, those of her line who had moved south and established themselves in the thinly populated region beyond Ruain and east of the great mountains.

Vivie's progeny were a thoroughly magical offshoot of House Verek, and unique for that reason.

With the exception of Dalton the bachelor—who had no legitimate children, though Drisha knew how many by-blows that womanizer had fathered—each of Lady Vivienne's siblings had married mortals and raised mortal families. Those offspring generally had talents that surpassed the ordinary, but seldom did a child with only one magian parent possess true wizardly powers. In old letters from home, Nina had read of a few young adepts sired early on by Legary, or more often by Galen in those first years. But over time, such births became rare. Jacca was the first truly magian offspring for either man in generations, and the brightness of that girl's flame might be ascribed in part to a trace of the Gift in her maternal line—her mountain-born, gemstone-dowsing grandmother.

Nina was looking forward to telling Vivienne's brood about the new adept in the Ore Hills, but then realized she probably ought to keep mum and say nothing of Jacca. It was Galen's place, after all, not Nina's, to share his family news with such of his relatives as he chose. As Nina contemplated riding into the midst of a coven of *wysards* she had never met, it came to her that discretion might be called for in all things, until she knew the temper of these unknown relatives. They had been away from Ruain for a long time, most of them, and perhaps they had come to feel little or no allegiance to House Verek. Though Vivie had likely sent word that Nina would be passing through on her grand tour of family places, Nina had no assurance that her visit would be welcomed.

She was ruminating on all of this when a shadow up ahead caught her eye. Nina reined Trav to a halt and sat studying the roadway stretching before her—in particular, its disappearing verge. The narrow strip of land that lay between the road and the ridges was tapering to nothingness. In front of her, a tall cliff of jumbled rock hung directly over the roadway, crowding close against the path and obscuring it in featureless shadow.

"My friends," Nina muttered, addressing her horse and the wolf, "I do not like the look of that passage through the gloom. Let's get off the road and seek a path through the trees."

Such a detour proved impossible, however. Nina had barely veered aside from the road's packed surface when Traveller began to flounder: she'd ridden him into a bog.

Leaping from the saddle with the reins in her hand, she landed with one foot on solid ground but her other slipping into the ooze. Nina twisted and went to one knee. Still gripping the reins, she squirmed free of the muck. As she sprawled sideways on firm soil at the bog's edge, she hauled on the reins with all her strength.

"Come to me, Trav!" she shouted. "Get clear of there."

Snorting with alarm, the horse struggled to find solid footing. Nina's heart was in her mouth as Traveller thrashed about, splattering himself and Nina with muck and mire. But then he planted a hoof on the firm ground beside her. With a visible bunching of muscles, Trav heaved upward out of the bog and stumbled a few steps onto the road. There he stood with his head down, huffing and blowing.

"Beggar all!" Nina swore, scrambling upright. "Forgive me, Trav. I never saw it." Even now, after the churning the horse had given the wet, spongy ground, the bog was invisible to any but a close inspection at eye level. How many riders and horses, she wondered, had met their deaths in this quagmire?

"Fiendish place," Nina muttered as she caught at the reins she'd dropped when Traveller cleared the morass. With a glance at the looming cliff that seemed to frown over the roadway up ahead, she reversed course, backtracking for a mile or so, listening for the sound of a running stream. She would retreat for now, back to the last place she had found drinkable water.

"Let's get cleaned up," she murmured to Trav when she'd located the stream that flowed down from the ridges. It had formed a pool alongside the road. Cautiously, mindful of the undetectable bog she had just escaped, Nina circled the pool, feeling with her muddy boots for hints of squishy ground. But no edge of the pond gave way, and soon Nina had her mud-caked gear stripped from the back of her equally bespattered horse.

She stripped to bare skin herself, and scrubbed clean in the small pool before she bathed Trav in it. The rest of the afternoon was devoted to cleaning and oiling her horse tack, and most especially to caring for her weapons. Her bow had been in its saddle scabbard when Traveller plunged into the bog up to his chest. Upon finding that the weapon and her quiver of arrows had come out of the muck still secured to her saddle, Nina offered up thanks with particular fervor in her daily devotionals to the Powers. The sling she wore around her neck had escaped a wetting, but her belt pouch of stone projectiles was mud-smeared. Nina dumped out her ammunition, washed the canvas pouch, and hung it to dry with the clothes she'd also laundered.

As daylight dwindled, supper became a rushed affair of dry cheese and hard bread from her packs. The wolf got the same, for Nina had bagged no meat that day. Disappointed though the creature might have been with its hunk of cheese and the bread that Nina softened for it in a little water, the wolf would have fared no better even if a carcass had been at hand and ready to roast. Nina built no fire large enough for a spit, only a flame so tiny, it would barely heat water for her nightly cup of tea.

Before dusk fell, she'd extinguished the fire and done what she could to secure a campsite that felt dangerously exposed. She was very close to the ridges above the pool, and uncomfortably aware of the narrow, overhung roadway that waited ahead like a trap.

"If there is to be an ambush," Nina muttered to the wolf that crouched where the stream trickled from the slopes above, "that ribbon of road under the cliff is where it's likely to happen. Trav and I made enough noise getting out of the bog, to announce our presence to any rogue skulking in the ridges. If they don't attack tonight, we may expect them tomorrow."

The wolf regarded her steadily, then rose from its crouch and climbed higher. As evening closed in, Nina glimpsed the creature sitting on a rubble of boulders above the road and her camp, where it had a clear view of anything that moved either in the ridges or along the road.

She slept little. In the small hours of the night, noises drifted down from the ridgetops, but Nina could not tell if her wolf had a part in whatever made the sounds. She might be hearing only a wild pig dislodging stones as it rooted for grubs and tubers. Even so, she lay awake listening for the sounds to come nearer, or to become recognizably the creeping footsteps of an attacker. Well before dawn, however, the noises ceased, and Nina slipped into a light doze.

She was up before the sun, her horse saddled and her gear loaded. Quietly she rode for the pitch-black lane that was so narrow, her sling would be useless. Under the looming brow of the ridge, she would not have room to whirl it. Her other weapons, however, were ready, including her most potent. Nina rode with her right hand raised, prepared to conjure a wall of water.

Her dark-adapted eyes saw the man the moment he straightened in a crevice cutting straight up the ridge. He rose high above her, the arrow on his bowstring aimed at her heart.

Nina's magical wave materialized in the crevice behind the man. It roared into him with force enough to break bones. The wave knocked him forward, out of his lofty perch. The bowman screamed as he fell to his death. Nina heard the impact like a pumpkin rupturing, the man's skull smashing into the road's hard surface.

She heard but she did not see, for her attention had already swiveled forward to where a second attacker had appeared from behind a jutting boulder. This man's weapon of choice was also the bow, but Nina was faster. Her arrow pierced the man's eye and entered his brain before he could loose his shot. He crumpled backward, dead as he hit the ground.

"Anyone else?" Nina shouted as her horse responded to the pressure of her legs and turned a complete circle in the roadway. She craned her neck, surveying every inch of the broken cliff overhead and to both sides. She swept her gaze along the shadowy lane that ran into and out of this place of ambush. The bare soil of the road appeared pale in the first hint of dawn ... pale, empty, and motionless. Nina stilled her horse and sat listening, but nothing disturbed the silence except the scolding of birds that the brief but deadly skirmish had jolted awake.

Satisfied that she had met the immediate threat, Nina was starting to dismount when she nearly came out of her skin at the sudden howl of a wolf. She twisted around to see her follower standing over the body of the first bowman. For an instant, Nina thought the wolf was howling with sadness, as though mourning the man's death. But then the animal lowered its head, sank its teeth into the corpse's shoulder, and gave the body a vicious shaking.

"Enough!" Nina exclaimed. "You don't like blood in your mouth, remember? Back off."

So savage were the wolf's throaty growls as it mauled the body, Nina kept her distance until the wolf had obeyed her and stepped away. Then she summoned witchlight and went to view the body. Or more precisely, she went to collect and dispose of the dead man's weapons. She felt no need to look upon the face of her attacker, but she meant to keep his weaponry out of the hands of other brigands who might pass this way and rob the corpse.

As Nina stooped, however, to pick up the man's bow and yank his knife from his belt, she couldn't help but glance at his dull, dead eyes. The man lay face up. The back of his skull was crushed, but his features were mostly intact.

Nina gazed at him, staring as an unexpected sense of recognition came over her. Could it be? *Him? Here?*

"Let's have a look at your friend," Nina muttered to the corpse. She swept up her orb of witchlight and walked to the second man where he had fallen behind the boulder.

The arrow through this attacker's eye made identification more difficult, but after a moment of study, Nina was certain. These two men had sat at a table not far from her own in an outdoor eatery that Roddy the merchant frequented when he was in Plainsboro. These men, joined by a third, had sat leering at Nina, their predatory gazes and lewd remarks declaring their intentions, should they catch her alone. Other women present that evening had accused them of preying on any female they could corner.

Nina had so thoroughly thwarted the men's plans toward herself, the trio of toughs had landed behind bars. But that was months ago, and obviously they had gained their freedom, whether through escape or release from jail.

What in the name of mercy were these two doing *here*, so far west of Plainsboro? Were the Rum Ridges their outlaw lair? Did they come here to divvy up the spoils when their thieving succeeded? Or perhaps to lick their wounds when villainy failed and they were run out of town on a fence rail.

Nina stepped out of the shadows to run her gaze down the long ridgeline stretching back the way she'd come. The morning sun was up now, but it had not yet risen over the ridgetops. Even when it did appear, Nina doubted she could use the sun's position in the sky to accurately judge had far northward she had come since leaving the Ore Hills. She knew only that she was considerably farther north than she'd been in Granger, or in the desert, or the Hills. Had she ridden far enough to be on a northern line with Plainsboro, even though that town must lie far to the east of the ridges?

But not so far that desperate lawbreakers could not ride to this place. The men who lay dead in the shadow of the Rum Ridges attested to that fact.

Nina clicked her tongue at this odd turn of events. She stooped to collect the second attacker's weapons and flung them with the first, off the edge of the road and into the bog. The bodies, she left where they lay as a warning to other potential assailants. Perhaps the third member of the Plainsboro trio had not made it to these ridges. But he could be out there, biding his time.

As Nina remounted and reined Traveller north, she called to the wolf that had ducked behind the boulder and was mauling the corpse of the second bowman as it had the first.

"Let him be," Nina said. "He'll trouble no one ever again. Come, friend, and watch with me for a scoundrel who may yet lie in wait."

She rode on, not waiting for the wolf to cease its puzzling behavior. What drove its savagery toward the corpses? Had the animal once been someone's bodyguard? And having lost the person it was trained to protect—possibly lost to the men Nina had killed—had the wolf taken up with Nina because it instinctively sought to fulfill its duty?

Whatever its motivation, she was glad when the creature came trotting up behind her. Once they were past the constricted place in the road and the verge had reappeared, to again put a little space between the road and the foot of the ridges, the wolf resumed its former habit of pacing along in that verge. It weaved its way through a sparse stand of trees and stayed slightly ahead of Nina, a vanguard of one.

The day passed quietly, but Nina remained alert for any renewed attack. She stopped before sundown and took her usual precautions: weapons at the ready, and no evening blaze to mark her location.

She was not surprised, however, when a fierce struggle erupted that night so near at hand, she did not bother grabbing her bow as she came out of her blankets. She unsheathed only her knife. This would be close combat.

Nina emerged into a starry darkness to see the shadowy form of a man grappling with the wolf. As the animal lunged for the man's throat, he stabbed downward. Starlight glinted from his blade.

"No!" Nina screamed.

Left-handed, she conjured Ercil's fire, hurled it at the man, and by its light found her target. The orb had barely left her fingers before she was throwing her knife, hard and true, at the man's temple. The blade buried in his skull at the same instant the wolf sank fangs into the man's throat. Together they went down, the man's body crumpling, the wolf on top of him. Growling viciously, the animal ripped into the corpse, flinging bloody chunks into the night.

Nina did not attempt to dissuade the wolf. There would be no reasoning with it in its frenzy. Gradually, however, when the corpse was mangled beyond recognition, the wolf raised its head from its gory work and howled at the stars. Again Nina heard the note of melancholy. But the sound also conveyed triumph.

"Are you hurt?" Nina asked when the wolf ceased its howling and lowered its head to look at her. "Did he stab you? Let me examine you for injuries."

In response, the creature turned away and walked to the stream beside which Nina had camped. It lowered its muzzle and opened its mouth, not to drink but to swish its jaws in the water. The act had a deeply human quality to it, like someone wanting to rinse a bad taste from their mouth. Then the wolf stepped into the stream and crouched, allowing the flow to flush blood from the creature's fur. By a second conjured witchlight, Nina had seen that the animal's coat was wet with blood. But was it the man's or the wolf's?

After minutes of soaking, the wolf rose from the stream and shook itself vigorously, slinging water in all directions. Then the creature came to Nina. Calmly, exuding no wariness, only a confident trust, the wolf sat on its haunches with its spine to her.

"Did he get you in the back?" Nina murmured as she gently parted the wolf's barely damp fur. By a floating orb of witchlight, she located the injury. The man's blade had sliced the backstrap muscle, but had reached no vital organ. Nina cleaned the wound with her strongest disinfectant, talking to the wolf all the while, telling the creature what she was doing. The wolf yipped at the remedy's sting but did not pull away from her. Before suturing the wound with catgut, Nina applied the same deadener she'd used on Corlis's thorn punctures and Jacca's blistered skin. The wolf flinched at the prick of the needle, but as the deadener took hold the creature allowed her to finish closing the wound.

"Well done," Nina said as she packed away her medical kit. "You're a better and more sensible patient than many I've had."

She paused as the wolf stood and turned its head to regard her. On impulse, she reached to stroke the animal's ears, but drew back as a look of startlement came into the wolf's hazel eyes.

"Your pardon," she muttered, dropping her hand. "I meant no offense. Whatever you are, friend, I perceive that you are not accustomed to being petted. I will not touch you again without your permission."

The wolf continued to stare at her, in a manner that Nina would have found unnerving from an ordinary carnivore. This animal, however, could lock gazes with no show of aggression. Something in the wolf's expression was profoundly human. In its eyes, Nina saw the hopeful sorrow that she had detected earlier. Longing was there also, and other emotions she could not read.

Nina dropped her gaze at the same instant the wolf did. The animal padded away into the night, beyond the reach of Ercil's fire. It did not stray far, for in the starlight Nina glimpsed the paleness of the wolf's muzzle and throat.

She could also see the dead man's remains. Unappealing though it was to spend what was left of the night so near the mangled corpse, Nina made no attempt to relocate her camp. She only pulled her knife from the man's skull, washed the blade in the stream, and returned to her blankets, to doze fitfully until dawn.

Chapter Twenty-Two

The wolf healed quickly. Nina fed the animal all the meat it could eat. No day passed that she did not hunt. Rabbits remained plentiful, and as she continued northward she found deer taking the place of antelope and pigs. Venison was a welcome change. It seemed an age since Nina had tasted it.

She remained on watch for new attackers, but none came. The road that arrowed to the north began to open up. It parted ways with the Rum Ridges, the road running straight while the ridges curved away eastward. In the thick woods to either side of the road, pines now outnumbered hardwoods, another sign that Nina was leaving southern climes behind.

Autumn edged toward winter, with nights so chilly that the wolf often slept with her, always atop her blankets but pressing so close that Nina benefited from the animal's body heat. The presence of the wolf was a comfort to her, but also mystifying in the way the wolf's nearness evoked memories of Nina's deceased husband, and even more vivid recollections of Corlis.

She sometimes woke to find herself curled against the wolf's back much as she had nestled with Corlis in the cold desert nights of her final week with the nomad. Awaking with the wolf in such a manner made Nina want to blush. She threw off her blankets and launched self-consciously into her morning routine. The wolf sprang up and darted away into the woods, almost as if it too were embarrassed. On such occasions, Nina had to remind herself that the creature *was* an animal, not a person. Some part of her, however, was not convinced.

Though the road remained deserted, Nina continued her habit of pulling aside each evening, off the packed surface and into the trees, to make her nightly camp alongside a stream that flowed some distance from the road. So ingrained was this practice by now, so much a matter of course rather than conscious thought, she was nearly surprised out of her saddle when she reined Traveller into the pines one evening, and after a dozen steps the horse balked. Trav stopped in his tracks as if he had hit a wall and would fling Nina into that invisible barrier.

"Whoa!" Nina exclaimed as she recovered her balance. "What's happened, Trav? Are you caught?" She scanned the forest floor but could see no impediment, no vines or stemmy briars in which the horse might have become entangled.

Dismounting, Nina checked Trav over, feeling for swollen tendons, lifting his feet, looking for stones in his shoes or anything of the sort that could account for his sudden standstill. She ended her inspection at the horse's head. Traveller regarded her without alarm or visible sign of distress, but he had planted his feet foursquare, giving an impression of inalterable immobility.

"What's going on here?" Nina muttered as she turned from the horse to the piney woods that Trav refused to enter. The sun hung low in the west, bathing the trees in hazy amber light. It picked out nothing except the stream flowing between low banks, and beyond the stream a rock outcropping. Was something hiding there?

As Nina stepped in front of Trav, seeking a better view of the rocks, she smashed face-first into an unseen surface that yielded just enough to avoid bloodying her nose.

"Drisha!" she swore, reeling backward into the horse. She caught her balance against Trav's shoulder. When she had her feet under her again, she advanced once more, but cautiously, keeping tight hold of the reins with one hand and putting her other out in front of her.

Her fingers met the invisible wall that had balked the horse. Its surface was smooth to the touch, and slightly warm. Nina pushed against it with her knuckles and felt the surface dimple under the pressure. She pushed harder, and broke through. Except there was no breaking—the surface rebounded and tightened around her wrist. Nina jerked her hand back through the unseeable hole she had made, and heard the hole close with a *pop.*

"This is wizardry," she muttered as she stood contemplating her discovery. "I have found the land of my relatives. They seem not to welcome visitors."

Nina rubbed at her lower lip, aware that her knowledge of magical barriers was limited. She knew of the ancient spellwork that kept the province of Ruain secret, isolating it from the rest of Ladrehdin. But as a daughter of that realm, she could come and go at will, unhindered by those spells. She had certainly not expected to find magic of that sort raised against her as she sought to make a friendly visit to the home of her blood kin.

She touched her fingers to the barrier and gave a shout, so suddenly that Traveller, standing behind her, jigged a step and snorted. As Nina reached back to calm the horse, she continued in a loud voice:

"Greetings! I am the eldest daughter of House Verek. Your ancestress, Lady Vivienne of Ruain, is my baby sister. I am senior to you all, and I have come far to make your acquaintance. Be pleased to drop your wall, kinsfolk, and allow me admittance."

Nina waited a moment, giving her words a chance to penetrate. Then she balled her fist and punched the barrier. Her fist popped through it, as before, but this time there was no sensation of the surface rebounding and encircling her wrist. She'd knocked a gaping hole in the wall, a hole that did not close. Nina kept punching, enlarging the hole and feeling for its unseen edges as she went. Several minutes went by and the sun was nearly set before she had beat a way through, a gap wide enough to admit herself and her horse.

The wolf paced nearby, watching her and occasionally rearing up to put its paws on the invisible wall. The creature clawed, and sniffed, and even licked the barrier. The instant Nina stepped to the other side, leading her horse through the breach, the wolf bounded through as well, close on Traveller's heels.

"That was a lot of work," Nina muttered, shaking her sore hand as the wolf trotted up beside her. "I hope these unsociable relatives of mine are worth the effort."

She made for the outcropping of rock, it being the only landmark in what was an otherwise featureless woodland. Aided by the wolf, who explored every cranny in the heaped stones, Nina determined that the rocks hid no threat. She made her camp at the base of them, using the stones for a fire ring and sparking a blaze big enough to be seen for miles. If Vivie's descendants had not felt the beating she'd given their magic, then they must at least detect her bonfire.

Nobody came, however, until late morning of the next day. Nina had plenty of time to hunt for meat. She and the wolf made a good breakfast on rabbit.

Then she endured a bath in the stream, shivering in the morning cold but determined to tidy herself for her first meeting with Vivie's brood. By the time her relatives arrived, Nina was wearing the best clothes her packs could yield after so long a journey. She had her knife on her belt, her rapier hanging at her hip, and her sling draped around her neck in full view over her tunic. In her left hand she held her bow, and at her right her quiver rested, propped against the rocks. Traveller stood behind her, saddled and loaded with her gear. The wolf sat on its haunches a little in front and to one side of Nina.

That the three of them made a striking picture was clear as the emissaries of Vivie's clan approached from the west. Four individuals rode toward Nina at a brisk trot until the lead rider seemed to get a good look at her. That man threw up his hand, signaling to those who followed. The foursome reined to a halt under the pines, keeping distance between themselves and Nina. They sat on their horses in silence, eyeing her as she studied them. Two of the riders were men; two, women. All seemed young, but that was to be expected of *wysards*.

More surprising than their youth was their style of dress. These adepts made no secret of who and what they were. Magical symbolism covered their clothes. Celestial motifs abounded: one woman's flowing black cloak sparkled with silver stars and crescent moons. On the jacket of the man beside her, double triangles and staring eyes were outlined in embroidery of every color. The morning sun picked out metallic glints of gold, emerald green, and crystal blue. The other two riders sported various representations of acorns, willow leaves, seashells and snowflakes. Among the mass of Nature symbols, Nina spotted a bear claw and a three-fingered hand. The hand was splayed across the crown of a tall hat that tapered upward, ending in a point. Nina nearly choked, trying not to laugh at the pointed hat, such a ridiculously old-fashioned and long-abandoned bit of wizardly attire.

Her amusement faded as she looked past the foursome, to survey the mounted troop that came up behind them. Twenty riders, male and female, carried swords and bows, reining in a tight formation led by their captain. That man cut an imposing figure on the back of a powerfully built horse with a coat the color of pale gold. He had the look and carriage of a warrior.

This show of force was not the welcome I expected, Nina thought as she turned back to the ostentatiously dressed foursome in front of her. Mindful of her initial difficulties with Corlis—his reluctance to speak unless first spoken to—she broke the increasingly tense silence.

"Greetings!" she called out, and then repeated a version of what she'd said at the barrier last evening, identifying herself not by name, but as Lady Vivienne's senior sibling and the eldest daughter of House Verek.

"Perhaps you have been expecting me?" Nina added with raised eyebrow when none of the four lead riders responded. "Did Vivie not send word from Ruain?"

The mention of that magical place seemed to breathe life into the still and silent foursome, and to fill the armed guard at their back with awe. As one, riders front and rear dropped from their saddles and went to their knees.

"Welcome, Lady Karenina!" cried the woman in the star-speckled cloak. "Indeed, we were told to anticipate your arrival." She held her arms up toward Nina in a gesture almost beseeching as she added, "But I never thought ..."

Never thought I could get through your wall? Nina wondered as the woman seemed unable to continue.

Aloud, however, she replied diplomatically, "Did you doubt that I would get here before we all grew old?" The foursome tittered at this, their laughter timid. All the company rose to their feet when Nina motioned them up. "I thank you for riding to meet me. Your escort does me honor," Nina added, choosing to regard the armed troop as a compliment rather than a threat.

"The honor is ours, Lady," offered the man with gold-rimmed eyes on his jacket. "Our people await to receive you. But ... the wolf?" Hesitantly, he pointed.

"The wolf is with me," Nina replied, her firmness brooking no argument. "Only brigands and assassins have cause to fear the creature. On the road here we encountered certain of those sorts, but I trust your lands are free of them."

Various avowals and murmurs of wonder rose from the foursome as they remounted. Nina cased her bow and shouldered her quiver, then swung into the saddle. She shot a grin at the wolf as the creature rose from its haunches to trot beside her. During her brief conversation with Vivie's brood, the wolf had never taken its eyes off the four. Now those riders made a nervous knot, reining their horses away from the wolf and keeping Nina between themselves and her silent bodyguard.

The captain of the armed troop also led his riders aside. As Nina crossed in front of him, the man ran an appraising gaze over herself and her weaponry. She pretended not to notice either his glances or the shining mane of his hair streaming upon his shoulders, as blond as his horse. Secretly, however, Nina vowed to test that warrior's sword arm before she left these lands.

None of her nearer companions spoke much as they rode through the woodland, escorting her westward away from the road and the ridges. Nina tried making small talk, hoping to loosen tongues. The foursome seemed willing to speak only of the weather, the changing seasons, the bountiful fall harvest. From their polite but restrained comments, Nina surmised that Vivie's descendants had made a comfortable home in this region between Ruain and the southwest hills.

Just *how* comfortably they had established themselves behind their magical barrier became apparent in late afternoon, when Nina's escorts brought her to a stone-walled city towering above the pine trees. Heavy wooden gates opened to reveal three-story structures of granite and limestone. Tree-lined lanes wove between the buildings and led to open spaces like parks. Despite the lateness of autumn, flowers were everywhere. Blooms spilled from trellises and window boxes, painting the fronts of the buildings in vibrant colors. Strangely, however, no floral fragrances wafted past on the breeze. Nina smelled pine sap, wood smoke, and the odors of cooking. Those things were real enough. But the flowers? Were they illusion?

Once through the gates, her four companions turned sharply along a lane that followed the wall. The way took them past a large exercise paddock to the stables. There the four alighted and handed their reins to the grooms emerging from the stalls.

Nina dismounted as well, but she declined with a brief shake of her head as a stableboy reached for Traveller's reins. "I'll see to him myself," she murmured. "I owe him that after all the miles he's carried me."

Stepping inside the stable with the wolf at her heels also gave Nina a chance to observe the other horses' reactions in close quarters. They proved to be as untroubled by the wolf as Traveller had been since first encountering the animal. While Nina unsaddled Trav and gave the roan a rubdown, the wolf sat outside the stall, alert to every coming and going of grooms and riders but showing aggression toward none.

Nina took reassurance from the animal's calm demeanor. The wolf appeared to sense no threat. Something about this magical place made Nina jittery, however. If the flowers were illusion, what other kinds of artifice might she encounter here?

"Allow me to escort you to a guesthouse," murmured the woman in the starry cloak, who had stood outside waiting with the others while Nina tended her horse. "Sumner has gone to announce your arrival and arrange for dinner. But first you may wish to rest and refresh yourself."

"I've been looking forward to a real bed," Nina replied, smiling. "A blanket on the ground gets old. Your hospitality is welcome, and so is the prospect of visiting with my kinfolk." Nina looked around, wondering if she were tied by blood to each of the dozen or more people within view. Several of them cast sidelong glances at her before hastening on their way. Whatever their magical powers might be, the people within the walls went about unarmed. In the absence of the mounted troop—those riders having circled the exterior, presumably heading for their barracks—Nina's bristling weaponry marked her out.

"In my travels, I have often needed bow and blade," she commented, turning back to the cloaked woman. "Here among family, however, I shall be glad to lay them down. It is not your custom, I perceive, to wear arms within your city gates."

This seemed to be the correct thing to say. Nina's companion relaxed visibly. "That will be well, Lady Karenina," the woman murmured.

"Let us not stand on ceremony," Nina said as she shouldered her saddlebags. "I am happy to be known as your 'Aunt Nina' … if I am indeed your aunt," she added with a chuckle. "I confess I'm somewhat overwhelmed by the idea of so many nieces and nephews." She gestured at the people who walked along the streets and sat on benches under the pines.

The woman picked up Nina's medicine kit and beckoned for her companions to bring the rest of the gear that Nina had unloaded off Trav.

"Not all of us are related by blood," the woman said, glancing quizzically at Nina as the four of them walked together up a lane leading away from the stables. "Though it is true that many here are direct descendants of Lady Vivienne, we also have master *wysards* who have come to us from the western mountains. The young people who work in the fields, stables, and kitchens are apprentices drawn for the most part from non-magian families." She inclined her head. "Some have no trace of a magical gift. Nonetheless, they are valued members of our community." The woman gave Nina a thin, tight-lipped smile. "What an inbred lot you must have imagined us to be, if you thought we closed ourselves off from all except our blood kin."

I am your blood relative, and I had to force my way in, Nina thought. But aloud she exclaimed in unfeigned relief, "Oh! So that's the way of it." She nodded. "I thank you for dispelling my misapprehensions. In truth, I had wondered how a society of long-lived *wysards* could sustain itself if entirely cut off from the world of the mundane." She smiled at the woman in the cloak. "I perceive that I did not ask enough questions of my little sister."

They had reached the porch steps of a cottage that fronted a tree-shaded, parklike expanse of green. Here, as everywhere, flowers blossomed. Nina dropped her saddlebags and bent to sniff a magnificent red rose. It had no fragrance. She straightened, and looked a question at the woman beside her.

"Wizardry," the woman said. "Though it is magic with little substance, it's good practice for the apprentices. Each is charged with the upkeep of a garden plot or window box."

"I shall wish to meet the gardener who tends this patch," Nina said, fingering the soft petals. "It's beautiful spellwork. Glorious color."

While they stood by the steps talking, the two who had come with them from the stables slipped through the cottage's front door to deposit Nina's baggage. Now those two—the youthful man and woman draped in nature symbols—waited silently on the end of the porch as if anticipating further instructions.

"I will leave you now," said the woman in the cloak. "If you need anything, Deidre and Bastian will be here." She nodded at the pair on the porch. "Perhaps you might offer refreshment to our honored guest?" the woman added with a pointed look at the one called Deidre.

"My pleasure!" exclaimed the girl so addressed. She turned to smile at Nina. "I'll run get cakes and things, and be right back to help you unpack."

Deidre was gone long enough, however, that by the time she returned, Nina had largely settled into the three-room guesthouse. In its small bedchamber she divested herself of most of her weaponry, but retained the knife at her belt and the sling around her neck, wearing the knife visibly but hiding the sling under her tunic. Nina had emptied her bags, hung up her clothes, and made tea in the cottage's tiny kitchen before Deidre reappeared. The girl came in carrying a wicker basket that overflowed with apple bread, barley muffins, and oatcakes.

"Those smell wonderful!" Nina exclaimed as Deidre set the basket on the table. "Long it's been since I've had fresh bread." For emphasis, she tapped the table with a hard biscuit from her saddlebags. "I've been living on this and wild game."

"Ugh," Deidre grunted, attempting to sample the hardtack but finding it impossible to break open. "I've never been a traveler, and I don't think roaming is in my future, if this is what you have to eat." The girl had a friendly air about her, but also a distracted one. She stepped from the kitchen to stare out the front door. "My Bastian is nervous about your wolf," she said, speaking to Nina over her shoulder. "He's on one end of the porch, and the wolf's on the other."

"I saw," Nina replied. "The wolf won't come inside. That creature has been keeping watch over me for many a mile. Evidently it is not prepared to cease the practice, here in your city. I count it a privilege to call that animal my friend."

"How extraordinary," Deidre murmured. "I've known *wysards* to keep ravens and falcons and sometimes owls. We've cats here, too—they come and go as they please, calling no one master. Occasionally we get a wayfarer with a dog, and I remember one had a pet goat. But a wolf?" The girl shook her head. "Wolves are rare within our borders. They stay mostly in the mountains, or in the high north. Always they run in packs, not alone." Deidre left off staring out the door. She returned to the kitchen table, to join Nina in nibbling on cakes. "Did your wolf get lost, do you suppose?" the girl asked, looking thoughtful.

"I have wondered that," Nina said. "From the moment it joined me on my northbound road, I have sensed a deep loneliness in the creature."

"Might you try to return it to its own kind?" Deidre peered at her over a half-eaten oatcake. "If you were to travel onward, I mean."

Nina returned the girl's gaze. "The wolf will be welcome to accompany me for as long as it wishes. Like your cats, it is masterless."

* * *

As evening fell, Nina answered a knock at her cottage door to find the starry-cloaked woman bearing an invitation to dinner, and full of apology for not having introduced herself earlier. She was Marsial, a granddaughter of Lady Vivienne—one of several in the community who had the distinction and the privilege, she said, of direct descent from the youngest child of House Verek.

Under her speckled cloak, Marsial now wore an elegant black gown. Nina still sported trousers, tunic, and riding boots, but she had unbraided her long hair and brushed it till it shone. With help from Deidre, who showed a knack for such things, Nina had pulled her hair up into a sleek triple-twist.

Nothing more could she do, for she had no formal attire with her. The gown she'd worn to dinner aboard Dalton's ship was long gone. Besides, Nina would not wish to be encumbered by skirts, going into an unfamiliar situation with unknown people. She caught Marsial looking at her belted knife and slanting a glance toward the wolf that stood guard on the porch. But the woman did not speak of either, and Nina offered neither explanation nor excuse.

As the eldest of House Verek, I outrank everyone here, Nina thought as she walked with Marsial through the flower-filled park, heading to a three-story house on the green's far side. *Let my juniors make of me what they will.*

For her part, Nina would be appraising every individual she met tonight, trying to plumb the undercurrents that moved in this place. Except for Deidre, everyone she had so far encountered seemed uneasy about her. The fellow in the embroidered jacket and pointed hat—Sumner, he'd been called—had disappeared as soon as he rode through the city gates. The young man named Bastian had fallen all over himself, bowing so low he nearly smacked his nose on the porch when Nina answered Marsial's knock at the cottage door.

Marsial herself was stiffly formal and reserved, offering only polite chitchat as she escorted Nina to the house across the green, the wolf trotting alongside. Candlelight blazed from every window on the building's ground floor. Torches burned in silver holders beside the massive front door, where a trim watchman snapped to attention when Marsial approached with Nina. The fellow pulled open the door, then drew back, his eyes on the wolf that stepped smartly over the threshold.

Nina and Marsial followed the wolf into a grand space that was half ballroom and half dining hall. Thirty or more individuals were gathered in the open half toward the front, while another dozen worked around the elegantly appointed dinner table farther back. Those workers were laying out the meal, putting bread on the table and pouring wine, while the guests stood around in conversational knots. A hum of chatter had filled the room as Nina entered, but the hum diminished when people began to spot her. They nudged one another, trying not to point but showing no compunction about staring.

She and her bodyguard glimpsed the ancient *wysard* at the same moment. A knot of people opened to reveal a lanky, white-haired old man. He wore a purple robe and stood leaning on a staff topped by a crystal orb. Nina knew at once: This was an Old One, a *wysard* who had survived the bad centuries by hiding in the highest, most inaccessible peaks of the far west. Only since Lady Carin's restoration of Ladrehdin's magical potency had the Old Ones begun venturing down from their mountain hideaways.

That this ancient magician held a place of honor among his younger colleagues was evident by the way people clustered around him, acolytes in attendance upon their master. Now they drew apart, splitting the knot to allow the old *wysard* an unobstructed view of the newcomers at the door.

Nina was starting to drop a curtsy, but she shot bolt upright as the wolf launched into a sprint. With frenzied barking, the creature raced toward the old *wysard*, its claws clattering and slipping as it sought purchase on the polished floor.

"Wolf!" Nina shouted. "Stop!" She had her hand up and her powers gathered, ready to petrify the creature with the spell of stone. From the corners of her eyes, she saw many other hands go up too. The wolf was in mortal peril from this assembly of *wysards* who would not hesitate to kill the creature rather than allow it to harm an Elder of the craft.

The Old One had also flung out his hand, but in welcome, not menace.

"Wolfram!" the *wysard* cried. "I'd given you up. Despairing I was, that I'd ever see you again." The Elder glanced around the room, waving down all the raised hands before fastening his gaze upon Nina and Marsial at the door. To Nina he said, "Thank you, my lady, for bringing me this lost fellow."

Then he turned to Marsial. "Young woman, may we have your cloak over here? He'll be starkers."

The old *wysard* was having to shout to be heard above the frantic barking of "Wolfram." That creature raced in circles at the Elder's feet, yipping hysterically, crouching on its belly, then springing up in a show of delirious joy. As Nina and Marsial approached, the latter doffing her cloak as they came, the Elder spoke soothingly to the creature, calming it with a touch between its ears.

"Patience, boy," he said as he brought the wolf to heel. Most of the people who had clustered around him had hurried aside at the wolf's frenzied approach. To those few who remained close by, the old *wysard* said, "Be pleased, all of you, to turn your back. Respect the boy's dignity."

As Marsial held her cloak out to him, the Elder shook his head. "I'll be needing you to hold that up and spread it wide. Make a screen of it." He tipped his head to Nina. "Help her, my lady. Take an edge and stretch it across. For modesty's sake, I would normally work this spell behind a closed door. But I think Wolfe won't wait for that." At the Elder's heels, the creature was whining, crying with anxiety and eagerness.

Nina did as instructed, raising one side of Marsial's voluminous cloak while the woman held the other side.

"Now close your eyes, ladies," the old *wysard* said. He stooped to lay one hand on the wolf's head, keeping firm hold with the other on his magical staff.

Nina shot a glance at Marsial and saw the woman standing with bowed head and tight-shut eyes. Her own curiosity was too great, however: Nina had to look. Through narrowed gaze she peered past the cloak's edge.

Under the *wysard*'s touch, the wolf had grown still. The old man began to mutter, chanting what was unmistakably an incantation, but in a singsong voice too low for Nina to catch the words. A light flashed in the crystal atop the Elder's staff. The glimmer began as a watery blue, then shaded into spring green. Steadily the light grew more dazzling until it burst forth in rays of pure white.

Nina could not look at it. She dropped her gaze toward the floor at the moment the *wysard* brought his incantation to a climax. The low murmur of his voice rose with the brightening of the crystal until his final words burst out as brilliantly as the light:

"Come back!" he cried.

In that instant, the wolf transformed.

At the *wysard*'s feet there now crouched a bone-thin youth. The boy's brown hair fell around his face. But Nina glimpsed the familiar hazel of her wolf's eyes as the youth straightened from his crouch. He clawed his way to an upright position, leaning for support on the *wysard* much as the old man leant on his staff.

As the Elder struggled to keep on his feet, Nina swooped in. "Give it here!" she exclaimed as she tugged the cloak out of Marsial's hands. She threw the garment around the stark-naked, shivering youth, then wrapped her arms around both the boy and the Elder. Easily she held them up, for both felt light in her embrace. The old *wysard* was frail, and the boy stick-thin.

Nina judged the youth to be not more than seventeen. Despite all the rabbit and deer she'd fed him when he'd walked on four legs, the boy was bony. Through the cloak, she felt his ribs. She hugged him and whispered, "I suspected there was more to you than met the eye. I'm glad to see you for what you really are, my wolf cub."

She said that last with a smile, but her words provoked a torrent of tears in which relief, gratitude, and exhaustion blended.

"My lady!" the boy gasped out between sobs. "I can never repay you. You have saved me from torment."

Nina shook her head. "You owe me nothing, child. If there was a debt, you discharged it many times on our journey here. Every night along that perilous road, you watched over me."

She shifted her gaze from the boy's tear-streaked face to the wrinkled visage of the old *wysard*. "Forgive my impertinence, master," she murmured. "Normally I would not fling my arms, uninvited, around an Elder. Particularly when we have not been introduced. But I feared, sir, that you were about to topple over."

The old man chuckled. "I commend your swift action, my lady." His faded blue eyes twinkled as he added, "It's seldom that any raven-haired beauty sees fit to embrace me these days, with or without invitation. But now I'll thank you to help me to my chambers. It's not easy magic, getting a shapeshifter unstuck and back to his true self. I need rest, and so does Wolfram."

"Of course," Nina muttered. She looked over her shoulder for Marsial. "Honored niece, please give the Elder your arm while I assist the boy. I beg you will lead the way to suitable quarters where master and novice may be at their ease."

The last words were not out of Nina's mouth before Marsial was hastening to support the old man. When Nina could be sure he would remain upright without her, she released his shoulders and gathered the cloak tight around Wolfram. The boy shivered violently, more from shock, Nina thought, than from cold. She half carried his thin frame upstairs, following behind Marsial and the Elder.

Racing ahead of them were three of the individuals who had previously been setting the table. That trio topped the stairs and disappeared down a dim hallway. When Nina's slower progress brought her along that same corridor, supporting Wolfram, she found the three busily lighting lamps and preparing the old *wysard*'s quarters to also accommodate the newly arrived novice. The Elder's chambers had two beds, but the second of these was covered in unfinished weavings, skeins of yarn, and a small handloom. Evidently the old man was a weaver, and he had been using the second bed as a work table.

The clutter was soon cleared away, allowing Nina to tuck her wolf cub under the bed's soft coverlet. The boy had not relinquished Marsial's starry cloak. He remained wrapped in it, under the covers. That lady seemed too concerned with the Elder, however, to give present thought to her garment. The ancient *wysard* now lay stretched upon his own bed, already snoring under heaps of blankets. It had cost him an effort to free the boy from a wolf's skin: sleep claimed the old man as soon as his head hit the pillow. Marsial perched on a stool beside the *wysard*, an anxious frown on her face.

"I am a trained healer with many years' experience," Nina said as she crossed to stand at Marsial's shoulder. "You may safely leave the old one and the boy in my care. Go down to dinner and reassure your guests that all is well." She smiled. "Unless you are much accustomed to watching shapeshifters transform in your dining room, I daresay the gathered company is abuzz with this evening's events."

"What a marvelous thing to have witnessed!" Marsial softly exclaimed, twisting on her stool to look up at Nina. "I thought shapeshifters were things of legend, long extinct—if they ever existed at all."

Nina tapped her teeth with her thumbnail. "I remember my father saying that no *wysard* of Ladrehdin had been capable of shapeshifting in five thousand years. And here I've been wayfaring with such a being. But the greater surprise is that a *wysard* still lives who can work a countercharm against such ancient and powerful magic." Nina gazed down at the sleeping Elder. The old fellow's hair lay upon his pillow, fine and white as gossamer. "He came to you from the mountains, I assume?"

Marsial nodded. "About four months ago, Master Gelgeis arrived at our western gate. He came on foot, packing little more than his weaving frame. We took him in without hesitation, for he appeared exhausted. Moreover, he carried a letter of introduction from Master Welwyn."

"Welwyn!" Nina exclaimed. "He is known to you?"

"Certainly. Many of us were apprenticed to Master Welwyn at one time or another. He established a school for young adepts. It continues here to this day, with the most proficient among us teaching our apprentices in the way that Welwyn taught us."

"How long ago did he leave you?"

"Oh, he's been gone many years." Marsial's frown deepened with the effort to remember. "As I recall, he meant to go south ... perhaps even beyond the Southern Seas. He never tired of searching out promising new adepts. Teaching is in his blood."

Nina smiled. "My parents used to say that the mastering of rambunctious apprentices was what kept him young. The man is ancient beyond all reckoning, yet still he travels abroad and seeks adventure. My brother in the Ore Hills told me that Welwyn had visited him, some time ago. I presume that was after he left here."

"How is Uncle Galen?" Marsial asked. "Occasionally we get word of him, carried here by travelers. The last I heard, Master Galen was happy with his home in the Hills—and with the smithcraft that has made him a fabulously wealthy *wysard*." Marsial laughed lightly, an expression of admiration in which Nina heard no trace of resentment or envy.

Nevertheless, she resisted the urge to put her hand in her pocket and pull out the necklace Galen had made for her. Reassuring though it was to hear Marsial speak freely and fondly of the metalsmith, Nina meant to continue in a cautious vein with these relatives of hers, until she could fathom the uneasy currents that she had felt since encountering their magical barrier in the woodland. To Marsial's question about Galen, therefore, Nina replied only that she had found him cheerful and well. She offered similarly vague tidings of Dalton and Legary, omitting any mention of the sea captain's flings or the stonemason's griefs. The younger generations need not know intimate details from the lives of their elder uncles.

Marsial seemed satisfied with the family news Nina imparted, skimpy though it was. "How wonderful that you have been to see them all!" she exclaimed. "I cannot imagine undertaking such a journey." She rose from her stool. "Now that you are here with us, you must think me a poor hostess. Do allow me to send for our resident apothecary. He can watch over Master Gelgeis and the boy while you go down to dinner."

Nina shook her head. "I feel a responsibility toward the young man. I would not be easy, leaving him to another's care." She glanced at Wolfram, who lay curled up and sound asleep in the second bed. "Pray attend to your other guests," she said, turning back to Marsial. "Have my dinner sent up on a tray, and I shall be content."

All was done as Nina requested. Marsial departed, and within minutes one of the smartly dressed young attendants was at the door, bearing a tray piled high with meats and breads, fruits, and all manner of vegetables. The room filled with mouthwatering aromas.

As Nina sat eating at a table beside Wolfram's bed, the boy's nose twitched. Though restored to his proper form, the youth seemed to have retained his wolfish senses. The smell of food brought him out of deep sleep. His eyes flew open, and he looked wildly confused. Then his gaze fastened upon the roasted vegetables that Nina was picking from a skewer. His hand shot out from under the bedcovers and grabbed the food from Nina's fingers.

"Steady!" she exclaimed as Wolfram devoured the cooked tubers and onions. "There's plenty here." She picked up another skewer. "It's good to dine on something other than rabbit, is it not?"

"Mmm," Wolfram mumbled with his mouth full. "I'll not eat meat again. How I have longed for turnips and radishes!"

The boy ate for the better part of an hour. He stuffed himself with vegetables and fruits, cooked and raw, and turned up his nose at every dish of meat, while Nina enjoyed the herbed chicken and fried pork. Although her introduction to Vivienne's clan had not proceeded as she had anticipated, she could not fault her relatives' hospitality.

Sated, Nina sat back and sipped tea, and watched Wolfram. When he'd gotten enough vegetables down him to blunt the sharp edge of his appetite, Nina began to coax forth the boy's story. Wolfram spoke in fits and starts, pausing often to chew and swallow. Mostly he found the words he wanted, but sometimes he struggled, as though his tongue had to relearn the trick of shaping speech.

It had been a wolf's tongue for longer than the boy could say. Wolfram knew only that the weather was warm when he and his wizardly master took the road under the brow of the Rum Ridges. They had heard nothing of the road's reputation as a perilous place. Their first inkling of danger was the arrow that pierced the heart of Wolfram's beloved master, killing that *wysard* instantly.

"I could do nothing," the boy mumbled, setting down a bowl of greens and avoiding Nina's gaze as he recounted the murder. "Moments before the arrow struck, I had taken wolf form. I'd been practicing my shifting under the eye of my teacher, Master Eymir. With him I had come down from our home in the mountains. He was curious to see the wider world. If we kept to ourselves and traveled remote ways, he thought we would avoid trouble with people who might still fear magic."

Nina sighed. "You found a road so solitary, murderers have taken it for their own. What did you do when Eymir died?"

The boy whimpered. "I hid. It shames me to say it. But taking the shape of a wolf leaves me helpless for an hour or more, each time that I do it. I had already shifted twice that day. Master Eymir was helping me to shift more readily, but every change wearied me to my bones. When he fell dead, I barely had the strength to crawl on my belly into the rocks."

Nina started to offer a comforting touch, but stopped when she recalled how Wolfram had reacted that time she'd unthinkingly stroked his wolf ears. "But you vowed revenge," she murmured, dropping her hand. "Is that not why you stayed in the shadow of those bleak ridges? You might have turned back and headed for home. But you lingered alongside that road."

Wolfram curled his lip. "I did seek revenge, and I began to take it. One of that pack of murderers had already fallen to my fangs before I met you, lady." He looked up at her. "Seeing you riding that road, carrying many weapons with the confidence of someone who knew how to use them, I wanted you for my ally against the others."

"So that's what became of Eymir," said a voice from the other bed.

Nina and Wolfram turned together to discover Master Gelgeis sitting up, propped against pillows. The old *wysard* shook his head sadly.

"When I heard that Eymir had gone wayfaring and not returned," he said, pushing himself farther into the room's lamplight, "I set out to find my old friend and rival." Gelgeis raised a long-fingered hand and pointed at Wolfram. "You remember I was there, boy, on the day Eymir made you his apprentice. You were just a pup, but even at a tender age you'd become known throughout the mountains as the first true shapeshifter to appear in this world since time out of mind." Gelgeis heaved a sigh. "I had wanted you under my wing. But I didn't get down in time to stake my claim, so high in the peaks is my hermitage. Be that as was, I never begrudged Eymir his good fortune in winning you. He had the skills and the knowledge to help you realize your Gift. It is a great one."

"Thank you, sir," Wolfram mumbled. "Your words honor me more than I deserve. Without my master, I found myself incapable of throwing off the shape of the beast. Had you not taken pity on me, I would still be howling at the moon."

"Nonsense, boy." Gelgeis threw off his blankets and grabbed the staff that had been left at the head of his bed. Supporting himself on it, he tottered over to scoop a bread roll off the dinner tray that Nina and Wolfram had nearly emptied. "No young adept could be expected to master shapeshifting without help from a good teacher. In Eymir, you had an excellent one. But now, boy, you're stuck with me. As far as I'm aware, I am the only living *wysard* who knows the spellcraft that you need to learn. Let us honor the memory of Eymir by continuing the work which you and he began. What say you, boy? Will you accept my tutelage?"

"With deepest gratitude, sir!" Wolfram exclaimed. He made to rise from his bed. But as he struggled out from under the covers, the boy tangled up in Marsial's lovely cloak. Before Nina could rescue the garment, he had torn it. Moreover, the youth had forgotten that he wasn't wearing a stitch. Only when he dropped to one knee, to offer obeisance to his new master, did Wolfram seem to realize that he was buck naked.

"Apologies, my lady!" the boy cried as he grabbed the now tattered cloak and covered himself. "I beg your forgiveness." A deep flush of embarrassment spread over the skin that until recently had been fur-covered.

Nina laughed. "Be easy, cub. Everything you've got, I've seen before." She stood up from the bedside table. "I must carry the news to our hostess, that both of you have rallied from tonight's extraordinary spellwork." Nina cast an amused glance at the youth who knelt before the Elder, stock-still under the torn cloak as if afraid to move a muscle. "I will see if clothes can be found for you, young man, and ask that a meal be sent up for Master Gelgeis."

Marsial's other guests had finished their dinner by the time Nina got downstairs. She found several of them gathered in a knot, clutching wine glasses and speaking together in low voices. As Nina approached, the knot unraveled and an awkward silence filled the room. Marsial covered it with inquiries about the Old One and the shapeshifter.

Nina gave her the gist of Wolfram's story about the murdered Eymir, and how the boy had been trapped in wolf form, unable to resume his proper shape without the aid of his wizardly master. Eyes widened and spines stiffened among her listeners when Nina described in detail how she and the young adept had exacted vengeance on the brigands of the Rum Ridges for the murder of Eymir. Over the tops of their wine glasses, the assembled company exchanged glances, and all seemed relieved when Nina put down her own barely tasted drink and took her leave of them. They bowed her to the door, and Nina felt their stares as Marsial walked her from the dining hall and across the greenway to the guesthouse. The woman's manners were impeccably, unyieldingly formal when she said good-night and left Nina at the cottage.

As she stepped into her private quarters, Nina noted the continued presence of Bastian on the long porch under the eaves. The fellow tried but failed to hide in the shadows, leaving her wondering if he had been posted there as her general dogsbody and errand-runner, or more as a sentinel who was charged with alerting the others to her movements.

Sighing, Nina shut and locked the cottage door, and went to bed with all of her weapons arrayed close at hand.

Chapter Twenty-Three

Nina was several days into her visit with Vivienne's apprehensive brood before she saw an opportunity to chat privately with Master Gelgeis. He, too, was an outsider here, but he seemed to have the trust of these people. Nina turned to her fellow wayfarer, hopeful that the old *wysard* might shed light on the nervousness her kinsfolk displayed toward her. On a sunny morning when the city streets were nearly empty, she spotted Gelgeis sitting on a park bench, working his handloom. She joined him, intending to ply the Elder with questions.

Up until now, Nina's mornings had been occupied with learning her way around this surprisingly large and active enclave. Her reserved but attentive hostess Marsial had shown her a library that housed innumerable books of magic, many of them copied by hand from the holdings of the Weyrrock library in Ruain. Sumner—he of the embroidered jacket—had ventured from hiding to give Nina a tour of the city's workshops. Crafters occupied studios that turned out everything from pottery and baskets to boots and candles. Gelgeis, resident master of weaving, held daily classes in his own studio and could coax artistry from even the most fumble-fingered novice.

Everywhere Nina went, Bastian followed, at a discreet distance but always keeping her in sight. By the third morning, however, Bastian had picked up a tracker of his own. Wolfram trailed the young man, sometimes in his true guise but often in wolf form. His daunting presence distracted Nina's shadow so she could slip away unnoticed.

She was blissfully on her own the day she discovered the city's armory and the large practice field behind it. These proved to be the domain of the armed troop with which Marsial and Sumner had "greeted" Nina. Just outside the city's walls, archers and swordfighters trained under the eye of their captain—the blond warrior who had coolly appraised Nina but spoke no word to her at the barrier. Now he introduced himself as Odhrán, and he asked about the sling that peeked from under Nina's tunic. His blue eyes lingered on the open neck of her shirt, but Nina pretended not to notice.

She commandeered a corner of his practice field for a slinging demonstration. Odhrán knew the weapon but had tended to teach it only to those recruits who showed little skill with bow or blade. Nina's prowess, however, elevated his opinion of the sling—especially when every archer and fighter abandoned their own practice and raced to Nina's corner, drawn by the scream of Legary's whistling bullets. Intrigued by this new twist on an old weapon, Odhrán set the city's masons to shaping and drilling stones on the pattern of Legary's work. Within a day, Nina had a fresh crowd of novices begging to learn slingcraft.

On the morning she joined Master Gelgeis in the park, however, to sit and talk for an hour, neither she nor the weaver had pupils to teach. Every able-bodied resident of the city had walked or ridden to the fields beyond its walls, to help with the final haying of the year. The bales they cut and stored this autumn would be fodder through the winter for the community's horses and the animals they raised for meat and milk. The last haying was a long-established holiday, when every person dropped their usual pursuits and went to enjoy the sun and the communal effort of final harvest.

Gelgeis was excused from fieldwork on account of his age and his exalted rank. Nina excused herself, for she would not pass up this opportunity to speak with the old *wysard* with all her relatives absent. Gelgeis had been here long enough to have a finger on the pulse of this place and know the reasons for the palpable uneasiness Nina provoked in most of her kinsfolk. He broached the matter with no immediate answers, however, but with a question.

"Is it true, my lady," he asked as they sat side by side on the park bench, Nina rebraiding her sling cords and Gelgeis busy with his weaving frame, "that you have come here to assert primacy over these descendants of your baby sister?"

"*What?*" Nina dropped her sling and scooted around to stare at the old fellow. "What a notion! Where in the world did you get such an idea?"

Gelgeis did not look up from his work. He was weaving a new winter cloak for Marsial, to replace the garment Wolfram had ruined. This one would have the silver stars and crescent moons woven into the fabric itself, rather than added as embroidery. The old *wysard*'s hands flew with magical speed as he interlaced the silver threads with the black.

"It's what they're saying," he replied. "I've heard it everywhere. These relatives of yours are acutely aware that their ancestress is the youngest child of House Verek. They worry that you, the eldest and thus the natural heir, will assert your birthright, now that you have returned from distant seas. They think you have come to be sovereign over them. Quite frankly, my lady, they fear you. You broke magic they considered unbreakable—a barrier spell that I myself would have thought unbreachable. They find you terrifying." Gelgeis said it with a smile, leading Nina to believe that he didn't think her an ogre—a view that placed him in the minority.

For a moment, she could only stare at the *wysard*. Then she sat back and laughed. The laugh rose from her belly, shaking her body as it spasmed upward and burst from her lips with a choking, spluttering sound.

"So *that's* it!" Nina exclaimed when her amusement had subsided enough that she could form words. "From my first meeting with these people—at their barrier—I have felt their disquiet, the undercurrent of trepidation that oppresses almost every interaction I have with them." Nina shook her head. "They have worried themselves to no purpose. I came here only out of curiosity to know these people, to strengthen the ties of blood, to honor our common heritage." No longer amused, now she scowled. "By the Powers!" she swore. "Their presumptions do me insult. I have no need of Vivienne's clan. I am matriarch to a brood of my own."

"Beyond the distant seas?" Gelgeis murmured, not looking up from his weaving.

"Immeasurably distant."

Nina watched him work, then added: "I'm not sure how much you know of House Verek and its affairs, but I can assure you, sir, that Vivienne's status as our father's heir-apparent has been established for decades. Or perhaps it's centuries now. I confess that my travels to faraway shores have addled my sense of time. I cannot keep track of it, for time seems indefinable when viewed from a magian lifespan. But my point is: Vivienne will inherit our father's sovereignties. All her siblings recognize her as the rightful successor. I have no interest whatsoever in coming between Vivie and her descendants or usurping anyone's authority, either her own or the established order of this place."

Gelgeis continued to weave more quickly than Nina's eye could follow. Without breaking his rhythm, he said, "I knew your sister back when she and Welwyn had their school at the foot of the mountains, where they taught the Creed of Archamon to all manner of apprentices. Some of those adepts became great *wysards*, while others have excelled as artisans. It pleases me to know that Ruain will be Lady Vivienne's without dispute. I esteem her highly. She will make a fine successor to Lord Verek."

"She's better suited to it than any of the rest of us," Nina said. "Her brothers are too single-minded, interested in their own elemental spellcraft to the exclusion of all else. They know fire, and wind, and stone. I am a creature of water. And like it I am restless, always moving. But Vivie? She has mastery of all."

"Such was my impression," Gelgeis said. "When I knew her at the school, Welwyn sang her praises. He claimed that Lady Vivienne had the greatest range of any adept he had ever trained. That's saying something, for Welwyn has been teaching young *wysards* for a very long time."

"I understand you carried a letter of introduction from my old tutor," Nina said, "when you approached the gates of this place. How long has it been since you last saw Welwyn?"

Gelgeis crinkled his brow, still bent to his work. "I've not laid eyes on the fellow for an age. Last I heard, he was heading down through the foothills. Some say he's gone east, out to those seaports on that distant coast." Gelgeis shook his head. "Who can say? The fellow is a mystery even to the oldest, those who have known him for centuries. He'll stay in one place for what seems forever, teaching generations of apprentices. But then he'll up sticks and take to roaming, and he'll put on such a guise that even his greatest friends won't know him."

"Indeed," Nina muttered, recalling her suspicions about Nimrod the merchant.

Gelgeis stopped weaving with a suddenness that startled Nina, so unfailingly had his hands moved for much of the hour they'd sat together. He held up his work for her inspection.

"See them?" he asked. "At the top?"

Nina ran her gaze over the exquisitely worked pattern of sparkling stars and crescent moons, constellations woven into the fabric in silver thread. Then she saw a break in the pattern. Along the topmost edge, no celestial symbols appeared. There, ocean waves crested, curling and foaming, throwing off silver sea-spray.

"They're beautiful," Nina exclaimed. "But master! Do you think it wise to weave the mark of *my* element into a garment that is meant for my niece? She may read the symbol as proof positive that I have come to subjugate her."

Gelgeis chuckled. "It betokens no more than your visit to this place. When the cloak is finished, the waves will curl beneath the collar, out of sight. I doubt Marsial will ever notice them. Nevertheless, my lady," he added, again taking up his loom, "you may wish to clear the air with her and all your kinfolk. Might I suggest you prepare a little speech for dinner tomorrow? I am told there is to be a feast to celebrate the harvest. You will be guest of honor, and I believe many here are anticipating an announcement from you. They're expecting to be put on notice that you're in charge now."

Nina huffed a breath of exasperation.

"I'll give them notice, all right," she muttered. "While they've been worrying themselves over nothing, I have been giving thought to a different matter altogether. Tomorrow, they will hear what I've got on my mind."

* * *

Nina prepared carefully for this second formal occasion at the house of Marsial. With Deidre's help, she donned a gown the girl had borrowed—filched—from Marsial's own wardrobe. The slinky blue fabric showed off Nina's figure to advantage, and emphasized her firmly toned muscles. To leave no doubt in anyone's mind that she came honestly by her swordfighter's physique, Nina strapped on her rapier. She'd polished the weapon's hilt until it shone like jewelry against the deep blue of her gown. Deidre showed particular creativity with Nina's hair, forming the raven tresses into waves that fell over her bare shoulders like cascades of black silk.

Galen's necklace made the finishing touch. Framed by the gown's plunging neckline, the pendant's blue steel, polished silver, and pure gold threw off sparks with every breath Nina took. As she walked into Marsial's dining hall, Nina looked every inch the warrior-*wysard* who would brook no opposition.

She smiled benignly on the assembled company and kept up a light, frivolous patter all through dinner, enjoying the effect she'd created. Her relatives were so unnerved, the poor things hardly ate. Nina, however, partook liberally of every course, and was glad to see Wolfram, seated a few places across from her, pack away the vegetables with an unblunted appetite. He was filling out well from the lean times he had endured as a wolf who disliked meat.

At last the meal was done, and the moment came for Nina to speak. As she rose, the room was silent: the wingbeats of moths could be heard as they fluttered around the candles. The fabric of her gown swished as she moved, sounding loud in the tension-filled stillness. Unspeaking, she stood surveying the faces that expressed various degrees of anxiety, resignation ... along with dark resentment, here and there.

That's enough, Nina scolded herself, fighting the grin that tugged at the corners of her lips. *You've had your fun. Put these people out of their misery.*

"Honored family," Nina began, then launched into a nearly word-for-word repeat of what she'd said to Gelgeis about Vivienne being Lord Verek's acknowledged and unopposed heir. Nina swore on the oath of her House, that neither she nor any of Vivie's siblings would challenge their baby sister's sovereignty in Ruain, or seek to displace her as the eventual head of the family.

"The matter is settled," she said. "Be easy, you nieces and nephews of mine, and all who bear allegiance to the Lady Vivienne. Through my sister's wizardly line, House Verek will live on uncontested, far into the future." Nina smiled at all the gaping mouths she saw around the table. "If I have distressed you by my presence here, know that I never intended such. A craving for family brought me to you, and will carry me onward. My journey continues, for I wish to know what—and who—awaits around the next bend in the road."

For the space of three heartbeats after Nina concluded this speech, the room remained silent. Then it erupted in thunderous cheers, exclamations of delight, and more than a few "By the Powers!" Those mingled with lesser oaths. In the uproar, Nina heard "Drisha blind me" and others she had grown up with, including her mother's mild "Sweet mercy." Everyone was on their feet, shouting and applauding. Minutes passed before Nina could again make herself heard.

"Sit!" she yelled. "I've more to say. There is a matter we must discuss."

As she waved the crowd back to their seats, Nina signed to the attendants to bring tea, not wine. She meant to raise a sober topic with them, and wanted them sober to hear it. When all were resettled around the table and looking puzzled by the teapots, for plainly they thought the occasion merited something stronger, Nina revealed what had been on her mind for the past several days.

"The nonsense about me coming in and taking over began with that hole I knocked in the magical barrier on your eastern flank. You were deeply alarmed—were you not?—by the manner and the boldness of my arrival. If I dared such effrontery as that, what else might I dare?"

Around the table, heads nodded agreement. "The way you breached the wall armed like a warrior queen—," Sumner began in an accusatory tone, but Nina cut him short.

"With that barrier," she snapped, "you offended me as few have. What a shockingly inhospitable way to greet a daughter of your ancestral house."

"We'd no thought of raising it against you!" cried Marsial from the head of the table. "Never against you, Honored Aunt."

"We had expected you to arrive at our western gate—as all other *wysards* have entered here, coming by way of the dependable road through the mountains," put in Sumner again, from the table's far end. "We were quite unprepared for such a distinguished visitor to emerge from the wilderness."

"From the ridges, you mean," Nina said. She rested her hand on the hilt of her sword as she added, "When I encountered your barrier, I first believed it fully enclosed your lands and was meant to turn away *all* visitors. I thought you must be a hostile lot, even warlike." Nina raised her hand to quell the murmur of surprised defensiveness that rippled around the table. "I now know that I misjudged you. That barrier, I suspect, rises only in the shadow of the Rum Ridges, and it has only one purpose: to ward off the outlaws who infest those bleak heights."

"They raided us," Sumner said, frowning. "Those brigands murdered field hands, stole horses, despoiled our crops. To defend ourselves, we called upon the Powers to raise an impenetrable wall. Impenetrable, at least, to any mortal," he muttered, looking at Nina. "My lady, you cannot fault us for protecting ourselves against marauders."

Nina gave him a nod. "It's entirely right that you should defend yourselves. But you are too comfortable behind your barrier, too isolated from the outer world. What of your mortal neighbors who have also suffered at the hands of those villains? As I ventured up that road, I saw settlements which had been burned to the ground, their occupants likely murdered. Do not forget that your brother *wysard*, Master Eymir, also met his death on that chancy road. What I find fault with," Nina said, "is your neglect of your duty toward those who need your protection."

She looked from Sumner to Marsial, and then across to Odhrán, who sat opposite Nina and had spent much of the evening studying her cleavage.

"You have the fighters and the weaponry," she said, raising the captain's eyes to meet hers as she spoke directly to him. "You can clear the ridges of the scum that collects in those heights. Wolfram and I made a start." Nina glanced at the boy who sat between Odhrán and Gelgeis. The cub was hanging on her words, and his hazel eyes shone with eagerness. Out of respect for Eymir, he would take up the cause, Nina had no doubt. But could she persuade the others?

"I call on you," she said, "to finish what Wolfe and I began. Drive the outlaws from the ridges. Make that road safe for innocent travelers. Accept your duty toward your mortal neighbors: Use your gifts, and your might of arms, for their benefit. Will you?"

Odhrán and Wolfram rose as one. "We will!" they cried.

Others around the table also shot to their feet, some of them known to Nina from the practice field at the armory. Odhrán's fighters seemed keen to use their skills out in the wider world. Nina suspected they were bored with years of inactivity, and had only needed a push to take responsibility for restoring and then keeping the peace in the non-magian realm that adjoined their borders.

Odhrán took charge from that moment, rallying his fighters to him and making Wolfram his lieutenant. At dawn of the day after the dinner party, those two rode out, leading an armed company. Nina rode with them, and Marsial and Sumner tagged along but only as far as the invisible barrier. Without dismounting, those two traced patterns in the air, working the spells to open an equally invisible gate that was large enough for the company to pass through. Nina watched closely, asked questions, and satisfied herself that she and Odhrán could repeat the spellwork upon their return from today's foray.

They headed south, staying on the road until noon and encountering no resistance. Then half of the company dismounted and went on foot into the ridges, climbing to the peaks.

Nina stayed down on the road, watching Wolfram leap up through the rocks as surefooted as the animal he had been at their first meeting. Several times over the past week Nina had seen the boy in his transfigured form trotting along the city streets, or racing Traveller across the freshly cut hayfields. Wolfram had sought and received Nina's permission to take the horse out for daily exercise. Sometimes he rode, but often he ran as a wolf, making with the roan a picture of freedom that filled Nina's heart with gladness, but also a sense of loss. The boy and the horse had become such fast friends, Trav was no longer hers alone. Often when Nina checked on him in the stables, she found Wolfram there. The boy would sit with his shoulder braced against the door of Traveller's stall and commune with the horse, speaking no word but holding Trav's rapt attention.

Even now with Nina on his back, reined to a halt at the foot of the ridges, the horse fretted as he watched Wolfram leap through the rocks. Trav would be up there with his friend if Nina would let him.

In late afternoon, the scouting party returned to report no sightings of their quarry, but they had discovered the remains of an outlaw camp. Odhrán judged it to have been abandoned a week ago.

"Winter's coming," he said to Nina. "I doubt we will find many stragglers in these heights, not from here on northward to where the ridges curve away toward the scrublands. The scoundrels we seek will have fled to warmer climes by now.

"Were you aware, my lady," he added, "that the line of these ridges continues to the south, uninterrupted to the edge of the desert badlands? All along its great length, this broken country has been a haven for thieves and murderers for as long as I can remember." Odhrán touched his hat brim. "I thank you, Honored Elder, for showing us our duty. It is past time that we came out from behind our walls and met our wider obligations. Had we been patrolling this road in the springtime of this year, Master Eymir might still be alive." Odhrán sighed, then grinned. "I would have enjoyed watching him and Gelgeis fight over Wolfram. What magical thunderbolts those two might have thrown at each other, vying for the right to train a shapeshifting youngster."

Nina laughed with Odhrán, picturing such a battle between two ancient *wysards*. No doubt she, Odhrán, and every other fighter in the ranks would have learned a thing or two from witnessing hand-to-hand combat between two old masters.

But Nina also smiled—or grimaced—at being called "elder." Had Odhrán meant only to acknowledge her as the eldest daughter of House Verek? What of the hints the tall, blond captain had been dropping, that he'd noticed her as she had noticed him? Despite her discreet nosing around, Nina had been unable to ascertain the degree of kinship between them. If he was her nephew, descended directly from Vivienne, then maybe she'd seen amorous intent where none existed. Nina had not considered—until now—that Odhrán might view her as truly elderly and thus have no interest in a dalliance.

She sighed, and reined her horse around to ride with him back to the magical barrier. Together they traced the patterns and worked the spells to open a passage.

But as they locked themselves within the wizardry, making the magic together, Nina caught a glimmer from Odhrán that was definitely not nephew-ish. When all the company had passed through and were riding homeward, with Wolfram at their head, Nina stayed behind with Odhrán to shut the gate. As they restored the invisible barrier, she again felt a spark hotly suggestive of desire. Perhaps he did not think her so old, after all.

They turned their horses toward the distant city, leisurely following the company that had gone on ahead. As they rode, Nina told Odhrán about her trek through the southern desert, and how she had been led to believe she could only reach the Ore Hills from Granger by passing through that badland.

"But from what you have told me about the ridges reaching to the desert," Nina said, "and judging by a map I saw in your city library, I'm thinking there's a different route I could have taken. But none would tell me of it, for that route cuts through the ridges—a place my advisers must have regarded as even more perilous than the scorched canyonlands, since no one mentioned it to me."

"Their silence is unsurprising," Odhrán replied. "The entire length of the Rum Ridges, from low desert to upland forest, is a no-man's-land. Decent folk would choose *farsinchia* over any part of that evil country. Your advisers were right to send you the way they did." He smiled. "I am pleased, my lady, that you came safely through the badlands, and then survived many miles of yonder bad road." Odhrán gestured back toward the byway they had patrolled today. "Just north of here, a fork of that road climbs into the ridges, becoming hardly more than a footpath through the crests where they curve away east. Eventually the ridges dwindle to nothing. But the road continues, and comes in time to Plainsboro."

"Plainsboro," Nina mused, remembering the scoundrels she had bested there, and their fatal mistake in coming this way to face her again. As she mentally matched Odhrán's overview to the map she'd studied in the library, she slowly nodded. "I could have done it—I could have ridden that route." She turned to him. "But with family on either side of the ridges, I might have backtracked for months and not seen them all. It's best that I came the way I did, through the badlands."

Not least, Nina thought, *because I never would have known Corlis, had I shunned the desert.*

The sun was setting by the time she and Odhrán reached the city gates. At the stables, Nina found Wolfram anxiously awaiting her arrival. More precisely, the wolf-boy wanted her horse. Traveller was of similar mind. The roan chafed at the bit until Nina dismounted and handed the reins to Wolfram. She stood watching as the boy unsaddled Trav and rubbed him down.

"By the bye," Odhrán said, pulling Nina out of her thoughts. He brushed past her, touching her sleeve as he led his own horse to its stall. "The other day when I was in the library, I checked the genealogies they keep there on long rolls of parchment. Just curious, I was, to know how you and I might be related."

"Oh?" Nina responded, attentive to only him now, and trying to sound casual. "What did you learn?"

Odhrán smiled, and arched a pale eyebrow at her. "Strangely enough, I could find no blood ties between us. Your wizardly lineage and my own have never crossed in the whole of recorded history."

"How fascinating," Nina murmured. "In that case, captain, would you care to join me this evening for supper? In my cottage. Alone."

Odhrán doffed his hat. "Lady Karenina, it will be my pleasure."

* * *

Weeks passed as Nina prepared to continue her journey. Master Gelgeis gifted her with a blanket into which he had woven magic so invincible, the cold of winter would not reach Nina in the fiercest blizzard. Lady Marsial—all smiles now that her status was secure—outfitted Nina with more winter clothes than she could fit into her packs.

The excess, Nina gave to Deidre to ensure that she and her suitor, Bastian the former spy, would keep mum about Odhrán's nightly visits to the cottage. From his errand-runner's place on the guesthouse porch, Bastian watched at sundown for the captain's approach. When he saw Odhrán cut across from the gate that opened out to the armory, he tapped on the kitchen window to alert Deidre. The girl then laid a light supper on the table, poured the wine, and left the cottage, taking Bastian with her. Each evening, the pair disappeared into the flower-filled park as Odhrán vaulted onto the porch and let himself in through Nina's unlocked door.

Their lovemaking was magical in the way of two *wysards* together. It lacked the intimacy she had known with Corlis, but it was unreserved and muscular, and wrapped in erotic spellwork. Odhrán knew Nina would soon move on. This dalliance would leave behind no broken hearts. For the remainder of Nina's stay, they simply enjoyed each other, both by day in the practice field, crossing swords, and by night in Nina's bed, entwining limbs. They made magic together, and it was enough. Nina had never before coupled with a *wysard*, and the tricks Odhrán showed her satisfied her curiosity about magian lovemaking.

It was everything the legends held it to be. But with her mortal husband and her nomad lover, Nina had known transcendent pleasures. Odhrán would not linger in her memories the way Makani and Corlis did.

As departure day neared, Nina sought out Wolfram. She found him, as expected, in the stable. The boy and Traveller had become inseparable. Though Nina would journey onward from this place, she would not ride forth on the back of the horse that had brought her here.

"He's yours, Wolfe," Nina said. "If you're to patrol the Rum Ridges next spring when outlaws return to these parts, you will need a good horse. I caution you: Do not allow Traveller's great heart to lead him to a broken leg. Such is his love for you, he would attempt to leap through the rocks as the wolf does, imperiling himself with every jump." She fixed her gaze upon the boy. "Remember what he is, even as you hold tight to your identity. Be the wolf, but never forget your true form."

"My lady," the boy mumbled, too overcome to speak. He bowed low, from the waist. Then with a sob, he went to his knees. "I beg your forgiveness, lady, for any offense I might have caused by daring to lie with you at night, atop your blankets, when we journeyed together. In my loneliness, I pretended to be only a wolf—or more a pet dog—so that I might sleep next to you. My deception has weighed upon my conscience. For weeks I have sought the courage to beg pardon for behaving toward you in a manner so unseemly."

Nina wanted to laugh. But she would not deepen the boy's embarrassment by doing so. The tears on Wolfram's face and his quivering lip said he meant every word of his confession. Nina rushed to offer absolution.

"You've no need to apologize, Wolfe," she said, stooping to draw the boy to his feet. "During our travels together, you behaved as a perfect gentleman."

Well, maybe not always, Nina silently amended. She recalled a time or two when she'd stripped off her clothes in front of the wolf, and those hazel eyes had not looked away. No matter. She had never been rigidly constrained by female modesty. From her first naked swim in an ocean at the age of five or six, Nina had enjoyed the touch of water, sun, and fresh air on bare skin. Let Wolfram harbor in his memory any detail about her that he found memorable—including the way she had responded to the warmth of his wolfish body atop her blankets.

"As I recall," Nina said, lightly holding the young man's arm, "I, too, wanted to snuggle on those cold nights beside the woodland stream." She allowed herself a wistful smile. "Someday you will fall in love, and one thing will lead to another, and then you'll understand why a woman who had a husband in her bed for many years, and who then found herself alone every night, might dream of her lost mate. In her dreams, she might reach without conscious awareness for whatever warm body lies nearest. Especially when she knows, deep down, that the body of the beast beside her holds the mind of a man." She released his arm. "Do you understand me, wolf cub?"

Wolfram nodded. "I understand, my lady. I thank you. It eases my heart to hear you say that my near presence in the night did not offend you."

This time, Nina did not suppress her laugh. "Be assured, boy: Had I been offended at any hour, you would have known it. My honored mother taught me to accept no insult from any man, be he manor born or wolf whelped."

* * *

Nina needed a new horse. Her relatives offered her the pick of their herds. She chose a buckskin mare with a pedigree that traced back to the fine mare that had once been Lady Carin's. These descendants of Vivienne had not only kept meticulous genealogies of themselves and their unrelated novices, artisans, and fighters, they'd also traced the pedigrees of their most prized horses. Bloodlines went back to the breeding stock of a long-deceased but still honored Ruainian horseman named Ronnat. Nina found it satisfyingly appropriate that she would be riding her new mount, called "Mischief," back to a land that was the mare's ancestral home as well as Nina's.

She spent a few days getting to know the buckskin, riding across the empty fields and going out on patrol with Odhrán's troops. Odhrán saw to it that the mare was properly shod for the journey ahead. Nina would go cross-country, following the course of a perennial stream that flowed from headwaters in the mountainous north. The stream would guide her onto an edge of the Plain of Imlen, and from there she would make for an ancient town that nestled in the northland's old forests.

Called Deroucey, the town lay within striking distance of the wild, unmarked border of Ruain. From Deroucey, Nina could follow her nose home. No mortal could make the journey and cross safely into the hidden province. But the magic which kept Ruain secret from the rest of Ladrehdin would admit a daughter of House Verek without a flicker of opposition.

In the final hours before her departure, Nina arranged a last talk with Master Gelgeis. The old *wysard* was a font of archaic knowledge, and Nina wanted to know what he might know about beings of the underworld. She asked Gelgeis: Did the early legends of Ladrehdin speak of rock trolls or any sort of powerful race that lived below the surface world?

"Trolls, eh?" Gelgeis said, his hands ceaselessly working his magical loom. "Aye, the legends are replete with tales of mountain trolls and cave ogres, sea monsters and lake goblins. In olden days, many a traveler claimed to have met with them."

"As I have done, but not in days of yore," Nina said. "My present travels have brought me face-to-face with a king of the underworld."

"A story worth the hearing!" Gelgeis exclaimed. "You've startled me so that I have lost my pattern. You must make it up to me by telling me your tale."

Nina obliged. She gave the old *wysard* a long account of Grog, starting with what Roddy had said about finding the fellow lost in the Easthaven harbor. She told of Grog's descent into the smoking chasm at Winfield, and how he had resurfaced hundreds of miles away, bursting up through desert sands, swimming to her on an underground river of life-giving water. Nina described the differing ways in which people had perceived Grog: how he had reminded her of an ocean leviathan, but Legary had thought him a huge mudpuppy, and the merchant Nimrod saw him as a rock troll—a form that Nina herself glimpsed at the moment Grog leapt into the abyss.

"Nimrod knew him the longest," Nina said, "and perhaps he came closest to knowing Grog's true nature. My months and miles of travel have given me ample time to consider all that I saw and learned while in company with the merchant and his 'bodyguard.' It is my belief, Master Gelgeis, that Grog issued from the underworld. For a time, he wandered lost in this surface realm that is so familiar to us but holds few comforts for a being like him. Moments before he threw himself into the burning crevasse that had opened in the grasslands, Grog spoke to me—a single word signifying 'home'."

Nina raised her hands in a questioning gesture. "Do you think me mad? Can you credit such an improbable account?"

"I can," Gelgeis replied, his hands flying over his loom. "Much of what you have said finds its echo in the ancient stories. Our own wizardly shapeshifting traditions trace their origins to the early legends of creatures that could transform within rock and fire and water. They were said to live in the bowels of this world and in its deep ocean chasms."

Nina rubbed her lower lip, gazing thoughtfully at the old *wysard*. "First I meet the lost king of the underworld. Then I encounter a young adept who is the first shapeshifting *wysard* to appear in Ladrehdin in millennia. Is it possible, master, that the two events are connected?"

Gelgeis smiled. "I judge both of those happenings to be the singular work of your honored mother, the Lady Carin of Ruain."

"How so?" Nina knew the answer, but she wanted to hear Gelgeis say it. "What has my mother to do with any of this? Lady Carin has not traveled beyond the borders of Ruain in many years."

"But her influence is felt the world over, and will be felt until the end of time," Gelgeis said. "When your mother restored this world's magical potency, that renewal reached to the very core, to the beating heart of Ladrehdin, and from those depths to the highest mountaintops. Consider a legendary race of underworld beings, and how they might have slumbered during the long ages of Ladrehdin's magical decline. Might they not have been stirred awake by the flush of new magic that pervaded every rock and hidden watercourse in their secret chambers, deep below our feet?"

Nina nodded. Gelgeis was adding the weight of wizardly scholarship to the speculations that she and Legary had entertained during their rambling talks in Granger.

"In one young adept," she commented, "that same flood of reborn magic renewed the gift of shapeshifting. Perhaps we will soon be seeing more like Wolfram."

"I count on it," Gelgeis said. "It is my life's ambition to train up a wolfpack of apprentices like that boy."

Nina laughed. "May you enjoy grand success, Master. Just think of all the shed fur you can get from a pack of novices. Spin their wolfish hair into yarn and weave yourself a blanket. I can attest that wolf fur is very warm."

Chapter Twenty-Four

At supper, it was only Nina and her parents. Vivienne was away, visiting family in the east of Ruain. She had invited her newly returned sister to go with her, but Nina wanted no more wayfaring for a while. It was good to be home, to be sitting at the old familiar table in the kitchen of Weyrrock and eating leftovers from a huge Mydrismas feast.

Nina had arrived home in time to celebrate the holiday with Lady Carin, Lord Verek, Vivienne and Vivie's husband, and even Dalton, ship's master and chief steward of Ruain. Dalton had contributed many seafaring tales to the long evenings of storytelling that were a traditional highlight of the winter festival. None of his narratives, however, came close to matching the accounts Nina gave of her travels. She had held her listeners spellbound, even while skipping over the parts they didn't need to know.

Now the festivities were over, and Nina's siblings had gone about the business of their lives, leaving her to enjoy a quiet rest at home. At supper, she tucked into a warmed-over meat pie and a remnant pudding. Never mind that they were a day or two past their peak flavor. The leftovers tasted like Mydrismas, like holiday fun and family. They got her thinking about a similar holiday that she had observed annually with family and friends on her island home across the void. A centerpiece of that celebration was an evergreen tree, gaily decorated with ornaments of silver, gold, and red.

In Nina's roving thoughts, the memory of the festive tree sparked another recollection from her years on the ocean world. Into her mind came the image of a very different tree, a peculiar twisted thing that bore no fruit or flower. It grew solitary in a lonely spot some distance from the house on the bay that had been her family residence during her sojourn on Earth. So forcefully did the memory come to her, Nina felt compelled to share it with her parents. She described in detail that tree of strange appearance.

Her father sat back in his seat and folded his arms. Through narrowed eyes, Lord Verek studied her. Then he demanded to know exactly where that tree grew.

"Drisha's knuckles," Verek swore when Nina had answered him. "I cannot help but think that the lonely spot you have named is the very place in which I burned the magical amulets I once carried there from this world. So great was the danger those objects posed to Ladrehdin, I could not leave them here. It smote my conscience to bury their ashes in the soil of another world, but at the time I had no choice. And now you're telling me, daughter, that a tree has grown out of those burned remains, and it's a thing not native to your ocean world?"

"I never saw anything remotely like it, anywhere else in my islands," Nina said. "If it did sprout from the seed of a native tree, it matured into something so odd that it looked altogether unnatural." She shrugged. "I had assumed that a seed blew in on the wind, or a bird brought it from a faraway land, and that was why the tree appeared alien to my island home."

Lady Carin and Lord Verek stared at each other.

"What if it *is* alien," Nina's mother said, her voice low. "If that tree grew out of an artifact from another world, then it might make a bridge to that world."

"As you and I have seen, my lady, in the fraught times of our early years together," Verek muttered, "otherworldly bridges permit the comings and goings of dangers unimaginable."

"By the Powers!" Nina broke in, swearing as she looked from one of her parents to the other. "Are you suggesting that the strange tree up behind my old house could let a deadly alien threat into my beautiful ocean world? Beggar it!" she exclaimed, borrowing one of her mother's stronger expressions. "I'll have to go back."

She saw Lady Carin start to object. But it was not her mother's decision to make. Nina had family in the world beyond the void. Generations of her descendants lived on its islands. Perhaps by now some of them had spread to the far shores of the great ocean that ringed the archipelago. Nina *would* go back there, to keep them safe.

And she would look in on her relatives while she was in the islands, chopping down the alien tree. With a pang, Nina realized that some of her older children might have now reached the end of their mortal lifespans. While all of her offspring were talented in ways beyond the ordinary, making them exceptional healers and herbalists, fishers and sailors, not one of the children she'd had with Makani was truly magian. Each would go the way of all mortal flesh. That knowledge had driven Nina from Earth while all her children yet lived. She had dreaded to witness the death of first one, then another.

Had her flight been an act of cowardice? Her brother Legary had outlived generations of his mortal offspring, as had Galen. Neither had forsaken their homes. They had endured their grief. They had taught her that it was a *wysard*'s fate to see their children die, and bury their spouse if they took a non-magian husband or wife. The death of her Makani had nearly ripped Nina in two. She had deserted her family rather than go through that with a child. But from her brothers, Nina had learned it was the price a *wysard* paid for the sweetness of mortal love.

She would go back, and if any among her Earthly family lay dying, she would comfort them.

Nina's mother must have read some of this in her face, for Lady Carin withheld the objection she had started to make. Instead, the lady perplexed Nina with a warning about some lost piece of Earthly writing that held a potentially dangerous incantation. Then Carin proposed to help Nina dress for her return to the ocean world.

"I thank you, Mother, but I have the clothes I need," Nina said, smiling. "While I was in the Ore Hills, Galen's ..." *Mistress,* she started to say, but quickly amended: "Galen's friend gave me garments that are perfect for the sunny warmth of the islands to which I'm bound. The embroidery on the tunics is lovely. Come upstairs and see."

* * *

Nina bathed in the springwater pool that adjoined the blue bedroom. The chamber at the head of the stairs had been hers for several years in her girlhood, after she'd been deemed too old to continue in the suite of rooms that Master Welwyn occupied with his younger apprentice, Galen. The blue bedroom had been Nina's private domain until just shy of her thirteenth birthday. Then she'd summoned the magic of the springwater pool and crossed the void to Earth, riding upon a wave of her own making.

Soon she would repeat that magic.

But first, Nina had a final leave-taking to attempt, though with little hope of success. There had been no sign of her enigmatic friend since the lake in the desert. And yet, as she had followed the stream northward from the lands of Vivienne's descendants, Nina had seemed to feel Grog's presence ... as if he followed the icy watercourse with her, but from the other side: from the underside, the steamy down-below.

She dived deep in the springwater pool, plunging to its rocky bottom. Nina found the irregular opening through which warm water welled up, continuously filling and refreshing the pool. Then she did something she had never dared to do as a child. She stuck her hand in that dark hole, down into the netherworld where underground rivers gathered heat from molten rocks.

There—

Nina felt something smooth and slick like the skin of a salamander. Grog's webbed fingers? She gave a squeeze but got no response. Perhaps she touched only the moss that grew among the rocks.

Nina shot to the surface, out of breath and gasping from long submergence. With a puff of disappointment she left the pool and toweled off, and pulled her wet hair into a loose braid. Outside, beyond the single window of the blue bedroom, a winter storm raged. But in the chamber of the hot-spring pool, Nina stayed comfortably warm even with wet hair. Her braid would soon dry in the tropical heat of the islands where she was headed.

She dressed in lightweight trousers and embroidered tunic, the Ore Hills costume Taji had given her. Nina strapped on her throwing knife and the belt pouch that held stones for her sling. She did not loop the sling around her neck as was her usual practice, but tucked the weapon inside the pouch atop the sling-bullets Legary had given her. For neckwear, Nina chose instead her pendant of blue-steel waves and silver whitecaps—the talisman of water magic that Galen had crafted especially for her.

The necklace had spent more time in Nina's pocket than around her neck. During her travels in the shadow of the Rum Ridges, she had not wanted to risk entangling the pendant with the cords of her sling and interfering with the weapon's deployment. But on the journey that lay ahead of her, she anticipated no immediate need for her sling. She could arrive on Earth properly elegant, as her mother wished.

Nina had her bow in one hand and her other hand raised high, ready to summon the wave that would carry her across the void. But then she saw it:

A scrap of cloth floated in the pool.

With a gasp, she knelt to scoop it up. She put down her bow and wrung the water from the fabric two-handed. The cloth's silky sheen and iridescent colors were unmistakable. With a low bow of respect, Nina saluted the king of the underworld, unseen in his hidden throne room but constantly present, an emissary of the Elementals.

Smiling, she took up her bow and conjured her wave. Nina rode the magic with the strip of fabric tied like a ribbon around the end of her long, damp, raven braid.

END of BOOK 5 of WATERSPELL

About the Author

CASTLES IN THE CORNFIELD provided the setting for Deborah J. Lightfoot's earliest flights of fancy. On her father's farm in Texas, she grew up reading tales of adventure and reenacting them behind ramparts of sun-drenched grain. She left the farm to earn a degree in journalism and write award-winning books of history and biography. High on her bucket list was the desire to try her hand at the genre she most admired. The result is Waterspell, a complex, intricately detailed fantasy comprising the original four-book series *(Warlock, Wysard, Wisewoman, Witch)*. The current volume, *The Karenina Chronicles,* is the first book in a new series also set in the Waterspell universe.

Having discovered this world, the author finds it difficult to leave.

Deborah is a professional member of The Authors Guild. She lives in the country near Fort Worth, Texas. Find her on Instagram @booksofwaterspell and peruse her overflowing, catch-all website at waterspell.net.

Milton Keynes UK
Ingram Content Group UK Ltd.
UKHW010858081223
434021UK00001B/92